DINING ON STONES

'Sinclair's prose is in a class of its own . . . it's hard to imagine there'll be
a novel out this year more deserving of the Booker' Nicholas Royle,
Zembla

'Brilliant' *The Times*

'Sinclair (painfully, brilliantly, fancifully) knows everything' *Time Out*

'Hypnotic, unnerving . . . Sinclair knows how to spin a good yarn'
Sunday Telegraph

'Vivid and sardonic, describing a world as idiosyncratic and
recognizable as Greene's or Ballard's' *Guardian*

'Energising and exhausting . . . anyone who cares about the
possibilities of English language cannot afford to pass him by' *List*

Iain Sinclair is the author of *Downriver* (winner of the James Tait Black Memorial Prize and the Encore Award); *Landor's Tower*; *White Chappell, Scarlet Tracings*; *Lights Out for the Territory*; *Lud Heat*; *Rodinsky's Room* (with Rachel Lichtenstein); *Radon Daughters*; *London Orbital*; and *Dining on Stones*. He lives in Hackney, East London.

Dining on Stones

(or, The Middle Ground)

IAIN SINCLAIR

PENGUIN BOOKS

PENGUIN BOOKS

Published by the Penguin Group
Penguin Books Ltd, 80 Strand, London WC2R ORL, England
Penguin Group (USA) Inc., 375 Hudson Street, New York, New York 10014, USA
Penguin Group (Canada), 10 Alcorn Avenue, Toronto, Ontario, Canada M4V 3B2
(a division of Pearson Penguin Canada Inc.)
Penguin Ireland, 25 St Stephen's Green, Dublin 2, Ireland
(a division of Penguin Books Ltd)
Penguin Group (Australia), 250 Camberwell Road, Camberwell, Victoria 3124, Australia
(a division of Pearson Australia Group Pty Ltd)
Penguin Books India Pvt Ltd, 11 Community Centre, Panchsheel Park, New Delhi – 110 017, India
Penguin Group (NZ), cnr Airborne and Rosedale Roads, Albany, Auckland 1310, New Zealand
(a division of Pearson New Zealand Ltd)
Penguin Books (South Africa) (Pty) Ltd, 24 Sturdee Avenue, Rosebank 2196, South Africa

Penguin Books Ltd, Registered Offices: 80 Strand, London WC2R ORL, England

www.penguin.com

First published by Hamish Hamilton 2004
Published in Penguin Books 2005
1

Copyright © Iain Sinclair, 2004

The Acknowledgements on p. 451 constitute an extension of this copyright page

Typeset by Rowland Phototypesetting Ltd, Bury St Edmunds, Suffolk
Printed in England by Clays Ltd, St Ives plc

i.m. Joseph Conrad & Arthur Sinclair

Contents

ROAD

Andrew Norton

Estuarial Lives

GRANITA BOOKS

LONDON

The eyes are hammers.

– Ceri Richards

Coast

Three flies, they might have been there all winter, exhibiting themselves on my kitchen window. Doing what they do, trying to get inside. Stuck to stickiness, salt. A low-level irritation, between my headache and the view of the roofs and brightly painted terraces, that drove me, almost immediately, into the other room. Where I pressed, in perverse imitation of my tiny, blood-sucking cousins, against the cool panel of the sliding door. If I was inside anything, it was glass.

So much experience, I thought, and so little of it experienced, lived through, understood. The sea, early light on grey water, does that, makes us melancholy in the morning, dissatisfied with our satisfaction. So many years on the clock, despite surreptitious winding back, the reinventions, the lies. Obliged to go over the details of a dull history, for a man sprawled in a chair, whisky glass in hand, you invent. A journalist worried about train times, his dinner. You smooth over unforgiven betrayals, hide shame. Jealousy. Impotence. Or boast of it. Bad reviews, which I pretend not to read, are quoted verbatim. The mike isn't picking up my whisper. The journalist booms and cackles.

'Tell me about the auditory hallucinations.'

I was waiting for something. And it was slow in coming. I'd done the walks, bought the local newspapers, sat in afternoon bars with an empty notebook. Pass sixty, sixty-five, and you can't sustain an erection beyond eight and a half minutes. So I read. Is that a promise? Eight and a half minutes, of the right intensity, sounds good. Novelists have managed books on less. Eight and a half minutes is epic to a minimalist (no flashbacks permitted). There were no women on my stretch of the coast, not for me. No car, few clothes. Finite resources and small knowledge of the set on which I found myself: no more excuses.

7

Joseph Conrad managed three hundred words on a good day. There weren't many of those. 'The atrocious misery of writing,' he moaned. A few miles to the east of here in a rented farmhouse. Labouring over *Nostromo*. The manuscript had elephantiasis. He was sick, sweating, characters mumbled in his ear, stalked him on afternoon walks.

Light is all memory, but it's not my memory. Nothing personal. A concrete shelf above the busy coast road. Furniture from an Essex warehouse. Fresh paint. Screaming gulls. Shingle shore. The English Channel.

Standing, nose against that cold surface, was the extent of my attempt to break down conventional distinctions between dream life and real life – if such distinctions could be said to exist outside London, beyond the hoop of the motorway. On the south coast. Do we have free will? Is it our choice to give up choice, to ape our grandfathers? The same retreat, getting away from debt, from creditors and family. Aberdeen in his case, Hackney in mine. The compulsion to write.

I came here in pursuit of a Greek woman, a photographer who only worked at night. It was a commission. Which I couldn't fulfil. I lost myself in the prints. She was an extraordinary storyteller and then she took the narrative out. Her photographs were the residue: colour, texture, neutralised gravity. So that specifics become universal. The tenderness she had for the world shocked me. Love letters that always said the same thing: 'Goodbye'. When you spend time somewhere with an artist (a thief) of her quality, you can't go home. I didn't think of it that way, at the beginning, but the task I'd given myself was to put the fiction back into Effie's documents. To pick up the stories that she abandoned. Her theatre of the coast was perfect. Deserted. A place of heavy drapes, shapes beneath tarpaulin, lit windows of empty rooms. Clubland calligraphy turning puddles of piss into blood.

Effie wasn't part of the story. That much was clear. She introduced me to a location she had a thing about once; she'll return as a friend, a tripper.

'So the first time I ever came here,' she said, 'it was by train, at night. I walked from the station to the main part of the town. Everything was deserted, I couldn't believe my eyes. I kept walking, hardly anyone to be seen. The restaurants were getting ready for the night. But who are they preparing these tables for? The ghosts? The dead? At night everything is transformed. Anything can happen. Nobody will blink, nobody will hear you.'

I was ready to audition. I could become one of those ghosts. I saw Effie to her train and I stayed put. The next morning I walked into an estate agent's office in the Old Town: the woman was preoccupied, servicing the thick tongue of a rubber plant with a Slavic thoroughness. You could hear the rubber squeak. The man, jacketless, tilted heavily onto one elbow, was giving handshakes on the telephone. Amused eyes weigh me up: timewaster. They know I don't have the equity, but they slide, without breaking away from plant or phone, through the motions.

'What are you looking for – exactly? Low forties? Sixty ceiling? We specialise in cheeky offers. Never know your luck.'

'A second chance,' I wanted to reply. New birth certificate, clean passport. Less pressure around the skull, fewer bills. And I'd like to meet the woman described to me by another woman. A writer, artist of sorts, whose name is mentioned, with awe and affection, in an off-highway shack, a breakfast bar in West Thurrock. Red and green sign – THE LOG CABIN – reflected in rainwater on the indented lid of a blue tin drum. Oily beads plipping from hanging basket, the bar had style: rusticated Americana. Estuary ambiguous: the flavour of the times. Perfume from the soap factory infiltrated our damp coats. We felt – as a consequence of walking, through successive rain curtains, along the riverbank in the direction of the bridge – as if we'd taken a warm shower in a gay bathhouse. I watched bright prisms in the bubbles that formed along the seam of the shorter girl's shiny black jacket. Her smooth cheeks, pink from the hike, were sticky with curls of dark wet hair.

Jimmy Seed brought us out here, two of his girls, mature students with charm (and, I guessed, private or undisclosed sources of income) and myself. He was grafting his way down the A13, from Aldgate to Southend – like those old-time economic escapees from the Whitechapel ghetto. You know the sort, two sweatshops, bit of property, revised stationery. The move I would make, a couple of years later, trading in one brand of dereliction for another. Drug-dealers in fancy cars for drug users in hooded sweatshirts. Dead grass for dead sea. The same desperate survivalists with bricks in their bags. The same ambulances and sirens.

Seed had the eye, no question. Native intelligence and the steady hand of a good painter, painter and decorator. Like Hitler: without the compulsion to have women shit on him, the urge to invade Poland. Jimmy let Poland come to him, by way of Rainham Marshes: Europe's last great apocalyptic highway, rumbling trucks, discontinued firing ranges, spoilt docks, poisoned irrigation ditches, mounds of smoking landfill and predatory seagulls. Property and prophecy, that was Jimmy's game. Nosing into territory with the vagrants who are about to be moved on. *So paint the vagrants, the canal bank lovers.* The drinking schools. Whores. Night footballers. Dogs on chains. Sell a painting, buy a share in a slum. Sell the renovated flat and option a burnt-out pub. Photograph the pub, copy the photo. Sell the painting to the hustler who risks a wine bar on the same site. Sell heritage as something to hang in the Gents.

Jimmy flitted from Glasgow in short trousers. He chased his old man's unemployment as far south as Derby. But when, like Charles Edward Stuart (the Young Pretender), the easily discouraged boiler-maker lost his nerve and turned for home, brave little Jimmy stayed put: a job in a garage, flattening oil cans with a hand-cranked device that left him knackered. One arm, like a Limehouse barmaid, thicker than the other. Young Seed saw art as a way of accessing women who had expectations of property. His third wife (second launderette conversion) carried him as far west as Roman Road. Social life tracked the flight of the sun (Clerkenwell, Soho, Bond Street), while his art travelled in the opposite direction; greater savagery, blanker canvases. By the time his scouting expeditions reached the Queen Elizabeth II Suspension Bridge, between Purfleet and Dartford, content was a shimmering zero. He laboured like a Whistler franchise: project image (outline of bridge) onto screen, bucket of whitewash, slap in a few lorries with fine badger brush and leave the rest misty and impressionistic. Let the buggers see what they want to see in a tribute to absence.

Jimmy ran a beat-up Volvo with tinted windscreen. The A13 looked much better that way, schizophrenic, two thirds grey and the rest tropical sunset. Grungy Brit realism invaded by Florida noir, plastic palm trees in Basildon Festival Leisure Park. Hanging an arm out of the window that wouldn't shut, Jimmy snapped away: snooker halls, cinemas, drinking clubs with Mafia lettering on necrotic plaster. Tough weeds splitting tarmac. His roadside portfolio, the scale of it, played well in New York. The venerable critic Manny Farber, deaf but still feisty, himself a painter now, visiting England to check out the Turners, said that the only place he recognised, in a couple of weeks being schlepped around the culture, was the A13 beyond Dagenham. 'Let down the window, kid,' he growled, 'I wanna smell it: New Jersey.'

Jimmy's new style (degraded Highways Agency promo) was taken up by a gallery in Dover Street, one of those plush operations where immaculate young women find ways to pass the day on the telephone, sitting, stretching, smiling by appointment. Further in, desks are not quite so large, but they're covered with a better class of green leather; gentlemen of a certain age, florid, drop in for an hour before lunch, without removing their overcoats. Upstairs, in private suites, the real players are as still as papal portraits (and twice as oily): sharp enough to freeze gin by looking at it.

For a season, wild man Jimmy enjoyed the status of a recommended window-cleaner. The small change he earned – around £40,000 a pop – barely covered his expenses: catalogues, private views, coke and champers for collectors. A new Dubliner, brickdust on his brogues, came over, two or three times a year (Cheltenham was one of them), tieless, white-shirted, to make a purchase against tax liabilities: another monster A13 canvas. Art with muddy footprints.

'Takes Paddy back to the years he spent with a shovel in his hand,' one of the grandees sneered – making sure that the brown envelope, stuffed with readies, that he slid away into his inside pocket, didn't spoil the hang of a loose-fitting jacket. 'Black bag merchant from Dagenham Docks. Tarmac-layer to landfill magnate in two generations.'

I was supposed to shadow Jimmy, write him up. The gallery slipped me a couple of hundred for expenses. The germ of my A13 book, *Estuarial Lives*, started there. The usual accident. Jimmy belonged in the first chapter, a Virgil with no staying power. A run in the Volvo and it was over. I took the decision that the road would have to be *walked*. Every yard of it, Aldgate to the sea: through memory, mess, corruption, dying industries, political scams, satellite shopping cities buried in chalk quarries. Defoe, Bram Stoker, Joseph Conrad. Elements were predictable, I was working from a very familiar script; elements were unexpected (the Plotlands of Basildon, the ruins of Barking Abbey surrounded by furniture warehouses and windowless blocks that peddled carpets). I wrote at pace, struggling to keep up with Jimmy Seed's production line, working to repopulate his programmatic emptiness, those huge blank canvases.

Magazines ran extracts – and then, when every word of the thing had been sold twice over, I delivered the typescript to my publishers. One of those decent, penny-pinching, heart-on-sleeve operations that are hoping to be taken over by the Germans or Japanese. Their reps are borrowed, the chains won't see them, but they achieve review coverage far beyond their weight (sympathy for the under-dog, journalists with uncommercial projects to peddle). My riffs were posthumous but ripe with déjà vu. The culture classes, pro-fessionally lazy and ill-informed, are only comfortable when the job has been done for them. Having absorbed, without noticing it, earlier versions of the A13 walk – as art criticism, psychogeography, anthologised fiction – they greeted my book with tempered enthusi-asm. Copies didn't leap from the shelves and nobody copped a hernia unloading stock. Broadsheets echoed each other, leading to radio fillers, talks at recently upgraded polytechnics: the University of Clapton, the Swanley Interchange Arts Festival, a Sunday afternoon recital in an otherwise engaged Finchley Road chainstore.

Estuarial Lives, measured in column inches, was a success; just enough to be a nuisance. Students from Paris and Milan (with bulging folders). Thesis brokers from the Cambridge fringe (stern questions about unread French philosophers). Freelancers on the nod from skateboard magazines. I didn't make any money, but I felt the burn of scorched time. The loss of anonymity. Locally, my wanderings were interrupted by cyclists eager to tell me about their projects: video surveillance of empty buildings, albums of rephotographed graffiti, underground streams tracked to source. A nervous woman, catching me at a petrol station on Mare Street, where we are all nervous (with good reason), presented me with a padded envelope that contained the evidence of an extraordinary art work. It anticipated, and surpassed, as the author rightly asserted, my crude urban expeditions. The man whose magnum opus the Mare Street woman was promoting, peddling around town, had cultivated a massive brain tumour, which pressed angrily on his optic nerves. He had X-rays of the intruder – which he superimposed over a map of medieval London, the walled City. He walked the shape of his pain, his unlanguaged parasite, into the map. His tiny script, pages of it, was harder to read than my own. But I caught the drift. I didn't want to be suckered into another malign fiction, in which his story became my story, my reading of his cuneiform text. Occultism, at this heat, was too oppressive.

It was time to go.

I pulled in to an empty bay, near the air machine. An Asian man in a big car needed my slot. He was very polite. He didn't honk. He waited as long as he could, then got out to tap, quite gently, on my window. The walker, the one with the dead foetus in his brain, believed that his pilgrimage would heal the hurt, free his spirit. By carving a mark into an historic landscape, he would exorcise the ancient thing that was devouring him. If I accepted the gift, walked his walk (X-rays in hand), I would activate my own demons. I would cultivate a duplicate tumour, a Smithfield thalamus. Brain-meat wrinkled in an opaque bowl.

'You staying long, mate?'

I reversed, swerved out of there, into the maelstrom of Hackney traffic. A12, Blackwall Tunnel, A2, M25, A21. Let the car drive itself. As a book-dealer, I made the run to the coast on a regular basis. Retirement colonies, modest shops packed with plunder. Fish supper, stroll on the beach. Home. Suspension groaning. A cloud of filth, shaped like one of M.R. James's demons, followed me onto the High Weald.

I was never going back. Easy as that. I wasn't interested in houses, investments, potential. The night walk with Effie the photographer was all the confirmation I required. I snatched at the sheet the estate agent didn't want to show me, a building that looked like a boat, a Thirties cruise liner. Such a monster would never be allowed again. They'd knocked down a hefty chunk of Regency development, so the man said, an archway and a hotel patronised by royalty. Balconies, windows, walkways. Looking straight out on the sea. One flat, old man taken into hospital, was on the market. But it wasn't for me, not worth going down there. Wouldn't waste my time. A mess of art magazines, tubes of paint, pigeon droppings, brown envelopes. Very nice properties in the Old Town. Catherine Cookson lived here for years.

The glass was smeared, clean it as often as you like, the same pattern of suicidal insects. As if there was something wrong with my eyes: no middle distance. I'd lost that register. Flies and clouds. Heavy sky-fleece mimicked the breaking-up of ice floes, seen from under deep blue water. On the horizon, twelve miles out, a procession of toy boats on their superhighway voyages.

There were other rooms. From the kitchen, I could gaze at the Old Town, cliffs, marine architecture, bourgeois and full-skirted in the French style (discreet behind flapping polythene); the sun, on good days, climbed out of the sea behind a skeletal pier. A bright rule across the crests of ever-shifting wavelets. I stood at that sink for hours – until the sun moved on towards Pevensey and Beachy Head. I watched, with autistic fascination, lines of stationary traffic, red lights and dirty gold. I noticed windows, shadows of strangers, blue television screens; the occasional solitary stepped out on a balcony, yawning, to test the evening air. There were always couples, all ages, moving along the seafront. Drinking schools kept to themselves, in caves and shelters beneath the promenade, out of sight, unrowdy, working hard at the daylong business of taking the edge off things.

The blight of vision: tide-race, scoured sand. Each morning the shingle combed like a gravel drive. A rattle of pebbles in the night. Weary mortals drawn to the shoreline. Resistance drained, they hooked themselves over the guard-rail, white-knuckled against the pull of the wind. Modest in bus shelters. Boarding houses. At high windows.

My reflection, in towelling bathrobe (think Joseph Cotten, age thirty-six, playing a sick old man in *Citizen Kane*), is convalescent. Solid to the shoulder, a thick white ghost looking for its head. A reflection that stays lodged in the glass. I can't move away until the job is done, the dreams of Hackney extinguished. Warm breath smears the gap where my face should appear. I creep, soundlessly, across rough matting, relishing the Weetabix texture. Down here, it's all sea news, crinkles.

What was her name? The woman Jimmy's students were always banging on about, their model: Marina? A bit of cultural freight there, be careful. A woman liked by other women, her attitude, her way of dressing. Fur hat with charity shop coat, fingerless gloves, workman's boots. The feeling that she'd got away with something, taken risks they appreciated without daring to imitate.

To the west, a black stone table set in a flowerbed, opposite the hotel. Table or altar? I cricked my neck to find it, get it into focus. I would have to do something about my eyes, keep the appointment I'd made with the optician. And then on, no choice, to the meeting with Kaporal. Jos had been on the coast long enough to pass as a native: no papers, no previous, no attachments. A sleepwalker with no short-term memory, misinformation on everything. Kaporal was a human computer, redundant but functioning perfectly – if you treated him with respect. Cash in advance. Wedge folded inside a used paperback, a novel by Ivy Compton-Burnett that he would never read. My first choice, a Patrick Hamilton, I decided to keep. The strolling pace of the narrative appealed, crimes were cruel but casual, fitted to a period and a location that solicited them. Stupidity was punished. The crimes Kaporal logged in my adopted seaside home were random and merciless: a vicar chopped into pieces and scattered over the county, a builder's yard dug up to search for missing gold bars from the Heathrow bullion robbery, a shipment of Samurai armour hijacked on the coast road, lorry dumped in a retail park outside Bexhill.

Kaporal told his tales without animation, heavy features sagging, thick fingers grooming a bald spot. I felt like a monster for disturbing his hibernation. Seated alongside him in a bar or café – he wasn't a drinker, but he perked up whenever he had a fork in his hand – I thought about a remark the critic David Thomson made about a 'maverick' American film director: 'Henry Jaglom is not a good enough actor to play Henry Jaglom.'

It had been a long time (and several unearned advances) since *Estuarial Lives*, my meditations on borderland psychoses, land piracy. I had to come up with something fresh (more of the same). Sixty miles out, on the leash, still attached to the hot core of London, but far enough away to appreciate the red glow in the sky, I lost my soul. What I needed now was an easy strike – six weeks max – doctoring Kaporal's research. New territory, salt in the air, small mysteries to unravel.

Coffee cup in hand, I limped down the corridor to my writing room; I cramped. Seizure of the bowels. Postpone the evacuation to catch that rush of energy and insight. Scribble notes – standing up, rubbing belly – in ruled notebook. Light a cigar, step out onto the balcony. Leave the smoking stub in an aluminium ashtray, scamper to the bathroom.

A necklace of stones, picked up from the beach, my morning

swim, hangs from the wall. A yellow-beaked gull lands on the balcony rail. The screech of another gull, swooping on the jagged spine of rocks, now revealed by a retreating tide, dissolves into the urgent bark of a chained dog, a city beast. Sixty miles away, where the real story begins.

Hackney Road

One dog barked but nobody heard it. The sound was part of the immediate acoustic landscape: aircraft circling, waiting for clearance, drills, sirens. A hair-trigger seethe of vehicles on Hackney Road (the only place in London where pedestrian crossings operate on a twice-daily basis). Restless humans. Groups forming, breaking, touching knuckles, outside the pub (the pool hall), grunting obscenities into unfamiliar mobiles.

The second dog, an Alsatian with dry snout and the eyes of Neville Chamberlain, was being teased, through the bars of the gate, by a young girl whose boredom was encroaching on hysteria. She poked, prodded, smooched endearments, made kissy-kissy sounds. The dog stayed aloof. But its smaller associate, given the run of the yard, went crazy: yelped, bounced off the wall of tyres, rushed at its tormentor, skidded, rolled, wallowed in mud, shook itself, backed away to the shed ... leapt, snarling, at a frayed end-of-rope, hanging from a tarpaulin sheet: so that a puddle of trapped rainwater cascaded over its filthy fur. The girl, who might have been as old as eight or nine, turned her back on the spectacle, to bum a cigarette from her distracted mother. This woman, not dressed for outdoors, the weather, rattled a warder-sized bunch of keys ... smoke-breathing, staring at her little pink phone: a powder compact mirror with the wrong face. The gates to the yard were open but the woman wouldn't go inside, move out of sight of her vehicle. Chilled nipples, mature, prominent, the colour of rich chocolate, diverted a carload of excitable Brick Laners.

Parked across the ramp, neither in nor out, denying access to other potential customers, primed for rapid retreat, was a motor stacked with ostentatiously hormonal Asian males. Senior rude boys. Fat, white-wall tyres: the nearside front, detumescent. Windows like gun-ports. Loud anti-music: a challenge. The youths twitched, suffered, the cranked-up adolescent's inability to sit still: three out, one in. All in, all out . . . And down the road towards the pub, back. Shoulder-shuffling, nudging. A quick dart to the shed at the end of the yard. No sign of the mechanic. Peep through dirty window, return to base, whack up the sound system. Scratch scrota. In unison.

Nothing is happening here and happening very fast. A soap opera badly mangled in an editing suit. Vital plot lines have been lost or suppressed, leaving a non-specific aura of panic that seems to hinge on the missing tyre technician. Alternate frames of *EastEnders* cut against structuralist slomo.

While I'm watching all this free television, Jimmy Seed is tapping a coin on the pad that cushions his hobbled electric window. The unofficial armrest has a groove fitted precisely to the shape of a pound coin, leading me to assume, by the deductive methods of Sherlock Holmes, that he keeps a mistress, or hideaway, on the south coast. The coin is the fee for the QEII Bridge, Purfleet to Dartford. But I was wrong. He did cross water on a regular basis, but his purpose was speculation: ex-industrial properties in the Thames Gateway zone. Bounty-hunting with a Polaroid. Jimmy had a talent for sniffing out units that would otherwise be wasted on housing economic migrants or Balkan sex slaves.

The girls on the back seat didn't talk much, the only still points in an edgy scene. They lounged: I stole a surreptitious glance in Jimmy's driving mirror. They whispered, tracked the tight-skinned youth who circled the Volvo on his bike, before looping back to the pub. This was an establishment where punters stayed outside, anyone who drank at the bar, in a jacket, a shirt, was a nonce. Or a fixture. Under-age lads played pool. Strays, remnants, the unlanguaged: they stared at a large screen that showed 24-hour football from elsewhere. The cyclist was their outrider, snaking into the world, bringing back news. Which he kept to himself.

'Explain again exactly where we're going.'

The tall young woman who asked the question might have been American, once. She had the kind of face in which you could trace the history of a solitary child coming to terms with life, haunted by atavistic fears, standing at the edge of town, watching a river. Thick red hair bravely unattended. An embargo on cosmetic enhancement. Her friend – I made that assumption on very little evidence – was English, ex-established. The woman she would one day become vividly present in her features; an inherited smoothness that would remain, points of colour on sculpted cheeks, dark lashes and a small pert mouth: the limits of her tolerance of Hackney inadequately disguised. They were both attractive. To me. To Jimmy (childlike and paternal in his off-hand courtesies). And also, perhaps, to each other.

'There's no exactly about it,' I said (when Jimmy stayed shtum, measuring the mother with the dark-brown aureoles). 'The A13 is a tributary of London's orbital motorway, the M25. But unlike the M25 it goes somewhere. If you can call Southend somewhere.'

'I thought,' Jimmy mumbled, 'Dagenham. For starters. Well, Ford's. Sheds, warehouses. Then the marshes, for Livia, engines buried in mud, all kinds of stuff. Ditches, channels. It's mysterious. The fiddly details you like to enlarge and . . . Sorry, that woman. I can't believe her.'

'Her *what*?' said the American, sharply.

'Stance. Attitude. The gate and the dog. If I did people, I'd have the camera out. That's prime, that is. Absolutely fucking amazing.'

I listened, I looked, but I wasn't part of it. I was reporting on something I'd left behind years ago and could barely remember. We met, early, in Jimmy's studio, under the arches, striplight, stacked with wine bottles, racks of prodigious canvases, estate agents' brochures. Three or four paintings were always on the go. He was a traditionalist, a hardworking artisan. Want a petrol station, on Burdett Road, to fit a space on your wall? He's your man. He'll do it. Better than the real thing. Call back Thursday. Chop off a couple of inches? Certainly, sir. A different car? No problem, give you a bell as soon as the paint dries.

Jimmy had this pitch he always came out with when he ran up against artists who wanted to talk art: 'If you were fixing the wing of a Cortina, you wouldn't leave brush strokes in the body filler, now would you? Fibreglass sticking out to show how fucking clever you are?'

Jimmy solicited: absence of signature, a solid frame around an innocent chunk of the world. His truth was thin as prison soup, smooth as satin. More real than the real. Rattle of trains overhead. Car alarms. A private world.

In this studio, which Jimmy had taken over, so he said, from a crew of over-ambitious crack cocaine dealers (blood on the walls), was a record of everything that was missing from East London: grandiose cinemas, open-air swimming pools (Lansbury's lidos), Underground stations. There were no people, people gave away the secret, they belonged in a particular time frame. Jimmy's graffiti-dense canvases, layered in carbon, cheap emulsion, virtual and actual mould and moss, didn't represent anything; they *were* that thing. Ugly, mute.

Here was the source of Jimmy's unease, his coin-tapping reflexes at the gate of the Hackney tyre yard. All his metaphors belonged to the period when he'd laboured in a garage in Derby. His art confirmed his failure to become a body-shop craftsman, covering up flaws, respraying insurance scam motors. Jimmy, who was short and damaged and hungry for fame and status and property, modelled himself on Steve McQueen: do the art stuff, yes, then get back to a man's business of bikes and cars, stunting, dirt-tracking. Playing chicken with the Grim Reaper.

The exiled Scottish painter was one of those unfortunates who had reached the stage of giving up everything that mattered (drink, cigarettes, bad behaviour with women). He felt better, was able to get out of bed in the morning – with absolutely *nothing* to get out of bed for. Work was never more than work. The steady accumulation of paintings that stood in for a past that was no longer visitable. Good things, houses, families, food on the table: none of it meant as much as the feel of that first glass in the hand, the sudden whiff of cinnamon from the spice warehouses, the muddy drench of the river.

Lines of cars on Hackney Road stretched back to the boarded-up Children's Hospital.

A West African, in a business suit, with his daughter, white ribbons on her pigtails.

Two geezers taking turns to roll a monster tyre.

A lad with a beaker of steaming coffee and a bag of rolls.

He has been tipped off about the arrival of the mechanic. Who leaps from his car, talking: 'You wouldn't believe the fucking A13, artic gone off of the ramp at Thurrock, gridlock. Roadworks. Three hours, no word of a lie, from Billericay.'

Estuarial Lives: the newsreel.

We wait. The American woman is scribbling in a notebook. Livia is staring out of the window in a freeze-frame reverie. Jimmy's whistling. I get out, stretch my legs, amble across the yard: steepling walls of tyres, all shapes, sizes and conditions, pressing back, bowing out the brickwork. Mud and oil. Old canvas so gone in colour that Jimmy could chop it into units, nail it onto stretchers, flog it to his collectors without adding a brushstroke. I lift the tent flap over a rickety lean-to, revealing a clean, well-maintained, top-of-the-range powerboat. A craft that would have you across the Channel, from Maldon to the Dutch dunes, in a short night, no questions asked. Fishing trip. 150 hp Yamaha engine, the sort Jimmy would admire. Work being done on extra fuel tanks. No wonder the man in the shed didn't have time to waste on punctures.

By now, most of Hackney is waiting. It's what we do, what we're good at: post offices, doctors, Town Hall. This little mob, with their various punctures, gathered at the gates, amuse themselves on their mobiles, sending out for coffee, making a run for the pub. Tribal scars. Moustaches and stubble. Hoods. Bleached blondes in loud leather. Chinese families on outings. All with cars slowly sinking into the slurry. Waiting, patiently or otherwise, for the solitary mechanic – who wants to be rid of them, with their favours and credits and promises, so that he can get back to his boat.

In the Volvo, Livia interrogates Track (the American woman).

What on earth is she drawing? What could she possibly find to memorialise in this slow-puncture entropy?

A sketch for Marina. For Marina's book. The book Marina was supposed to be writing. A possible illustration. Something Track had noticed in a shop window as they waited at the lights, Westgate Street into Mare Street. A pair of giant spectacles, painted with bright blue, unblinking eyes. Quite surreal. Marina will *love* them.

That was her project, gathering random images for a book that Marina hadn't finished, might never finish. A book that seemed to anticipate the road trip we were never going to complete. Never begin.

The Missing Kodak

I was superstitious about lost or undeveloped films, how they displace more memory than faithfully preserved albums of family portraits. They don't decay. They are imminent. Their potential is absolute. Lost films are dreams that anybody can steal.

Not trusting my ability to download names, signs, shifting skies, I always carried a small camera in my pocket: Canon Ixus L-1, forty exposures, idiot simple. With time, and Japanese technology, the cameras got smaller, lenses sharper – but it didn't help. Photography was still, as the man said, 'a form of bereavement'. The recording instruments shifted from awkward black boxes to silver toys (credit cards that ate light). My snapshots had no pretensions towards art or duplication, they logged a day out, evidence for narratives I would later subvert.

Photography, in its brokered aspect, is about exclusion: the high-contrast theatre of Bill Brandt, Eugene Atgèt's deserted Paris with sharp-prowed buildings like transatlantic liners in dry dock. Keep out the inessential, stay alive to significant accidents. I understood the theory, but I couldn't live by it. Once you break free of the traditional one-eyed stance, everything loosens up. You breech the middle ground. I abandoned my viewfinder as much too risky in Kingsland Waste Market, Clapton High Street, Green Lanes. The click of a shutter would alert the minder who watched over the contraband peddlers (the Albanian women, the man with one word of English, his mantra: 'Cig-ar-ette, cig-ar-ette, cig-ar-ette'). The unrequired flash reflected in the dark glasses of the Black Muslims with their sinister suits and bow ties. The hooded tollers on bikes. The fat man, on his knees behind the video stall, unpacking two carriers of hardcore. The loungers in the doorway of the Kurdish football-club café. The rock sellers yawning outside the newsagent.

The police, in their white van, eating pies, ignoring the ratty scavenger who is making off with black bags of clothes donated to Oxfam.

If photography is a form of masturbation, then exercise your wrist. Imitate the gunfighter, shoot from the hip. The eye in the palm of your hand deflects the victim's curse.

I deactivated the flash and learnt to frame by instinct. The result was a pleasing, slapdash, unmediated aesthetic. The prose I contrived from these snapshots would be more provocative, so I hoped, than the awkward blocks of verbless sentences 'inspired' by the many thousands of diary-images I'd gathered during the years of my compulsive logging of London and the river. What are we *really* doing with those handheld obituary lanterns, our cameras? Despoiling virgin topography. Forging, on stiff card, autobiographical confessions. *I witnessed it*. Every picture a story, every story a lie. Look at them now. Look at the captured rectangles in their prophylactic envelopes. This person, raking over mounds of paperback books, left when the market packs up, is someone I once was: predatory, stooped, close to the pulse of the city. This building charts my ruin, wrecked knees, twisted spine. A failing heart. The fouled stream skulking through Rainham Marshes, a piss-trough, is my lost optimism, my childhood. When the local was eternal, water (clear and fresh) always flowed towards some larger, busier river, a cold grey sea.

The photographs that haunted me were the ones that got away. The new mountain range of smouldering waste, lava trails of burst black bags, between Rainham Marshes and Dagenham, reminded me of one roll in particular. A strange story, a voyage out from Limehouse to Southend, to the mouth of the Thames, the North Sea, in search of an off-shore fort. Our craft, a fishing-boat brought back from Yarmouth, was on its last voyage. The skipper, drunk at the start and getting drunker, was preparing himself for that lashed-to-the-mast *Dracula* gig. Most of my shipmates, it soon became apparent, had signed on to locate and confront their demons. And they were making a very good job of it. A shivering photographer, inadequately accoutred in a thin T-shirt with cutoff sleeves, having puked himself dry, was hidden (from the rest of us, from the sea) under a dog blanket. A video director, incapable of taking his camera out of the satchel, droned through the long night, an Ingmar Bergman recital of dreams, phobias, confessions, visions of existential horror. He hated boats, loathed the river (with reason: accidental deaths of loved ones, drownings witnessed at close hand). He suffered from a recurrent nightmare of being trapped for hours, midstream, watching the dim lights of a shoreline he would never reach. This moment, he informed us, recognising the never-extinguished fires of the Rainham Marshes landfill site, was the realisation of his trauma. Talked out, the man slept, tossed and turned, returned to the borders of consciousness – and *there it was*: the oil refineries. Canvey. Prospero's island, abandoned by its devils, left to burn and smoulder for ever.

As the only photographic amateur aboard, strong stomach, no imagination, I kept on snapping. Registering the details of this lunatic voyage. But I didn't secure the rolls of completed film. What was the point? We were never coming back, onwards and outwards. I saw those little black plastic containers floating ashore, in Suffolk or Denmark, with their obscure messages. Like suicide notes in miniature whisky bottles thrown over the side of a Channel ferry.

By the time we reached Leigh-on-Sea, the neurasthenics had given up their ghosts; you could hear teeth chattering like ill-fitting computer keys. The photographer was laughing hysterically and banging his head against the deckboards. I wanted a couple of shots of the women – bad luck – who had smuggled themselves aboard to keep the captain company, to steady the wheel while he opened another bottle. He demanded oral satisfaction while he dodged oil tankers in the narrow channel off Gravesend. But there was no film left. I decided that, in the circumstances, I'd have to reuse a roll I'd shot in Howard Marks's borrowed flat in West London. A pity, really, but the random superimpositions would give whoever found my floating canister something to analyse. Derrida or Sontag. Let them quote their way out of that mess with Walter Benjamin and

Schopenhauer. Howard, it was generally acknowledged, dues paid, was the acceptable (out-of-focus) face of cannabis culture, reform of soft drug legislation. New Labour's favourite anarchist. On the road, on message: on the money.

Marks had been in splendid form, talking freely, exhaling dense clouds of herbal nostalgia, saying nothing. The London light was exquisite, verging on excess. It seemed to imply: you *can* get away with it, walk free, sunshine on old wood, interior jungles, quiet streets. You *can* come home again to make a career out of bent memory; telling it how we'd like it to be. Howard twinned nicely with Alex Garland, Irvine Welsh, Danny Boyle: he anticipated the era (pre-terror) of hallucinogenic tourism (Thailand, Bali, Edinburgh). Sheiks and falconers sharing a lift in the Cairo Hilton. Airports, massage parlours, record collections and favourite paperbacks: *Lord of the Flies*, soft punk, Bill Wyman barnet. The ideal is to stay in prison – or smacked out of your head – long enough for retro to come back as this week's tendency. J.G. Ballard-lite: tropic beaches, tourism as a life style, business-class flights, the discretion of the suburbs (where all the best conspiracies are hatched).

It was as difficult to dislike Howard Marks as it was to take the right photo. That's why I left the film so long in the camera, an abandoned essay. Huge smile (new teeth better than the originals), expansive gestures. A girl in a scarlet PVC raincoat, bottle blonde, sitting with him at the table, was pretending, for the purposes of a documentary film, to be the interviewer. Neither acting nor reacting, she was a more potent reality than the Marksian hologram with its Mediterranean tan, twinkly eyes and contradictory semaphore of hands and shoulders. The mobile bleeped at regular intervals.

So our night voyage on the Thames, dark dreams, lapped over this sunlit room in Earls Court: arbitrary juxtapositions. The film, lost in the bilges, was busy in my memory. Soft evidence transformed into fiction. The image you don't have, mislaid by chemist, stolen camera, retains its malignancy. It is unappeased. Marks talking, girl listening (with an expression of cynicism, boredom, that is impossible to quantify). The passengers and crew on a small craft, making no headway against a running tide, are tormented by fantasies of death by drowning.. A blank sheet in my typewriter. Two stories lost. Two stories that got away. The burning chimneys of the Esso oil refineries at Purfleet. The spontaneous combustions of the landfill site on Rainham Marshes. Seen from the river. The yarns Howard Marks spun, conspiracies, coincidences, scams, going up in smoke. Sound lost with image.

Marks was one story, but the other was more poignant. More personal. An early Kodak portable with a curious history. It was not the film that was missing, this time, but the camera. My great-grandfather, money dissipated through bad investments, property threatened – he moved south for the winter, from Aberdeen to the English Riviera, Paignton, I think, or Bournemouth – took off on what turned out to be a last, mad journey into the Peruvian interior. The tea interests he'd served so effectively in Ceylon wanted to know if this unmapped territory would be suitable for the cultivation of coffee. With a young man from the company, a small library of botanical books, odd volumes of De Quincey, quinine, salt, pen and ink, rifle and Kodak, he set out from Lima, through Chicla and Tarma, to the Rio Perene, towards land designated for potential exploitation by the commissioners.

Diaries and photographs and faithful camera were brought back by young Mr Stevenson, when the search for my great-grandfather was abandoned. A second expedition, funded by his widow, found nothing. The Indians retreated into the forest. A terse and unreliable account of the ill-omened river trip was assembled from unposted letters and journal extracts, which my great-grandfather had revised and polished during a month's stay with a renegade Franciscan, in a district called Chanchamayo, while they waited for the weather to break – and for contact to be established with King Chokery, the Chuncho chief whose goodwill was required for any voyage on the upper reaches of the uncharted Perene.

The expedition, from the moment the ship sailed from Tilbury, was wrong, malfated. My great-grandfather, softened by the years of his retirement, missing wife and children, paced the deck, struggling for breath, feeling all of his fifty or so years. He was an abstemious man, he took a whisky or two with his dinner and a cigar with the first officer after it. His eyes were still sharp. They watched the stars.

The first officer, a stocky European with a literary beard and waxed moustache, quoted the painter Delacroix (as my great-grandfather noted in his journal): the light from the star Vega, hurtling through space, set out on its epic voyage twenty years before Monsieur Daguerre invented the process whereby its arrival in Cambridge could be recorded as a pin-sized impression on a metal plate. Something of the sort, so the merchant mariner suggested, should be applied to his conversation. To the tacit understanding that my great-grandfather would record his remarks. And that those insignificant blots on the page would, at some future epoch, be the source of unimaginable revelation.

Panama was a sink, Colon lived down to its name. The Scots Calvinist felt as if he were crawling into the continent by the back door: caecum to rectum, a yellow worm in a hunk of rotten meat.

Colon, our first landing port, apart from its luxurious vegetation, is a very wretched spot. It is only in a Spanish Republic that the existence of such a pestiferous place is possible. It is not merely the disreputable appearance of its degenerate people, nor the frequent squabbles dignified by the name of revolutions we have to fear, but the ever present filth, which is much more dangerous to life. Fortunately, a fire has recently burned down and purified a large portion of the town, rendering it, for a time, less dangerous to sojourners.

Driving east down the A13, past Creekmouth, with Jimmy Seed and the girls, the mess of the sewage outflow, filter beds, new retail parks, coned lanes, uncompleted ramps, I took the Peruvian journals as a literal guide: like for like. A shifting landscape of equivalents. The River Roding, disgorging in a septic scum into the Thames, became the Rio Perene. The man-made, conical alp of the Beckton ski slope stood in for the foothills of the Andes. Stacked container units in dirty primary colours hinted at the roll of film on which

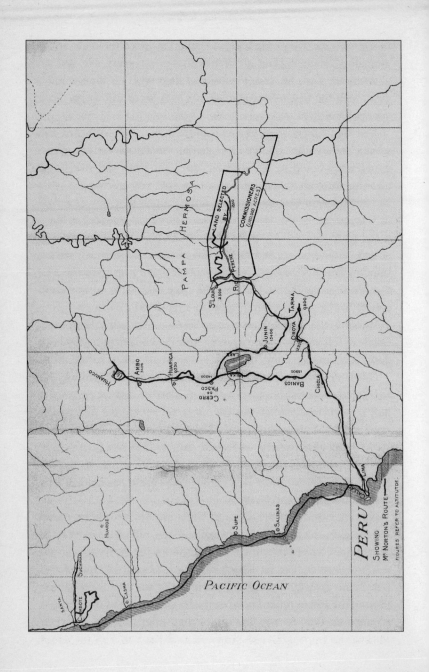

PAMPA HERMOSA

LAND SELECTED BY COMMISSIONERS (162,500 ACRES)

S^T LOUIS 2300

RIO PERENE

TARMA 9800

OROYA 12000

JUNIN 13400

LAKE

MULA 14200

CERRO DE PASCO

AMBO 7400

HUARICA 9730

HUANUCO

BANIOS 13600

CHICLA

CALLAO

LIMA

SUPE

SALINAS

HUAROZ

SANTA

CHIMBOTE

CASMA

SUCHIMAN

PERU

SHOWING
MR NORTON'S ROUTE

FIGURES REFER TO ALTITUDE.

PACIFIC OCEAN

my great-grandfather made his survey of the missionary settlement in a jungle clearing.

The road was a villainous rut at a gradient of about one in three, a width of about eighteen inches, and knee deep in something like liquid glue. Before we had gone five miles one-half the cavalcade had come to grief, and it was some weeks ere we saw our pack mules again; indeed I believe some of them lie there still. We soon found out that the padres knew as little about the path as we did ourselves, and the upshot was we were benighted. Shortly after six o'clock we were overtaken in inky darkness, yet we plodded on, bespattered with mud, tired, bitten, and blistered by various insects. Whole boxes of matches were burned in enabling us to scramble over logs or avoid the deepest swamps. At last there was a slight opening in the forest, and the ruins of an old thatched shed were discovered, with one end of a broken beam resting upon an upright post, sufficient to shelter us from the heavy dews. It turned out to be the tomb of some old Inca chief whose bones have lain for over 350 years, and there, on the damp earth, we lay down beside them, just as we were. Our dinner consisted of a few sardines, which we ate, I shall not say greedily, for I felt tired and sulky, keeping a suspicious eye upon the Jesuit priests.

The Peruvian interior in the late nineteenth century, filtered through the prejudices of a weary Highlander of discounted Jacobite stock, a self-educated plantsman and jobbing author, was a more convincing mindscape than riverine, off-highway Essex. My great-grandfather's notebooks were livelier than my own, more dyspeptic; he covered more ground (somebody found it worth their while to commission him to do so). The picaresque elements were the by-product of a very practical quest: could coffee be cultivated, cheaply, on this land? The Pampa Hermosa took precedence over the Dagenham Levels. Sepia photographs on wilting card, brought back by Mr Stevenson and spread across my desk, outranked my anaemic Polaroids. A 'balsa' on the Perene: loose-robed Indian with pole, great-grandfather squatting low to the water, rifle in lap, boy in prow watching out for submerged trees. The skeletal remains of a burnt-out Ford by the side of the road that led across Rainham Marshes to the landfill site. An orchid on the banks of the turbid

stream, decadent, pale, carnivorous. Small blue flowers, soap-bleached, beside the Thames path, in the shadow of the Procter & Gamble factory at West Thurrock. Two of the wives of King Chokery. Jimmy's postgraduate students, Track and Livia, posing beside an irrigation ditch.

Three months into the expedition, weak from dysentery, dehydrated, shivering with cold sweats, cursing the Jesuits who had come with him so far, and would go no further, my great-grandfather followed the example of King Chokery's subjects, the guides who punted him down the dark, creeper-enclosed tunnel of that Stygian river: he took to chewing the leaf.

Coca, from which the invaluable drug, cocaine, is obtained, is a native of this locality. It is a plant not unlike the Chinese tea, though scarcely so sturdy in habit, growing to a height of from four to five feet, with bright green leaves and white blossoms, followed by reddish berries. The leaves are plucked when well matured, dried in the sun, and simply packed in bundles for use or export. Of the sustaining power of coca there can be no possible doubt; the Chunchos seem not only to exist, but to thrive, upon the stimulant, often travelling for days with very little, if anything else, to sustain them. Unquestionably it is much superior and less liable to abuse than the tobacco, betel, or opium of other nations. The Chuncho is never seen without his wallet containing a stock of dried leaves, a pot of prepared lime, or the ashes of the quinua plant, and he makes a halt about once an hour to replenish his capacious mouth. When I decided, driven by physical necessity, to make a trial of the native habit, I found the flavour bitter and somewhat nauseating at first, but the taste is soon acquired, and if not exactly palatable, the benefit under fatiguing journeys is very palpable. Cold tea is nowhere, and the best of wines worthless in comparison with this pure unfermented heaven-sent reviver.

No leaves on the Eastbury Level, the Hornchurch Marshes, the old firing ranges with their overgrown butts and tattered distance markers: hybrid vegetation, unloved, ungrazed. Thorn bushes. Nettle beds. Nothing to chew. By river, through Tilbury and Silvertown, doctored coca, a synthetic, is smuggled ashore. By container transporter, by white van, by Special Boat Squadron inflatable: sustenance and stimulation for Sherlock Holmes and Dr Freud. Cargo for illicit Range Rovers.

The balsa, a few twigs roped together, is punted, now drifting, now spinning on the current, towards the white zone. The blank on the map. Noises of the jungle. Shrieks and long silences. The pole sticking in mud. Jimmy parks his Volvo beside Rainham Creek, sleek black crows gather in a naked tree, black plastic flapping on razor wire.

Like my lost roll of film, out there on the Thames, two journeys overlap: Peru and Essex. Mr Stevenson was in no condition to make his report to the com-missioners. He recuperated on the coast, prematurely aged, mimicking the old men, staring for hours at the Channel. Salt-smeared windows framed by faded velvet curtains. Persuaded to take the air, an afternoon constitutional, Stevenson refused to walk along the promenade; he turned his back on the sea, retreated uphill, under an ornate arch, into a small park. He liked the flowers, their

teasing scents, regimented profusion: rhododendron, hibiscus. The park, with its gentle microclimate, was a grey-filter Ceylon.

He reached into the pockets of his long chalky coat and drew out my great-grandfather's pen-and-ink sketches; as if, by handling them, he could remember what happened, those last days on the Rio Perene. The photographs – King Chokery, the Cholo Highlanders (like dwarfish and displaced Scots), the grave goods, the cathedral square in Lima – had returned to London with Stevenson's overheated and incomplete report. Acting on some nervous instinct he retained the botanical sketches. Now, in the early-evening chill of an English park, the drawings brought back happier days in Colombo, visiting tea-estates to gather material for articles published by the local press, the *Ceylon Observer* and the *Tropical Agriculturalist*. My great-grandfather's minimalist representations of humble verbena, lobelia, oxalis, calandrinia, substituted for the empty beds in this south-coast garden, the tin labels that designated future plantings.

I took the phone call late on the Sunday before Christmas, suicide's eve. You can hear the third gin being poured at the other end of the line, as old folk, solitaries, survivors, work through outdated address books. The second wife, tennis partner, of my great-grandfather's second son's only boy, had inherited that early Kodak portable. There was no one else. It should come to me. We'd never met, but my number was in the book. The old lady was in sheltered accommodation, very nice, very warm, a jolly Christmas in prospect: I could hear James Stewart ya-yawing in the background. The camera, that came back from Peru with Stevenson, had passed down through the generations, looked after, polished and put away in the cupboard. Then this woman, no connection of mine by blood, a lovely, no-nonsense (by the sound of it) South Londoner, took her prize possession to a charitable Antiques Road Show, in the church hall. It was certainly worth something, the man with the bow tie said, not in cash necessarily, but as part of a 'fascinating' tale. It should be placed in safe hands, the memory should be preserved, of that adventure in . . . where was it? . . . South America, Mexico? And, by the way, he enquired with studied emphasis, did she realise that there was *film in the camera*? Unexposed film. This was the thing that haunted me, that kept the Peruvian expedition running alongside my trip with Jimmy and the girls to Rainham Marshes. The impulses responsible for those pictures, the heat that caused the shutter mechanism to be pressed, was still active. Floating, unresolved, along the soft verges of the A13.

'Lovely to talk to you, dear, so lovely. One of the ladies here, her daughter's getting married at Easter, in church, will send you the camera. My husband, your father's first cousin, wanted you to have it. He always said so. But we weren't in touch, were we? And then when I heard it might be valuable, well . . .'

I was caught off-guard. I stood with the phone in my hand, long after the connection had been broken. I knew that the parcel would never arrive. And I knew that the mystery of those final undeveloped images would never be solved. Next morning, back from a short walk, sitting at my desk, glass in hand, gesture to the season, I remembered. I hadn't asked for a number, an address. I didn't even know the old lady's name. The nuisance of it, my stupidity, ruined my Christmas curry, the traditional cigar and tape of Bresson's *Pickpocket*.

Rainham Marshes

The girl Track had disappeared. On the marshes. After searching for thirty or forty minutes, until the rain forced us back to the car, we left her to it, retreated to a truckers' café in Thurrock. Track did this all the time, Livia said. Jimmy, in loco parentis, was unfazed. Track was five years older than his current wife. She'd grown up on European art cinema, Monica Vitti stalking Lea Massari. In her Oxfam way, the American was a bit of a drama queen. Right set, right reaction: absence.

In Hackney it was cats. Nailed to trees, photocopied portraits. Rewards. People didn't disappear, not for a second time: they were the disappeared, it was their vocation. Bodies showed up in parks and squares, killers vanished. Crimes were unsigned, uncredited. Random conjunctions inspired by the location. Women, men too, travelled to the coast if they wanted to shed their identities. You saw the faces, years older, in shop windows.

Track was a premature ghost. You couldn't pull this number on Rainham Marshes. Nobody would notice.

Monica Vitti, so Track had informed us, when we sidled, collars up, around a breakers' yard, got her start dubbing an actress called Dorian Gray in Antonioni's gloomy Po Valley drama, *Il Grido*. Echoes of echoes of echoes. A counterfeit name for a forgotten performer. Oscar Wilde's fable twisted: a production still staying forever young and enigmatic in a film buff's attic, while the freckled sleepwalker Vitti (who always seemed to be taking instruction, a few beats after the event, from an earpiece disguised by a lustrous tumble of hair) succumbs, in gentle increments, to the pull of mortality.

Out on the road, Jimmy's spirits lifted; he understood precisely how to play the part of the man at the wheel. Humming, tapping his coin, doing the voices: a replay of last night's television, a documentary about a stuntman who'd broken every bone in his body, but who kept on pushing it, wilder and wilder outfits. Clenched fist, cigar in mouth, as they wheeled him away on the gurney; wink for the camera. Jimmy, his biker days behind him, was impressed by the fatalism, leather and tassels, of this once dirt-poor hillbilly. An Appalachian astronaut who jumped buses, took flight across canyons, hurtled to earth. A gravity addict. The absence of a helmet that would interfere with an exquisitely engineered hair-style, raven black and aerodynamic, was a red badge of stupidity. But what Jimmy liked best in the film were the empty roads, dawn shots of a dusty nowhere, the clapboard whistlestop where the stuntman grew up. Coal heaps, coal dirt as a filter. Lone dogs picking at road-kill in the parking lots of drive-in convenience stores.

Half listening, I could tolerate Jimmy's monologue, float it across the aspirant-Americana of the A13. New Jersey's reed beds translated to Newham: sideflash of carney show Millennium Dome. Marginal enterprises (failed) giving way to hopeless future projects, retail suburbs, development scams, ski slopes sculpted from toxic waste, the inflorescence of entropy. (With his spare hand Jimmy snapped a high-rise trio on the outskirts of Dagenham, seen from a flyover, pale sun rising, downriver, beyond Ford's water tower and the pylon forests.) Heroic English cottages, grace-and-favour for workers in the motor plant, were terraced hard against the sub-motorway, this sluggish tributary of London's orbital hoop, the M25. Front windows were boarded over. The back gardens, in the days when these dwellings were habitable, concealed the front door, the way in. You learnt to live with noise, dirt. You looked north, away from the river, towards the slopes of the Epping Forest fringe, the Italianate tower of Claybury Mental Hospital.

Jimmy's immodest canvases, stacked in his Hackney lock-up, were a memory bank for everything that was missing, damaged or destroyed: gangland pubs where retired dockers talked contraband with chalky villains, swollen knuckles, liver spots, back from a seven in Parkhurst. Carpets of scrunched up betting-slips. Metal ashtrays from which the ash could never be rinsed (nobody tried). Size implied defeat. Caverns for excursionists who weren't there. Riverside palaces of ruined gilt occupied by two or three old men, leaking smoke and watching the door. If these pubs aren't taken over by ravers, for all-night noise fests, they're finished. Abandoned to Jimmy and his swollen replicas.

Track and Livia disregarded the low macho of the stuntman replays, they looked out of the window, passed soft-voiced comments, noticing things. Jimmy needed an audience, needed us with him: he switched to a Los Angeles murder mystery, the reinvestigation of a slasher crime. He did Nick Nolte, drunk, table-hopping with a bunch of homicide cops at a reunion in a Chinese restaurant; Nick's fame-clubbed head too heavy for his shoulders. Jimmy did the obscenities, panty-sniffing creeps, masturbating peepers, Vice Squad jokes with canned laughter. And he did them with furtive glances in the driving mirror.

I suggested, feeling the first pangs of hunger, that we come off-road at Rainham. The Thames marshes, bordered by semi-legit businesses, Portakabins, slavering dogs, were a lacuna Jimmy could effortlessly exploit: a bit of fence, rubbish lorries hiccuping down an unclassified highway. A single striking object – concrete barge, bridge disappearing into the clouds, motorbike wheel peeking out of sluggish stream – would be enough, a focal point for the composition. The rest was suggestion. A sprayed undercoat, a bucket of emulsion, detail touched in with a fine brush.

'Like welding,' Jimmy said. 'The garage. Everything comes back to that. Access boredom and march right through it.' Five hours a day, radio blaring. Knock off in time to pick up the kids. Evenings free to network, go on the piss. Even if the binge lurched on for a week and Jimmy woke up in a flat above a barber shop in Portsmouth, he never failed to bring home the numbers. Mobile and ex-directory. Name, rank: neatly inked on the flapping cuff of his once-white shirt. Antony Gormley. Man from Tate Modern. That architect who does the long, thin glass coffins, shoehorned into cracks between Clerkenwell lofts. Woman from *Modern Painters*.

Howard Jacobson, Will Self and Rowan Moore, the journalist whose brother is the editor of . . .

We pulled up broadside to a phone kiosk that some humorist had slapped down in the middle of nothing. The police car that had been trailing us, since the mountain of multicoloured container units (we clambered out with our cameras), cut across our bows in a whip of dust and rubber. The driver yawned, his oppo tapped on Jimmy's window. 'Where do you come from?' 'What are you?' 'Where are you going?' The second question being the tough one.

The uniform talked to Jimmy and stared at the girls. I did my halfwitted, middle-class TV researcher act, flashing a laminated ID card (Apollo Home Entertainment, Bethnal Green Road). They weren't interested. What we hadn't noticed – preoccupied with extreme manifestations of local colour – was the distant line of beaters working their way towards us across the mud flats. Wellington bootmarks filling with yellow squitter. Nuisanced crows perched on wire.

The search was now in its critical third day, a schoolgirl from Purfleet reported as missing: last seen at the bus stop, 8.30 a.m., grey flannel skirt, blue jersey, no coat. Fourteen years old: no form, no suspect connections. An occasional clubber at 'Tuesdays' in Basildon. Tuesdays: as in 'shut on'. Apostrophe sacrificed in homage to Ms Weld, the peppy ingénue of *Rally Round the Flag, Boys*, the depressed mom of *Heartbreak Hotel*. Clubland in Essex had slithered down the fantasy casting couch from Marilyn (shaking it for Jack) to Raquel (fur bikini) to Teen Queen surf bimbos (sub-Corman). Weld deserved better. In her day she was pretty good. We were the same age, but we'd matured at different speeds. She got to play Scott Fitzgerald's wife round about the time I was scratching dog shit from the base of the pyramid in Limehouse Church. In the film dictionaries you'll find her between Johnny Weissmuller and Orson Welles.

Sad that Tuesday had become estuary slang, mouthed by groups of young males, on walls, on bikes, shouting after schoolgirls. 'See you next Tuesday.' C-U-N-T.

The Basildon club was the kind of place where they employed

bouncers to chuck you *in*. To keep you wired. Blood flowed, at the burger stall in the early hours, when grudges were sorted; cold night air, big men with small psychoses, rucks over minicabs and gash. The local filth were so bent, there was no point in putting them on the payroll. They paid *you*, for part of the action. They stored excess stock, drugs and porn. You worked for them, if you were lucky, as a salaried distributor.

Beyond the cordon of police and volunteers, searching the wetlands with their sticks and poles, we saw, as the rainbelt moved on, the full span of the QEII Bridge: a set of silver dentures. Traffic stalled on the M25. Incident, accident, weight of numbers overwhelming the Dartford poll booths.

The police car put on its siren and flashing blue lights. I watched it race away down the long straight road, shuddering over bumps, swerving and flashing to warn off the convoy of approaching landfill lorries. The secret cargoes of London.

Livia found a piece of engine, submerged in the claggy ground: cut hoses, valves, cables. The lumpy metal heart looked like something ripped from a living body, by surgeon or contract killer. The young woman brushed away mud. She stroked the proud letters of the manufacturer's name with her naked fingers, before lifting the specimen up to her face and sniffing it.

'Livia, no,' Jimmy warned. 'Use the camera. We're artists, not dealers in scrap metal. The boot's full.'

The formal description of this thing – size, weight, odour – went into a moleskin sketchbook. Hand-drawn panels. Like a Manga strip, an angry Japanese comic. A machine brought to life by a woman's love. Oil for blood. The soul-meat of a murdered android. Only then did Livia use her camera. For the final rites, before Jimmy tossed the abortion into the creek.

'Breakfast now. Ahead of that mob from over the river. That's where Track will have gone, you'll see. The café.'

The Log Cabin at West Thurrock was long and low, hanging baskets dressing a theme park timber facade. Narrow bays for rep cars out front, space at the back for the white vans and lorries that served the riverside industrial units: soap, petrol, paper.

The interesting thing, as the three of us faced up to the consequences of ordering up numbers, heavy platters of beans, bacon, airfixed sausage, blind egg, tin-flavoured tomato, grease raft of fried bread, was that Jimmy, in his PLASTERCASTER T-shirt and black leather waistcoat, was comprehensively discommoded by the scale and immediacy of the feast. The Glaswegian hardman, beetling eyebrows, red-gold fleece of thinning hair, hadn't been inside a workman's caff for years. And it showed. His hand trembled as he reached for a fork.

'Christ,' he said, puncturing the sawdust-and-pig's-foot condom, 'is this thing still *alive*? I don't, I can't, I mustn't . . .'

Pink-cheeked Livia, having wolfed down the potent slop, salty strips of doctored meat substitute, was wiping her plate, a clover leaf of thick scarlet smear. 'Good,' she said. 'Very good.' She burped. Jimmy amused her.

'I sold my soul to join the fucking middle classes,' the painter moaned. 'You're wiping years off my CV, I mean it. Dragging me back to the gutter. Phowarrr! Sorry. I've got to drop one. The beans. I haven't *seen* one of those plastic sauce dispensers since I was in New York.'

'You don't seem very bothered about your friend, about Track,' I said to Livia. While Jimmy lurched up the aisle, running the gauntlet of scornful tabloid-grazers who took their tea in pint pots. Signature flatus lost in the amnesty of rain-fug and fry-up, loosened belts and squeaky seats. A veil of cigarette smoke and steam from donkey jackets.

'Happens all the time. She calls it: "my fugue". Jimmy thinks it's attention-seeking. He's wrong.'

Livia didn't look at me when she spoke. She was staring out of the window, head on hand, patterns made by raindrops in the accumulated grease, human leakage.

'Why?'

Livia rummaged in her satchel.

'I thought I had a photograph. Wrong bag.'

'Of what?'

'Marina. Marina is Track's great passion. Marina is ahead of the game. A studio – in Dagenham? A residency in Grays, paid for by the riverside developers, to come up with an essay on Conrad in Stanford-le-Hope. A creative-writing fellowship at the Bloomberg Centre. You know that place in Finsbury Square? "London's first post-paper environment," Marina called it. Curtains of floating images. Live-feeds from the seaside washing under your feet. Banks of monitors in every pillar. 24-hour cable transmission into world-wide financial centres: liquid art. Bloomberg wanted writers without writing, text as presence. So Marina used books like computers. Slim, elegant ones: Beckett, Borges, late DeLillo. Flip the lid and read vertical word-columns as prophecy. "They saw his glasses melt into his eyes." Marina filmed books. She would stand there, behind one of the pillars, watching them watching her work. DeLillo fables about men losing billions of dollars. No future. The poetry's been left out. Marina is a poet.'

'Marina who?'

'Marina Fountain.'

'Where is she now?'

'Postcard last week: a ship burning on a beach. Other than that, nothing. Could be anywhere. Track thinks that if she walks out of the story somewhere around the area where Marina was last seen, she'll find her – by mimicking her actions. Psychogeographical possession.'

I sighed. Too old for this stuff.

'Another coffee?'

Our chauffeur hadn't reappeared. Jimmy was the latest disappearance, groaning in the Portakabin out back; horrified by where he found himself, an empty soap dispenser, a hot-air blower that didn't blow. Piss stains on the soft suede of his desert boots. Holes in the floor.

'Actually,' Livia muttered, when I was already on my feet, heading for the counter, mugs in hand. 'Marina used *your* road book' – I sat down again – 'for her Bloomberg piece.'

'What road book?' I hadn't written about roads. What did I know about roads? The A13, it's true, was a possible future project – but I'd kept pretty quiet about that.

'The one about Lakeside, Chafford Hundred, Essex gangsters, Dracula's abbey, bullion robberies. The walk.'

'I've never, *ever* been inside the perimeter of Lakeside. Ikea is a four-letter word that brings me out in a cold sweat.'

It was crazy, this woman was describing a book I was incapable of writing. Another jolt of caffeine-scum on watered milk might do the trick.

'Marina left a folder of stories. She asked me, when she heard you were doing a piece on Jimmy, to show them to you. I could bring them round if you like. To your house?'

This was altogether too much. The face, innocent of distinguishing features, of the woman behind the counter, was a relief. I basked in her aura. Her physicality. The way she moved and talked and knew herself. It went with the décor. Basic transactions: request, cash, ticket, coffee. Wet windows. Hiss of frying bacon. Steam from a kettle. Radiant horseshoe (white light within blue) of a shoulder-level heating device. Mute TV giving out pictures of traffic jams, rain on the road. Jukebox synthesising sunshine, beach bars, golden sands.

'Hello, love. What's it this time?'

'Two coffees, please.'

'Gone off of us? You ain't been in this week. You found another woman then? You hear, Den? The prof's found another woman.'

'*What?*'

'Research, your mate said. The TV. You're going to put us on television.'

Openmouthed, she laughed. Shook.

'I've never been in Thurrock before. I'll be back for sure.'

Her Lana Turner bosom agitated the tight sweater. Hooped earrings jangled.

'Hear that, Den?' She said to the cook, the flame-eater in the string vest. 'What *never* been in? That's your second this morning, mate. I said to Den, "Where's he bleedin' put it?" Full English twice over. I thought you was back cos you fancied me.'

She turned to scoop three portions of freshly singed toast from the machine, to scoop margarine from a catering pack.

'Toast. Number 12. Number 12, your toast's done.'

Something was dripping into my coffee, staining it. The plipplip-plip of raindrops from the overhanging greenery. I rubbed my chin, blood coursed and spouted. I stared into the steamed mirror with the *Coca-Cola* logo. A small shaving-nick was pumping out absurd quantities of very red blood. And this on a morning when I hadn't shaved. I couldn't accept the evidence of my own eyes. I took off my glasses to get a closer look. When I tried to stretch the sockets, achieve sharp focus, clear this milky softness, I succeeded in smearing more blood across my cheeks. Turning an everyday, slightly bemused, slightly weary expression into urban werewolf, cornered sex criminal. The Beast of the Marshes. *They saw his glasses melt into his eyes.*

Coast

At the high window, above Warrior Square, Kaporal shut one eye and then the other. The statue of Queen Victoria with the red traffic cone perched on her head slid left to right and back again. He was the director. The grey, sea-facing monarch looked like a Hobbit. Kaporal approved: surreal contrivances tempering anomie. This was the first time, in twenty years, that he'd lived in a room without a phone. A mobile. He had a TV but never switched it on. The view from the window was better than electricity. He had to believe that if he kept clear of the Old Town, the Stade, the beach-front winkle bars, arcades, clubs, he wouldn't run into O'Driscoll, the Sleeman brothers or Phil Tock.

Basildon villains weren't troubled by Mafia memories. They never crossed water: Southend, not Margate. Canvey before Sheppey. If they couldn't sort it, pliers and industrial meat-mincer, within forty-eight hours of the original insult, the supposed absence of respect was history. 'Me bruvver, 'e wouldn't hurt a sparrer.' Maybe. Good news for Bill Oddie and the twitchers of Rainham Marshes. But Alby Sleeman, with the fat neck, musculature over-developed to the point of deformity, buttonhole eyes drilled into a snowman, had plenty of harm, discriminations of dentistry, on offer for those who badmouthed his family and associates. His sponsors. Alby was old school: not merely illiterate but anti-literate, books were suspect (school, Borstal, greenpaint office of psychiatric assessor). Writers were worse. He'd top the lot of them, mincing ponces. Grasses. Weasels who bent the truth, stole the words out of your mouth and twisted them.

Take that Kaporal. The geezer looked genuine when you met him, a face. Thick skin hanging on a skull that seemed to have shrunk overnight; scarlet earflaps (straps dangling from flying helmet), beaky snout poking through wet pastry. The scars, the wrong side of a shattered windscreen, were shallow and non-specific, giving the appearance of a character who'd seen it all. And kept it to himself. Kaporal had the walk, shoulder roll, sucked-in belly. The man could put it away, no question. He knew the story. You could talk to him. It was only later, much later, you realised Mr K wasn't on the nod, that bulge was a tape-recorder hidden under his shapeless jacket.

Kaporal used his contact with Alby's little brother, Reo, to get into the back room with the CCTV monitors at Tuesdays. Reo was a throwback with a couple of O levels, he'd been to college (for a week). He ponced off Alby, was into martial arts, John Woo, David Carradine, harmless exotica: steroids, speed, girls from art school. Black stockings and too much mascara: Reo borrowed them when he could, to go clubbing down Hoxton. He was dangerous, hair trigger, as Kaporal realised, when Alby asked him, as the kind of favour he couldn't refuse, to detach the boy from the posh bird who was leading him astray. Reo was losing it. Talking about employment, moving up west (to Poplar), living with the bint, sharing a futon. Bad habits like books were sure to follow.

It was an awkward position in which Kaporal found himself. Alby was an arm-breaker who took his calling very seriously. Reo was a nasty little psycho (just smart enough to enjoy the panic chemicals he provoked in the women he slapped around). The student in question *might*, Kaporal couldn't remember, have been one of his own mislaid fiancées. A photographer, definitely. He'd rather gone in for those, back in the Nineties. But now, the Sleeman tapes transcribed, he was on the verge of a real scoop: the M25 conspiracy theory.

Here's how it went.

Maggie's orbital motorway changed everything; amen, goodbye and good riddance to Ron and Reg. Adios neighbourhood heavies, blaggers of Bethnal Green. The old firms were good for nothing except heritage TV: suits and wreaths at Chingford Mount, gravel-voiced killers schmoozing the camera. How we butchered Jack, blasted the Axeman (heart of a lion, brain of a budgie), buried Ginger. Lady Thatcher's superhighway dried those crocodile tears. Instant access to everywhere: South Ockendon connected to rock-star Weybridge, dodgy Dartford to dormitory Radlett. New motor-way and mobile phone: the perfect marriage. Leading, immediately, to rave culture, ecstasy franchises, the apotheosis of the humble doorman. Gold bars, laundered after a bullion robbery at Heathrow, funded pill manufacture and distribution in Essex. Chancers like Mickey O'Driscoll started with a pick and shovel, digging the road in Surrey, then moved to transporting smiley tablets in their Y-fronts (Basildon to Canning Town), hauling human landfill (Kurds and Afghans in sealed containers). Onwards and upwards to respectable middle-management: waste distribution (small fleets dumping black bags on Rainham Marshes). Nouveaux businessmen and chemical entrepreneurs of Tower Hamlets, Deptford and the Old Kent Road, transplanted themselves into the suburbs, crossed the motorway: all roads led to the Epping Country Club. Gay TV comics, footballers, bodybuilders, ponytails who fronted lap-dancing establishments, celebrity cooks and page-3 crumpet. Muscle: on the piss. Larging it. Hawaiian shirt, medallion, clenched fist, bottle. Eyes, all pupil, flaring red in the photoflash as someone (Kaporal) frames the group, thick arms around temporary best mate's shoulder, the ghosted memoir.

Only a ghost would *want* to remember what Kaporal knew, what he had found out. Every story, every crime, every unsolved hit (used-car dealers, video distributors) played back to one man: Mr Mocatta. Non-playing golfer, Freemason, property developer. Mocatta was working his way downriver. 'Thames Gateway', the politicians called it (formerly: Grays, West Tilbury, Greenhithe, Northfleet). The last wilderness. Like a Brazilian robber baron, Mocatta was clearing the jungle; his minions taking on local labour to spoil what was left of their undervalued inheritance.

Associates who crossed Mocatta disappeared. Blown away in the car park of the B & Q in Dartford. Buried in a shallow grave, bloody but breathing. Butchered at the foot of the stairs in a New Georgian estate on the fringes of Croydon.

The most recent biography of Mocatta ('The inside story of Britain's Public Enemy No. 1') was unusual in not being written (gummed together) by James Morton. But what sent Kaporal diving for the porcelain halo was the list that vintage hack James Colvin (author of *The Deep Fix* – 'Drugs took him into a nightmare world where logic ceased to exist') appended to his final chapter. The obituary roll-call. Twenty-seven names with a timid rider: 'There is absolutely no suggestion on the part of the author that Declan Mocatta played any part whatsoever in the deaths of the following persons.' The detonated Range Rover in Sydenham. The Bromley doorstep. The Brighton firebomb. The investigative journalist run down in Lewisham High Street. Mocatta was elsewhere. A charity bash with Denis Thatcher, Shirley Bassey at the Festival Hall, Whitstable Oyster Festival with Janet Street-Porter.

Colvin didn't live to enjoy his royalties. Drink taken, he fell off the Portsmouth–Fishbourne (Isle of Wight) ferry. That was when Kaporal decided his paranoia was justified, when he stopped reading newspapers, taking calls, watching TV. The one drawback with retirement to the south coast was the fact that minimarts run by Bangladeshis stocked the London *Evening Standard*. Cornershops didn't bother, a dozen video boxes (tapes under the counter), a shelf of stale Eccles cakes and the weekly fright-sheet comprised their working stock. NO CASH KEPT ON PREMISES. PREMISES PROTECTED BY CCTV.

The final story Kaporal transcribed, verbatim, before he left Streatham for the coast, concerned a small-time hustler by the name of Sid Rawnce. Rawnce had been in Chelmsford, later HMP Hollesley Bay, with Phil Tock and Alby Sleeman ('built like Beckton Alp and half as bright'). Rawnce came out first, boasting of his connections, hanging around the door at Tuesdays in Basildon, cautioned for affray, a bun fight in a drive-through McDonald's.

Rawnce started seeing Tock's wife, Debs. Totally out of order. Tock wasn't bothered, he was looking at another five. And happy with it. 'Tick' Tock, they called him, when he palled up with a pretty boy from Eltham, a semi-pro racist. Phil was a fatalist,

Debs had never been much of a housekeeper. But Alby, he went mental. He lay on his bunk rehearsing scenarios of revenge, involving jackhammers, shower units, car batteries and drums of bad chemicals.

The debriefing – with Kaporal (car to car, window to window) – took place at Thurrock Service Station. Rawnce, giggling in terror, ranted, riffed. His teeth shipwrecked but very white. Despite the cigarettes, the American sticks.

Kaporal was shocked by the sight of Rawnce's motor, scrapyard reject, Vauxhall Astra held together with mismatched paint and black-taped Cellophane. Three sessions, cash in hand, more promised, and still no lead to Mocatta. Rawnce couldn't be persuaded to use that word, the name. He outlined, in tedious detail, cross-Channel runs to Belgium and Holland, the travellers'-cheque scam in Silvertown. Nights when the filth pulled them on the A13 ramp, Junction 31 of the M25: deal done, product transferred. Divvy up or jump sixty feet over the parapet.

Rawnce sniggered nose juice. Knuckled it.

It was always next time. Tomorrow. Dirt on Mocatta, photographs, files. Data that would finally resolve Kaporal's unified field theory of everything: oil, blood, arms, property. M25. M for Mocatta. M for Murder.

Two Thursdays in succession, Kaporal slept in his motor. Waited all day at Thurrock Services (where every minute is a week anywhere else). Rawnce didn't show. Seven months later the story made p. 20 of the *Standard*, five terse paras. MAN FOUND DEAD AT BEAUTY SPOT. July to February, he hadn't budged. The A3, near Wisley (woodland favoured by sex cruisers, peepers, gays, suburban Satanists), he went off-road and into a ditch, 'yards from a busy dual carriageway'. Headlights, full-beam, sweeping through the undergrowth, launched a Surrey myth: 'Phantom Lights in Forest'.

The body was discovered by a green-lane hiker who had wandered a long way from the nearest pilgrim track. Rawnce was reduced to essence: a fat watch ticking on a skeletal wrist. He was like one of those Battle of Britain pilots dug out of a Kentish hop field. Bone-man lolling on red leatherette. Devoured by rodents, flies, picked clean: grin was in place, the fine strong teeth by which he was identified. Cheap trainers and rags of leisurewear. St Christopher medallion, the gilt gone from the holy man's staff. Six cans of extra-strong lager, four drunk. In the glove compartment, Kaporal's card stuck into a copy of the *50 Miles around London* map. Along with a lump of something nasty – later identified as the indestructible plastic element from a cheeseburger. 'I've seen more appetising mummies,' said the DS from Guildford.

Kaporal drove straight to the coast, dumped his hire car, found a room. A good decision to quit the A13, the Sleemans, O'Driscoll, their crazed vendettas. Sooner or later the Essex boys would implode, destroy each other in a frenzy of steroid-induced rage. Ecstasy binges, with vodka chasers, didn't do much for your short-term memory. Where better to hide than Mocatta's backyard? The rarely seen dandy was rumoured to be building a grotesque mansion, 'bigger than Blenheim', somewhere near Paul Merton's place on the Pett Levels. Mocatta had a marine property empire, 'slums for bums', that ran from Seaford to Hastings. Given his start by Rachman, he'd recognised, very early, that asylum-seekers and urban unfortunates (banished from the Smoke) were a major asset, the coming commodity. Better than oil. Better than – or twinned with – drugs. The coast would have died without his vision. A couple of dim heavies and a filing cabinet, two dogs, that's all it took. To keep Declan Mocatta, dandy and aesthete, in crushed-velvet suits, snakeskin waistcoats, elastic-sided Chelsea boots. In gold-topped canes and car coats. Silly hats. Leave out Chris Eubank and Mocatta was the best-dressed male south of Croydon.

The view from the high window, on the semi-formal gardens, was soothing; no people. A town at the edge of Europe, in dim weather, container ships and oil spills just over the horizon. Or – it was that time already – small groups of bareheaded men in bright leather jackets, jeans, white trainers, being turned out of crumbling

Victorian buildings (salt-eaten facades, loose window frames); turned loose to slouch on broad pavements. Knowing better than to occupy dew-damp park benches, or to hang about the bowling green. Unwelcome in seafront cafés. Suspect in post offices and charity shops. Pissing in doorways.

The council operated a regime of benevolent social control: keep out of the way of the paying punters and do what you like. We'll put a roof over your heads and supply you with vouchers. You won't starve. Want to work a number, off the books, with the builders who are patching up Mocatta's ruined hotels and mid-Victorian terraces? Fine. No insurance claims, no additional benefits. Keep quiet, keep clear of the public streets and make your own sandwiches.

Melancholy men from the Balkans watched the waves. Kurds followed young women, silently, hungrily, at a respectful distance, never quite becoming a nuisance. Glaswegians and third-generation Paddies (expelled from Kilburn and Kentish Town) staked out the lower promenade and took it on themselves to get the drink in, to act as informal social secretaries, keeping the scene lively and open to all-comers (bring your own carrier).

Survival, the economic migrants had cracked it – why couldn't Kaporal? Wrapped in a long scarf, letting rainwater seep through cracked shoes, he mooched among the naked beds of the out-of-season gardens. Cashmoney, where was it to come from? As he reached the seafront, he looked west towards the pale outline of Beachy Head, the double cliffs of Bexhill; no light shone from the A13 author's kitchen. The building in which this man lived, trellised in scaffolding, roosted by predatory gulls, was a tribute to misplaced sentiment. Ugly as it was, a sort of marine cousin to Jack London's 'Monster Doss House' in Fieldgate Street, Whitechapel, nobody had the bottle to pull it down. The exiled writer might, yet, prove a lifeline. Kaporal was to meet him outside the optician on London Road, ostensibly to give him the tour (actually to pitch the Mocatta book, to get someone else's name on the cover).

Only the dead can help the dead. The writer was a back number.

And the A13 book, *Estuarial Lives*, was ancient history. Transient fame, no royalty statements. London lost. You wouldn't find a copy of the hardback in a year of combing through the charity shops that clustered around the station, preying on incomers. (It went out of print, modest expectations surpassed, shortly after J.G. Ballard gave it a plug as a Christmas selection.)

Drin and Achmed, the Albanians, were in the usual place. Kaporal had an hour to kill. They greeted him warmly, shaking him by the hand, individually, then together, slapping him on the back, pummelling his shoulder. One of the Scotch boys was off on a fugue: 'Yus a grafter, grafter. Mmmah reet, Jimmy?'

This Jimmy, the universal Jimmy, smiled. A lovely man with one white eye. He spoke no English, less even than the Scot. The whole bunch of them, misfits and tolerated outlaws, women with kids in plastic-covered prams, gathered at beachside, above the shingle, under the promenade, in a sort of open-sided temple or viewing platform. They started drinking early, chucked their cans over the parapet, keeping their spirits up until darkness fell. Then they dissolved into the shadows. In half-decent weather, this side of hurricane, they made fires, cooked something, gull or scavenged meat, and slept on the beach.

The film director Stephen Frears can't have taken an awayday to the coast when he said – of a lowlife romance he was promoting – that asylum-seekers and economic immigrants were 'invisible', the unseen of the city. If this lot had been any more visible you'd have to stick a preservation order on them; they made indigenous scroungers and petty crims feel good about themselves. Keep your eyes open and there is always someone to look down on, scapegoats for hire, giving a dull resort a touch of colour. Beach Boys, locals called them. Their timing was all wrong, they were asylum-seekers at a period when there were no asylums left. The Victorian and Edwardian mental colonies at the fringes of London had been made over into Barratt estates and gated oases for the upwardly mobile. But the tide was turning, forward-planners had decided to grant the supplicants their wish, access to the biggest asylum of them all. A great V-shaped barrack on the Dartford Salt Marshes was being converted into a holding centre, a place of detention for the men from Sangatte.

Achmed, short in the gum and long in the tooth (garlic chewer), gave Kaporal, who no longer smoked, a cigarette.

'My friend, English friend, you come always at good time. We decide. To go. Of course to go *back*. What we are knowing. Tradition, you understand? Be again bandit.'

Drin nodded, stroked his moustache. He didn't speak. He left that to his brother, his patron.

'You also, Mr Joseph,' Achmed continued. 'With us. Take thing for money. Take thing, keep thing, sell thing.'

Kidnapping? Why not? Kaporal had tried everything else, as instructed, except Morris dancing and incest.

'You mean kidnap someone, hold them for ransom?'

'Kidnap – who is this?' said Achmed. 'We honourable men, *banditti*.'

'Who? Who will you kidnap?'

By now Achmed was on his feet, affronted, patting his knife pocket. Drin put his arm around his brother's shoulder. He too was disappointed in Kaporal, the Englishman's obtuseness.

'*Dog*. Take dog, find dog. For money. You love dog, more dog than woman, sons. Take dog.'

So this was the great scheme. The drinkers were unimpressed, they listened to such boasts by the hour, fantasies of revenge, sudden wealth. But the communality of the underdeck was powerful. Post-terror families clung to their small span of allotted territory. Steaming, piss-soaked men with boiled faces. Women dropping ash into prams. Salt-scoured, wobbly on their feet, the tribe wouldn't hear of any exploitation of canine dependants. If there was a barbecue going on the beach, a sausage to burn, stray curs took first bite.

Drin and Achmed hadn't wasted their months on the coast. They made a careful study of local customs, how the English emerged from their houses and pinched flats to walk their animals – in all weathers, bent against the wind, clinging to the leash, shovelling warm faeces into a plastic bag (with a trowel they kept for the purpose). The Albanians were fascinated by this obsessive behaviour. They tracked one family for miles, west, till the promenade ran out, along with any attempt at civic revival; this was a savage landscape, as the bandits recognised. Broken metal pillars, cancelled cafés, broad concrete steps that led to nothing. Threadbare grass, a railway cutting, gulls congregated around the sewage outflow.

It was the dog that held their interest, a shaggy, spindle-legged, toast-rack-ribbed beast, part greyhound, part lurcher, taller than the kids. The dog galloped, ahead of its owners, zigzagging over the shingle path, scratching for dirt, straining unsuccessfully at stool, battering against the chainlink fence, returning to check on his tardy masters, and away again. Painful to watch. The costive animal had nothing to excrete, one heave and its intestines would be coiled on the path.

Dogs and Englishmen. The obvious career until something better came along, a move to the city. Kaporal, needing to shake off the Albanians, before his meet with the A13 writer, improvised a better plan. Kidnap a celebrity.

The White Queen Theatre, across the road from the pier, under which the drinking school passed the day, played host to a glittering roster of TV names. All dead. Or worse. Every Albanian from Dover to Margate had descended on the town when they thought Sir Norman Wisdom was going to do a turn. Kaporal had to explain, the White Queen featured tribute bands, fame Xeroxes, animate waxworks. Think Floyd in Concert. The Beatroots: 'All You Need Is Lurve'. The Maori Elvis. The Yowling Stones. With a leavening of sharkskin spooks from Limboland, the once notorious, the Undead of *Hello!* (misremembered for the tabloid scandals that brought them down: Freddie Starr, Michael Barrymore). The White Queen showcased glove-puppets with replacement hands up their backsides. Impressionists, no sense of self, offering hit-and-miss caricatures of politicians nobody recognised. Some acts were compulsory, like National Service (but not as much fun). They appeared everywhere at the same time – Brighton, Blackpool, Cromer – sweat-soaked in frilly shirts. Yellow eyes frantic for cue cards. Panstick ghosts with a road-kill rictus. Caught in the headlights of involuntary amnesia: Jim Davidson, Chas and Dave, Mike Reid ('Adults Only, Plus Support'). Slippage from soap operas, pensioners of the rubber chicken circuit. And one real star, Bermondsey's own: Max Bygraves.

The name was on the bill. It couldn't be the real one, Kaporal was sure of that, not here. Max had sold out the Palladium in his day, written books about it, done the chat shows, played the golf. So why not punt him to the Albanians? He must have retired to Australia years ago.

Achmed liked the sound of it, a superstar, heavy zeros on the ransom fax. The nation would demand Max's return within days, hours. A cultural treasure. Drin could keep observation on the joint. They would stake out the pier, climb the rock from which the theatre jutted, check the stage door, the entrances and the exits. Pal up with roadies.

That should keep them quiet, Kaporal thought, as he cut through Warrior Square, faded glories and new scaffolding, and headed for London Road.

Eyes

Print was getting smaller, areas of the map were blank: every page I tried to read reminded me of the A13. So much of London's liminal territory, if you drove towards the rising sun, wasn't there: pending, in abeyance, a future development site. That's why the clapped-out arterial road was tolerated: it was somewhere to cook the future. A rogue laboratory in which to undertake high-risk experiments, mix-and-match surgery, retail facelifts.

The sea still worked. It had no fixed shape, it shone. I could feel the play of light on my face, even when I couldn't bring distance, boats and cliffs, into focus. I *knew* they were there. Things got better when I gave up my spectacles (lenses greasy and scratched) and trusted to memory.

Were I to write another book – *Sixty Miles Out*, I planned to call it, a pedestrian circuit around what was left of London – I needed to be able to interpret road signs, graffiti, menu boards in grease caffs. No point in lifting a camera if all I could locate in the viewfinder was smoke, vortices of dazzle. Pertinent ectoplasm. The visual world had become an unbreakable code. Photography, more than ever before, was an exercise in wish fulfilment, projection. The convex lens, distorting reality, took me into a zone of ghosts and phantoms: the middle ground.

Into places like Hunter & Harris, Opticians.

IS ONE PAIR OF SPECTACLES ENOUGH? SPORTS & HOBBIES? DIY? FORMAL WEAR? CASUAL WEAR? FASHION & COLOUR CO-ORDINATION? BRANCHES IN BATTLE, BEXHILL-ON-SEA, POLEGATE. SPECTACLES ARE ALSO A MOST IMPORTANT STYLE & FASHION ACCESSORY & HAVING MORE THAN ONE PAIR IS AN AFFORDABLE OPTION.

If I could read that, things weren't too bad. Disposable copy was still within my remit, the gobbledygook of ad men, admin, address. Reading matter that nobody reads. Folded pamphlets in green rooms where we wait for bad news.

Hunter & Harris kept a chained library of spectacles. On London Road, they were taking no chances. They ran to a rubber plant, a postive-discrimination matron behind the desk – but no customers. No clients for fashion accessories. The optician, a smooth and unflustered Asian gentleman, jacketless, would see me shortly: he smiled and nodded on his way into the small office, surgery, where he made his phone calls.

I've never minded waiting, sitting down in a warm, dry place – with no expectation to perform. But I wondered how Hunter & Harris took the decision to go with a window display of World Cup (Mexico City) T-shirts, blue gravel and yellow parrot-in-tree. I suppose the shock of working out what possible connection this surreal arrangement could have with eye problems was enough to get punters in through the door.

Not today. The receptionist filed her nails. I picked up a magazine – because it had a big CU of a Sony Precision Projection Zoom Lens. Plus the name JIMMY SEED (top right) on the cover. 'Photography & Painting: Hockney, Handke, Sontag, Seed. Interviews, Features.'

The magazine was glossy, the illustrations lavish – and strangely familiar. They looked, to my admittedly unreliable eyes, like the missing portions of the A13 landscape. Frame-pulls of travelogue painted over in lurid acrylics. Worse, the hack responsible for this essay had stolen my title: 'Deadpan! Jimmy Seed & the Illusion of Sustainable Existence.' I began to read, with mounting horror, a garbled version of my own words, the profile of the Bethnal Green painter I'd abandoned three years earlier. Seed, once he climbed into his Volvo and set off for Rainham Marshes, moved out of documentation and into fiction. He was a future novel, not a deleted monograph. But some hack, name of Norton, had found and pirated my research. And without the courtesy of shifting a comma – or making any form of acknowledgement (share of the cheque).

This is what I read:

DEADPAN!
Jimmy Seed & the Illusion of Sustainable Existence

The position of the realist painter, the detached observer of metropolitan life, is increasingly complex. Life doesn't work in the city. Roads are clogged. Buses don't arrive. There's a bug in the system. Marginal landscapes drift, swallowing all trace of their previous history. Jimmy Seed's bingo palaces and snooker halls don't disappear, they're just not there. It's a nice paradox, but a hard one to accommodate, permanent impermanence, loud ghosts that won't go away. Everywhere we try our vacant and preoccupied gaze, there are widescreen holes. Blank walls to fill in Shoreditch. Rubble. Vacant lots. Women, wearing bright new leather jackets over saris and shalwarv, wait on the pavement outside locked doors under railway arches. The buildings Seed nominates, new ruins, don't know what to do with themselves. They are untransformed, fossils of chipped plaster, deleted trade names; white ferns growing from weather-damaged courses. East London is haunted by a sense of non-specific embarrassment, of having outlived its liberties. Too much message, not enough content. Traffic lights hold trapped motorists, travellers, in a time warp.

'It's a memory game,' Seed confesses. Over a cup of tea. In his restored artisan's cottage, opposite the Camel pub, in a tributary at the west end of Roman Road. 'You train yourself to remember the order of objects removed from the table.'

Jimmy Seed, Glasgow born, is comfortable with his long-term exile in this working/not-working district that used to be jellied-eel London. Bethnal Green is for plutocrats. Hip film-maker Danny Boyle stands at the school gates among knots of everyday folk, working mums, freelance dads. He is distinguished only by the quality of his leisurewear. Or so Seed reports with a certain relish. He's amused by the notion of having his grungy epics exhibited in

Dover Street. Young artists, travelling home to Leytonstone and Walthamstow from the latest Hoxton opening, glance enviously at old-timers like Seed and his mates. They are the scruffy survivors of the generation that followed Bacon east to Limehouse, Gilbert and George to Spitalfields. Second-division chancers who managed to infiltrate Shoreditch or the environs of Columbia Market at the right time, late Sixties, early Seventies. You could nobble a two-up, two-down in Wellington Row, Bethnal Green, back then, for less than a year's council tax in Hackney now.

Seed's neighbourhood crawls with Buddhists (soup and candles), BritArt print facilitators, hairdressers, but still finds room for the fabulous cave of Les the junk-dealer. With a business that opens at whim, for a few brief hours during which he does his genial best to repel all cash customers, Les is both artist and curator. He accumulates rubbish, postmortem clothes, records, books bought as ballast. And he packs them, with no sense of arrangement or hierarchy, into his filthy window. Display rather than trade. Frustrated book-runners, threadbare connoisseurs, beat against the padlocked door. Here are the real memory traces of London, lost lives, greasy suits with the imprint of dead bodies still on them. Les runs his shop like a franchise from the old Victoria Park Cemetery on the south side of Roman Road. A grim field to visit, the cemetery was once condemned for over-stacking verminous proletarian hordes. There are entire streets hidden beneath the uneven grass. But Les doesn't discriminate. If an artefact has no fixed address, he will crowbar it into his cabinet of curiosities. This is where he breaks from Seed. Les deals with the madness of the city by incorporating *everything*: a conglomerate of deletions and residues, ash, fur, plastic, bamboo. Landfill with a modest price tag. Jimmy Seed, the area's sanctioned artist, makes careful measurements. His memories are selective. He'll take off on wild journeys of discovery, down the A13, in the direction of Dagenham, Rainham Marshes, the Estuary. He'll park the Volvo, snatch a photograph. And then, in the privilege of the studio, he will work on a thirteen-foot canvas, very fast, using a 'wet-on-wet' technique;

paint thinned with spirit, blotted with old towels, attacked afresh. Broad brush and sable brush. Large gesture and intricate detail. Thumbprint and bootmark.

The displaced Scot, having known poverty and the grind of manual labour, now suffers from a lust for ownership. He owns the building in which he paints. And several others: Edinburgh, Normandy, Folkestone. The bricks and mortar of his studio, I soon realised, meant more to him than the paintings themselves. Seed gestured derisively towards packed storage racks. Unsold canvases are so many oversized cheques, collateral for a future property portfolio. The chilly, ex-industrial space in which I found myself was the sort of killing ground familiar to British gangster films, victims slung from meat hooks in *The Long Good Friday*. Seed digs out awkward canvases, trundles them across the floor. Vast slabs of Aldgate East Underground Station become windows on a parallel world. 'I paint the bits I want to possess,' he boasts. His new paintings are unpeopled. The rush of cripples, skinheads with festering love bites, with which he achieved his early notoriety, is over. The lowlife have been expelled. No more dogfaced BNP supporters. No more pit bulls hanging from trees in Victoria Park. No minimally covered slags propping up Whitechapel walls. The Seedian underclass has been banished. Status revoked. You no longer see them, but they *are* still there, choking for breath under a casually applied emulsion wash. Uneconomic immigrants. Headache substitutes. Desperate and bestial forms cannibalised from Francis Bacon, Seed's early mentor and – according to legend – drinking partner. Bacon travelled downriver for the hardmen, dockers and villains who knew how to wield a belt. Seed came for property. Decommissioned sets that he could paint, before the developers moved in.

It's quite a spooky thing to stand in the great empty ice-box of Seed's studio, and to find your exit barred by canvas windows: a monstrous facsimile of the Queen Elizabeth II Bridge, a slapdash account of three tower blocks on the road to Dagenham. These flats have been, on my successive visits, purple, scarlet, Chinese gold and the silver-pink of something in a foil carton waiting for the kiss of life. Locked away in this Hackney warehouse are all the missing parts of the jigsaw. Jimmy Seed's privatised subterranea is the true Museum of London: piss-stain yellows, bruised blues, the grievous harm of jealous ownership. Jimmy wants it all, a comprehensive list of the city's mysteries, its unrecorded and unloved margins. The official topography, energies stolen and exploited, is bleaker than ever. More abandoned. Seed doesn't paint people because their time is done. He anticipates the coming age of restlessness, boredom and terror.

The wonder of Seed's current work is how he discovers and defines borders, roadside memorials, ways out (of his own dilemma). *Mare Street Snooker Centre* and *Mare Street Top Rank* are imposing facades, more considered, more themselves, than the buildings which have now been demolished. Sentiment, loss of heat and sweat and civic argument, spit and smoke, is displaced into arrangements of texture, low-key virtuoso tricks to re-access memory. The precise lettering. The little green man on the pedestrian indicator who stands, Lowry-like, for all those earlier Seedian gargoyles, Ensor masks of the canals and street-markets.

The large-scale depictions of Hackney and the A13 are properties: in the film sense. They come with unreliable narratives (the story of their composition). What goes on *behind* the canvas is none of our business. Set against information overload, the multi-channel digital noise of Mare Street (Kurdish, Vietnamese, Jamaican, Irish, Jewish, Cypriot, Afghan), Jimmy's cool minimalism is perverse. The story doesn't stop where he leaves it. It spills onto the floor, out of the window. Gunfire, siren, road drill. It's not the artist's business to deal in social comment. No sermons, no history. Jimmy's stance, so he says, is 'deadpan'. Literally so: the panoramic shot of the vanished liberal-leftist documentary film-maker frozen in its tracks. *Stopped dead*. The city, once revived by waves of immigration, is finished. So Seed proclaims. Get in the Volvo, move on. 'I think of the sea, always,' he says. 'Waiting behind those brick cliffs.' The pull is in one direction: towards the rising sun. A13 and out. Like a

Victorian explorer, hacking through the jungle, he is searching for one last colony to exploit.

There's nothing better, Jimmy asserts, than to hit the road. Early and often. Into the unknown. One jump ahead of the politicians and hole-diggers, destroyers of memory. From his days motorbike-scrambling on Beckton Alp, he learnt to love the junky inconsequence of the A13: industry, enterprise, mutation. Old poisons colouring present neglect. He operates like a resurrection man, bringing landfill back to life. The Essex paintings catalogue this debris: a burger shack, a drinking den, a discontinued filling station, the car park of a hypermarket under an enormous and agitated sky. The toxic gaudy of a culture of transition. These works have a morbid fascination. We feel for them as our great-grandfathers felt for impressions brought back by Roberts from the Holy Land. A landscape of myths and dreams fallen into decline. Seed deals in trophies − like giant Polaroids − produced for Bishopsgate aesthetes, masters of the commodity market who no longer have the leisure to travel. But who have wall space to dress in Spitalfields and Shoreditch. Better to own a Seed than to look out of your window. As you stroll through the atria of the temples of finance, shadowed by gently panning CCTV cameras, you will be close to a Seed − without realising it. Hung as an element in an architectural scheme, beside the escalator, overseeing the receptionist's desk, the huge paintings are blots of noise. New London, global stopover, treats the old, dirty, lost London as an abstraction. We aspire to the condition of a club-class departure lounge, with low-intensity/high-definition art as a palliative, something to take our minds from the horrors of flight. Artists like Seed can do the travelling for us.

The A13, as revealed in Seed's paintings, isn't London. And it isn't anywhere else. Moving out, riding the fairground humps of the arterial highway, catching glimpses of retail weirdness in your wing mirrors, is to submerge yourself in a pill-popper's vision of New Jersey: McDonald's, Warner's, Ford's. Hungry apostrophes and empty paddocks − like deserted airfields, where unsold cars (Seed would specify the brand, year of manufacture, engine capacity) once waited to be shipped out, by rail or down the Thames. To the world market.

By shaping his work so remorselessly in landscape format, Jimmy Seed delivers something like the curved view through the windshield of an American gas-guzzler. It's easy to read his recent paintings as an extension of the credit sequence of *The Sopranos*, mid-Atlantic reverie. Compositions stacked in three bands: road, obstruction, sky. 'Tuesdays', the Basildon club, is the perfect signifier: imported Scorsese, melting around the edges, impregnated with burger smoke. A punishment block in which (unseen) Essex heavies practise the body language they acquired by watching bad TV in prison. Seed loves Tuesdays, the calligraphy, the nakedness of the plaster, the black-slat blinds. 'Nobody in London, in this day and age, would try and get away with those,' he says. 'That's style, baby.'

To cope with such retinal blight, artists have to reinvent themselves as businessmen. Of the Basildon type. The sharper operators cosy up to developers and architects who don't wear ties. The big cheeses, Bacon, Freud, Auerbach, are not only the painters whose work commands a premium in the saleroom, they are the ones who copyright a mystique: an art that is better than money. The kind of lavishly framed painterly display that can – if stolen – underwrite a drug deal.

Seed, a sensible man, juggles his property portfolio. A flat here against a farmhouse there. An old garage, abandoned by villains, in which to operate – in which to store the back catalogue. We live in an age of remote-controlled security shields, barriers that curl up on themselves at the touch of a button. Private worlds, secret spaces, hidden behind a frontage of dying commercialism. Standing in the nether reaches of Roman Road, lacking the magical device with which to gain entry to one of Seed's studios, I realised why those huge canvases were so provocative. They were, without disguise, doubles of the coloured photographs in the estate agent's window. Right alongside the door of Seed's warehouse are the premises of Naz Ringblatt Property Services. Naz's big punt was an image of 'Hollywood Lofts', a '1930s cinema complex' on Commercial Street. 'Penthouses from £1650 P/W. Gates to Garage Electronically Controlled. One-minute walk to Spitalfields' Famous Market.' The computer-enhanced promo snap, all redundant detail eliminated, gave off the same rush I get from confronting, unexpectedly, one of Jimmy Seed's austere A13 panoramas. It's hard to draw breath in the gap between nostalgia and exploitation. But it's as good a place as any to work out the price of behaving with 19th-century diligence in a fast-twitch electronic multiverse.

Don't believe I waded through this bilge while I waited for the optician to get off the phone. I skimmed. Taking in just enough to infuriate me. Some person had nicked my file and submitted the aborted Seed piece under a version – A.M. Norton – of my name. I slid the magazine beneath my coat, to take it back to the flat. I wanted to check Norton's text against the carbon copy that I had preserved, with all other duplicates, against the day when I ran out of fresh material. When I was too knackered to walk, lift a camera, or try a new town.

I struggled to focus on an author photograph that looked like a polished silver implant, a tiny mirror revealing . . . what? Awkward head, heavy, balding, wincing from the light, falling away to one side; lolling like an idiot. No question, it was my face. As I was *then*, in historical Hackney, when an American woman, New Yorker, walked me down to the canal for a photo shoot (results never used, filed as: 'unlikely to help publicity campaign'). Wrong age, wrong sex, wrong race. Wrong shape: crinkled around the eyes, but somehow in shock, in recent receipt of a large brown envelope. Mouth buttoned. Lips sealed. Neck like a turtle. Like Ronnie Reagan (in *The Killers*). Norton had raided the album. Not content with pilfering ancient hackwork (good riddance), he was using *my* photograph. For all I knew he was out there now, taking the radio gigs, picking up cheques from the *London Review of Books*, banging on about congestion charges (thirty seconds) on Channel 4 News. I certainly wasn't getting the calls.

These days, opticians don't do white coats, or jackets, or those shiny disk things you used to see in American comic strips. I was a minor inconvenience: sit down, read the bottom line, chase the light across a vertical bar, keep your eyes open while they're assaulted by puffs of cold air. The Asian man had an offhand elegance to his movements, crisp white linen, cufflinks that flashed.

'For now, nothing to be done. Incipient cataracts requiring surgery in a year or two. See the receptionist on the way out.'

The phone bleeped in his pocket. He was soon rattling away. I was alone in the cubicle, listening to laughter in the next room. I thought of those black-and-white photographs of James Joyce with bandages around his head – like the Invisible Man (jaunty homburg and dark glasses). I thought of pain. Of reports I'd read of laser surgery which involved 'having your eye clamped open and a flap cut from your cornea, which is then wedged under your eyelid so that a surgeon can carve up your eyeball'. The worst moment, the woman reporting on the experience said, was when she could *smell her eyeball burning*.

I thought of *Un Chien Andalou*. Weak simile, strong image: cloud across moon, razor across eyeball.

I thought of Ernest Bramah's blind detective, Max Carrados. I thought of the film, *The Dark Eyes of London*, based on an Edgar Wallace story: Bela Lugosi (dope-fiend and former vampire) running a home for the unsighted. And wasn't there – back to *The Killers* – an asylum peopled by blind folk? Where John Cassavetes waited for kindly fate in the form of Lee Marvin and Clu Gulager. The bullet.

Cataracts were for old men. I remember them, coming from my father's surgery, shaken but brave. Born with a howl, assaulted by light, circumcised (on grounds of hygiene not religion), inoculated against this and that, tonsils out, teeth drilled, until daylight turns to milk. Worsdworthian cataracts foam, things lose their shape, outlines blur. 'Cataracts most commonly occur in the elderly (*senile c.*), but some are congenital. Cataract is treated by surgical removal of the affected lens (*c. extraction*).'

I'd rather keep the details a mystery for now.

The man Kaporal was lurking outside, eyeing up a cashmere coat in the Blind shop (ouch). The cut was generous (it needed to be), but the price was steep: £6.

'Any chance of a sub? The days are drawing in.'

I laughed and we set off together up the hill.

My one advantage, where unpleasantness was concerned, was my ability to put the future aside, as inconsequential, when I chased a story. Kaporal was in a teasing mood: he pointed out the dank premises, chipped busts, foxed prints, alopecic furs, of an antique dealer who was rumoured to fence. He was in on the Samurai weapons raid, the lorry hijack. I couldn't summon much enthusiasm. The whole town was in hock, shops were either empty or crammed like Noah's Ark (with all the animals stuffed). Cargo was in perpetual transit; men with blue chins, cheeks like the sides of matchboxes, staggered through the streets with bundles, cardboard coffins, roped rugs. Women pushed prams packed with shoes and empty LP sleeves.

For want of anything better to do, we climbed. The houses aspired to villa status, colonial (verandahs, sloping lawns). My great-grandfather, back from Colombo, en route to Tasmania, contemplating Peru, brought his family to one of these south coast cemetery rehearsals. The hillside, with its rundown squares, Regency terraces (restored at front, decayed at rear), gave me the creeps; a mortal fear of predestination, having to repeat, without script, some ancestor's misguided life. Flagged passages plunged towards the railway station, Robert Louis Stevenson (who did time near Bournemouth) called them 'wynds'. A good name. Suggesting twist, the labyrinth, with a chill breeze always at your heels. Steep steps vanished into the rain.

'Do you know about Marcel Sulc?' Kaporal asked.

I read the local paper with its list of random killings – 'Man, 33, charged with murder of ex-soldier' – rapes, affrays, pages of colour photos of holiday flats and investment properties. Sulc was a regular topic.

Mr Sulc, 40, owns over 50 properties in Hastings and others along the south coast and in London, Manchester and Liverpool.

It was claimed he used 'shady business practices' and intimidation in building his property empire.

He said he legally took possession of the leaseholds after owners refused to pay outstanding bills and ground rent due to him.

'It's called peaceful re-entry,' he said.

'Yes, I know Sulc. He owns my building.'

'Well, forget him. Small potatoes. The real man's called Mocatta. M-o-c-a-t-t-a. Mocatta runs everything. He started in short trousers with stamps and Old Boys' magazines. From his mum's back bedroom in Norbury. And he doesn't, until you get very close, look a day older. The Dracula of Winchelsea.'

'Promising.'

'Better than that. The loose ends you left in your A13 book, I can tie them into a noose. The girl on Rainham Marshes? Mocatta supplied paedophile porn to the guy who killed her, the uncle. The road-rage killing? The kid was running Mocatta's pills. The decapitation in Thurrock . . .'

What decapitation? I don't remember writing about that. Missing girls, there were so many. And girls who appeared from nowhere with preposterous tales to tell. Without that art student at my door in Hackney, I might never have started on *Estuarial Lives*, the A13 walk. I'd have logged it as another potential project, a book sold to a small publisher in the expectation that they'd go belly up before delivery date. I had dozens of phantom titles all over London. I lived on the pitiful advances.

If the girl hadn't brought that packet, if she hadn't been so persuasive, I'd never have got into this. I'd be at home where I belong, in London, and not beating through the rain with a madman on the south coast.

We trudged a road, splashy with evening traffic, that they called, for obvious reasons, the Ridge. It was in every sense the end of civilisation, the end of the town; a drizzle of headlights, beaded beams, between hospital and woodland. Kaporal led me down a gravel drive to the saddest house in England. It was his *Psycho* moment, I suppose. Urban Gothic. Turrets, dark windows and the steady drip of water on our bare heads from an overreaching chestnut tree.

'You know where this is?'

'The Hammer House of Horror?'

'This,' said Kaporal, doing his Edgar Lustgarten bit, 'is where he lived. And died.'

'Who?' I said. 'The vicar they chopped in pieces and scattered around the county, the one who collected marine paintings by Keith Baynes?'

'Vicar of a kind, yes. Vicar of Satan. East Sussex's authenticated Antichrist. When he came to "Netherwood", he was on his last legs. A Patrick Hamilton boarding house. His guests sucked Brown Windsor soup, pushed cold tongue around the plate, while he excused himself to take a shot. By the finish he was up to eleven grains of heroin a day, enough to kill a clubload of Hoxton revellers.'

I remembered the book, gilt dustwrapper and a pair of demonic, Tony Blair eyes. Lights out. The Great Beast skulking coastward to die. Letting the final programme play out as bleak comedy, tapioca and congealed custard. The notice the landlord placed in every tall, cold room: 'Guests are requested not to tease the Ghosts. Breakfast will be served to the survivors of the Night. The Borough Cemetery is five minutes' walk away (ten minutes if carrying body). Guests are requested not to cut down bodies from trees.'

Slow walks to the chemist's shop (where they still treat cash customers like al-Quaeda suspects); long, lonely evenings not reading Walter Scott. And wishing that he'd learnt to play solitary chess. A deathwatch from a deep armchair. In a brown room where magick doesn't work.

'Aleister Crowley,' Kaporal said. 'He came here to shift dimensions. ''The Wickedest Man in the World''. The trick of invisibility rubbed off on horsehair sofas and tasselled tablecloths. He's gone, the house remains. A holding pen for incontinent geriatrics.'

Hackney

Let me call myself, for the present, Andrew Norton. Call me Norton (*never* Andy). But call me, summon me into existence. Distinguish me from the sprawl of the city, the winter grey. Having little or no money in my purse, and nothing particular to interest me on shore, I thought I would sail about a little and see the watery part of the world.

'Not at home. Nothing to report. No message.' Said the answer-phone. In another voice (female). Nobody called.

I sat in the house, alone, in the tragic heap of things, not writing. Taking exercise by climbing the stairs to the attic, picking out an old paperback, stealing a sentence. Scribbling quotations in a ruled notebook, composition by default: elective affinities. Surrogates.

I reread and it was never the same book, Simenon, Highsmith. A chapter, a couple of pages, a sentence. Highsmith quoting Kierke-gaard in her journal (1949). 'The individual has manifold shadows all of which resemble him, and from time to time have equal claim to be the man himself.'

A photograph, cut out of a magazine, used as a bookmark: Highsmith, aged twenty-one, naked. The eyes don't change; the fat lower lip, the lipstick. Raised arms, shaved armpits, no surrender. Small breasts. Dusty pucker of body pores like sand on a wet sunbather. Shocking. The writer exposes herself: as a secret.

I thought about doubles, duplicates, fetches. I dipped and filched, wrote letters to myself in a tiny, indecipherable hand. Remember the poet George Barker in Chelsea? Footsteps behind him, speeding up? *Don't look now*. He was my age, crow's-feet of mortality biting into the once-arrogant profile (lip chewed off by fractious lover). Aches in the knee, twisted spine. The two sides of the body working against each other. Left leg longer than right. No stalking shadow,

Georgie boy, a black dog. Seasonal melancholy. That dog is fate, London. The thing that has no contrary.

A loud ring at the door. Gasman, bailiff? I don't move. I can't move, my back is in spasm.

I made notes for *Estuarial Lives*, the A13 book: Aldgate, Limehouse, Dagenham, Rainham. Blank chapters. Headings on empty pages. No characters, no story, no narrative push. Pedestrian in every sense. I read my Stevenson, my Poe. How did they do it? What possible connection was there between those masters of prose and Essex, the road out?

Ford's water tower.

I love that tower, its great white bowl, up in the air; blue lettering. Romanticism of the badlands seen from the ramp, as the road climbs and the sky expands, moist air over Purfleet. Railway lines. The empty paddock where export vehicles once stood, gleaming and optimistic. The altruism of high capital: good for England, good for the world, sheen on metal, paint reflecting high clouds. This nation knew how to make things. Now the plug's been pulled and the car park finished with a topdressing from the burning stacks of the London Waste Company at Edmonton. Bottom ash and fly ash mixed in a potent cocktail, one hundred times more powerful than the Vietnam defoliant, Agent Orange.

Dagenham. Ford's. Ford Madox Ford. His book, *The Soul of London*, published in 1905 (three years after Jack London's descent into the abyss of Whitechapel). 'One may sail easily round England, or circumnavigate the globe. But only the most enthusiastic geographer . . . ever memorised a map of London. Certainly no one ever walks around it.'

Walking restores memory. So why was I hanging about? Bad back or no bad back, I needed to be in the weather, on the move. The ring at the door was repeated, finger held on button. I remembered. I was waiting for that girl, the photographer. Jimmy's protégée, Livia. She made some excuse for invading my privacy, a manuscript she'd been asked to deliver. I had an excuse too. I wanted to see her again. My life lacked complication.

'You got a towel?'

It was the wrong voice. And the wrong girl.

'Pretty wet out there, right now. I walked from Jimmy's place. We had a big night watching biker videos.'

She was taller than she should have been, broad-shouldered, dripping; a woollen cap and less hair than the first time. She took off her coat, hung it over my bedroom door and made her way, uninvited, undirected, to the kitchen. She seemed to know where the kettle would be. She dumped her sad rucksack on the floor, opened cupboards, the fridge, looking for something.

'Not working?'

'Preparation is work,' I said. 'Reading, research.'

'Your icebox. Yurrgh.'

The 'lost' American from Rainham Marshes. What was the name?

'Track,' she said. 'Ollie couldn't make it.'

'Ollie?'

'Livia. A residency in Hastings, you know? Photographs. The town at night. In colour. Says, hi. Meet with you another time. She's just awesome, Livia, but so petite. I'm pure Viking. Jimmy's kids start calling us "Ollie and Stan". The wrong way. Ollie's down on the coast right now, finding locations where a dead guy made his paintings.'

Tall coffee, cold hands around a warm glass jug. Edible aroma. An interlude. Time and place frozen, slipping into other times at the same table. One of my wives wanted to do a book on tables. As a focus for the kind of life that no longer exists: post-Elizabeth David, country in town, cut flowers, blue-and-white bowls from the Algarve, black olives and Welsh dressers. Two cats. Slow cooking, shopping in street markets, conversations that ran into the night. Ever seen anyone *peel* chestnuts? This table still had the hieroglyphs carved into it by a Sixties painter who couldn't quite make up his mind to paint. Or to give up painting and move on. I can never think of Elizabeth David without flashing to the image of her – in a biography (review of a biography) – naked, lashed to the mast, literally lashed, by a caddish lover, a loved wrong 'un. Cruising the Med, siren of the bedsits, necklace of garlic bulbs, illustrated by John Minton. 'Another era altogether, John,' as the villains say.

Prisms of remembered sunlight. Kitchen passions, summer parties. Old film, 8 mm, flickering on a dirty sheet. Prized babies crawling through uncut grass. Wine in wedding-present goblets. Cider in petrol-station beakers. Picnics under the cherry tree. Table as tent. Kids playing with squashed cardboard and sacks of oats. Table of meals and quarrels, friendships launched, renewed, cancelled. The central leaf, which was never needed, now that communal feasts were a thing of the past, was pristine, a lovely, honeyed yellow. The rest of that surface, with the join down the middle, greasy, scripted with nicks and stains, a patina of unearnt nostalgia.

Tables and kitchens, so the architects say, are finished. Workers don't have time to eat. Builders don't have space for anything more cumbersome than a microwave. Kitchens are a design feature: to be admired, not used, somewhere to park a display of cook books by celebrity chefs.

'Marina had to be sure you got this. I'm under oath. Put the bag, personally, right into your hands.'

Track was nothing like my caricature, less brash, less American. More Scandinavian. Freckles and a chipped tooth. Eyes that watched your eyes.

'Would you read them, the stories? I mean *really*. Don't just say it.'

She worked, hard, on her hair – with the best towel I could find, flecks of blue lost as she spun the rag into an improvised turban. Very little makeup, so far as I could see, translucent skin. The business of the hair dealt with, Track slumped in her chair, suddenly modest about her size. She talked softly, but she talked. Which suited me very well. I half listened, went back to my reverie: the pale table, coffee jug, two broad shallow cups with small red flowers painted around their border. The window. The sodden, shapeless garden in which no human had set foot in two years.

I slid the manuscript out of its yellow-and-blue Ikea shopping bag. It was thick, text hammered into cheap paper by some ancient portable. *A book on the table, unopened*. I got that far (first sentence) and let it go. The woman in the story was on a train, leaving London, heading off to the Estuary. Women and trains, I thought, quit while you're ahead.

'Marina, she didn't . . . not in words. Just: "Stan, you know what to do." And she walked up the steps into the train station, Fenchurch, and . . . I guess that's it. No call, no message, nothing. That's why I came in the car with Jimmy. Why I went off. Marina had *all* of your books in her apartment. Find her for me, please.'

Why not? The woman had the rucksack, the boots. Why not invite Track to come along, as a character? A foil for the A13 walk. The pain had shifted from my lower back, a fault in the lumbar region, old damage, to my left shoulder. A good omen for the coming adventure.

'Would you like to see where the A13 is born?'

'Sure,' she said, reaching across the table, a gesture left in air. 'What are you waiting for? Let's go.'

Actually, now that I thought about it, this was *not* the original table. There had been at least three others. The first, at the period of brown rice and afternoon smoke, was chipped tin. Uneven legs, it rocked every time we sat down. The kind of cold surface on which dogs are castrated and tomcats have their wounds cleaned. The second, pine, was solid enough to take the weight of two bodies, love in the kitchen. This one, the last, came from Tottenham Court Road: it expanded, the immaculate central leaf was for the dinner parties that never happened, the children who stayed out there, refusing to be born.

Wife/Wives

At this point, if you are trying to picture the house, its layout, the way you walk in from the street past a bedroom door that won't close (swollen timber), the storeroom (books, film cans, laundry) in which I worked, down a couple of crooked steps, kitchen (where I sat with Track), I should tell you about my wife. Wives. Historic. As I remember them. About the quirk of serial monogamy that I never managed, despite several never-to-be-repeated short-lived attempts, to suppress. I was faithful to the concept. And to the fact of the thing. There were no children, none that I was aware of, certified and living under my roof. But there was always a wife. The better part. A local mystery. Someone around, doing her thing, a steady beam of super-critical intelligence, unspoken support, to confirm as I woke in the marital bed that I was still the same person who fell asleep, book on face, the previous evening. Eight hours, precisely. Waking, to check the clock, at intervals that expanded incrementally through the night: forty minutes, one hour, one hour ten. Tossing, turning. Best sleep before dawn. Hearing her, whoever, enduring my horrors. Living my nightmares. That was the root of the trouble, out of sympathy (unfeigned), my wives walked in my sleep. Dreamt my dreams. They anticipated fictions and future territories – before, just before, I began to exploit them.

I would get on pretty well with my first wife, the writer, I was sure of it – as soon as I found the third. That seems to be the rule, checking around, lecturers with access to the gene pool, painters like Jimmy Seed (taxable income): by the time they get out of the registry office with a bride who is two years younger than their eldest daughter, they're best chums with the original. The church-married one (fellow student). The second wife is demonised, the bitch. Thief. Nympho. Big mistake. 'She's barking,' they say. Using the new, young wife's money (old wrecks trade up, socially, financially), they will have her predecessor committed. Then let out, chastened, scorched around the temples, sedated, to look after the kids. Second wives have a very rough time of it. But they can work out OK if the sequence stops there, at two: early mistake, impulsive passion, smoothed over. Bruises slowly healed. Long and blissful union between suitably tempered and experienced lovers.

I was in that awkward stage of having lost one, mislaid another, and not knowing if I was going to have to go through it all a third time. Tempted, but wary, I wasn't ready (yet) to dislike Hannah, my second, the psychotherapist. She might not have decamped, entirely; the stopover in the settlement-house in Bow might be no more than an overdue sabbatical. Problems to confront that were more dramatic than anything I could contrive. Space. A room of her own. And a view over the entrance ramp to the Blackwall Tunnel, the eastward sweep of the A13, the hallucinogenic glitz of Docklands. How could I compete with that? Erno Goldfinger's grim tower block, once representing a beacon of blight glimpsed from the A102, now had a preservation order slapped on it; artists (video, light bulb) cohabited with media drones (cycling distance to Canary Wharf). One floor had been given over, by a council run with a sharp eye on public relations, to some of the more interesting dispersees from Victorian and Edwardian asylum colonies around the fringes of the M25 (Shenley to Belmont, to Horton and Long Grove in Epsom).

Hannah, on the phone, taking in that glorious view, above the brown pollution belt, high in the troposphere, quoted the poet Douglas Oliver. *Holes in the bedazzled.*

'Holes in the bedazzled,' she said. 'Who needs Hackney? There's not one solitary person walking through this landscape. The river, the road. And *light*. I'm falling into the bedazzled. It's all I've ever wanted.'

My first time, with Ruth, was very much a case of falling into the bedazzled. We met at the Marylebone Magistrates' Court. Upstairs, in the gallery. A dispiriting morning of pathetic hustlers, electrical-appliance thieves, sad prostitutes of both sexes. She had a friend up on a drugs charge (cannabis possession in Notting Hill, it was that long ago) and I was hanging about as part of a megalo-maniacal project: I decided that I had to penetrate, or bear witness to, all the strands of urban society (mortuaries, abattoirs, law courts, Parliament, rag-trade sweatshops, white-lines-on-Hackney Marshes).

I'd recently dropped out of the Courtauld Institute. I was enjoying it too much; contemplating Cézanne slides, dozing through dis-criminations of Cubism, soothed by the weird precision of Anthony Blunt delivering, on gin and tranquillisers, his annual Poussin ser-mon. I was too dumb to realise that all I needed to form a picture of the city, its machinations, corrupt establishments, smoothly oiled liaisons between disparate social groups, was here, under the dome. From Blunt's eyrie to the marble hall with its checkerboard floor, grand staircase and fine art, this palazzo of privilege, training ground for Sotheby's shysters and culture brokers, had the lot.

Typical, I thought. I have the ant heap at my mercy, top to bottom (plenty of that), Queen Mum's transvestite routs, Blunt's rough-trade pick-ups (diversifying dockers), future ivory-finish novelists, the passport to the secrets of London – and I flounce out, nose in air. Graham Greene, Guy Burgess, Ronnie Kray, Lord Boothby, Anita Brookner, Brian Sewell: I missed them all. The men from MI5 and MI6, shuffling in through the tradesman's entrance, pipes and macs, for their free tutorials. The Saturday night parties when the students were safely removed to South Ken, Fulham and Battersea.

That quarter of the town, those pavements, wide, clean, discon-certed me. I couldn't get the hang of it: how to walk without looking like a CCTV suspect, all hunch and hood. How to stroll without expectation of being shoved against the fence by a teenage toller, a crack fiend with a Stanley knife, a foam-flecked outpatient preaching madness. Manchester Square happened behind closed doors, padlocked gardens, quilted service flats fading into sepia. Assignations took place in the Wallace Collection; elderly romantics, creaking gentlemen and vamps with purple lips and nicotine teeth. Tired spies going through the motions in the last rites of a discredited system. Music and medicine, specialists in surgical and orthopaedic instruments. Blue-plaque Georgian properties leaking Schubert. Fetishist furniture, German, for the electively crippled. Sadists and masochists with the income to support their refined tastes.

What had this to do with David Rodinsky? Rodinsky: the White-chapel hermit, the mysterious figure who vanished from his locked room above a synagogue in Princelet Street, sometime in the Sixties. He left a friable *London A–Z* that was marked, in red Biro, with a number of routes, possible pilgrimages. One led to Claybury Hospital, where his sister died, the germination of the still-to-be-conceived M11. One meandered, in a fugue of forgetfulness, stopping and starting, through Dagenham. And another, the most enigmatic, moved from the ghetto, through Clerkenwell, over Holborn Viaduct, to Bloomsbury and Oxford Street. Why? What possible business had the orthodox scholar, holy fool, joker and accumulator of rubbish, with Portman Square, Manchester Square and the Courtauld Institute? A calendar with a reproduction of Millet's *Angelus* hung on the greasy wall of Rodinsky's garret. Did he, sniffling, snot on sleeve, attend an open lecture at the Institute? Did he know Blunt?

These questions were far ahead of me when I met, and was dazzled, by Ruth. Do you know that stomach-turning shock of recognition? Impossible to take a breath, lift a hand. To speak in your own voice. Every detail of how she looked, brown top dressed with a clasp made from three small silver coins, grey skirt, stays with me, displacing a certain shape, shaping a hole that can never be filled. The way she sat, crossed her legs. The hair. The turn, the smile. I wouldn't have said, before this coup de foudre, that she was my type – if I had a type, beyond the waifs and strays, pub occasionals who would break away from the group for a single unremarkable night. Hair (infrequently washed), long and tangled. Mascara. Eyes like a road accident. Black clothes or improvised layers of fabric, charity-shop coats. Yellow fingers. That smell of multiple-occupation chenille and patchouli oil. Drink you into a coma. Tears at bedtime. I had to fake the cruelty they were searching for, the stamina to listen to the tale.

During those few, unreal weeks at the Courtauld, a pattern was set; the weather was good, autumnal, provocative, and I walked, after lectures, for hours through quarters of London that I'd previously seen through the windows of moving vehicles. The people who lived here were invisible. The ones I noticed were, like myself, tolerated visitors: tourists, Arabs, gallery users with undeclared motives, the diseased and damaged soliciting verdicts, panaceas of expensive furniture, heavy curtains. Tanned specialists with clean fingernails and pocket handkerchiefs that matched their heavy silk ties (in the style perfected by Lord Bragg).

I took Ruth to the Museum of Mankind in Burlington Gardens. There might have been some loose cultural connection between John Golding's lectures on Cubism and my instinct to wander through this quiet building with its walls of tribal masks and glass cabinets of delicate whalebone carvings. It was where I spent most of my afternoons; drifting through the galleries, scribbling illegible phrases and uncertain facts in my red notebook, thinking about my great-grandfather's expedition up the Rio Perene. I meditated an impossible and very soon abandoned work in which I would blend – in imitation of Paul Metcalf (great-grandson of Herman Melville) – Peruvian travel journals from the nineteenth century with lecture notes on Cézanne's obsessive reconfiguring of Mont Sainte-Victoire (the thing seen from a pine-fringed distance, his Beckton Alp), and walks taken through the topography of Mayfair and Marylebone. In Metcalf's 1971 book, *Patagoni*, he shifts very smoothly from the Detroit of Henry Ford to his own Peruvian journals: 'A man is anxious, restless, a pressure on the breast – the frame shudders, limbs tremble.' It can't have been easy, I thought, to have Melville peering over your shoulder.

We left the court together and, later, the pub. Ruth's friend escaped with a fine. Back in Westbourne Park, they picked up a few mates and headed off to a dive at the scruffy end of Portobello Road. I wasn't fond of the area, even then, but I tagged along. Drinks on the table, they lit up: part of the general amnesty. Traders with gear to sell, wobbly writers, sessions men between sessions. Ruth didn't do pints, as the others did, regularly on the quarter-hour; she hugged the joint. The afternoon stretched.

Talking, we brought our conversation out into the street, away from the others, routes I didn't know. We wandered through the park to her basement flat in Cornwall Gardens. Straight to bed. And stayed there for the weekend (the sheets had pale-yellow stripes). At some point on Saturday afternoon, when I slipped out for food (rollmops, crusty bread, cheese in plastic, two leaking cartons of that exotic culinary newcomer, yoghurt), I made up my mind. I asked her to marry me.

Better to marry than to yearn.

Ruth suffered from several disadvantages that I was prepared to overlook: she was English, a country family, Lincolnshire. Established and orthodox in opinions. She'd done school, university, a pass at Goa, and was now working in the office of an impressively foul architect, somewhere in Paddington. In London, she never ventured east of Tottenham Court Road. She wouldn't give me an answer, too politic to make a decision in the derangement of the present, rumpled sheets, pillows on floor, shared bath, midnight coffee and rolls in the Cromwell Road Air Terminal.

She didn't know anything about Marcuse or Foucault, had never heard of Jung or Brecht, never read *The Waste Land*. Never been a member of CND or the Trots. I thought she was joking, it was too good to be true. None of that stuff came up until we'd been together for a couple of months, Chinese restaurants, bistros like the Ark in – where was it – Palace Gardens Terrace? Not far from Bernard Stone's poetry bookshop. And the guy who sold Aleister Crowley material to Jimmy Page.

Black-and-white photos of Parisian vagrants on bamboo walls. Beef stews with French names, cheap red wine.

Males couldn't help themselves. They stared at Ruth, waiters in aprons and advertising men in loud striped shirts. Noise levels dropped as hearts missed a beat. I stared too, when I could, her reflection in speckled mirrors. Through curtains of smoke and noise, I listened to her life, the factored anecdotes. Small confessions. Her sense of family. Men trailed after Ruth in the street. Knocked, late or early, at our door; dry-mouthed, twisting with awkward-ness, they asked her out. Asked her to pose. Offered modelling contracts. Film parts. Begged her to move in with them. She had a particular appeal for large, smiling Nigerians and thick-necked squires in hairy suits.

Women like Ruth happen once in a generation.

'Yes,' she said. 'You're on.'

She gave me her answer in the pre-Colombian room at the Museum of Mankind. Grave goods: monkeys with spouts coming out of their heads, panther pots, shallow red-brown dishes, blood-stained idols whose concentrated malignancy shone through the glass. Through time. Aztec, Toltec, Maya. She said, yes. *Yes*. Against, I felt, the spirit of this place, the still-potent negation. The stopping of the sun's pump. We kissed, opened our mouths. She came back, for the first time, to Hackney.

While she continued to take the bus to the architect's office, everything was fine. I had the house to myself. I hacked away at film reviews for *Time Out*, research projects for published writers, uncredited script rewrites. Afternoon strolls to Mare Street Library or along the canal. We shared a glass or two of wine in the evening and I nodded over the horrors and humiliations of her day, before improvising a meal from leftovers. In summer, we sat out on the stoop, waiting for the stars. Friends came around for meals. Otherwise: we went to bed early and slept close.

It started to go wrong, I'm ashamed to say, when a shiny yellow Jiffy bag arrived; Ruth's maiden name on the printed label of a respected independent publisher. She was at work. I opened the package, 'in error', and found a proof copy of her first novel. She'd written the book on the bus, travelling backwards and forwards to work. I was mortified at the betrayal, her secret life, and spent the rest of the day rehearsing my spontaneous enthusiasm at the wonderful news. I even bought a bottle of Spanish fizz.

Then we were both at home, writing. We couldn't discuss our projects over the reheated spaghetti. Ruth was modest, superstitious of outlining a plot before it was properly cooked. I was blocked (Jack Nicholson in *The Shining* – without the Yukon shirt and wolf grin). I sat at my desk reading other writers, making collages of quotations.

Susan Sontag: 'To quote from a movie is not the same as quoting from a book.'

The house shrunk around us. I assembled monster files of cuttings and photographs, everything that could be known about the worst of London, the A13. Company histories, geologists' reports, traffic-flow statistics, gangland memoirs. Luke Howard's classification of clouds over Plaistow. I walked the Northern Sewage Outflow. I haunted burial grounds. I cycled along scummy canals and lost rivers. If I found a good pub, a promising ruin, I came back with Ruth. I shared the best of my research, the bits you'd highlight in an off-beat guide book. And I suppressed the evil stuff. Hoarded it for use at some future date.

My spoiling tactics worked, no second novel appeared. I smothered Ruth in sympathy, let her waste the grit that might have made a pearl. She couldn't lose face by returning to the office. She took on a series of short-term jobs: bus driver (outpatients and special-needs citizens), cook in a children's hospital (she never tried it at home), tending flower beds in Victoria Park, compiling useless statistics for the fudging of government white papers. But this was worse than before. Ruth was out there, archiving the city, getting her hands dirty, acquiring at first hand information I had to dig from books and newspaper archives, depressed local libraries.

I started to hang out with a cell of leftover Laingians, remnants of the Kingsley Hall settlement, marooned in Bow – with no collateral beyond tall tales about the final excesses of David Cooper, face-down in a foil tray: game over. They fought like cats and dogs. Letters of resignation were waved around like final demands from

Hackney Council. The psychotherapists and free-range social workers certainly knew how to hate. Tenderly, they cultivated discriminations of slight, never-forgotten gestures, insultingly positioned cups of tea. Their days were spent composing rebuttals for injuries that had not yet been attempted. They were always looking for worse properties, on the edge of chaos, in which to set up independent principalities (where they could strut like cardinals). They auditioned crazies. Nobody was mad enough. Shit-painters trumped by swallowers of cutlery. Spoon-chewers devalued by men who set fire to their hair and ran naked after buses.

I became a sort of unofficial freak-wrangler, shunting visionaries, poets and all manner of the urban possessed, towards these very unsafe havens. Hannah rewarded me, for the gift of a ketamine-addicted multiple-personality railwayman (who could – and did – recite the whole of Sax Rohmer's 1919 shocker, *Dope: A Story of Chinatown and the Drug Traffic*), with a bone-shuddering, marrow-sucking blow job.

Women in antique markets took Ruth for Jewish, she had a thing for jewellery, scarves, hats, pink or yellow stockings. Her colouring was slightly sallow, Mediterranean, and she had lovely almond eyes, a generous mouth. The faintest of moustaches. But she was turnip-belt England: peasant to tenant farmer, to gent, to over-educated middle-class unemployable, in three generations. Hannah, on the other hand, was the genuine article, a London mongrel: Jewish, German, Polish, Irish, Geordie. Every piece of her arguing with its neighbour, heart and soul, vendettas, battles for and against the dispossessed, slapping kicking gouging attacks – instantly healed in hot embraces. She danced in notorious breeze-block clubs, with Yardies and Rastas, until her feet bled.

There was no row. Ruth didn't know about Hannah. Hannah didn't concern herself with Ruth. Things muddled along as usual. And then, one evening, Ruth didn't come home. There were no calls. I declined to check out the new hotels around Waltham Abbey (roundabouts off the M25), where she told me she was attending a workshop for health-food reps. A few weeks later, after I'd tidied away Ruth's stuff, put it in storage, Hannah moved in. And madness became the stuff of my existence. Bigamy was the least of it.

I absolutely refused my new partner's psychoanalytic overtures. I wouldn't, *couldn't*, on pain of death, reveal my dreams. The raw material of future books. 'You operate,' Hannah told me, 'an extremely effective schizoid defence mechanism against exhibiting signs of your evident clinical depression.' We could barely sleep in the same room: Hannah dreamt my unwritten narratives. She saw the Hackney house as a boat, washed over by giant waves – three weeks *before* my first trip to the coast. My deposit on the seafront flat. Hannah said that I lived too compulsively in the visible (boxes of photographs, paintings). She made me listen to music, gloom, moaning, Schnittke (as performed by the Kronos Quartet).

'Spirit,' she announced, 'has no eyes. After death, in the cosmic stream, you're blind.' She touched invisible shapes, described biographies for my savagely repressed alternate lives. I felt like a child-killer, aborting better selves. I suffered from ontological insecurity. I used the false avatar of city-as-body as a way of avoiding a deep-rooted conviction of impotence.

Hannah didn't read novels. Poetry and Marxism. She was fantastic in bed, generous and greedy – with a European dignity and relish for dirt that I had never previously encountered. But she would *talk*. She insisted upon equal use of my work room. For her therapy sessions. I could have 8.30 a.m. to 1 p.m. Afternoons were hers. The walls, the floorboards, the curtains, the fabric of my chair: infected by hours and hours of deranged monologue. Lies. Confessions. Fetishes. Regressions. Rebirths. Language that drove me to the borders of alcoholism. Instead of taking off for my afternoon walk, I hung around the house, trying to eavesdrop on Hannah's intimate séances.

Second-wife syndrome. This time *I* disappeared. Without a word. I hid out on the south coast. I knew that silence was the worst thing I could do to Hannah. Now there would be no dreams. She would have nothing to interpret, nothing to complain about. If I left it long enough, phased it right, before I came back to Hackney, she'd be gone.

And she was. Leaving a long, closely argued, loving, vituperative letter behind her. I read the first dozen pages and put it aside. I didn't deserve this. Hannah had too large a soul for me. I regretted Ruth (bitterly, bitterly), airbrushed Hannah from my CV. And wished her well in her trashed flat, her excrement-smeared, needle-carpeted corridor in Goldfinger's tower block overlooking the flood pool of the A13.

Brick Lane

By the time we crossed Bethnal Green Road and started down Brick Lane, I knew Track was a walker. The look, dress-in-the-dark potluck with stout boots and rucksack, was reassuring. She didn't talk too loudly or make a fuss about curious details she'd noticed. She was alongside, on the move, keeping her own counsel. If she didn't know what I was on about, she had the grace to let me run with it, uninterrupted.

I wanted to find out about that name, Track, where it came from, so I asked about her work instead.

'I'm making a real change right now.'

What Seed told me about Track, his enthusiasm, set me off in entirely the wrong direction: Jimmy liked painters who ran variations on his own style and scale. Make it *big*. Loud. Expensive. I wasn't used to disinterested patronage. Usually, when a Sixties veteran, survivor on the circuit, deigned to notice the work of a young painter, to call me over to visit the studio, there was a disguised agenda, a payoff. 'I'll get this old fart to write you up in *Modern Painters* and you'll let me into your knickers.'

Track, by her own choice, nothing to do with Jimmy's recent landscapes, operated on boards or canvases that could rarely be manoeuvred out of the locations where they were painted: fire stations, cooling towers, fish-packing sheds, municipal swimming pools. She slept where she worked. East London, Hackney to Poplar, Shoreditch to Stepney, had been colonised, peanut factories, fur warehouses, printworks, by self-described artists (ie., non-citizens). Transients. They incubated prospects for 'socially responsible' architects (stable conversions, brewery renovations, synagogue make-overs). Wolfish developers with collarless shirts and an interest in rewiring history.

Jimmy conformed, his best canvases looked like blow-ups from an estate agent's digitally enhanced display panel. He used the cameras they used; he projected industrial ruins, cinemas, pool halls, onto a screen. And he painted by numbers. In New York, where the sites he favoured meant nothing, they *loved* his work: for the colour (absence of). So English! The space-filling potential. Possessing a Jimmy Seed was the best way to visit London, Europe. A price tag that guaranteed respectability.

Track recorded: manhole covers, curls of paint peeling from warm pink brick, Victorian tradesmen's faded boasts. Graffiti. FUTURE EVENTS. ANGEL LETTING. FAT BOY / HUSBAND. RUHEL SUCK ON YOUR MOTHER. STOP DIRTY WAR IN KURDIS-TAN. FUCK MY HEAD IS MELTING. NO BLOOD FOR OIL. NOT CRICKET, SCREAM.

'What really sucks in this neighbourhood,' she said, 'is the spray-can guys, they're all pros.'

She was right. Brick Lane was a permanent exhibition of look-at-me graphics, stencils, retro-Situationism. Track did not, she announced, buy into the current Birkbeckian vogue for psycho-geography. Goldsmiths, the RCA. That mob, over the river in Lewisham. They were awash with it. Stewart Home and his chums didn't realise what a monster they were liberating when they started to rip off Guy Debord and the Lettrists. French philosophers have never played over here; not on their own terms, not in French. But they get their revenge, in the Brits they choose to honour. In Paris they adore the psychotic nightmares of novelist Derek Raymond (Edgar Wallace noir), a London of rain, festering meat beneath Catford floorboards, rats up the rectum, serial killers with Shelley on the brain; we suffer wankers spouting Baudrillard, Derrida, flannel about flâneurs.

Tiny, luminous panels. Miniatures too complex to read as discrete items. Words. Symbols. Tracings. That was Track's current method: bring the work down in scale, a level of abstraction that can be accommodated in a moleskin notebook. Each page a block. Each block a world.

'London won't fit in my pocket? I'll try someplace else.'

'In my day,' I said, playing the crusty (barbers were already offering pensioner's discount), 'self-respecting artists worked in the brewery as labourers, they didn't sit around drinking espresso and fantasising about a show at White Cube. The only white cubes they understood were impregnated with acid.'

'Right.' She smiled. 'I love the old standards too.'

From her rucksack, Track produced a fat book; a novel, written in the last typewriter decade, that described a walk down Brick Lane. The journey we were now making, a parallel tracking shot. A once-familiar *dérive* into Princelet Street, past the synagogue where David Rodinsky lived with his mother and sister in a small cluttered room. And then, alone, with fifty cases of books. Wind-up gramophone. Millet calendar. Bus tickets. *London A–Z*. Bundles of sodden newspaper.

They were queuing, school kids in beanies (David Beckham) and oversize battledress, outside the brewery, for a freakshow. Body parts. Plasticised, waxwork flesh: in all its contemporaneous, stop-frame banality. A Dr Strangelove franchise. The twenty-first-century equivalent of the Elephant Man, blanket around shoulders, huddled over a heated brick. Or, tidied away in his London Hospital apartment, visited by the great and good: the Exhibit.

In Track's battered old novel, pages loose as a junkie's teeth, Brick Lane was adrift in time, unanchored; much as it had been at the time of the Krays (the Ripper, Mayhew and the Quaker philanthropists). Two characters – Track detached the relevant sheet – set off to visit the Princelet Street synagogue, relishing the exoticism of the area, its connections to Polish ghettoes, *shtetlach* in the Ukraine.

The turn into Princelet Street, from Brick Lane's fetishist gulch of competing credit-card caves, is stunning. One of those welcome moments of cardiac arrest, when you know that you have been absorbed into the scene you are looking at: for a single heartbeat, time freezes.

We are sucked, by a vortex of expectation, into the synagogue, and up the unlit stairs: we are returning, approaching something that has always been there. The movement is inevitable.

As is the prose. I could have written it in my sleep. I remember doing a very similar piece for the *Guardian*, commissioned by that wise man, Bill Webb: on Rodinsky. As usual, I took it far too seriously, months of research, nights sleeping on the floor of the weaver's garret, cultivation of feline characters from the Spitalfields Heritage Trust. All for nothing. Webb retired to Oxford. The new people at the *Guardian* didn't know what I was talking about. The guy who produced Track's novel must have stolen my notes and given them a language spin. Words like 'vortex' betrayed a background in Wyndham Lewis, a Cambridge connection. A post(humous)-modernist, cocky, slumming it for a season: straight out of Liverpool Street Station, research file bulging with John Rodker, Mary Butts, Isaac Rosenberg, Aleister Crowley. Ten minutes in Elder Street, curry pit-stop in Brick Lane, drink in the Seven Stars (Jimmy Seed sketching strippers), and they think they've cracked it.

Track pointed, with distaste, to a stencilled artwork on the mustard-yellow brick of the old brewery, a Thatcher figure embracing a bomb: the artist had *signed* his cartoon!

Shamed, we turned west into Princelet Street, self-consciously waiting for the hit the novelist described, the Wellsian time jump. And it was still there. Like a quotation. Brick Lane graffiti had itself been graffiti'd: base ground for ruder signwriters. A demonic dandy (heroin Goth, cockscomb) customised with a pair of purple wings. Awarded a chalk spliff. Tagged. Then made to spout political slogans. The level of visual sophistication was absurd. BNP / ROCK AGAINST RACISM polarities: faded as the boasts of defunct hairdressers, radio-valve salesmen, furriers and tailors. Posters peeled from posters. Cheap glue wrinkled torn paper like elasticated stockings on the ghosts of bin-searching old ladies.

Blue plaques, boasting of poverty and benevolence, Jewish boxers, forgotten politicians, infested restored Georgian properties. Satellite dishes for the heritage classes (commissioned from

Wedgwood). A kind of life – afterlife – had returned, behind the period shutters, the authentic doorcases.

'Only in Spitalfields,' said a local architect, stopping off between projects, 'are householders, whatever their wealth, just two inches, literally, from ordinary folk. No porch, no barrier. We may have fine wines, furniture, libraries, but there's absolutely no separation from . . . streetlife. We can smell the market, hear the voices of children.'

Princelet Street was deserted. The synagogue, which now enjoyed an ambiguous status as a potential display case of immigration, appeared to be closed. I imagined it, in a fever of impotent fury, as an archaeological museum in Baghdad, after the Second Gulf War, looted, cleaned up, handed over to an occupying power with no interest in deep-culture traces. It awaited funds (millions) for restoration. And, meanwhile, to pass the time, it hosted occasional, by invitation, media events. Rodinsky's room had been scoured, the rogue scholar tidied away. The stairs were unsafe, visits were discouraged. A young artist, carrying out a memory project, eager to gain access, was required to put up a £2,000 bond.

My wife Hannah (whose status was even more ambiguous than that of the museum) knew Rachel Lichtenstein, the woman who uncovered the mystery, Rodinsky's life, death, burial place. Hannah and Rachel grew up together in Southend. They clubbed in Hackney, worked on a kibbutz, attended conferences in Kraków. I visited the room with them. Saw poetry readings, heroically cold, orange flames wavering from the candelabrum in the draughty synagogue. Shots of pure Polish spirit laid out on a table in the entrance hall. Shrouded objects stacked in dark corners.

Skin like alabaster.

I tried, when Track lifted her arm, brushing warm brickwork, to scan the revealed flesh. Was mainline addiction the origin of that curious name? She saw me looking and pulled down her sleeve.

The peeling pink door, at the far end of Princelet Street, hadn't changed. In appearance. Its continued existence, its knowing distress, was perverse: Wilkes Street (named after Nathaniel, brother of John, the radical, champion of the mob, editor of *The North Briton*) gave shelter to Tracey Emin and a raft of merchant bankers and art moguls. 'Wilkes and Liberty!'

The house sold itself by a strange act of impersonation, continuing to be what it never was – outside time. Wall panels, dark timber, candle-holders; the narrow, twisting staircase up which comic-book genius Alan Moore, backlit like a Dürer Christ, climbed to his fate: the discovery of a legendary magical primer, the summoning of those demonic entities, the Vessels of Wrath. A long-forgotten drama.

I'd been involved in a minor way with this film, directed by Jamie Lalage, at the point where he'd dropped out of features, out of *Morse*-type travelogues for the Tourist Board, into late-night TV. Taking me on, as untrustworthy guide to the labyrinth, was seen by his peers as a suicide note, a cry for help. Jamie was expelled from the Barbican and deposited in a carpet warehouse in Archway: the confirmation of their thesis.

I won't bore you with full-frontal nostalgia. This is a slasher précis of the yarns I threw at Track. Spitalfields had worked its old magic, I rapped like a speed freak. Lalage's film, *The Cardinal and the Corpse* – 'Too many corpses, not enough cardinals' (*Time Out*) – was a wake for Whitechapel, a party for the near-dead, a hooley for vampires who'd just heard that the blood bank was foreclosing. The best of the London writers: Derek Raymond (RIP), Alexander Baron (gone but not forgotten), Michael Moorcock (vanished into the Texas badlands). Mythic book-runners: Dryfeld (disappeared) and Nicholas Lane (relocated to another dimension). All present in that secular synagogue, the house with the peeling pink door.

There were two stories: Moore's magical primer that held the secrets of the city and a search for the journals (confessions) of a man called David Litvinoff, who had been 'dialogue coach & technical adviser' on the film *Performance*. Litvinoff, it seems, grew up in Whitechapel. He knew everybody, Krays, Lucian Freud, Jagger. And Joey Silverstein (we'll come back to him). Joey the Jumper was definitely in the film, rueful at a Formica table as his long-suffering partner, Patsy – who had the lovely, brittle style of middle-period Christine Keeler – blew the whistle. Joey had the copyright on paranoia; bitten fingernails, hand through greying hair. Withdrawn smile. Another cigarette. Deep drag. Smacked lips.

There were no journals.

Joey had been Litvinoff's lover, there at the finish, the suicide in the country. He admitted as much. There were reel-to-reel tapes, hours of them, covertly recorded telephone conversations, as Litvinoff worked his way through a cardboard box of vodka bottles. He wound up his victims, cruelly exposed their pomposity, greed, their ambition to get into Jagger or Nigel Weymouth or Christopher Gibbs. Then he yawned in their faces, fell asleep, phone in hand. He wasn't well. He had money, cashmoney, the wad, and was flash with it. He had nothing. The kind of negative equity that had gangsters hanging him out of a window with a shaved head (useful research for *Performance*). Litvinoff was the conduit, more runs (east–west) than the Circle Line. Just as unreliable. He died and must have been buried somewhere, the tapes with him. Nobody knew. Only a few film anoraks, paperback collectors in places like Canterbury and Hastings (great for charity shops), cared.

The house with the pink door twinned itself with Prague and started to appear in Dickens. When Alan Moore's Victorian Gothic, Jack the Ripper deconstruction, *From Hell*, was filmed by a pair of black brothers ('it's a ghetto story'), a facsimile of the house, of Princelet Street, was constructed in Poland.

At the time of *The Cardinal and the Corpse*, Joey's dad, Snip Silverstein, was still working (off the book) in an unrestored upstairs room in the Princelet Street house: smart suits for hoods, for City sharpies who strolled across from Bishopsgate – and parody 'Fifty Shilling Tailor' streetwear for Gilbert and George. Snip started as a barber, obviously, given his size (diminutive), his gift of the gab. When Raphael Samuel passed on, he was the last working Jew in Elder Street.

The little barber was the reason for my baldness. His stories, in the chair, were so enthralling, I kept coming back. I demanded a trim every afternoon: to find out what happened next. He'd learnt his trade in the army, during brief periods in camp, Colchester, Catterick. Most of the time he'd gone over the wall, getting away, not from the red caps, but from an irate husband or father. He took up hairdressing, so he said, to make sure he had an adequate supply of rubbers for the weekend.

Spielers were Snip's undoing. The old Whitechapel double act, industry and indolence: periods of hustle (Hoffmann presser, gentleman's outfitter in Shaftesbury Avenue, bookie's runner) undone by lost Sundays gambling with Jack Spot: gangster, razorman, hero of Cable Street. Fabulist. Jack and Snip were like – *that*. Blood brothers. With one difference. Jack kept his loot, relocated, up west, south coast, abroad. Snip stayed put: dapper, shiny shoes, lemon waistcoat, trilby. He attended shul with small businessmen and television personalities he'd known since they were snotty-nosed kids thieving from the stalls in Middlesex Street.

'I could kill for a tea,' Track said.

I wanted a bacon sandwich. Thinking about Snip made me peckish. Snip and Joey, father and son, Pellicci's in Bethnal Green Road, like refugees from Alexander Baron's novel, *The Lowlife*. Joey was a voracious reader. Snip never got beyond the racing pages and the Torah. But Joey deferred, treated his old man with slightly shocked courtesy: he presented him to outsiders as a great wonder, an oracle from a vanished world. Battles with Mosley's blackshirts, runs out to Brighton races, stitch-ups in Denmark Street. The fortunes Snip lost on a turn of the cards were replicated by the great books Joey held in his hands – before peddling them for a necessary pittance in Camden Passage or Cecil Court. Pre-war Faulkners in pristine wrappers. A beautiful run of early Waughs. The Colin MacInnes trilogy: all inscribed to Joey (a late friend).

Snip told me about a visit the pair of them made to David Litvinoff, when he was in hospital, after a savage and unexplained beating. Snip brought a bunch of grapes and ate them. Joey brought a second impression of Canetti's *Auto da Fé*, which Litvinoff left in a drawer at his bedside, when he skipped. Never to be seen again, until he walked into a club in Stoke Newington with a floor-length vicuna coat and a Wykehamist film director in tow.

When we needed them, there were no caffs. Even the Market Café in Fournier Street, supported by Gilbert and George, much-photographed regulars, had folded. No market. Now everything was public, visible, self-conscious. You could sprawl on a distressed couch, sucking Pernod disguised as absinthe. The tweeting of cellphones replaced the Huguenot canaries, the birds in cages hung outside rookeries. A generation of narcissists transmitted miniature photographs of themselves, doing nothing, back and forwards across cyberspace.

Remembering Rachel Lichtenstein's account of the hermit David Rodinsky playing the spoons, in a workmen's café in Hanbury Street, we tried that. It was still there, hanging on, deserted in mid-afternoon. One little old man, his back to us, nursing an empty cup.

I couldn't explain to Track how much the area meant to me, how inspired I was by the current changes: it was like regressing to those fondly recalled Thatcher days. Spectacular corruption, land piracy, North Sea oil revenues given away to underwrite arms deals. Wonderful stuff. For a writer. A jobbing dystopian. Blair and his gang were doing great business, bringing it back: horizon-to-horizon mendacity.

When you get into the zone, as sportsmen describe it, your book writes itself. Every phone call keys up the next chapter. Imaginary creatures, borrowed from Stevenson or Machen, beckon you from doorways. Succubi wink and flirt. London and the Estuary become extensions of your immune system. But you are *not* immune, you are wide open to all the viruses, syndromes, germ cultures: you twitch and fret, rant, sweat, ravish.

I had to prove my wild assertions. I took out a letter I'd received that morning from the poet Lee Harwood. Another escapee, another seasider. Lee belonged in the noble age when poetry and poverty were happy to acknowledge their blood ties. The same sound, the fatal contract: *live it*. Lee was in Brick Lane before any of them.

Strangely your writing of Cable Street, Wellclose Square, etc., took me off into memory land. I suddenly remembered lying in bed with my then wife Jenny in Brick Lane on New Year's Eve 1961/62. (We had a top floor room and kitchen on the east side of the street a block up from the old synagogue/Huguenot church.) There came a loud low droning sound – and to me (forgotten childhood memory) it sounded exactly like the bombers flying over in the war. I thought our end had come. Then the noise suddenly stopped – and eventually I realised it was all the ships sounding their sirens in the docks to mark the New Year. That, of course, was when London was still a port and St Katharine's Way and Wapping High Street were lined with spice warehouses, and not fancy flats and offices. That seems an age ago, though the number of years isn't that many.

By the time I'd finished reading this letter – I'm an easy touch, it happens at the end of every chapter in *Bleak House* – my eyes were moist: conjured images of Hasids sleeping in stone coffins in the crypt of Christ Church. Photographs of the 'Monster Doss House' in Jack London's *People of the Abyss*. Memories of Derek Raymond and Michael Moorcock (last seen limping out of the Princelet Street synagogue).

Tea swallowed, local colour entered in notebook, Track asked the cruel question. 'What's this *stuff* got to do with the A13?'

'Every road,' I improvised, 'but especially one as unlucky as the A13, carries a freight of memory. It starts somewhere, goes somewhere, keeps on until it has purged its contempt. The A13 is Whitechapel in an open charabanc.'

'Aldgate Pump?' said the man who was tapping his spoon against the rim of his empty mug. 'Stand us a cuppa, guv, and I'll show yer where that bleedin' road starts. I'll tell you a story you'll never forget.'

I hadn't recognised him. He was small ten years ago, now he'd shrivelled into his hairy overcoat like a ferret into woodchips. Snip had trimmed his banter and cultivated a nosegay of nostril hair. It took him a minute or two to get me into focus, to crank up to speed.

'Blimey, it's Joey's pal. The book geezer. I fort you wus dead. Joey's not too clever. Ain't seen him meself – not since his mum's funeral.'

The three of us, pace tailored to Snip's canted hobble, headed sou'-sou'-west, navigating an uncertain path towards Lord Foster's half-peeled gherkin, the Swiss Re tower. And Aldgate Pump.

Aldgate Pump

White stone. A traffic island. Unexpressed water.

The Aldgate well was bricked up, cholera risk, but that didn't stop freelance antiquarians searching for it. In Mitre Square, a hobbling, hunched man in excused-games windbreaker was chasing phantoms. That is: he hung on to L-shaped handles, golden rods, as he skidded, small feet in sections of black tyre, trying to keep up with the pull of the stallions of unreason. On the diagonal, corner to corner, he rushed and stumbled – until his rods crossed (the eyes of Ben Turpin). He mapped the dull square in a lined notebook, registering geological shifts (every stratum with its own acrylic colour). An urban dowser, cousin to the metal-detecting fraternity of the south coast, this man pursued his hobby with the vigour of a committed careerist.

'In orf the pavement Jack went, dahn the stairs, pulls out a razor – *whoosh*, *whoosh* – stripes him, the blackshirt on the door. That was the start of it, Jack's name. Put five of them bastards in 'orspital.'

Snip Silverstein saw history on cable, his own private channel. Instant replay. All time, one time: Jack Spot, Colchester barracks, fitting Matt Monro with a lilac three-piece, spin to Portsmouth (mob-handed in a borrowed two-tone Zephyr).

The afternoon was drawing in, vapours from heavy clay creeping through the mantle of paving stones. Snip, who had brought us through Whitechapel to Aldgate Pump, was running out of gas. He had returned to a place that was no longer there. Bones ached. His back was out of alignment. Shoes pinched. The angle of his hat was jaunty, but his nose dripped, faulty washer, long silver droplets absorbed in the greenish black of anachronistically severe lapels.

'So long, son. Miss. I should be gettin' indoors. Shalom.'

He shook my hand, winked at Track and left us to it: the point where Leadenhall Street meets Fenchurch Street, the prow of a boat cutting through waves. The fabled launch of the A13: Aldgate Pump. A heritage token shunted and shifted for the convenience of developers with greedy eyes on a steady march to the east.

A dog's head reared from the stone. A titular spirit.

'More like Jack London's wolf,' Track said.

Bronze: buffed like coffin handles. Erect ears. A flattened brow in which you could watch the traffic divide into two streams. The wolf, fangs bared, was road hungry. He tried to hurdle stone – and found himself trapped within it, a token of the wilderness that lay forever beyond his reach. He strained, struggled, snarled. In silence.

'Let's get out of here.'

Lord Foster's smooth glass tower, the Swiss Re building, gave me vertigo. It pulsed provocatively, a sex toy someone had forgotten to shut off. A fishnet condom skinned over an Oldenberg vibrator. Foster's gherkin dominated London's approaches, reconfiguring the energy spirals of the labyrinth; it glowed like a sick bone in a soup of dollar bills. No wonder the dowser fled. No wonder Snip Silverstein scuttled home for *EastEnders*. Swiss Re, a reinsurance operation, were quitting their current premises, alongside Aldgate Pump, to occupy this retro-futurist blob, a misplaced salute to fibre-optic technology.

Track wanted to record the thing. It would play much better as a photograph. She stood foursquare in the road, a sturdy figure dwarfed by recent buildings, slabs of light; offices in which figures sat, or rose from their desks to talk to other seated figures, to stare *at* the windows, not out of them. There was no out, a moving screen, a future that belonged to a religion still waiting to be defined; a priesthood honouring the City's persistent duality, a Manichean creed of darkness and light. Greed and fear. Flesh and spirit. Love and death.

London, I thought, regretting Snip, and sensing that I would never see him again in this world, belongs to barbers, tailors, gamblers. Cut, stitch, risk. Shave and shampoo. Send the corpse down the chute in best pinstripe, clean underwear, polished shoes.

Accidental survivors like Aldgate Pump filled me with an inexpressible melancholy. Better let them rip the relics out, burn John Stow and his surveys, dismiss scholars and memory-men, Bill Fishman and his ilk. Characters like our Mitre Square dowser worried at a rind of pain, made lists, catalogues of the lost. Track was more sensible, no truck with nostalgia. She trotted beside me, headset pumping out Jah Wobble's anthem to the A13 as celestial highway, a benediction to sales reps and Ikea warehouse persons in bright overalls: a smile on her face and a notebook to be filled.

New buildings meant old bones. Without development, Quatermass pits in London clay, there would be no hard evidence of plague deaths, helmets, brooches, Elizabethan theatres, coins, rings, oyster shells and broken clay pipes. The yellow dead, in their gaudy, would sleep for ever in the choke of claggy earth. Bulldozers fetched them out. More to display, more skulls to house. A louder story to narrate.

We were on the outside of the City gate where Geoffrey Chaucer was Keeper of Customs, a salaried bureaucrat. The original Swiss Re building housed, in its basement, a section of wall, a medieval arch from Holy Trinity Priory. The arch had been constructed from stone salvaged from Jewish houses, demolished after the expulsion ordered by Edward I in 1290. Or so the sign said. Swiss Re decorated their prize exhibit, all that was left of 'one of the most powerful institutions in the Capital', with prompt cards, genealogies, checklists of significant dates.

Track read aloud facsimile extracts from Victorian newspapers, pre-tabloid horror stories based on the Whitechapel Murders. The invention of that entity now known as Jack the Ripper. A more recent cutting must have been placed here because of its casual references to Swiss Re and the Holy Trinity Priory. This was a review of the film *From Hell*, in which the journalist argued that US global capitalism had nowhere left to invade – except the past. Regime change in Mitre Square and Berner Street was the preferred option.

History is there to be captured and colonised by a commando unit of highly trained and skilled professionals, using the most advanced technology known to the Western world. The military/industrial state sees film as an efficient way of burning (laundering, re-investing, alchemising) money. Great Britain, that drifting, off-Europe aircraft carrier, is tolerated as a generator of exploitable myths: Dracula, Frankenstein, Sherlock Holmes, Harry Potter and the runic menagerie of J.R. Tolkien.

The arch in the basement of the Swiss Re building, close to where the body of the murdered prostitute Kate Eddowes was found in Mitre Square, is preserved — as a conversation piece. The arch belonged to one of the ten side-chapels where masses were sung for the souls of the City's dead. Its provenance is explained on boards hung alongside Ripper caricatures and expressions of horror that such events could occur in the world's greatest and most civilised metropolis.

From Hell, as a film, returns us to source, the penny-dreadful, the shilling shocker: a marketable product crafted to compliment the wave of predatory development that maligns history and treats the past as the final colony in the American world empire.

'Standard riffs,' I snorted. I'd used them myself, more than once. The problem, at my age, is that every statement sounds like an echo of something written or read. The worst of it, for journalists who stick around too long, is that we self-plagiarise to the point of erasure, quote our own quotes, promote fresh new talent, buried for years in Kensal Green or Nunhead. The madness of seeing London as text. Words. Dates. Addresses. No brick that has not been touched, mentioned in a book.

In a gloaming of wheelspray, wet light eddying around Aldgate Pump, we navigate a complex system of pedestrian crossings, underpasses, islets on which you could perch for a moment, reeling from fumes, before hazarding a rush at the next high kerb. Yellow fences, too tall to vault, have been designed specifically to balk random hikers. There never was a landscape so much factored on confusion: LOOK BOTH WAYS. Double red lines. Contradictory arrows. Taxis hauling business folk a hundred yards between meetings. Creased suits returning, flushed, from wine bars. Repmobiles trundling back from the dirty worlds of Dagenham, Rainham, Basildon. Sports commentators in loud shirts, airfixed hair, hoarse from calling the arrows in the Circus Tavern, Purfleet: 'One hundred and eighty!'

The Hoop & Grapes public house is a marker on the old road. We spotted the Mitre Square dowser coming out, unintoxicated, crackling with crisp packets like a Bacofoil-swathed marathon runner, in danger of imminent dehydration. Lips crusted with salt. The signboard swung, a heavy vintage of green grapes caught in a golden hoop, like another Ripper prompt. A nifty back reference to Stephen Knight's eccentric notion of chief suspect, Sir William Withey Gull, feeding doped fruit to compliant Whitechapel whores, while they jolt over the cobbles in a closed hansom.

So indulge that theme for a moment, if you will. Old man (ex-hack) buying wine (white and sour) for young female artist, as the lights of the City come on and haloes form around the hot bulbs of streetlamps. The stolen hour when Track, three drinks in, remembers a story her mother told about trying to retrace the steps immigrants took, after coming ashore near Tower Bridge, walking to Heneage Street in Whitechapel.

The mother's friend, a gentile from across the water, spoke 'incessantly' about the lavender fields of her youth, between Mitcham and Croydon. And how the smell stayed with her even now, through all the dirt and noise and bluster; it only took a pinch of lavender on her fingers to bring back the blue hills of Surrey.

It had been raining that day, and coming towards Fenchurch Street, crossing Commercial Road, Track's mother was delighted to find the speckled-granite basin of a drinking fountain filled with water. An old lady was washing herself, her face, her hair. And singing. And some of the vagrant drinkers, the ones she had seen earlier, angry, affronted, were singing with her. Track's mother loved that moment.

We were following the thread of the aboriginal A13, no question. Another leaping dog. Or, if you want to be pedantic, a South American jaguar. *Jaguar.* The bronze hound of Aldgate Pump transformed into a showroom token, guarding a display of £40,000 motors. (A direct swap, I thought, for one of Jimmy Seed's paintings.) Vagrancy and conspicuous consumption loafed side by side in the tradition of this territory. Poverty and flash shacked up. If you haven't got it, spend it. £62,725 will secure you a nice green car in a glass box (polished tile floor). Car as sculpture. You'd never risk one of these on the A13. Why trash your investment? Leave it in the gallery until it achieves its full market potential.

This hinterland – river, ghosts – won't let Gothic themes fade; everything zooms back to the karma of the Whitechapel Murders. Kelly's Foodhall commemorates, for slasher freaks, the name of the final victim, Marie Jeanette. PLEASE PAY HERE. The Minories trigger spectral sightings of the unfortunate Montague Druitt, Ripper fall guy, stones-in-the-pocket Thames suicide.

A red smear is sinking slowly, rubbing itself against the blind windows of an anonymous block-building on Commercial Road. We can't move east without brushing against sticky webs of memory, a sense of being crushed, even on this broad highway, between the murder sites of the so-called 'Double Event' killings: Elizabeth Stride in Berner Street (ahead of us) and Catherine Eddowes in Mitre Square. Sepia photographs of human figures: so stitched and blotched they look like representations of tribal trophies, shrunken heads from the Amazonian rainforest.

The nicotine prints, that made such horrors acceptable, re-form on paving slabs like pools of dried blood. Sepia is an older weather. My great-grandfather spurned such impurities, favouring solid blacks and radiant whites for his Kodak portrait of the supposed skeleton of a conquistador.

The conclusion come to was that the identity of the body was absolutely established, not only by general indications, but by evidence of the wounds on the neck and elsewhere, which, after lying three and a half centuries, the mummified corpse clearly disclosed. The conformation of the cranium has a very marked resemblance to that of the typical criminal of to-day. The lower jaw protrudes abnormally, a certain sign of a brutal man. The chief peculiarity, however, is the knee joints, which are so unusually large as to look like a deformity. The total length of the mummy is fully six feet. After having been scrutinised, the precious relic was handed over to the care of the Metropolitan Chapter, who placed it in the Chapel of the Kings in the Cathedral of Lima, where the curious may now see all that is mortal of Pizarro resting on a couch of crimson velvet, the whole being enclosed in a marble tomb with glass sides.

Another glass box lifted our spirits, a display of virtual reality, silver-thread, Bollywood/Motown outfits: Teddy Boy jackets in shimmering sequins, aluminium shirts with pearl buttons, brothel creepers in scarlet suede. Wedding outfits for a resurrected Messiah. A comeback by Michael Barrymore. The window, strobed with red and green lightbulbs, was a shrine to swank: the idea that dressing up, posing in front of a cheval glass, makes the world a better place. Travolta Scientology for a sugary Day of the Dead.

And, boy, did Commercial Road need it. Rag-trade pizzazz (Kabbalah chic) to offset the gloom of housing offices (with no houses on offer), congealed commerce, economic slippage, offices that defined problems by getting you to tick the box for your confession of choice: substance abuse, social and antisocial diseases, convictions and offences (potential or achieved). And, over it all, the hammer of sewing-machines, hiss of presses, racks of chainstore-multiples shrouded in plastic (like a row of hanged flashers): bad air, thin light, rain you felt but couldn't see.

It was going to take a superhuman act of will to break out of the equilateral triangle formed by Commercial Road, Whitechapel Road (Mile End Road), the Blackwall Tunnel Approach. Dead ground: London's version of the Bermuda Triangle. Unwary voyagers breezed in and were never seen again. Tower Hamlets

Cemetery: overgrown paths, erased memorials, obelisks. Jack London took photographs and Joseph Stalin lodged in Tower House, Fieldgate Street. The Elephant Man is still imprisoned in the London Hospital (albums of photographs, X-ray Martyrs). Hamlets Way. Ackroyd Drive. Empson Street. Jimmy Seed's old studio in Turners Road. The unrecorded (and over-recorded) voices of Stepney and Bromley-by-Bow.

Commercial Road and Whitechapel Road begin as kissing cousins, but they soon part, moving further and further away: as upwardly mobile A11 (heading off to Epping Forest) and as our old friend, the sluggish east-flowing A13. Decisions, casually made, can never be undone.

Twilight, neon-licked, brought another sighting of our dowser. Posed against a window of decapitated humanoid models, he was heavier, slower, shorter in the leg. He limped, weighed down by a black bag that might once have belonged to a doctor or plumber.

We scanned the sign: HENRIQUES ST (FORMERLY BERNER ST). Our man was still on the trail, heading towards the railway and the river, quitting the A13, paying his dues to a Victorian crime scene; one jump ahead of the ghouls, the video tourists. Named-and-shamed 'Berner' might have been struck from the map, but they couldn't let it go; this once-and-future killing ground was part of the heritage route. Working-men's clubs, schools, debating societies. A red-brick mansion with breeze-block doors. TAFFY'S BARBERSHOP: the only going concern. Step away from the brightly lit boulevard of Commercial Road and you flounder in Miltonic darkness.

A man, soft-shoed in rubber, weighed down by a black bag. Sealed doors. Suspended charities. The first whiff of the Thames, unspiced, on chill evening air. We followed, keeping well back, staying in the shadows.

This was another London, occupied by invisibles, secret hordes in tenements, low-level flats with gauzy curtains. Cars, left on the street, winked with security lights. They outranked the rundown properties. Cars and ex-cars, accredited wrecks with shattered wind-

screens and no engines. The dowser dragged himself through this
territory, eyes fixed straight ahead. A long way from Brick Lane's
curry houses with their touts and greeters, from leather wholesalers,
minimarts, peddlers of slippers and virtual Meccas. Brick Lane was
the Oxford Street of these obscure warrens. Obscure to outsiders.

Out of nothing came nothing: a dogpatch, tired carpet of theoretical grass, sodden at all seasons. A cliff of unrestored flats. A rank
of devastated lockups.

Track loved it, this set. She saw it as a future art work. Her
camera: she wouldn't follow the dowser until she'd gathered evidence for a new grid. She didn't say as much, didn't say anything.
This is how I read it (freelance journalist, collector of trivia). And I
think now, sitting on my balcony by the sea, going over my notes,
that I was wrong. Track's behaviour was never calculating, she
went with her impulses: hundreds of lit windows, the termite
theatre of evening, this was something worth celebrating. For itself.
As itself. Proper artists know how to wait.

Squelching, unable to see where I was putting my feet, I waded
onto the grass. My actions, in response to the dowser, were influenced by the fact that we both fitted cosily within the spectrum of
autism: obsessive, unpredictable, hoarding twigs, locks of hair,
scraps of paper, cigarette packets, bus tickets. In black bags and
awkward rucksacks. We laboured with kit. Faces of strangers,
faces of friends, faces of celebrities, they were equally unfamiliar.
Meaningless. We scarcely knew ourselves.

A rugged boulder. Glacial debris, fallen monument. The dowser,
rods catching blue light from a television window, was circling a
rock. What was it doing in this wasteland?

'Like a try? It's not difficult.'

The man was waiting for me, holding out the rods. It was a
simple business, apparently, this dowsing. Easy grip, no clenched
knuckles. Don't rush it. When you pass over new material, cable
in earth, dull coin, the rods cross.

Was this megalith one of the unrecorded wonders of London? It
looked, in the half-dark, like a tumbled standing stone, a menhir in

the wrong place. A blood table. It hummed and throbbed: booster
for the journey on which we were about to embark.

'Concrete, I'd say,' the dowser replied. 'Could be, like, an art
thing. Without the holes. Or debris builders left behind.'

I stroked the surface and felt extremes of temperature, microwave heat and cold that would freeze your tongue to the rock.
Parts, it's true, were rough as concrete, fissured, fuzzy with moss –
but speckled veins ran through the rest, Peterhead granite transformed to gneiss, fractures of pure obsidian. The thing was a
geological anomaly, a freak. A rock designed by committee.

Quietly, without fuss, a revamped Stone Age culture was creeping across East London. We couldn't erect circles or astronomically
aligned spirals, so we tipped rubble into small parks, left boulders
in places where nobody would notice them. When the dowser
swept out, in wider and wider circles, dogging this rock, I had a
comic vision of municipal stone floating through the sky, Magritte-
fashion, like loaves of bread.

'It's getting a bit late, last train. Sorry. We could meet again if
you're minded. Or the lady. Tomorrow morning, tenish. I'll show
you how to dowse. Most people can. My pleasure.'

He gave us his name, as security, a parting gift: Danny Folgate.
Laid-off, voluntary-retirement paintshop man. Ford's at Dagenham.
Dowsing and local history, facts, provided Danny with a new life,
a reason to get out of bed. He kept his books indoors. He had
hundreds. And could lend us a few.

We might, this first day, have achieved a mile and a half, in
parallel with the A13. It was going to be a long haul – if I couldn't
learn what to leave out, which estuarial lives to ignore.

Danny limped off. Track disappeared. I picked my way between
fences boxed in asbestos and garages that barked. To Amazon
Street. A source place, left out of Nicholson's *Greater London Street
Atlas*, but found, by those who need it, at the back of Hessel Street
(caves of lurid vegetables, loud meat, its reek).

This, wrote my great-grandfather, *is the source of the Huallaga, or,
as some geographers say, the real source of the Amazon. The Huallaga is*

at least one of the chief tributaries of the king of rivers, and our immediate object was now to follow this streamlet until it became a mighty flood, upon whose bosom steamers of considerable magnitude may safely float.

Hackney

Putting our first day on the road behind me, I went to bed – but couldn't sleep. I thought about Ruth. Then Hannah (whose shape I could feel in the mattress). Whose smell was still in the sheets. Ruth, Hannah. Hannah, Ruth. Hannah was sex. Fear, respect. In that order. Ruth was sex too, on both sides of a deeper affection, shared experience; the unshakeable belief that we were meant, had known each other always and, after this time of testing, would again. Death and beyond. The hollow romanticism of an empty house and an empty fridge, a Brick Lane bagel eaten on the hoof. A washed-up writer without a muse.

I tried reading, American crime capers, Florida, New Mexico, New Orleans; it didn't take. The women. Men came in all shapes and sizes, steroidal cartoons, pondlife, scammers, scalpers, bigots and psychos; the women, young or old, were uniformly frisky, good-hearted, wisecracking, independent – an unholy blend of Howard Hawks and E. Annie Proulx. That and the ecology, the dolphins, bears, horses. The cats. Show me another alcoholic, living alone with his moggy, writing poetry, listening to the hip tracks, in an on–off relationship with a semi-reformed black prostitute, and I'll choose to stay awake, staring at the ceiling.

Thinking about Ruth.

Who was always there, like a nodule in the armpit. I thought about what Ruth was thinking. And about what she thought I thought (thinking about her). And what I thought she thought I thought when she walked away. I didn't understand, I'd never understand, where it went wrong. It wasn't Hannah, was it? The novel? It was something I was never going to touch, the look in her eyes, the place women go, when they're driving a car, in the kitchen, out for a walk: sudden unexplained absence.

'What did I wear?' she would say. 'Last Thursday?'

Meaning: did you like it? Can you remember?

Ruth's was the only face I carried in my head, the only woman I would recognise in a crowd (I did it most days, street, bus, bank). But it was Hannah's voice that shared my bedroom. Hannah slept in costumes that mirrored the cultural diversity of her background: naked with football socks (cold feet), a black slithery thing (mother's gift), thin strings that slipped off the shoulder, combined with a buttonless pyjama jacket I'd long since abandoned. She wore spectacles in bed, reading for hours, but took them off when patients called. (Ruth rested an open book on her belly, staring into space: 'Did we do that walk from Narrow Street on Friday or Saturday?')

Twitching and tossing, unable to find a position in which to settle, I started – shortly before dawn – to work my way through Hannah's bedside library. The books she didn't need in her tower block: Clancy Sigal's *Zone of the Interior*, R.D. Laing's *The Divided Self* and *Sanity, Madness and the Family*, Gregory Bateson's *Steps to an Ecology of Mind*, Foucault, Jung and Esther Leslie on *Walter Benjamin (Overpowering Conformism)*. A slim volume of poetry by someone called Anna Mendelson.

I read the poetry. It squeezed the pap out of me (until my eyes bled): Hannah's intensity brought to a flamelike pitch, scored and scoured. High lyrics of hurt. Everything I couldn't answer. The riptide of this verse, Slavic and unforgiving, sealed me in a sweating carapace. I was language-stalled and guilty. Impatient for death.

> Look my coat is threaded thin. I'm not robust,
> I don't know where life ends and dreams begin.

Two lines was all I could take. I tried Laing. Couldn't get it into focus, the print was too small. I remembered a story Hannah told, when she had a bunch of therapists and crazies around for dinner, about Laing's 'expert evidence' at the trial of former Postmaster-General John Stonehouse. Stonehouse was premature New Labour. He associated with bent businessmen, teased the media, groomed himself for the cameras, at a time – before Cecil Parkinson – when that wasn't done. With the Fraud Squad closing in, Stonehouse faked suicide by drowning (like a bad situation comedy), before skipping to Australia.

Laing's performance – substance-enhanced? – mystified the jurors and contributed to a guilty verdict. Stonehouse, he said, was unusual in that 'his two personalities were not really aware of each other, but were joined by an umbilical cord'.

I know that cord. It is wrapped around my neck: a lifelong obsession with twins, astral doubles, doppelgängers.

Poe's William Wilson, a moral conscience, a stalker, manifesting at moments of crisis, was a very different case. Wilson's etheric twin was horribly familiar, while Stonehouse lived in ignorance of his other self. Laing was sympathetic to the pain this caused. He suffered from the same syndrome. A residue of Scottishness. The Glasgow hardman (and suffering child) travelled with the charismatic psychiatrist to London. To fame and doom. To Hampstead.

Sleep wouldn't come. I worked on compensatory fictions: long boozy lunches and longer afternoons. Slats of sunlight across a blue bed. Ruth's face shifted. Ollie (the lost Livia of Hastings) auditioned in her place, arriving windblown from the beach. Hitching her skirt to climb into a small red car. Riding over the QEII Bridge, oil refineries, power stations, tractors for export, reed beds. Smoke and clouds. 'Don't do it,' I shouted. 'Don't trust a man with a ponytail and an Old Town tattoo. A snake with an inoculation scab for an eye.'

Dreaming was strictly competitive in the days when Hannah was in residence. Mug of black coffee in a pistol grip, she awaited my appearance – stiff-backed, shuffling, fiddling with pyjama cord – at the breakfast table. (Could I could reach the milk bottle before a spasm stopped me in my tracks?)

'Why, why, why,' Hannah started right in, tapping the rim of her mug with a purple nail, 'would you present me with a withered artichoke? Then inform me, as a matter of great moment, that you found it on a walk through . . . Dagenham?'

Setting the mug in a ring of stain, her spot, she reached under the table for a handbag, tipped out the contents, searching for loose cigarettes. Flashing green eyes. Like a cat? She marched across the kitchen, opening drawers, slamming cupboards, shunting tins. Matches. Fine, smooth hands (nibbled nails). I admired the style with which she dragged the matchhead, away from her, across its thin brown strip (smooth, printed with honeycomb design, not like the bristling, crushed-glass of old, that picture of a ship). Twice, three times.

Rush to the sink, rinse a wineglass, swallow water; back to the table where I am waiting, mouth filled with crunchy stuff, gaps in my bite wedged with detritus. Milk on the turn.

'Why? Why was that – do you think?'

'What?'

'The *vegetable*. Which, on closer inspection, turns out to be a head. Yes, head. Which then, as I watch, grows a body. Arms very thin and legs like . . . dental floss. This male creature is around three feet tall but has a very large *presence*. You know what I'm talking about?'

'I haven't the first idea.'

'Last night, a dream.'

'Did it say anything?'

'It moved towards the mirror, turning back to give me a very peculiar look.'

'It stared – at you?'

'It left. We sat down to dinner and my father joined us.'

'Your father? He's –'

'Dead, yes. So during the meal, one of your curries, I question him – to determine whether he *knows* he's still alive. Of course, he sees right through my strategy. And is supremely disdainful.'

'Was he alive?'

'That depends on your definition of mortality. If he's dead, we are dead too. He has a certain period in which to mediate the situation in which we find ourselves, our failing relationship. He can return three times, no more.'

Hannah had done it again, ruined my breakfast. I pushed the cereal bowl away, called after her as she strode from the room, leaving, as she invariably did, drawers open, tap dripping, oven on.

'What's it mean?'

'It means that our praxis must be resolved. My father went into the garden, sat under the cherry tree, and your wife Ruth walked in. She led me to the bedroom, which was no longer a bedroom. It was decorated with ceiling drapes made from an ancient silk parasol that spiralled outward as it unfurled on the floor.'

'Did she speak?' I asked.

'Not a word. Nothing. She kissed me on the lips.'

Walking through streets that were memories of streets, correct in some details, quite wrong in others, down through Bethnal Green and Whitechapel, to our meeting place (Track, Danny Folgate), the great stone that lay on the grass behind the Amazon Street flats, I slept. Dreamt. In micro-snatches. Dreams that night refused. Sleep I had missed.

By a dirty window, a closed shop that once sold surplus uniforms, daggers, calor-gas containers and rusty water-bottles, I stood alongside the man who had my face, who looked as I looked – in the days when I used mirrors to shave. Our eyes met, dream self and teasing double. Blood oozed from beneath a strip of plaster that curled from his chin. The stranger lost his nerve, first, dropped his gaze, moved off ahead of me, in the general direction of the Thames and Commercial Road. He never glanced back.

The White Stone

The stone hadn't moved in the night. Danny Folgate was in watchful attendance, a light dew darkening the shoulders of his pale retail-park windbreaker. Presented with this scene, as 'shot by amateur cameraman', my first thought would have been: 'Where are the blue-and-white ribbons?' Then: 'What did they find *under* that rock? How many bones?'

Folgate was a classic stalker: serial-killer beard (copyright Peter Sutcliffe), buttress nose supporting overhanging brow, worry lines like the aftershock of ECT, bottle-black hairstrands gelled over Klingon ears. Soft-strength, quivering hands and a rolling gait. A proper man, generous to a fault, courteous to strangers, prepared – without hope of reward – to talk me through the mysteries of dowsing.

While we waited for Track.

She would certainly show – if she managed to convince herself that yesterday's Aldgate walk was an actuality, the same stone could be found twice.

'Try this,' Folgate said, passing me a strip of rough blue tape, the kind they use to secure oversize boxes of white goods. 'A W-rod.'

Folgate's kit, fished from the black bag, was salvage; pendulums contrived from bath plugs, bent coat-hangers, acrylic divisions painted onto a metal disk that had been carried home from Ford's PTA (Painting Trimming Assembly) plant. In riverside Dagenham.

'I never use hazel, not since that first time.' Danny hooked back his upper lip to show me the missing lateral incisors. 'Kick like a Lee Enfield. You're much safer with brass or plastic.'

The W-rod, in Folgate's candle-white hands, twisted and writhed, locating a series of quite distinct energy fields around the grey boulder (folded schist with mineral bands).

'If we had the time,' he said, 'we might turn up –'

'Grave goods? Human remains?'

'Bicycle wheels. Foil dishes from the takeaway.'

Dowsing, in Danny's scheme of things, was not unlike plumbing. You called him in to find a lost ring, a betting-slip. He didn't charge. He had a notable collection of beer-bottle caps indoors. He kept hair in bottles. There was a model of Diana Dors made from scavenged watch-faces. Objects migrated but never disappeared. Black water, running beneath the city, affected those who lived above it, bringing cancers, blindness, loss of male sexual potency.

I spread my Nicholson's *Greater London Street Atlas* on the stone table and invited Danny to take a reading from the A13. His pendulum, with its moonstone splinter, responded vigorously, the axis of oscillation favouring the east.

'Oh dearie dearie me,' he said. Disturbed by areas where pylon forests, mobile phone masts and shooting ranges had the bath plug spinning. 'Sewage is prolific.'

My stomach rumbled.

'Don't take this wrong,' he patted my shoulder, 'you might be asking too much too soon.' The pendulum reeled over Rainham Marshes like a drunk from a Clerkenwell club hitting Sunday morning sunshine.

Folgate was tall for the Estuary, but hunched from years in the machine shop, the noise. Track with her excited hair towered over him. Beady rain, which had been falling for days, the kind Londoners don't notice or acknowledge, did wild things to her rampant thatch: it knotted, curled. Red as a Purfleet dawn over the soap factory. It kept the drizzle off the collar of her donkey jacket. She was smiling, as always. Moist-lipped, a Styrofoam beaker of coffee in her hand. The diluted aroma nudged us on towards the road, that phantom Americana of multiplexes (you can't access), burger joints (where Lee Bowyer hurled chairs) and Wal-Mart imitations with permanent fire sales.

'Danny, Hannah. Track, Alan,' I blurted. Introducing the already introduced. And getting it completely wrong, confusing Track with my second wife and Danny with a correspondent from Romford who had been very helpful in downloading Essex material from his computer: the Bascule Bridge over the River Roding at Barking Creek, Hadleigh Castle, conspiracy stuff about Templars at Danbury. Facts kept leaking into my fictions, the borders were insecure. Ask me how I recognised Track, what made her unique, and I couldn't tell you. The story required her presence and she obliged.

Is it a common experience? You come across an unexplained boulder in an urban backwater and you think: 'This needs a dowser.' You get home, there's a letter waiting on the mat – lined paper, blue Biro.

I have been told by a friend youre thinking of doing the A13 next can I help. I am a dowser I will meet and show you its very simple. I'm not working everyday next week is good. I must say Andy I enjoy your books about London when they are real and not too fancyful. Anyway Andy good luck mate.

Ponder a local mystery, the locked room of David Rodinsky, and the phone will ring: a woman with the death certificate, the location of the grave. It gets to the point where you daren't make a note, jot down a bright idea. That's why I gave up, years ago, any attempt to publish fiction. I understood that you had to be an established journalist, dictating a column, inventing contrary opinions, faking outrage, to get a novel published. I hung around too long doing the inches on pit bulls, CCTV, gangsters' tailoring. Novelty's the game, fresh blood. Ten years of sponsored discontent, sub-Orwellian engagement with society and its ills, sidebars on *Big Brother* and the Millennium Dome, left me in limbo. Commissioning editors lost interest. Hacks I'd trashed took their revenge. I should have recycled decades of research, foot-slogging expeditions up the Lea Valley and along the Thames, as fiction. But it was too late. I was as old as I looked. No serious convictions, no previous. No family. Never appeared on TV.

I envied Track. She did what she did, not caring if anybody came to the studio, if there were no exhibitions, no sales. The woman couldn't stop grinning. The only problem was finding space in which to work, putting up with constant relocation; being dispersed, deeper and deeper into Essex. Brick Lane to a Portakabin on Rainham Marshes in three years.

Danny Folgate, master of apparatus, was another contented human. His art was a craft, no editors or producers to appease. No foremen, union reps, cards to punch. Dowsing was an explanation of a liminal world that commuters and salaried slaves had no time to notice.

I read the A13 as a semi-celestial highway, a Blakean transit to a higher mythology, a landscape of sacred mounds and memories. (And endured the derision that brought.)

Danny smiled. 'The road's an irritant, really. More noise and nuisance than anything else. When you live on it.'

I had to interrogate the Nicholson myself, Danny insisted. 'Controlled subjectivity' was the name of the game.

'Don't take the map too personal, mate. Picture yourself walking *through* the symbols. Ask the right questions and the answers will come.'

The only question that came to me, quartering pp. 58–9 of my *Greater London Street Atlas*, was: 'why?' Why was the A13 as green as the artichoke from Hannah's dream? Crossroads, running south towards the Thames, were yellow. Understandably. Piss troughs. Rhomboid parks and playing fields were diamonds dropped in a swamp. And, south of the road, was an ice cap, blank as Antarctica. The terra incognita of Beckton and the Eastbury Levels. Waiting for the spoilers, the exploiters, spivs and politicians who couldn't abide white space.

I dowsed with a milky-green serpent stone, dangling on a bath chain, while they hired professionals to interrogate satellite scans, the virtual Estuary. The final frontier: Thames Gateway. New London: stilt cities, excavated chalk quarries, airstrips, amnesia. The beginning of the ultimate exodus. When the centre implodes and the fringes are populated with the Undead, dreaming of lottery wins and bright-blue seas.

*

'I'm concerned, you know. For Ollie. I mean, what kind of place is Hastings? At night? For a woman with a camera?'

I dropped back alongside Track, allowing Danny to follow his W-rod down the broad pavements of Commercial Road; she was off the pace, hands in coat pocket, no camera. I caught her staring at a bald mannequin in a wholesaler's window. The product was much more eccentric than anything on Brick Lane: no leather, no leopard spots, no Gulf War T-shirts.

The payback for movement, the launching of our quest, was a break in the cloud cover, low sun over the river, splintering on tall buildings, reflected in glass: tired stone brought to life. Warmth in the blood. A glint of silver where the grey paint was wearing away on Danny's colour disk.

'White is very strong here,' he said. 'Holy water. A chain of churches and statues. Virgin Mary, Clem Attlee.'

Water, apparently, was the medium of memory. Molecules of memory remained even when water had been purified. Like a beam of sunlight, I thought, passing through a stained-glass window.

'I tried calling Ollie last night,' Track said. 'And again this morning, nothing. She's hooked up with that freak, I'm sure of it, the gangster boy.'

Socialist ghosts for Danny. His childhood: rubble and unexploded bombs. A world without fruit and colour. Without cars. Lorries from the docks, the rumble, as the remembered soundtrack. The benevolent invasion of the borough by social planners, visionaries inspired by Abercrombie's 1943 *County of London* plan; foldout maps as pure as anything by Ben Nicholson or Mondrian. Neo-Romantic abstractions in thirsty greens and purples. Open Space plans. Diagrammatic proposals. Ring roads. Hospitals. Schools. Allotments. London squares: *The squares should be open to full public use. The removal of the railings, as a war-time measure, has brought them into the life of the community and destroyed their isolation.*

Space around buildings. Segregation of housing from industry. Combining rest with culture: *The Russians have adopted this principle of combining mental and physical recreation in what they call Parks of*

Rest and Culture. The largest one in Moscow is particularly noteworthy for its children's section, which includes a children's theatre, cinema, experimental workshops and a large-scale village.

River-front amenities. Direct action in deficient areas. *To conclude: a main task in the immediate post-war years will be to provide new open spaces in those areas which at present have an amount totally inadequate for the needs of the inhabitants – the East End, Islington, Finsbury and the south bank boroughs.*

The Las Vegas pyramid on the summit of Canary Wharf tower winked at such aspirations. Its near neighbour, HSBC, stole sunlight. But the names were still there, embedded in low-level flats, schools, projects: Lansbury, Toynbee. A black statue of Attlee outside Limehouse Library. They mean nothing to Docklands commuters for whom the distance between *this* and *that* is so much dead time; place as an irritant, figures ticking on the clock. Only grizzled socialists like Danny paid their dues, a wistful nod in passage. Limehouse topography, swept up in the dirty backdraught of the A13, was profoundly schizophrenic.

When I kept pace with Danny, I saw this stretch of Commercial Road as a tracking shot from one of the Soviet realists, a camera train, Dziga Vertov: sailors' dormitories, reading rooms, padlocked swimming pools (with an Eisenstein montage of culture hero statues, cranes, demolition balls, high-contrast clouds).

If I fell back to chat with Track, I saw threat in hooded lurkers in doorways, opium dens out of Sax Rohmer, needles underfoot, wrecked bus shelters, burnt-out cars.

Left to myself, I lifted my camera to record graffiti: RIPPER VICTIM WAS VICE GIRL. DRAMATIC ESCAPE IN GUN SIEGE. Long shadows behind a chainlink fence: a discontinued car-valeting operation, where a group of camera-shy Balkan men were doing something suspect with a white van. Indoctrinated by TV cop shows, you might read the situation as: kidnap, body cargo, kiddie prostitution.

My camera lacked a long lens. I could go wide or panoramic but I couldn't do close-ups. I logged saints, angels, madonnas, north-facing, on the roofs and pediments and porticoes of ugly, brick churches. Irish immigration was strong here and the traces remained in neighbourhood politics and pubs.

My most exciting discovery was a blue plaque for VICTOR ANDREW D'BIERE McLAGLEN. BOXER & OSCAR WIN-NER FOR *THE INFORMER*. One of John Ford's troop of drinkers and Beverly Hills saddle-bums. The cavalry sergeant on the edge of retirement. Plum-nosed brawler, kisser of ladies' handkerchiefs. The bully's maudlin tears for the thing he has crushed. Victor McLaglen: honoured, unforgotten, beside a road of drivers wanting to be elsewhere.

John Wayne, camping on a renovated minesweeper, was ferried to the set of his latest western in a military helicopter, to pistol-whip Dennis Hopper as a pinko fairy. Other sclerotic cowboys from the poker school – Ward Bond, Walter Brennan, Ben Johnson, Slim Pickens – were busy gumming charred steaks at Richard Nixon's benefit barbecue. And Victor McLaglen, god's Irishman, got his blue plaque in Limehouse.

A nice fable. Until I discovered that McLaglen had in fact been born in Tunbridge Wells. Print the legend.

The Stephen Hawking Special Needs Primary, a collection of haunted huts set back from the road: that's the next one into the notebook. Before Track comes back to life, back to the Ollie theme, when she spots a pub called the White Swan.

'Gimme a camera. *Quick.*'

An ordinary boozer, foursquare to the road, with a royal-blue turret addition, plasterboard windows.

'What's special about the Swan?'

'Ollie used to hang out with that creep Reo. Reo Sleeman. Reo knew his brother and the big guy, O'Driscoll, wouldn't show up in a gay bar.'

The Irish and the gays weren't mutually exclusive. I'd seen O'Driscoll and his mate Phil Tock, heavies I recognised from group shots in one of James Colvin's books, drinking with art faces and Kray-chasers in black shirts. Limehouse families like the Cashmans had a foot in both camps.

'I warned her, begged her, but she would give that scumbag another chance. The night Michael Barrymore came out. Tabloid guys three-deep at the bar. Reo was *so* panicky. Brother Alby was heading for a nasty shock with his cornflakes next morning. Ollie was oblivious of the whole scene.'

All in all, Track reckoned, the Swan was a good thing. Jimmy Seed was a regular. Top cabaret. Great bands. Lock-ins every night. The East End as they like to sell it, a right knees-up. You didn't know who you were shouting at over the decibels, hoodlum, painter, electrician, rapper or media drone slumming from Canary Wharf.

Reo was jumpy. Sucking plastic water. Lifting his T-shirt, slapping his abs, tweaking his pecs. Rocking his head in his hands – trying to hear the sound of the sea inside. Ollie was dancing, by herself. Talking to anybody who talked to her.

Ollie didn't catch the incident.

The bruiser, coming out of the Gents, rubbing a finger across his nose, zipping up, who smacked right into Reo, knocking him off his stool. He was about to stomp the little shit for disrespect – when there was a moment of hideous mutual recognition. Reo, reacting first, grabs Ollie, runs. The other man is too far gone to realise, immediately, what he's done, who the slag is. Alby's kid, his brother.

The shirtlifter was Phil Tock, worst of the bunch. Reo clocks him, clocks his chums, a pair of fairies with big grins and milky moustaches.

'What did you say to Ollie?'

'I told her to put right in for the Hastings gig. Like *now*. No time to pack. The coast, I'd drive.'

After Limehouse Church – neutralised, sandblasted to a heritage sheen – we tramped de Chirico avenues. Statues of forgotten men. The Evil Empire glittered on the horizon: cloud-reflecting panels on space-launch towers. Elevated railways. Diverted traffic. Inky black on the dowser's colour disk. Danny trembled, his decency affronted by cities that appeared overnight, out of the swamp, offering nothing to the now isolated holdouts in their doomed terraces and council blocks.

We were the kind, Danny and I, to give nostalgia a bad name. Track was amused by our growls and mutters.

'You *love* this shit. Trading horror stories. Without Blair and Livingstone, Conran and Foster, the landscape rippers, you'd wind up sharing a couch in an old folks' home, plaid rug over the knees, watching reruns of *Fools and Horses*.'

She was right. Track was so much younger than we had ever been; alert, amused, ready and willing to be unsurprised. I might yet propose to her, wife number three. Treat her to a haircut. And a bar of soap.

The park adjoining Trinity Methodist Church in Poplar featured a ravished memorial that reminded Track of Elizabeth Frink. A double-Ozymandias: four vast and trunkless legs of cancerous concrete, peeled to the iron sinews, stood in the desert. On a shallow plinth. A wonder that required our full attention, an art work that had come into its own through its dissolution.

'The Wrestlers,' Track called it.

The floor beneath the swaying gladiators was the kind of delicate green that calls for a decade of ill-directed piss. Feet were hooves, stripped of skin – as in an anatomical plate. The pubic thatch was grass. Acid rain, road grit and all-enveloping low-grade pollution had collaborated with the anonymous artist on an expressionist masterpiece, 3-D Grünewald: buboed, leprous, raw. Flesh as wood. As bone. Spraypaint leaked its black treacle from gashed groin and clenched rump.

Two large men, dog walkers, told us that the sculpture was a tribute to the nobility of labour, to men who had given their working lives to the West India Docks. I didn't need the lecture on the good old days of fiddles in export sheds, iffy manifests, contraband, insurance scams. I'd survived a cold winter, blacklegging, in railway yards at Stratford East, when container cowboys choked the last breath from dockers who had basked too long in restrictive practices. Enoch-supporting chants and inherited jobs for life.

'We knew what graft was, mate.'

So did I. 'The acquisition of money, gain or advantage by dishonest, unfair or illegal means.'

Graft? I'd shaved every inch of this park, along with the Catholic church behind it, madonnas on mounds. I'd shovelled dog dirt into black bags and harvested slippery condoms like so many fallen leaves.

Back on the A13, now rebranded as East India Dock Road, we went with the romance, the myths. Anchors and hostels. Ghost ships in relief on granite plinths. Richard Green (1866) with bronze dog. Tamed, domesticated and sniffing at his crotch. (When ownership of the East India Docks was divided in 1842, the Green family took the whole of the Silvertown side.)

Sunstreaks flashed from Erno Goldfinger's tower at the mouth of the Blackwall Tunnel. Approach roads spurned Poplar vernacular for the soulless Esperanto of US colonialism: off-highway blocks parasitical on Docklands. Buildings gave nothing away, sporting obligatory shades: Jack Nicholson returning to the Connaught in a cab.

A crisp shadow slanted across herringbone flags, kerb, cambered tarmac: a curtain of brown dust between old London and the clip-on *Blade Runner* set (in which everything was provisional, subject to immediate cancellation). A yard or so of this division between darkness and light was taken up by a granite rectangle, set flush to the pavement (where nobody walked). 'THE GREENWICH MERIDIAN LINE,' it said. 'ZERO LONGITUDE ESTABLISHED 1884.'

'So this is all that's left of it,' I thought. 'Enough thread to wrap a parcel.'

Before I could stoop to capture the memorial tablet, my light was stolen by a large car. I waited. The car didn't budge, it parked itself firmly across white paint that spelt out: A13. A mud-spattered Volvo, the kind I'd have described, seeing it in Whitechapel or Kingsland Road, as 'short-haul Hasidic'. Solitary driver in black coat and hat, wholesale transport. Not this time. A major ruck was in progress. The driver, arms waving, leapt out into the traffic.

'I'm supposed to find this fucking hotel? Yes, I can *see* it – on the other side of the dual carriageway, the crash barrier, you stupid bitch. No gap, darling. We've been through the Blackwall Tunnel *twice*. And over the Dartford Bridge. Get out, kids. All out, out. We'll walk. Just leave it. *Leave it*. Let them tow the bugger away.'

Clutching black bags, rubbish sacks which dragged along the ground and split, depositing clothes and toys all over the A13, straggled a column of small kids. An attractively spacey mother in beach wear, two coats, pink boots, dark glasses. And Jimmy Seed: distraught. Refugee plutocrats. Unhoused.

As he explained. When we helped him with books and wine and PlayStation and marine watercolours by other artists. The family Seed were temporarily banished from their new home. Property millionaires without a pot to piss in and nowhere to camp. The market, paintings for riverside flats, had peaked, then plunged. Teams of builders (electricians, tea-brewers, fetchers of bacon sandwiches) had trashed their latest acquisition, a Bethnal Green synagogue. The roof was off. Rooms were filled with rubble. There was no water and plenty of sewage. The Seeds had been forced to emigrate to the Travelodge. Where Jimmy could knock out a road triptych to trade against a couple of Victorian terraces in Hull.

If they could scrape together – milk money, kids' piggy-bank – £42.95 (one night's sanctuary). The Travelodge at the mouth of the Blackwall Tunnel, convenient for everywhere, was much favoured by reps and tourists who'd made the wrong booking for the Dome.

I saw the attraction: anonymous Eurostyle. A peacetime barracks in Germany. Small square windows, which open on the tilt, masked in gauzy drapes. No entrance on the A13 side. Nothing to draw attention to itself. The Travelodge concept was: filling-station fore-court in which you are permitted to sleep. Refuel, pass water, watch television. Pick up a complimentary map – on which the next Travelodge will be marked. Britain had been invaded by numbered flags. Like a golf course. Alton (Hants) to York (Central). 'A Travelodge for every occasion': slogan, not a threat.

Jimmy's mob, surrounded by possessions, slumped in the otherwise deserted afternoon bar, with its banks of TV monitors and unsynchronised lounge Muzak. Danny was uncomfortable indoors and fiddled with the zip of his bag. Track smiled, unfazed, eager to occupy whatever chair she found herself in. I tried to locate someone prepared to serve up drinks. Dying sunlight poured through picture windows: panorama of parked cars, strategic bushes, amputated lamp-standards, other buildings with much the same design. The only notable feature in this landscape was an attempt to introduce poetry. A sequence of slate-grey slabs with upbeat messages (reprised in doodles above the bar).

I watched, in the mirror, as an animated couple, impervious to the beauty of the car park sculptures, approached the Travelodge. The woman was familiar. At my age they all are. The lovers ambled into the bar, passing close enough for me to get the scent. Faces might not register, smell retains its potency. Hannah was never overfond of bathing – once a week, for an hour, a good soak, during which she read Laing, or took a hit of poetry – but she liked perfume. And was quite experimental about it, little bottles, picked up in transit to conferences, set out in a line on the mantelpiece. There was one bottle, squat, shaped like a glass eye, which gave off a rather heavy drench that reminded me of the Sixties, Gitanes and lemongrass. Hannah used that one whenever she expected sex. A Pavlovian trigger that never failed. So what was she doing doused with the stuff in a Blackwall Tunnel Travelodge? And who was the mouthy gimp in my father's coat? The one with his arm around her waist.

The Literate Jukebox

Elis, the slender man in the air steward's uniform, prowled the bar-zone on twinkly feet, staying within a ladder of imaginary lights that led to the emergency exit, his past life. He talked in semaphore (a second language), matching gestures to meticulously articulated words. Cheeks puffed, lips pursed around an emergency whistle, he kept back just enough breath for the inflation of a life-jacket.

'The lady's a regular, business class. You understand? She likes . . .' – he leant forward, dropping his voice – '. . . the window seat, plenty of legroom. Plenty of leg.'

'The man?'

'Never flown before, not with us. Madame is alone, a little farouche. I set a dish of peanuts, roasted. Freshen her drink every forty-five minutes. She lives, they say, up in the clouds, by the Tunnel entrance. Comes over most nights. To unwind. Where else should she go, person like that, around here?'

'She drinks?'

'Not to cause a problem. Kümmel with lemonade and ice, unusual. I had to order it in.'

'You know her well?'

'She likes to talk. Excuse me.'

Hannah was due a refill. Her companion, back to me, was a lush. Heavy, morose. Going at it steadily, soft Irish whiskey with Czech lager chasers. A bad drunk, I'd guess. Hanging on to his Hoxton pretensions (black wool beanie) in the Travelodge, London Docklands.

This A-road attraction, according to my complimentary coaster, was five miles from everywhere. Old Royal Observatory: five miles. Maritime Museum: five miles. Queens House: 5 miles. Royal Naval

College: 5 miles. Cutty Sark: five miles. A13 (aka East India Dock Road): fifteen yards.

Waiting for Elis to do his bit with tray, twist bottle, peanut pack, I watched twin monitor screens in the long mirror. An alternate world peopled by Dennis Hopper clones; by the worst Hopper imitator, Hopper himself. A short-arse in a dirty Stetson. A Hollywood coke-freak boozer who could no longer get the nuisance parts in Henry Hathaway westerns.

Hopper on a train. Hopper on a mountain. Hopper crucified. Hopper out of it. No TV network would run these films. One of them, I knew, because I'd been chasing it for months, had been deleted twenty years ago.

The bar stank: money burning into scratched light. No soundtrack. The narcoleptic of choice. Muzak: like piss fountains splashing on pink ice.

'I'm having a little bitty Hopper season,' Elis said. 'Bootleg VHS tapes from a Paris dealer. *The American Friend* and *The Last Movie*. What happened to Robby Müller? Great photographer. But slow, they say. Took hours setting up if he didn't like the cut of your shirt.'

It was much too late for a wallow in anorakia. Film history had migrated to a generic Docklands hotel (a place without memory). Film (self-destructive stars) was the barman's hobby. The manager didn't care. He could run whatever he wanted, so long as he killed the sound. Other screens hosed in news footage, soaps, football. Colours unknown to nature, scarlet faces (every interviewee a potential Alex Ferguson), grass like Sinatra's rug.

For a man who didn't drink, Jimmy Seed was having a famous session. Tabletop like a bottle bank. Jimmy and Track, notebooks out, talking tactics: who to hit on, which paintings to display, which ones to hide. Favours for favours. Philip Dodd, Tim Marlow, Jonathan Jones. Contacts to squeeze. Old lovers to reactivate. Curators with exploitable weaknesses, soft spots for rough trade.

'ICA?'

They both laughed.

'The Whitechapel?' Jimmy slurred. 'It's in the fucking charter, a modicum of exhibition space must be given over to gin-u-wine East London artists. Lifers like . . . me. Thirty years, man and boy, within sound of gunfire from the Blind Beggar.'

Track snorted. 'No chance.'

'White Cube. They don't give a fuck *what* you do. It's who you do, you are. I am . . . IT! In-your-face *truth*, adherence to . . . mat-erial-ity. Matter. Paint on canvas. Got to come back. Am I right, babe?'

Mrs Seed and the kids had cleared off, dragging their sacks, to argue over bed space in the single room they were to share. Danny Folgate, nursing his cordial, was unhappy.

'I'll kip in the motor. Keep an eye on it.' He didn't fancy spending the night in a place so bereft of spirit.

Jimmy yielded a set of keys. I walked out with Danny, to clear my head in the damp night air. If I stayed in the bar, drink for drink with Jimmy, I was going to do something stupid. Make an outrageous suggestion to Track. Ask her to marry me. I hardly knew the woman, would have difficulty recognising her if we came face to face in the aisle at Tesco's, but she had this vital quality: she was nothing like wives numbers one and two. Different era, different species. Different chat. That's the most important element in any relationship, sound. Voice. Does it grate? Does it wear away at your reserves? Ruth didn't say much, but you had to pin your ears back when she was on the phone to a relative or friend. Hannah talked fluently, aggressively, her words a challenge. I was forced to respond, drawn into the argument, made to perform when I wanted to hoard language, keep its potency secure.

Ruth was and is a mystery. But I know absolutely everything about Hannah's childhood, adolescent difficulties, flirtations, neuroses, sex triggers. Dreams. Nightmares. Fear of the sea crashing around the house. Fear of buttons. Fear of silence.

I cracked it! Prompted by one of the TV monitors, it came to me, the puzzle of that name. Track reversed gives Kat. The big hair, eyes, attitude: one of the Slater sisters from *EastEnders*. Students probably got themselves up for a party. Ollie as the soppy one and Track as Kat.

Riddle solved. Trouble was . . . I couldn't claim my reward, sleep with her, Track, without a marriage certificate. Out of the question. And sleep was so sweet a notion. Danny, yawning, rubbed his eyes, while we waited for a break in the late-night traffic flow.

Jimmy's Volvo, astonishingly, was still there. Unclamped. Nobody could be bothered. Danny, hunched over the wheel, was a smooth driver – by the standard of the journalists, painters and film-makers who gave me most of my rides. He understood this road and very soon, too soon (landscape a miracle of shapes and signs), had us back in the Travelodge car park. Where he folded his arms and nodded out.

His only remark, before he swung across three lanes of honking maniacs, was gnomic. A quote. 'Stones want to go on being stones.' He took a hand off the wheel to squeeze my arm. 'Remember that, Andy mate.'

I don't know if he meant it as a tease, something to sleep on. Or as a pensée that didn't require an answer.

'Beckton Alp tomorrow,' I said. Patting the roof of the car. 'Early start.'

Elis had retired. The screens were playing visual Muzak to go with the sound: waves breaking repeatedly on a golden beach. I'd missed my chance with Track, she was going to sleep in Jimmy's bath. So he said. Four or five brandy miniatures on the table, the bar shuttered.

I helped myself, before Jimmy arranged the rest on a tray. He was turning in.

'How would you rate this evening?' I asked. 'Average session? No dinner and a dozen stiff ones?'

'I can't do it anymore. Cholesterol, grease caffs. I find, if I'm working, I don't use food. A cheese sandwich or a chocolate digestive now and then. Plenty of water.'

'Water?'

'Oh yeah, back then, sure. The hair, the cowboy boots. Running off to strip clubs in Spitalfields with featured writers. I'd cover Bond Street openings, fizz in flute, and watch the clock. I had to make it back to Limehouse, Blade Bone in Three Colt Street, for the eleven-thirty lock-in. Serious drinkers, great crack. We were down there every night.'

'This was when you still painted humans?'

'Sure. Critics called me an Expressionist, school of Bellany. Bollocks. I never touched a drop before breakfast. Unlike John. Bottle packed on each hip at the bus stop, going to college, Chelsea. I painted what I saw from my window. Actuality, first to last. If I couldn't get the women, I'd dress up. That's why they stand that way, legs like croquet hoops.'

Animated, in the second flush, Jimmy swished brandy, using the liquor as a filter against subdued lighting. We had more in common than I realised: place not people, topography instead of narrative. Human figures treated like caricatures, rude cartoons. I'd junked fiction (and my soul mate, Ruth) around the time Jimmy treated his canvases to a thorough ethnic cleansing: no freaks, crips, dogs. No tarts propping up walls. A self-denying ordinance: no booze.

'First wife sent me to the quack, round the corner from here,' Jimmy confessed. 'You might have known him, London writer, old Trot, name of Widgery. "I'm a bit concerned about my drinking, doc." I said it with a straight face.'

'Any use?'

'Good bloke, but busy. Got me to write down my daily intake – seven or eight pints of an evening, couple of bottles of wine at lunch. Like we all did. A brandy, maybe, to get me on the road.'

'And?'

'Practically teetotal, Widgery reckoned. Wasting his time. He had real problems on his patch. Diseases unrecorded since the Middle Ages. Call myself a painter? I wasn't trying. That's when I shifted to landscapes. No mad eyes staring back at you.'

Tumbler in each hand, Jimmy lurched from the room, crashing against a slot machine that dispensed books. I followed, bladder burning, the night's drinking catching up with me. And nothing ahead, the wasted expense of a solitary Travelodge bed: 'Due to problems beyond our control, we have had to remove all telephones from rooms.'

Jimmy, shameless about these things, saw the book-dispensing machine as a future painting: the literate jukebox, cabinet of curiosities. Thirty-two portraits, cover designs, to be remade: melancholy woodland pools, waifs on rain-drenched jetties, barbed wire, skulls, cars, minimalist abstraction. In silver and gold. England, the culture, reduced to essence: a catalogue of favoured tropes, iconic views.

'Contemporary fiction,' I said to Jimmy, 'is either pod or ped. Left-hand rack, you'll observe, begins with J.G. Ballard, *Super-Cannes*. Pod-meister. Suburban solipsism: world in a windscreen. Right-hand rack is ped. The walkers. W.G. Sebald, *Austerlitz*, *Rings of Saturn*. Sit at your PC as you sit in the car: pod person. Lose yourself in the rhythms of the walk: pedestrian. Stately prose, Sebald.'

'Stephen King?'

'Pod. By instinct. He tries to walk down a road, a redneck runs him down. Know your limitations. Stick to genre.'

'P.D. James?'

'Pod. Outing to flint church. Body in ditch.'

The vision was sharp: Jimmy and I, stooping forward, superimposed over the glossy books in their display cabinet. It went all the way back through literature. Peds: John Cowper Powys, Gerald Kersh, D.H. Lawrence, James Joyce, Dickens, De Quincey, Bunyan, Blake, Rousseau. Pods: DeLillo, Updike, Flaubert, Proust. No precedence. Different strokes. I was far enough gone to appreciate the conceit, too sober to write it down. Another inspiration that would never see the light of day.

Jimmy tried to find the stairs. If there was a lift he'd never manage to summon it. He didn't fancy sleeping overnight in a stalled tin box.

'Tell me' – he jabbed my chest – 'are you gay?' His hands clutched my shoulders, then slipped. Boneless, he fell to his knees. I looked

down on a bright ring of male-pattern baldness, freckled scalp and
rusty wisps of wool.

'Not now, thanks.'

The night porter, an economic migrant, slid back into her cubbyhole. A redhaired Scotsman gripping another man's thighs, head in
crotch, mumbling incoherently, after midnight, was rather too
much.

'You're a fucking journo,' said Jimmy, 'and you never pull. That's
all wrong.'

I was uneasy about broaching the Gents, a plywood door with
one of those symbols you have trouble working out, sober. But
it had to be done. Relief was acute. I counted the seconds as a
steaming arc dissolved the blue chemical cork – while keeping an
eye on the dirty mirror, in case Jimmy barged in with another
monologue.

Ruth always hated those scenes on TV, bits of business enacted
at the trough, two tough cops nudging the plot, shaking the drips.
Male-bonding sessions: media sharks snorting coke, lowlife spilling
blood on the tiles. Television drama, without mobiles, laptops and
lavatories, would fall apart.

There were two of me in the mirror. Nothing unusual in that,
you might say: dodgy peepers, drink taken. 'Photographs are
mirrors with memory,' someone wrote. Untrustworthy, promiscuous things. You never know when they'll start to leak. But this was
no Marx Brothers routine. The impersonator was wearing my
father's funeral coat, the one I'd lost on the coast. And the cleft of
his Desperate Dan chin was pumping blood from the nick I'd given
myself, weeks ago, before I'd driven to Rainham Marshes with
Jimmy.

I grew perfectly sober in an instant.

That's Poe. You didn't think me capable of such a sentence? Even
drunk.

There was that in the manner of the stranger, and in the tremulous
shake of his uplifted finger, as he held it between my eyes and the light,
which filled me with unqualified amazement.

'You think it's clever?'

My mirror image shouted.

'Dodging through Whitechapel? The Hoop & Grapes? Staring all night at a woman drinking with me in a hotel bar?'

His eyes were bloodshot. He'd lost it. But his grip was powerful.

'What are you? Private dick? Journalist?'

He banged my face against the glass. The situation, if I accepted it, was absurd. The kind of novel that would never make it into the Travelodge display cabinet. The man was crazy, road crazy; nothing in the way of solid research to hold his world together. He'd come to believe that this portion of London, Docklands, A13, was his private fiefdom, personal property. Every splinter in the ground a nail in his hand. Every fast-food joint a trauma.

He wanted to shift, the insight came to me, as he hammered my face against the mirror for the second time, from being a character, someone I'd observed at the corner of the frame, to the teller of the tale. The author. Ugly word. Worse thought. There are places, the Docklands Travelodge in the small hours of the night is one of them, where fiction and documentary cohabit. Indiscriminately. Fetches appear and disappear in anonymous corridors. Dead actors work the bar. TV sets loop conspiracies. The future is optional – but it's out there, beyond the double-glazing, full-beam on a restless road.

I drove an elbow into his Adam's apple, loose cartilage in a flabby sock. John Fashanu would have been proud of the shot, blindside and very painful. When in doubt, go pulp, lift a passage from a forgotten book that has lodged, deep, in memory's sediment.

He doubled over and had to sit down. He laughed until the punch line sucker-punched him – then he froze.

That's James Ellroy. I downloaded *The Big Nowhere* from the book display.

Ellroy trumped Poe.

Ellroy plays the same game, he opens with a tag from Conrad: 'It was written that I should be loyal to the nightmare of my choice.' *Heart of Darkness*, what else? The only title available in California.

Brando refused to sample the novella before he landed, whale-sized (wrong movie), in the Philippines for Coppola's vanity project.

I polished my bruises. My impersonator had been sucked back into the glass – where, doubtless, a nest of spooks were recording the scene. Behind every mirror in every toilet in every Travelodge, ibis, off-highway motel, are ghosts. Succubi. Third Mind essences detached by acts of love. Road reverie. Tremors. Sweats. Karmic multiples, doubles of doubles, lost without trace, divorced from human congress. Eternally alone with the Muzak of the spheres.

I was wearing the other man's dark coat, won back, when I returned to Hannah. We kissed and went upstairs to bed.

Nightsweats

Nightsweats. Noises.

The woman, Katherine Cloud Riise, known as Track, lay in her cold bath (no water) and thought autopsy. Thought: photographs. Dead ones, females, in the crypt of Christ Church, Spitalfields, their names: Mary Jourdan, Mary Ann Pontardant, Mary Pearson, Mary Loader, Mary Tufnell, Mary Tagg, Mary Leese, Mary Ann Ball. Bones spread across the floor of the church. Persons in white, masked. The flash of: reality.

Nashville corpses, victims, in the coroner's office. A powder of fine snow on the fins of huge cars. Two Hispanics discussing Patricia Cornwell in the documentary a friend worked on, viewed in Bow. The radio in the next room: 'You can run but you can't hide.'

Wisconsin Death Trip: the book, not the film. Black River Falls, Wisconsin. Her Norwegian, German grandparents, great-grandparents. Everybody comes from somewhere. From photographs. The clothes and the eyes, how they argue; respectability and terror. Territories where death holds sway and warm-bloods trespass at their peril.

'How do you pronounce that name, Riise?' Jimmy had asked, their first tutorial. 'Like Ben Johnson in *One-Eyed Jacks*, in the cantina: "Greaser"? Nobody drawls like Ben.'

So she'd become Track. For her own reasons.

Scouring powders left their imprint on the smooth enamel of the Travelodge tub. No lid, no stars. Smell soap, think sugar. Think Silvertown, the Tate & Lyle factory on the river. One stroll down that marine high street and you'll never take sugar in your tea; solid air, a curtain of sticky droplets clogging the pores, filling the grooves of your fingernails, blackening them.

No sleep for Track, except this sleep, her life. What was she doing out on the road with mad old men? Her business, her choice. It amused her. This landscape, their failing memories. Sounds came through thin walls. She saw herself from above. As a photograph: *Woman in Bath*. She lay very still.

Jimmy's daughter calling, calling for him. The son for the mother. Jimmy snoring. The wife singing. Bedside clock ticking: a red heart. And on the other side, wild gasps, groans through the air duct, Norton howling in a way that shouldn't be heard, no connection with the man in daylight, his awkward amiability, his stories.

In the slit beneath the door, the light came on. The little girl: a pee, a drink of water. A chat. 'I like you.' Track wasn't asleep. She didn't want to dream about Ollie, Livia, her friend, getting into a car with Reo Sleeman. About the way Sleeman wouldn't talk or touch, how he drove with that unblinking, thousand-yard stare, full-beam headlights, away from the coast. Back to London.

One photograph, when Track fixed it, carried her from reverie to unconsciousness. Chest heaving, pupils chasing spectres, hands clenching and unclenching. Mouth agape, wine breath. The cold bath becomes the boat in that studio portrait, a family. From *Wisconsin Death Trip*. From River Falls, 1899. Inauthentic memories, her memories. Hatchet-cheeks, the man. Elegant eyebrows. *Black, pin-hole eyes that won't stop*. Hunger, winter diet. Woman in tall hat. Child – soft gaze – the only one looking directly at the camera. A painted craft in a painted landscape. Single oar: spike in the father's left hand. Water lilies. Wyatt Earp moustache drooping with gravity, black straw boater. Priestlike male with stiff white collar. Wavelets frozen mid-ripple. This phantom Europe – stairs, parks, ruined temples – conjured in a photographer's studio in the Midwest. Fierce father. The child, a girl, young enough to see what has been left behind. The woman, dressed in her finest outfit, necklace, high neck; an expression of tragic subtlety – ironic, wise, forgiving. Left hand, hard-used, exposed on the rim of the fictitious craft. Naked fingers. Ring lost, left to the fish.

Track sleeps. Jimmy sleeps. Norton and Hannah sleep; she is curved into him, her arm across his chest. Life continues, revived and resuscitated, until the next time. If they never share a house, it might still work, this argument of affection.

Lamps along the avenue, fuzzy haloes of riverdamp, illuminate a pedestrian passage between roadworks and mud creek.

Danny the Dowser sat on a metal bench, waiting for the first streaks of pink over the Brunswick Power Station, blue shocks of the elevated railway. The zone of transition soothed him. Wind in the reed beds. Birds on the shoreline. Traffic ramping a passage into the A13 obstacle course. Land given over for centuries to dirty industry, gas, chemical, bone vats, distilleries, was now the gateway to the future: Dome, towers, airstrips, underpasses, multiplexes, eco-friendly superstores with little windmills, the largest empty parking space in London.

The filling station, opened in anticipation of a promised fast-track future, was an oasis of artificial daylight in a desert of rubble, storm fences, tyre mounds, night security patrols.

Danny tapped on the window, asked for a chocolate bar, slid his coins into the tray; a complicated transaction – like getting cash from a Mare Street bank. Cameras swivel. The Asian, red-eyed, snatches up the coins, checking them for fingerprints.

Sticky Danny, choc crumbs in beard, returned to his creekside vigil.

Helicopters low over jungle, over Norfolk coastal wetlands. Thudding blades. Shuddering bed.

Hannah shook Norton, brought him out of his dream. They settled, folded in the old way, against each other, and very soon Hannah's apologetic, mousy snores were puffing the short hairs on Norton's neck. After love, boundaries shift, defensive reflexes are inhibited: the therapist dreamt and the hack, now alert, supersensitive to night's noises, suffered the visions of his partner. Intravenous cable TV.

'Most of you will go to Vietnam. Some of you will not come back.'

Vietnam, England.

English light.

Waterskies with cloud wisps, black Fenland earth.

Dreams don't discriminate, we are everywhere at once. We give ourselves up to long-suppressed lovers whose names and faces we have deleted. (The headless man in the torn Polaroid from the Duchess of Argyll's bathroom. A blow job. With pearl necklace.) We visit spine-tapped valleys, ocean depths of arterial blood, bone coral.

Hannah, that most urban of women, floated over a desert road that ran for hundreds of miles towards sharply outlined mountains, irrigation ditches. She penetrated forests, ankles caught in under-growth, wrists secured by lianas. Pressing herself against me, sharing body-warmth, she took on my obsessions, my vanished ancestor's Peruvian expedition. Arthur Norton and the lost camera.

She sampled films I had seen. And films I thought I had seen, sleep-edited from release prints, redirected by untrustworthy memory. Extracts from books. Lines of poetry echoing insistently when the names of the authors are past recall.

Next morning we were up betimes, and, after settling la cuenta, *which our ragged host seemed to have sat up all night concocting, we rode briskly off, leaving the lake, with its swarms of fat wild-geese undisturbed on the water, and the ill-favoured and milkless kine shivering amongst the coarse rushes on the margin. We zig-zagged over a preliminary ridge, had a smart canter for two hours over an undulating plateau, and reached by 9 a.m. the station called San Blas. Here there are extensive salt works in active operation, but no food for man nor beast procurable, so we pushed on.*

Lodged in her bath, Track dreamt of Livia, face shifting to another woman, also dark, also beautiful. To Marina Fountain, the writer who had taught them both, at college, at Chelsea. Marina's championing of such mysteries as Canvey Island, Sheppey, the Isle of Grain, Tilbury Town, Deal, Thanet, carried Livia and Track into their current projects: perversity, cutting against the grain, travelling with strangers.

'Pick a railway station,' Marina used to say, 'buy a ticket to somewhere you've never been, bring back the story.'

Marina was always late, smoking, books and papers falling out of her satchel, dressed by committee: jumble sale, designer collectables (prize money), extravagant and wildly inappropriate presents from admirers (curators, rich students, both kinds of bookie, turf and lit). Marina did scarves, coats, fancy boots, rings – but wasn't bothered with the rest, minimal suede or leather skirts on long legs, laddered stockings (black, purple, green), loose tops (food-spilled, mended). Hats.

The students, male and female, were in love with her. The schemes she proposed were never carried out, not by them. They were far too preoccupied with their grievances, getting from wherever to wherever, to have time for conceptual journeys.

Marina understood this, her expeditions were not intended for public consumption. They were a way of talking, obliquely, about her own work. Which she wouldn't, otherwise, expose. They were too lazy and impoverished to track down her unique published novel.

She pitched extracts from writers she liked, Djuna Barnes, Jean Rhys, Mary Butts, Nicola Barker, Denise Riley – and left them to it. Fine artists couldn't, for the most part, see the connection: what this had to do with a career, getting a first show. Track and Ollie shared a bottle with Marina, went to the cinema, but they never shared a train ride. Marina did that alone. So she said. If her trips to the coast weren't fiction, a provocation to get them *moving*.

When she didn't turn up one Wednesday, mid-term, November, they missed her. Track was jealous that Ollie had been entrusted with the folder of stories; Marina left them – by accident? – in her flat. She talked about giving the package to a journalist called Norton, a man who wrote about roads, urban Gothic, ill-favoured topographies. Norton was a brief vogue in London art schools, for those who lacked stamina for the real thing, Walter Benjamin, Baudrillard, Mike Davis.

Ollie wouldn't, and Track couldn't, read the stories. Marina knew that perfectly well, otherwise she would never have trusted them with the folder. Now that Norton carried the burden in his A13 rucksack, Track's duty was performed. She would stick with Norton, with the Jiffy bag, until Marina returned to reclaim her property. Until the typescript had been enacted in the Essex territory for which it was always intended.

Sweating, Norton rolled from the bed. It was his turn to sit in the bathroom, sleep was denied him, no hint of dawn through the gap in the curtains. Cars on the road. The soft electronic hum that is London, headache-hammers on rooftops and spires, radio masts, photovoltaic scanners. The yammer of acoustic landfill, idiot conversations, text messages, broadband signals. Sleep? Whose sleep? The Docklands Travelodge was an open dormitory – a hospital in the Crimea – through which Norton drifted, perplexed by the nightmares of reps and adulterers, cleaning staff, kitchen staff, unseen servicers of the virtual city.

Nothing to read.

Baths were for reading. Why else would you take them?

Not even a Gideon bible.

He rummaged, deep in his rucksack, dug out the package that Track had landed him with, and – well aware what he was letting himself in for – began the first story by Marina Fountain. First sentence. First fateful words.

Marina Fountain

Grays

A book on the table, unopened. Yellow canvas bag on the aisle seat. This was a woman who hadn't travelled in recent times. A client who had never made the acquaintance of the c2c service into the Estuary. The carriage was empty, lime green, futuristic in its conceptual cleanliness. A golden script, made from unstable dots of light, floated mirror-reversed across a shield of protective glass. Rubber-lipped doors closed with an hydraulic sigh. The material on which she sat was coarse. It cat-scratched laddered stockings. The tabletop bruised her knees. She wriggled to find space for long legs. She hadn't chosen her position with sufficient care. But she wouldn't change. She ran one finger down the spine of a book. Her nail varnish, too dark, had chipped. But that was another life.

She twisted in her seat, turned to read the mesmerisingly banal loop. <u>Welcome Aboard the c2c Service to Grays.</u>

Sea to sea.

A New England spinster with cobwebs in the throat. <u>And then the Windows failed – and then/ I could not see to see.</u>

Write it to know it. Use fear to stave off fear.

The point of this move was to be somewhere, somewhere feasible, in the region of Stanford-le-Hope. No, it wasn't. The point was to disappear. The point was to get out, not to stay. To become invisible. To avoid anyone who knew her face, her history. To deflect conversation with promiscuous strangers.

Forgive my long silence: I have been ill.

Her enthusiasm for Conrad, did it endure? The advance had been pitiful; the commissioning editor, a friend, had moved on. They never talked about the project. They sat for hours in the pub – while the editor, in spelling out her hopes, confirmed disaster.

Cora smoked, gave up smoking, stubbed a ruff of butts into a cracked white ashtray. As a woman with lousy taste in men, could she trust herself with a merciless account of Joseph Conrad's marriage? His life at Ivy Walls Farm. His wife's health. His agonising drudgery, his pride. The muffled sound of bells from ships on the river.

I married 18 months ago and since then I have worked without interruption. I have acquired a certain reputation – a literary one – but the future is still uncertain . . .

First, she learnt Polish. Then she tracked down the letters and began the slow, painstaking, much-revised process of translation. She travelled, validated herself. Another country, another woman (the original staying put, carrying on as before). Being alone in a strange city, visiting libraries, enduring and enjoying bureaucratic obfuscation, sitting in bars,

going at whim to the cinema, allowed her to try
on a new identity. A new name. She initiated
correspondence with people she had never met.
She lied. She stole from Conrad. She set up
meetings, back in London, that she had no
intention of keeping. She avoided affairs,
pleasured herself efficiently, without summoning the eidolons of previous lovers. She wrote
to English authors of the moment, teasing them.
She became a fiction. Solitude was an indul-
gence. Grays, she hoped, would be as melancholy
as Kraków. As the sentimental bond that did or
did not exist between Conrad and his childhood
friend Janina Taube. The name was the colour,
chalk and lead. A dull sky and a dead river.

Voluntary amnesia.

The moment she took her seat, turned up her
collar, caught her reflection, Cora recognised
that she was behaving as if she were still
outside, with the sunshine and showers. Subdued
artificial light left her slightly queasy. The
cabin seemed pressurised. She forced herself to
take slow, steady breaths. She blew on the
window, signed 'Janina', rubbed it out with her
sleeve. The emptiness of the long carriage was
the end of a ghost story. Doors that weren't
doors. Opaque windows. A cancelled landscape.
Everything in the wrong order.

'Journey from hell, isn't it?'

A Docklands drone in highly polished black
shoes. A suit and an anorak. He gestured, as if
to hold the door for the woman with the rings
and the industrial hair. They must have been
there all the time, in the far reaches, hidden
by high-backed seats.

Exterior varnish failed to disguise the damage of a cleaning job, rough hands. Long 'anti-social' hours removing evidence of occupation from still-throbbing trains. Drudgery at the outer limits of a legal wage. Cora had been there. Manual work was actually quite social; as close as she wanted to get to society. To the sisterhood of the put-upon; cigarettes shared on first-light platforms, the day's horrors rehearsed. A litany of cancellations, detours. Mechanically voiced apologies.

Wipe them.

Cora didn't need characters. Acknowledging their existence, granting them space, led to unwarranted projection, the invention of other lives. Empathy. Eavesdropping. Romance.

Stay with the window, the slight stickiness of her palm on the book. Cold, damp glass. Exploited streams. Breakers' yards. Miles of production-line cars that nobody wants. A water tower that belongs in New Jersey.

She was far enough out of London now to take off her gloves. She didn't wear gloves. Her hands were grey. The low-intensity light of that riverside landscape, the sickly green of the carriage. She scratched, trying to peel skin from her hands. The skin had died. She was wearing skin gloves that she couldn't unpick.

Conrad's Polish Background.

An infection had been transmitted from the author portrait on the cover. Creases and mud tributaries beneath the writer's tired eyes with their scrotal pouches. Spirals of hair around neat, bat-ears. Conrad's face was a map of the Estuary. If she held the book at the right angle, her reflection and the reflection of the great writer would marry with the desolation of the marshes. Gull clouds. Mountain ranges of hot landfill.

It was working. When they passed under a motorway on stilts, she felt the rush. Displacement. Her senses given up to blight, erasure. She couldn't remember who she had killed. Just where. The room. The position of the furniture. The sound of a running shower. The flattened shadow of a tumbler on a window ledge. She didn't know why. Or when. It didn't matter. She had everything she needed in the yellow bag – laptop, pills, a few clothes. The keys to the new flat could be picked up at the estate office in Grays. Meanwhile, she was happy to let it happen, shifts of geology, registers of light. The more sky the better. Keep moving and memories will be revised, reconstituted. The train window is the perfect screen. A cup of decent coffee and she can forget London.

A flooded quarry. The train had stopped. It didn't concern her if the landscape drifted or kept still. Train travel worked very well, so long as you didn't need to be anywhere at a particular time. The seat was comfortable. The view unobtrusive. She had a table and a book. Hunger was manageable – when you considered the alternative. A good strong coffee, the smell, the feel of the cup in her hand, was her dominant fantasy.

Cora could hear the driver, a woman, talking. Making excuses. The flooded quarry, with its abandoned industrial aspirations, was an official halt. A youth with ravaged skin was standing on the platform.

Don't catch his eye. Don't look. One client only. Why so many? White tongues hanging from the pockets of a tartan bomber jacket. He was unhinged. <u>Don't look.</u> Tongues of white plastic. The guy looks like a dispenser for carrier bags. You wouldn't say he suffered from eczema, that would be making light of the case. Inflamed skin shedding its ash in volcanic flakes: raw and scabbed. He couldn't keep still long enough to get on the train, couldn't commit to a destination. Also, it appeared from his writhing and hopping, his frantic groin-knuckling, he was in imminent danger of wetting himself.

There had to be better options than Grays. The pocked youth waited. The train, by this time, was unoccupied. He'd find a compartment and relieve himself, go back to his hole. You couldn't see him surviving anywhere beyond the railway network. He was never going to present a ticket. He didn't have the spring to leap a barrier. Or the clout to deck an official. He was a native, non-aspirational asylum denier. Not bright enough to compete with the car washers in the retail park, the ones with blue stubble who called themselves 'Persians'. And always finished their swab-downs with: 'Wanna sell? Very nice car. Very good in my country.'

There was a moment when, despite their best efforts, this odd couple came face to face through the train window. The boy had a terrible suppurating wound running from below his right ear. He was clutching the gash with his left hand. Let it go and he'd spill out on the platform.

Cora was doing it again. Responding to place by flattering fictional potentialities. The wound was the shadow of an arm. He was scratching, squeezing a spot. He wouldn't take this train. He lived in the station. She could open her Conrad and impale herself, yet again, on the barbed wire of black print.

The door hissed.

<u>In this way you live two lives. Over there, at Lublin, where life is hard, no doubt – and here in Stanford, Essex, on the banks of the Thames – under the spell of my words: for the one you have never seen, vous avez la douceur des Ombres et la splendeur de l'Inconnu!</u>

The stink of the swamp. It came with him onto the train, slept-in, sweat-stiff clothes. Cancelled adrenaline signals, fear.

<u>La douceur des Ombres.</u>

She wanted coffee to anneal the original perfume of the upholstery, the sprays the cleaning women used. Now she was nostalgic for that smell, furniture left too long in its own company – in too intimate a relationship with its protective wrapping. The boy was acrylic from the skin out, layered in accidents of fake wool, vests, waistcoats, rubber shoes with flapping soles.

He took his place on the other side of the aisle and he muttered. He emptied his pockets of paper, scrumpled each item, individually; then lined up the paper balls and flicked them onto the seat that faced him.

He mumbled. He swore. He shifted his position. Stood up, with nothing to put on the rack, sat down again. He reeked.

Cora turned away. There was a vast block building, windowless, and a burning chimney pumping out white smoke. They had stopped again. Grass grew between the lines, delicate threads, tough clumps, bushes pushing through small yellow stones.

This time she didn't turn from the window. It couldn't be worse. Any new passenger would improve the situation. The gibbering stopped, the smell reverted to an airline cocktail of dead air and randomly applied chemical agents.

At last, as they pulled away, the river asserted its presence. New housing, yellow-brick estates. Yesterday there was nothing, now this: a town brought into existence by the happy conjunction of corrupt brownfield wastes and an orbital motorway. Flooded quarries were being colonised. Car parks like game reserves. Ribbon estates that looked exactly like the demolished asylums they had replaced. This is where urban exiles, divorced or otherwise damaged, come to roost. Who would pay good money to be incarcerated in a flatpack hutch? Cora, that's who. Contracts exchanged, signature on cheque. Sight unseen. Purchased straight from the catalogue.

Untitled, her book was taking shape. The research was on the laptop. Documents, files, interviews, photographs. Skeleton outline. It would write itself.

She had to disembark. This was it, end of the line. A square brick tower, the word STATE stamped on it. She felt like reaching into her bag for a passport. Grays <u>might</u> work. It was more foreign than Poland. Disputed territory – like Gdansk. Grays belonged in the Baltic. All it lacked was the soundtrack, the verbigeration of the stinkhorn youth, the paper-crumbler.

Doors stay shut until potential tourists do something about it, find the right button to press. She is ready to unzip her bag, put Conrad away. She waits for the other passengers to take themselves off, before walking into her new life.

The bag wasn't there.

It wasn't on the floor, under the table, on the rack. The freak from the quarry halt had lifted it. She had been suckered by that old muttering crazy routine. She shut him out and he'd timed it beautifully. Two stops, close together: on, off. Vanished into a nowhere of unmapped roads and poisoned creeks.

She knotted the belt of her white raincoat, dug her hands into the pockets. The air was heady, soapy perfume from the factory, mud from the river. The sky was immense. All things considered, he had done her a favour. No baggage, no back story. A fresh set, a new chapter. The edge was there. She caught the ripple, fur growing down the sensitised ridges of her spine. The whiteness of her teeth. The horn of her nails, beneath that flaking black paint, curving into claws.

She put on tinted glasses, to flatter the blood in her eyes. She prepared a smile for the ticket collector. It wasn't required. He'd been replaced by non-functioning automated barriers.

She strolled through, crossed the tracks, and headed for the Thames.

*

I was never convinced that one of these nothing halts would have a bookshop. I overheard a conversation on the Saturday stall at Kingsland Waste, a runner flashing the contents of his bag to a punter, a woman in glasses. He didn't drive. He scouted the same routes, Maidstone, Margate, Ramsgate, Deal, Southend Railway. Anywhere with plenty of stops, charity caves, old-folk-death dross. But what he showed, and the price he was letting it go for, made me think. He said: 'Broadstairs.' So I knew I should start on the <u>other</u> side of the Thames, mirror image. He wasn't a very inventive liar. Simple code: Kent was Essex, Broadstairs meant Southend. Track down the line a couple of stops and I'd have it.

<u>Nada.</u> Mid morning and I hadn't pulled out a single carrier bag. Books? I couldn't find a shop. West Ham, Barking, Dagenham Dock. Shop? I couldn't find the town, the centre. Who needed books? The entire zone was an obituary. Which was promising. The developers would be in soon, architects, glass hangers. When you locate trash Americana, you locate the road: burger pits, multiplexes, dealerships. But Essex/America has no history, no memory to recover. No disposables: pulp paperbacks, records, tapes, <u>True Crime</u> chapbooks. A landscape without text.

I drank coffee, black, standing up in fast-food dumps with revoked franchises. I ran back to the railway. I was jumpy for a hit of print.

I read bills of fare with random apostrophes. I cross-referenced graffiti. I scraped the shit off my trainers to find a label to interpret. I tried to make up words from broken matchsticks. This was a territory without a written language. I snatched crumpled betting-slips from the gutter and crammed them into my pockets to have something to read on the train. I paced the platform like a caged cougar.

Dagenham was promising. The ghost of a town. Fat men in cars that aren't going anywhere, parked on bricks. I don't like cars. The hand on your head. The way you have to put your trust in a stranger. The certain knowledge that drivers don't understand, in their locked-off trances, that every road is made up from discrete elements. <u>It doesn't fit together until you walk it.</u> If you can drive to a bookshop, it's not worth stopping. They'll have caned it, the amateurs, the ones who pitch out, once a month, in Bloomsbury hotels.

Dagenham had the elements, the dereliction, the deadbeats. The mix of Old Socialist estates, garden-city aspirations, cashmoney from the car factory. There were broad pavements, grease caffs, charity caves near the station. But it didn't play. The town was waiting like a whipped cur for the next wave of exploitation. Two or three coffees, decaf diesel, and I was out of there.

By Purfleet, I was desperate. To piss. To find one shelf of books. A random three yards of printed matter. Dust. Yellow paper saturated with cigarette smoke. The feeble annotations of failed writers. Keep your back to the suspicious owner – who can't wait to engage you in conversation or to blank you. Laugh at your confounded expectations. Another sucker, hopping from foot to foot, wondering if he should carry on, or cut his losses and try elsewhere.

I was running out of elsewheres.

A train stopped. I hit the button, sprang aboard. Why didn't it move? A woman had my seat. I almost jumped into her lap. I always swing left around the door, tuck in behind that glass shield. At worst, I can avoid the view from the window, read reflected script as it loops across the screen. The Estuary service is as close as I want to come to cinema. This woman had spread herself in my slot.

I didn't notice what she was reading. That's how bad it was. I had to do something with my hands to stop myself grabbing for the book. It came from a library, most did, laminated plastic pressed over the original dust-wrapper.

Fists knotting.

I had to take out all the Dagenham refuse I'd collected, unwrap it, roll it up – as tight as it would go. Get rid. Flick flick flick. Paper bullets lodging in the sockets of her eyes. She had a smell that was the opposite of elsewhere. It made me dizzy. I had to breathe, gag on it. Bedroomy, lived in.

We stopped in a flooded quarry. I had to move to another compartment, closer to our destination. Get a head start on her. She had one book, she might want more. She looked the kind, very sure of herself.

The doors hissed, I ran.

Secured my usual spot, unmolested, in the

first carriage. My hand closed tight around the leather strap of my bag.

What bag?

It had been years since I'd travelled with such luxuries. Years since the weight of books had me leaning into the wind like a sailor. The bag had gone, along with its contents. I owned what I stood up in, borrowings, thefts, accidental purchases. The perfume had unhinged me. I'd lumbered myself with a bag I couldn't keep, didn't want. And I couldn't conceive of any way to get shot of it.

As soon as the train stopped, squealing, stink of brakes, I was away. Tensed finger on release button. I ducked behind a toilet Tardis and waited. She stood out, she knew where she was going – over the tracks and down towards the river. Unaccompanied by railway officials. There weren't any on this line. Perhaps she hadn't noticed. That's how I lost my own bag. On a train. It was only, three or four days later, when I tried to pitch a few of the items I'd picked up in Hastings, that I remembered. I never replaced the bag, never made it to that level of operation.

Bookshops, if any, will be parasitical on the station. I legged it, as fast as I could, in the opposite direction to the one the woman had taken. Away from the river. Even by Estuary standards, this was a hole. A labyrinthine shopping centre, a rat run for lab rats. Dead light. Blue chemical floods washing away piss streams. Wheelchairs and mechanised cripple-carriers surrounding an empty stage. Cardboard cutouts of forgotten entertainers.

I found the right street: bent solicitors, West African dentists, table-tappers. Curtains drawn against daylight. Linoleum polish and cheap massage oil. An open door with access to a loan shark. A cracked glass panel, wired over, through which I could see the books – tightly packed, triple-stacked on rickety, freestanding units. The glass was too dirty to make out individual titles. A phone number on a card, but the ink had run.

Out in the street, twisting my neck, I tried to see if it was worth kicking the door in. The owner would be taking the usual long lunch. He might be back to watch the sun go down behind the oil storage tanks.

Among the ratty paperbacks and Book Club ballast, photocopied topographic views, was the unmistakable yellow cloth of an early printing, perhaps even a first edition, of Bram Stoker's <u>Dracula.</u> I'd had dingy, exhausted copies through my hands but never dreamt of one as pristine as this. I didn't need to read the red lettering. <u>I knew.</u> The only copy in Essex, in England, had come back to source, to the fringes of Purfleet, Count Dracula's Carfax Abbey.

<u>Thursdays and Sundays Only. 12.30 to 5 p.m.</u>

I had arrived on the wrong day. I would have to come back another time. Or stay over. Find somewhere to kip, sleep rough. This was it. My one chance to get back on the ladder. In a cold sweat of excitement, I started walking. Keeping away from the river, heading out of town. Twenty-four hours to kill. Twenty-four hours to survive in Grays and environs.

*

Very new bricks, yellow. Buildings in blocks. Rooms where no sentient being ever lived. Rooms without ghosts.

Running water, the river. A hot shower needling flesh, splashing on tiles. Cora twists, contorts, trying to get her mouth around the tap. The muck and ooze of the shoreline. Lines of white globes, glowing palely, illuminating the empty avenues. Pools of light: the spaces between posts, along the perimeter fence, in a political prison.

She swallows, greedily. The taste is metallic, silver. Her mouth furred with gritty deposits. But skin, wet from the shower, is unblemished. The grey she discovered, looking at her hands in the train, has faded; hot pink. She bares her teeth to the bathroom mirror and the bite is regular, no wolverine incisors, no fangs. The prickle of fur down the length of her spine was an illusion. A fiction.

The thief had done her a favour. Taking possession of her clothes, documents, money, he became responsible for her memory. The laptop. Notes, translations, extracts. Everything had been transferred to that slim box. Now she was released from it, relieved of her past. Naked, in a room in which no human had ever slept, a riverside apartment, she slipped the envelope of identity.

Her successes, such as they had been, derived from an unusual psychopathology. An over-intense identification with books she read, authors and their characters. Cora, the woman: emanation of place. That's why she wanted to be close to Conrad, to the landscape in which he had lived.

 It is still more painful and hard to think of
you than to realize my loss; if it was not so,
I would pass in silence and darkness these
first moments of suffering.

She suffered. And it was bearable. Grays was the
manifestation of anonymity. Her clothes were
heaped on the floor. Not a stick of furniture. No
blankets, no bed. No towel. She dries herself on
her slip. The room is warm. She has no control
over the heating, the voices. Still damp, she
puts on a man's white shirt. She can't remember
where it came from. She holds it up to her face.
She sniffs, flinches. She sits, arms around
knees, looking out of the window. At the darkening river. The river which is becoming darkness,
becoming itself.

From the river, midstream: one by one, lights
in scattered windows go out. Faked balconies
shine.

*

Most of the afternoon, and the early evening,
was spent on the road; backwards and forwards
between the bookshop and the housing development on the lip of the quarry. If anyone wants
to update William Hope Hodgson's horror tale,
The House on the Borderland, this is the place:
pit, swamp, congeries of red-brick hutches
under a massive sky. A puff of wind and they're
gone.

I stayed out of the town centre, a chance of
bumping into the woman – but I couldn't risk
letting another runner get at the bookshop
before I snaffled the Stoker, the gold brick
Dracula. So I trudged alongside heavy traffic,

chemical works chucking out filthy smoke, flags shredded by wind, storm fences protecting the wildlife of a quarry; protecting the new development. Three or four cul-de-sacs went up while I walked. The Grays satellite was turning into a garden city without gardens. Every time I reached the first house, it was closer to the centre. It was new but it looked the same as all the others. There were more burnt-out cars on the verges of deserted avenues. Nobody bothered with 'Police Aware' notices.

Suddenly, I was exhausted. I had a bag, I was respectable: I could try for a room in a pub. The choice was easy. There was only one, Mexican/Californian; desert plants stripped by salt, battered by river winds, sticky with oil droplets. They took my money, in advance. They gave me a key. And a hard look. The manager said something to the barmaid and they laughed.

I went out later to look for food, chips, burger, a foil carton. The settlement was inhabited by youngish women with dogs, children at an awkward age. There were no men, no families. No shops or fast-food outlets. 'Try Lakeside,' a kid told me. But I didn't have time for fishing.

I brought crisps and peanuts up from the bar. And I drank cloudy water from a glass with a lumpy residue of Steradent or some other fixative on the bottom. Salty food left me hungrier than before and stung the raw sides of my cheeks, which I had the habit of chewing when I was nervous. The Grays bookshop had me spitting blood and gristle.

I stretched out on the bed, the yellow canvas

bag beside me. I didn't take off my clothes or roll back the covers. I wouldn't sleep. I put my arm around the bag, felt its bumps, tried to guess what was inside. Rather disturbing images assailed me, half-dreams. I always keep the light on at night – and also, in the unusual circumstances of finding myself in a hotel room, the television. Sound down. I like that blue glow and ignore the screen.

Something inside the bag <u>moved.</u> The woman from the train. Her head. Talking. I could hear her banging on about pain and loss. Meanwhile, I could see one of the politicians, a minister, being grilled on television. Nodding, smiling. Using his hands. Dark rims under his armpits. And I could hear the woman's voice: demanding to be let out. <u>Let out?</u> Keep this up and I'll chuck her through the window of one of the trashed cars. Into the swamp.

I touched the zip and it opened like a wound. Like, as I'm forced to picture, the back of a dress. The smell. Her presence is overwhelming. Underwear, nightclothes, a pair of skirts, stockings. Sponge bag, notecase. A metallic box that might be a portable computer. All of it grey. Every single item. I lay them out on the bed. I stand up, move away.

I don't like that box. I put it in the bag, zip it. Carry the bag to the cupboard. Close the door. I can still hear her voice: <u>Before the sun rises, the dew will have destroyed the eyes.</u>

I turn up the sound on the television. I go into the bathroom and run the taps. When I come back to the bedroom, the voice has stopped –

but her clothes are arranged with great precision on naked sheets. The coverlet has been
folded and placed on a chair. The red blanket
and top sheet stripped back. A grey dress,
underclothes on top, Italian shoes. With ice-
pick heels.

It occurred to me that – as the water was
running – I should avail myself of the shower.
It wasn't unpleasant. I stayed there for some
time. Until, despite the warmth of the water, I
began to shiver. I wrapped myself in a towel
and sat on the seat of the toilet. I could
spend the night here. Take off as soon as it
gets light, find a café in Grays. Hang around
the shopping centre until the bookman turns up.

I needed sleep. A few hours should do it.
Shut my eyes, forget about the woman and the
train. I'd worked myself up about the Stoker, a
real book after all these months. I returned to
the bedroom. The canvas bag was on the chair,
zipped. I opened the cupboard. It was empty.
The coverlet was back in place.

I made myself a cup of coffee. It wasn't bad.
You could almost taste it, the genuine aroma.
The cup in your hands, my hands. I lifted the
bag off the chair, turned it to face the
window. The quarry, at night, had a kind of
beauty. Street lights where there aren't any
streets. An Umbrian hill town. A red glow, low
on the horizon; the beams of cars driving
through clouds towards the suspension bridge.

I turned back the sheets. Slid in, naked.
Tried to find a tolerable position in which to
pretend to sleep. I twisted and turned on the
nylon pillow. Something stuck to my cheek, a

sheet of paper, a message from the management.
I felt for the bedside lamp.

It was a glove. A grey leather glove. I sat
up, wide awake. There were two gloves, one on
either side of me. Except that they weren't
gloves, not even the stretchy surgical kind.
The condom-fingered ones with which forensic
pathologists pick maggots from a wound. These
gloves were marked with veins and downy hair.
They had fingernails. Peeled hands. I pulled
them on, the left first (weaker, female) and
then the right. And they took, the graft took.
My hands, up to the prominent bulbs of my wrist
bone, were grey. And smooth. And cool as water.

*

She misread him badly, the thief. Cora started
when the bell rang. He should never have been
let in. She was paying for security. These
flats were supposed to be tighter than Paddington Green. He didn't generate enough energy
to register on CCTV. He was at the door, bag
lifted in front of his face, to ward off the
blow.

'So sorry. Used to have one just like it.
Your papers and stuff, inside. Address. Didn't
touch. Came straight round.'

'I don't have an address. I hadn't decided to
stay — until you stole my bag, leaving me no
choice.'

'I'm trying to explain. I'm a book-dealer . . .'

It was the middle of the night, early
morning. Neither of them had a watch. Dormitory
noises from other units, snoring and snorting.
The walls were cardboard. You could hear dogs

fart in their sleep. Milk pouring into thick glass.

She'd been quite wrong about him. He wasn't young. Bad skin doesn't fade with age, it weathers. Greasy hair stays greasy however many times you run your head under a cold tap.

'Must be important, I thought, the computer.'

'You said you didn't touch the bag.'

'Weight. I felt the outline. Had to carry it from –'

'You touched it? Felt it?'

'No.'

'Played with it?'

'No.'

'Open it now. Show me what you did.'

Rocking on his heels, he hugged the bag. It had been a mistake coming here. No colour in his skin. Nightdirt sticky in the corners of his eyes. She was only wearing a shirt. She scratched at the inside of her thigh.

'Take it out.'

I shall see Mr Wells in a few days and I will ask him on your behalf for permission to translate The Invisible Man into Polish.

For years, Conrad referred to his neighbour, Mr Wells of Sandgate, as L'Uomo Invisible. He never worked out how the front door at Spade House opened without the intervention of any human agency. As he stood there, with Hueffer, waiting to announce their literary collaboration.

Cora didn't want him here. She wanted to be invisible, to stay in this room for ever.

Reluctantly, the man set the bag down. The floor looked as if it were made from wood, but it was wood-print linoleum. The riverscape had already been translated into Polish. Her hand closing around her wrist closed on nothing. She folded her arms, anticipating his furtive glance at her breasts. She ordered him, again, to open the bag.

He lifted out the laptop. He wouldn't touch her clothes. She raised the lid, activated it. Checked her files.

'Go to the bathroom,' she said. He froze. He had been backing towards the door. 'Take the bag. Dress yourself in the clothes. And don't tear them. Take your time.'

Her hands on the computer keys, skin rough as an Aberdeen fishwife. A transplant that hadn't taken. The sun climbing above low clouds, over Northfleet and Gravesend – where, in the old days, East Indiamen waited on the tide.

In her bag, a smaller bag: lipstick, toothpaste, powder, tweezers, razor. An old-fashioned, barber-shop cutthroat.

She unbuttoned her shirt, took it off. Wrapped it like a surgical dressing around her arm. He would be standing in the bathroom, wearing the grey dress and the grey shoes. Her things on the glass shelf.

Her naked feet made a sucking sound. The acoustic memory of each footfall lingering in a brief interval of silence.

She closed the bathroom door behind her. When the steam cleared from the mirror she would see her own face. Her face over his shoulder. The sharp bones. The lifted razor.

On the laptop screen, in the empty flat, with the view of the river, words appeared. I must

close, it is already late. I only hear the
bells of the ships on the river, which remind
me how far I am from you all.

And then the photograph, the moist black eyes
of the Polish writer. And then the river.

The Highland Forest

'What a freak show!'

Start the day with a quote from the film *Performance*. Clear the throat, lower lip under upper teeth, tongue pressing: a rare line of dialogue attributed to David Litvinoff by cultural historian David Seabrook. Pertinent, I thought. On the button. As we wave goodbye to the Travelodge. Horizontal blight, vertical squalor. A rep's face in every window.

Breakfast skipped (no loss), burdens shouldered, we beat the road rats into the car park. Danny was waiting by the Volvo – where I left a note for Jimmy Seed, outlining our future plans (unreal as a premature synopsis punted to a publisher). Dagenham, Rainham Marshes, Purfleet and the M25: follow us. See you – camera, cash, car – at the ibis, West Thurrock. Book us in and I'll treat you to enough soap factories, pylon farms, railways, dredgers, oil tanks, bridges, to buy up most of Margate (Cliftonville, if you're picky).

Movement was what Danny craved, brass rods pulling him eastward to the vortex of the alp, the triangulation of sacred sites nominated by the writer C.E. Street in his geomantic prophecy: *Earthstars, The Visionary Landscape. Part One: London, City of Revelation*. The key sites were: St Mary the Virgin (East Ham), Barking Abbey, the 'lost' Miller's Well (top corner of Central Park). We didn't have the photographer with us, the lanky skinhead who had collaborated on my Thames book, so we were spared that terrible old Cockney joke about Chris Street being 'three stops beyond Plaistow'.

Bow Creek – its backwaters, reed beds, uncivil engineering – was the mess, the metaphor. And metaphors were what I wanted to discuss with Track. Metaphors employed by the Fountain woman. But not yet, leave it until we get a few miles under our belts. I had to sort out my own difficulties: first, why Fountain's story was so disturbing.

She hadn't written it without help, obviously. The tone was masculine, sure of itself, its pretensions; grammatically suspect, lexicologically challenged, topographically slapdash. A slash-and-burn stylist. But haunted: by missing fathers – Bram Stoker, S. Freud and Joseph Conrad. Clunky hints, based on autobiographical elements Track might be able to clarify, about writing and stalking, literary bloodsucking, gender, disguise. It was a tale that never worked through its confusions, never lifted from dirty realism to science fiction. Did Fountain understand, for example, the William Burroughs fixation with 'grays', as *X File* beings? Soft-skinned and seamless, the aliens among us. Returned dead. Doubtful, very doubtful. Her title, like much of the story, was accident.

Fountain wrote like a man envious of the vim and attack, the linguistic inventiveness, of the new lesbian novelists from the Celtic fringe. The praise heaped upon them, the advances. The film adaptations.

But it was the Conrad aspect that pricked me. Fountain had somehow got wind of my researched (incomplete, unpublished) essay on Conrad in Hackney. Her exaggerated prose, its shotgun sarcasm, jump-cuts, psychotic syntax, was an offensive parody of a manner of composition I'd left behind. But what I really wanted to know was where she'd come across the story of the *Dracula* first edition in Grays? Ruth was the only confidante who knew about that, pillow talk, table talk, kitchen chats while pots bubbled; gossip overheard one Saturday morning in Kingsland Waste Market.

Ergo, Ruth knew Marina Fountain. Ruth was using the Fountain woman as a way of communicating with me. Love letters, if you like, at one remove. Fountain had been given my Conrad files. She had been dosed on newspaper cuttings, photocopied articles, bought a ticket into the Estuary. Now she was out there, ahead of us, inventing fictions that anticipated – and, in some senses, neutralised – my more measured psychogeographical reports.

I had a powerful urge to get on a train. Marina Fountain on the platform at Fenchurch Street, a copy of *Conrad's Polish Background*, edited by Zdzislaw Najder, in her shoulder bag, setting off for the great unknown, for riverside Grays, is a very seductive image. The opening of a film. Red eyes, dark glasses. White raincoat. Isabelle Adjani. Anna Karina. Herzog's *Nosferatu: Phantom der Nacht*. André Delvaux's *Rendez-vous à Bray*. Chantal Akerman's *Les Rendez-vous d'Anna* ('A series of train rides, a series of tales ... A moving eroticism stemming from the everyday'). The woman had hooked me. I would follow her, vamped, vampirised, into the badlands. Into yellowback fiction. Just as soon as I could get shot of my fellow Beckton Alp pilgrims.

Danny drew our attention to a gateway. This, he informed us, was the true beginning of the non-metropolitan section of the A13. Grey concrete, flattened obelisk slabs with inset panels: the gate looked like the entrance to a forbidden city. The panels, I noticed, featured the caduceus symbol (my symbol, Mercury): twin serpents writhing around a magician's staff. Arthur Norton, my great-grandfather, left me his gold caduceus tie-pin (stolen in my first burglary, two weeks after arriving in Hackney). Three of his sons, by way of Aberdeen University, became medical men. Was this miraculous survivor, Babylonian fragment among craters and future walkways, a Crowleyite token from the chthonic city?

'Brunswick Power Station,' said Danny. 'Their logo, Mercury for energy. The rest's rubble. Derek Jarman, he was fond of this stretch, Canning Town, Silvertown. Helped him, didn't I, find locations for *The Last of England*? The Millennium Mills, remember? From the free train, Dalston to Woolwich North?'

I remembered the photograph, Jarman's production still. Hooded figures, holding flares, out on the river. I remembered the river. Long shadows of bomber squadrons coming in from the Estuary. The credits for *EastEnders* spontaneously combusting: water on fire, exploding gas-holders at Beckton.

Conrad, according to Ford Madox Ford, who tended to exaggerate these things, arrived in London by river; awed by wealth and dirt, miles of deep-water docks, spice warehouses, Portland stone steeples, the cargoes of the world. London was two cities, riverine development, narrow and dense, and that late addition, the City. Offices in which to pick up your wages, sign on for the next voyage out.

In fact, Conrad arrived by train. Lowestoft to London; first steps on English soil, 10 June 1878. Rivers and railways, they never fail: there is no better method of penetrating the mysteries of our Mithraic capital. The privileged stutter of privatised transport, views from embankments into secret spaces; constant metamorphosis, industry to park, synagogue to satanic tower. The breeze, the light, the stink of the slurry-coloured Thames: history too rich to be trashed by developers and explainers.

From his first marital establishment at Stanford-le-Hope, down-wind from the Travelodge, Conrad liked nothing better than mess-ing about in boats, dressing as an old salt, powerful shoulders, long arms, buttons and beard; out on the river in company with the former merchant seaman George Hope (dedicatee of *Lord Jim*). Hope, one of the exile's few English friends, brought him to the Estuary. Now a director of several companies, the officer who had sailed on the *Duke of Sutherland*, three years before Conrad, offered financial advice to the newly married immigrant: the impoverished author (word-slave) who was, as yet, unreleased from his status as a French-speaking, Polish-born, Russian subject. And premature Essex man.

A semi-detached villa in Victoria Road. Forget the Thames. Victoria Road, Stanford-le-Hope, offers unrivalled prospects of the A13 (the Gas Valve Compound) – and the A1014 (Manorway) as it swerves from the junction to the Shell Haven Oil Refineries at Coryton. Stanford-le-Hope has declined, since Conrad's day, to a huddled extension of St Clere's Golf Course; a strip of meaning-less ribbon development at the margin of the fabulously named Balstonia (a petrochemical oasis).

Ever restless, anxious and melancholy, subject to gout, Conrad relocated from his 'jerrybuilt rabbit hutch' to Ivy Walls Farm on the edge of Mucking Marshes.

The glamour's off.

'The glamour's off,' Marlow says in *Heart of Darkness*. Maps have lost their attraction (since they found their way, as a metaphor, into the mouth of George W. Bush). But Conrad appreciated them, their fictional possibilities. A shop-window in Fleet Street. Author peering over his character's shoulder, nudging him aside to get a better look at 'the biggest, the most blank' space on the map of Africa. A space now filled by busybodies and exploiters, the riffraff of Europe. Filled with rivers.

I visited, every time I walked towards Tower Bridge, a window of my own in the Minories: nautical charts, oceans of numbers. The conjunction, mathematical symbols and river, was provocative. Voyages I would never make, voyages I remembered (without having experienced them): Arthur Norton sailing from Tilbury on *The Albemarle*, 1858, bound for Colombo. The map he drew, in blood-brown ink, each week concluded with an X: 'Total distance 1,400 miles.'

The white of the map, that's what seduces us. Arthur's speculative, foldout version of Peru, the Pampa Hermosa, white as meat in a bottle. Red lines representing Arthur's route, Chicla, Banios, Cerro de Pasco, Huarica, Ambo, Huanuco. River-threads like skull cracks, brain fissures. The hours I spent poring over Arthur Norton's unreliable chart. The days on the road, heading for Beckton Alp, Creekmouth, the Eastbury Levels, London's empty quarter. Or so it appeared. At a distance. The map-makers found nothing to colour between the Royal Albert Dock in North Woolwich and Ferry Road in Tilbury. The last of England. The empty Custom House, railway terminal, disembarkation sheds. Deserted platforms and overgrown railway tracks.

It's not that there's nothing of consequence in the white bits, geographers are too lazy to see it: rifle ranges, landfill mountains, wild nature enveloping concrete, oil-spill on the shoreline, rock pools in threadbare tyres.

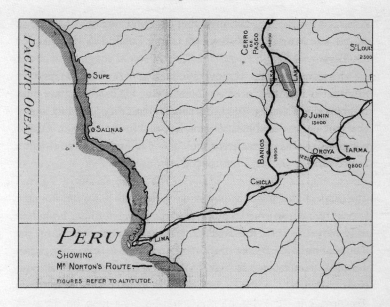

Conrad saw it, loved it. Going out on the river, in the yawl *Nellie* with G.F.W. Hope, kept him sane. (Fountain knew about this. That's why she picked Grays. For the *marina*, the squadrons of sailing craft, riding at anchor, in the lee of that distant monster, the Tilbury Power Station. And Hope himself, she knew about him. His name: George Fountaine Weare Hope. Fountaine Hope! Weary Hope! Marina was writing me a letter in code. And I was beginning to crack it. As soon as possible, I would make for Fenchurch Street, repeat her fictional journey.)

Hope and his friends, the accountant W.B. Keen and the lawyer T.L. Mears, we are told, become models for the frame-narrative of *Heart of Darkness*. Waiting on the tide at Gravesend, mother river, in the abeyance of twilight, spinning yarns. In parts of the map that are not overwritten, worked out, everything bleeds into everything, sea and sky, truth and legend; defences are down, faces merge into protective beards. We confess, we lie. We make up stories.

The essay I abandoned, as an act of homage, Conradian lethargy, elective malaria, opened in Hackney. Voice-over by Michael Caine at his most soporific. (Try for Caine, get Bob Hoskins.) Not a lot of people know that Joseph Conrad, taking London as the base for his life in the British Merchant Service, found lodgings in Stoke Newington. May 1880. Dynevor Road. Dynevor Road, a tributary running to the west of Stoke Newington High Street, is a near neighbour of Evering Road (running to the east). Hackney's own heart of darkness: the basement flat of hostess 'Blonde Carol', where Reggie Kray butchered Jack 'the Hat' McVitie. (Jack's trilby as mythical as Conrad's cannonball bowler.)

The Lambrianous started scrubbing the carpet with hot water from the kitchen. When the worst of the mess in the living-room had been dealt with, McVitie's body was wrapped in an eiderdown, dragged up the stairs and placed in Bender's car. Ronnie told him to drive away. Then somebody remembered McVitie's hat. It was his trademark and could easily identify him. When he dived at the window it fell outside. It was retrieved.

When I dived at the window, Polish darkness imported to Lea Valley Congo, the theoretical structure of my Conrad-in-Hackney essay fell apart. Free-associating connections hissed like a badly wired tenement in a thunderstorm. Gravesend. The port of Boma. Conrad's meeting with Roger Casement, the only sympathetic personality in a swamp of African madness and corruption. Dysentery. Fever. Soul sickness. Skeletons nailed to trees. Carpets of skulls. Broken in body and mind, branded with the mark of what he had witnessed, the future, Joseph Conrad returned to London.

This is what I discovered, this is what amazed me, a mad, undigested narrative of colonialism and fiscal voodoo, earthed in Dalston. *Heart of Darkness* brought to ground. Joseph Conrad taken to the German Hospital, Dalston Lane, London N16, suffering from malaria, rheumatism, neuralgia. And worse. The Congo diaries, as fantastic as the black forgeries presented at the trial of Casement, were kept at his bedside.

Saw another dead body lying by the path in an attitude of repose . . .

At night when the moon rose heard shouts and drumming in distant villages. Passed a bad night.

With many more to follow. It's not the same moon. I don't care what they say. From my window, writing the Conrad piece (raiding other men's books), I watched a cigarette-end moon, glowing ash, floating over the wet roofs of the German Hospital: one ward brilliantly lit. No Germans left. No hospital. An improvised film set. A Freudian drama. A naked patient being given the water treatment.

But that is not why I gave up, why I started walking, making reports from a real landscape. It was the discovery of the arbitrary connection – no accident, no remission – of Joseph Conrad, first officer, and my great-grandfather, Arthur Stanley Norton. (Names that shift, migrate. H.M. Stanley's painstaking travel journals dressing the piracy of the Société Anonyme Belge pour le Commerce du Haut-Congo. David Livingstone, febrile and driven: a Xerox of Robert Louis Stevenson. A divided Scotsman looking for the right place in which to die.)

Arthur Norton's fatal expedition to Peru resulted from the loss of funds amassed over years of labour in the Ceylon tea plantations. Conrad was also the victim of well-meant but devastating advice (if you have to pay someone to tell you what to do with your money, it's gone). South African gold mines. Two men, who find themselves, passenger and officer, on a voyage from Amsterdam to Java, *The Highland Forest*, 1887. Norton, amateur essayist, limping around the deck, talks literature. Conrad talks weather and money. Norton, who has a way of teasing out secrets, encourages the new Englishman, the cultural migrant, to read aloud from his first composition, *The Black Mate*.

Conrad talks of South America, 'the land of the ancient Inca', which extends 'along the coast for 3,000 miles, including what is now Colombia, Ecuador, Chili, and Bolivia'.

My great-grandfather remembered the conversation, made a note of it in his privately published pamphlet, *Arthur Norton: The Story of His Life & Times as Told by Himself*. He took Conrad for a Frenchman. From the south, Marseilles? The merchant mariner had the disconcerting habit of saying nothing, polishing his monocle, staring at you: butterfly on a pin. Chin up, beard primed, fists thrust deep in the pockets of his nautical jacket. Like Cutcliffe Hyne's Captain Kettle.

They conversed in French; Conrad fluently, rapidly, meridional emphasis, a whiff of garlic, Norton with painful slowness and an atrocious accent. My great-grandfather's shipboard 'Frog' is a footnote – I had to wade through suitcases of untranscribed diaries to fill out the details – in a section entitled 'Striking Personages and Eccentrics Met On Voyages in the East'. Norton has more to say about his 'fellow-passengers': Tindall, Wernham, Jock Hay and the brothers Rossiter. 'All gone now excepting one of the last-mentioned.'

Like Conrad, Arthur Norton retired from his first career, at around forty, and took to country living and occasional literary composition. Investments evaporating, he ventured.

The French-speaking Pole, come ashore at Stanford-le-Hope, wrote, grimly, remorselessly, every word wrenched from him, to keep his family afloat.

Arthur put the notion of authorship, this whim, aside: he went after gold in Australia, he tried Tasmania (sent for the family). I have a prize-book, Class V, Mathematics, from Hobart, awarded to his youngest son, my grandfather. *The Terror of the Indians (or, The Life of David Crockett)* by John S.C. Abbott. The frontispiece, a steel-engraving, depicts yet another black river, huts, smoke, coracles.

Scratching for gold was as foolish as taking shares in South African mines. Norton, so his journals reveal, felt his age – fifty-three – on a circumnavigation of Lake Sinclair. His leg was troubling him, he leant on a heavy stick. But there was one expedition left in the old man, his *Nostromo*: Peru. He would act on the hint dropped by the first mate of *The Highland Forest* on the passage out; the madness that did for Walter Raleigh, silver mines, cities of gold covered by jungle.

And here is the thing that still puts the shiver on me: Arthur Norton's bias towards the picaresque, the grand project that declines into loose bowels, fevers, hallucinations, *might* have touched Joseph Conrad – as the Pole's over-nice attempt to draw financial advice from my bearded ancestor, mistaken for a hardheaded man of business, was fatally misinterpreted. Could it be, I wondered, that Norton had infiltrated Conrad's fiction? A ghostly cameo, a line or two, offering a sort of immortality? The language of great writers, the order of words, mistakes, inspirations, is outside time. But the order never changes. If Norton was in Conrad, he lived. *Lives*. Outlasts the rest of us, sons, grandsons, great-grandsons. Hidden away in an Amazonian thicket of sea tales, silver hunts, redemption, loss of nerve – and flashing, dark-eyed women (unreal as miniatures in a locket).

I went everywhere in the canon, odd volumes, sets, battered first editions, before I tried *Youth: And Two Other Tales*. *Heart of Darkness* had been milked to death, they'd all been at it, Orson Welles, Nicolas Roeg, W.G. Sebald. It wasn't *Heart of Darkness*, although that played best with the situation I found myself in. So many of Conrad's tales begin at the hinge, the liquid edge of the A13: 'an enfilading view down the Lower Hope Reach'. The living and their fictional doubles yarning their lives away, 'not more than thirty miles from London, and less than twenty from that shallow and dangerous puddle to which our coasting men give the groundless name of "German Ocean"'.

The End of the Tether was a makeweight, thrown in to bulk out a volume, 40,000 words for William Blackwood, ballast for *Youth*. This was that famously unlucky manuscript, burnt in an oil-lamp explosion, lost, rewritten. Fiddled with by Ford Madox Ford. Critics talk of old age and *Lear*, 'assorted fools and grotesques'. *The End of the Tether* has been eclipsed by *Heart of Darkness*. But it was here that I found the sepia imprint of Arthur Norton, his limp, the heavy stick that supports him in the Peruvian photographs.

His age sat lightly enough on him; and of his ruin he was not ashamed. He had not been alone to believe in the stability of the Banking Corporation. Men whose judgment in the matters of finance was as expert as his seamanship had commended the prudence of his investments, and had themselves lost much money in the great failure. The only difference between him and them was that he had lost his all . . .

He had to use a thick cudgel-like stick on account of a stiffness in the hip – a slight touch of rheumatism. Otherwise he knew nothing of the ills of the flesh.

Arthur Norton, dragging around the deck, talking investments, blackguarding his advisers; his dry, Aberdonian humour misunderstood by the supposed Frenchman.

A burnt manuscript, months of graft, destroyed.

Norton's shot at immortality: a dodgy hip, stick, money-talk that sent him back into exile, that pushed Conrad towards the crowning achievement of *Nostromo*.

Different Americas, the same Essex. The Lower Hope Reach, in morning light (Conrad favoured dusk, redness over London), never changes. A poultice of yellow mud, a fast-flowing river, an immense and very English sky.

East Ham

We're moving, over ramps, along tolerated pavements – FOOT-PATH CLOSED – much faster than the morning traffic, which, in thin blue, first-cigarette tension, is not moving at all. The A13, everybody knows, is the future; the highway on which the sacred cities of Thames Gateway will depend. With the blessing of government and mayor, the one thing on which they agree, brownfield swamps will witness the beginning of a process whereby London is turned inside out. Centre as an inauthentic museum (haunted by authentic beggars, junkies, prostitutes), flexible rim as a living, working, vibrant economy.

Meanwhile: stasis. Avenues of red-and-white cones. Yellow, giraffe-neck cranes. Heavy-duty machinery exhibited but not used: two Irishmen with one shovel, down a ditch, the only action. Dozens of grey drums, stencilled MILTON: I like those. I photograph them – with a vividly decorated (pink, blue) tower block in the background. Mexican vivacity, Siberian weather fronts.

We can't talk. We have to creep, Indian file, backs to the wall. Noise verges on blood-from-ear levels. Not from the cars and lorries (thumping engines, exhaust fumes, radios, mobile phones), nor from road crews (drills, banter, radios again), but the sky. Traffic helicopters, weather helicopters, accident helicopters from the roof of the Royal London Hospital: a Murch/Coppola *Apocalypse Now*, wraparound-Dolby soundscape, without Wagner and the Doors. Sky fouled by contrails, smoke plumes, planes into Stansted, Heathrow, Silvertown. Crossing and circling, holding patterns and bumpy descents. Actual noise and the imagined noise of phonebabble, acoustic fizz, deregulated fibre-optic overload. Outgrowths on church steeples, schools, filling stations: dishes and masts and things that blink from tall poles. Scanners tracking the bands, trying to find a language they recognise.

When the traffic does stir, it comes straight at us, hating our independence. A blue dumper truck, ISLE OF DOGS, careering across mud, making up for lost time. White vans bombing over the crest of the ramp like breakaway fairground gondolas. We are obliged to press ourselves against scrapwood fences that obscure our view of the Canning Town estates and the Prince of Wales Park Farm.

When in doubt, quote Ballard: 'The continued breakdown of the European road-systems would soon rule out any future journeys'.

Track was unimpressed.

'You don't attempt future journeys. Every walk you lead disappears, very rapidly, into the past.'

She kept her eyes open, this girl. Crunched by wheels (taller than she was) of an articulated lorry, she swooped on something black and shiny. An old record, a seven-incher with rat bites taken out of it. 'My Oh My' by Slade. Log it, the absurdity. (For the grid, the only future that counts: the sketchbook.)

Log official posters: FREE COMPUTER COURSES. LONDON SCHOOL OF PROFESSIONAL STUDIES. FIRST RIGHT. Log fly-pitched posters in lurid red on yellow: PYJAMA CLAD PSYCHOPATHS. HARD KNOCKS ON YOUR XBOX! SEXY NINJA VIXEN. LYCRA CLAD WEBSLINGER.

Wing mirrors brushed our sleeves. We were the only pedestrians in a panning shot that took in discriminations of improbable and impossible human habitation, imposed-from-above housing schemes, cottages, demi-villas, low-level estates (neo-suburban or punishment colony), solitary tower blocks like periscopes surfacing to challenge the ruin.

There were Pupil Referment Units like battery farms with paranoid security. Galvanising outfits. Rusting gas holders. Stinking creeks. A yellow-blue Mercedes lorry, canvas-backed, stalled at the next section of roadworks, asked us for directions. The canvas billows suspiciously at the sound of English voices. The driver, heavy beard, dark glasses, is browner than anything achieveable on a Loughton sunbed.

We can't, by my calculation, be more than two and a half miles from Beckton Alp. In a straightish line. But there is no sign of it. Nothing untoward breaks the horizon: pedestrian bridges, cranes, estate agents' boards, communities severed by the great arterial road (five lanes ambitious for expansion). Little gardens with rudimentary planting (grass, privet) are used as parking lots (second, third car, another on the pavement).

A hundred-yard section, between aborted or incomplete engineering projects, threw us from our road-edge walk and into a brief transit along the boundary wall, red brick, of a Canning Town estate. The wall acted as a noticeboard for this abandoned settlement: trysts, declarations of love (or the mechanisms of love), threats, political and occult symbols.

ROBERT KEYS YOUR NEXT ... FUCKEN TRAITOR. HAPPY XMAS LONDON. LOVE + BEST WISHES. SINN FEIN AND THE IRA.

Such niceties are soon behind us. We're back in the virtual tunnel, of noise, remorseless traffic flow, cancelled pathways, detours, sand, yellow jackets and hardhats. It's cold and we feel the first flakes of snow burning against our faces, melting and dripping from upturned collars.

The alp, when it appears, is as unimpressive as the Millennium Dome, which, under a powdering of fresh snow, it resembles. As we advance, the mound becomes more dramatic, conical not humpbacked. Beckton Alp is a considerable event that nobody notices. They, motorists, are preoccupied with traffic lights that seem to change on a weekly basis, holding reluctant tourists under a flyover, alongside a series of piers and supports (supporting nothing but foul air). Precast concrete columns and elegant structural solutions – for which, as yet, no questions have been found.

The approach to the alp is by way of a parodic suburb, a single line of misplaced Hendon semis, grafted together to form a mile-long terrace, with bow windows, porches, stained-glass sun-rises, bushes and cropped evergreens at regular intervals. As if this vulgarity, the A13, wasn't happening, wasn't hurtling past the garden gate. (If those gates had not been removed to convert garden into garage.).

I'm struck by a pair of white horses' heads (manes, veins, bulging eyes) that stand, like chess knights, on gateposts. The missing ears are encouraging. It means that somebody, at some time, must have walked this route.

CLUTCH CARE CENTRE. NEW & USED OFFICE FURNI-TURE. DIVERSION.

We take it, willingly. Coffee would be welcome. East Ham must have a café. The transient amnesia of the road, keep moving, see nothing, builds up a powerful undertow of disenfranchised weirdness: it puddles and spills from ancient villages, pilgrim route stopovers. Anything human and messy that has to happen, happens here.

S. KOREA/BEAT & EAT/DOGS.

White transit van with red script: ISRAELITE CHURCH OF CHRIST.

A team of Kosovans working the lights.

The women, long skirts, headscarfs, smear windscreens with dirty water, scrape and scratch with harsh sponges and squeegees. The cold, the ice: it doesn't help. A young lad with a mobile phone keeps watch. I can't lift my camera without being spotted, abused. The men, minders, smoke in a flash American car, discreetly parked in Roman Road.

This is a major crossing point for the energies of London. Danny is excited. He takes out a black box that reads the health of the land-scape, electrical pulses, numbered keys. I don't need the box to reach a verdict: sick, possibly terminal. Purple and black. Ameliorated by snowfall.

Tides of sewage rush under the road, down the Northern Outflow, to Beckton Creek. Traffic grinds on an east–west axis. Travellers heading for the retail parks, City Airport, Silvertown,

Woolwich Ferry, wait for a break in the flow. The Kosovans have the whole thing covered. Head for the M25, Lakeside, QEII Bridge, Southend – or back towards the City – and you'll be hit by windscreen polluters.

Head for the Thames, on the A117, the old north–south road, and a troop of war zone performance artists will attack you. Like a George Grosz tribute band. Strong meat, this. Men, on a bitter morning (bitter themselves), rapping on car roofs, shouting, gesticulating, butting at windows, holding out their hands. No attempt to charm or to go for pathos. Trouser leg rolled up to reveal a livid stump, a limb the size of a knotted rope's end. Landmine deformities and mutilations pressed against the screens of Dagenham multiples, Mondeos, Capris, Escorts. Angry, handsome men with pieces missing. They move among the stalled cars like relic peddlers on the Mexican border. In T-shirts, they weave through lanes of captive motors, raging, pinched and shivering in the sudden arctic snow shower.

'You know,' Track said to me, across the Formica table in the neat East Ham café, 'you chew like an old man. At the front of your mouth, slowly. Like your teeth might fall out at any moment.'

'I am an old man,' I shot back. With feeling. This place, with its wall mirrors, was a shrine to memento mori. 'I'll eat any way I want.'

Danny didn't do food. He took his tea, sweet, by the pint. He sucked, wiped his beard, without comment from Track. Who was amused by my peevishness, my vestigial vanity. She hadn't meant her comment that way, it was a technical observation. She liked to know precisely how things worked.

'Do you live around here?' I asked Danny – who seemed very much at home, getting tannin refills on a wink at the hostess (ink hair, full slap), spreading his books and charts across neighbouring tables with no challenge from the authorities.

'No,' he said.

I don't know why I imagined that Danny lived anywhere. He

was the sort of man you meet on the road, lose on the road, find again: in field or ditch or stone circle. Or church. We'd walked past a good one, St Mary Magdalene. It was closed. And Danny, his bag and his reputation to consider, wouldn't go over the wall. Track had no such scruple. She reported that the church was built around 1130, Kentish rag, flints and chalk from Purley, Caen stone from Normandy, pudding-stone from local quarries. A Roman cemetery was close by: hence, Roman Road. A doctored wilderness, enlivened with overgrown memorials, ran down to the A13. At nine and a half acres this was, so the notice claimed, 'the largest churchyard in England'.

'I've got a place,' Danny admitted, when the subject had been abandoned, 'near Basildon. You've heard of the Plotlands?'

We hadn't. So he produced the book: *Basildon Plotlands (The Londoners' Rural Retreat)* by Deanna Walker. What a story. It brought tears to the eyes, the liberties that had been lost. Anarchist (Guild Socialist/Naturist/Up Yours, Squire) Essex men and women allowed to erect whatever form of shelter they chose, chalets and shacks, on land nobody could find another way to exploit (not then, late nineteenth century to utilitarian Fifties). A frontier cabin on the Langland Hills (they made the Beckton Alp look like the Matterhorn). Danny was the last open-range squatter. The rest had been swallowed in planning restrictions and the thrusting New Town – where so many pill-peddling gangsters and A13 pirates thrived.

I listened to his tale, gumming my bean-and-sausage mush. Another coffee. The ascent of the alp, in this weather, could be indefinitely postponed. Behind us, at the table next to the door, sat three all-day-breakfasters as unlikely as ourselves. A woman who used words like 'altruism' and 'atrophy'. A sallow dude who spoke of weekends in Milan and Venice. An older woman who knew how to cook. English was their common language, but not their native tongue, they used it to greater effect than anyone else in the caff. They treated the experience of English eggs and bacon ironically.

Let it go. Commentary is not compulsory. This isn't radio. You don't have to notice every colourful detail. Drink your coffee. And get back to the road.

Track read Danny's Plotlands book. Danny fiddled with his black box, adjusting dials, tapping keys, making notes in a ruled ledger. I prepared for the coming alpine assault by dipping into Arthur Norton's journals. Trying to find a clue to his state of mind at the time of his expedition to the Peruvian interior, the vanishing.

Retirement came early.

For the next ten years I extracted as much enjoyment out of life as perhaps ever falls to the lot of ordinary unambitious mortals; but at the end of this time I fell among thieves and, as misfortunes rarely come single, the Hemileia must needs play havoc with securities in Ceylon at the same time, so that I began to look abroad again for investments and occupation, resulting in a trip to Tasmania, an adventure much talked of with friends now gone, Skeat, J.W. Birch and L.J. Petit.

I resolved, a sum of £2,000 wasted, in the unrewarded pursuit of precious metals, to attempt the only remaining sub-continent that I had never visited, South America. My age and partial incapacity, a troublesome knee-joint, should have argued against the enterprise. Sensations of doubt and uncertainty, premonitions derived from the belief that no free-born Scotsman had any business in a land bedevilled by Papist rogues and cassocked inebriates, could keep me from Tilbury, and my passage, by way of the islands of Barbadoes and Jamaica, to the Isthmus of Panama. It remains my strongest conviction, however, that the great lesson of travel is that we learn to better appreciate the qualities of the land we have left behind; perhaps for the last time.

Beckton Alp

Beckton: a fake alp under real snow, a marvel. The ascent, Dante-fashion, is like unspooling apple peel, tracking ghosts. A man-made Glastonbury Tor with a ski-lift (hidden by boards, protective fences). Slowly, curve by curve, viewing platform by viewing platform, the wonder of the thing, the spread of ersatz London (much brown, some grey), is revealed.

Danny's brass rods, lightly held by frozen hands, swivel and cross, as he locates the spiral energy, the heat-core of the demolished gasworks. The alp's a true illusion. Built on rubble, stepped like a Mayan pyramid, this is a bespoke ziggurat designed to be lost, secreted in Guatemalan jungle. The alp is so much in the way that nobody notices it. They rush on, never appreciating its generosity. Being nothing in itself, a bump, a wart, the ski slope offers: prospects. Somewhere to pause, look back. Look forward. Weigh a life in the balance. Blue Surrey hills (Italianate water towers, TV transmitters) to Epping Forest. The cold, glacial torrent of the A13 doing the work of the antiquated Thames.

There is such clarity of light in the temporary suspension of the mundane, the after-effect of snowshowers. Arctic Albion. High air so clean that it hurts our lungs. The division of spoils, Docklands towers, sugar factory smoke over Silvertown, Upton Park football stadium, Jewish Cemetery beside outfall walk, is as blatant as a boardgame, a three-dimensional map.

Beckton, for me, completes one of London's significant triangulations. I'll leave the church, the abbey and the holy well, to Chris Street. And stick with Greenwich Hill, the missing mound of Whitechapel (to the west of the London Hospital) and Beckton Alp. Natural and manufactured elevations. Offering: vision. An aerofilm pattern of constructed things. The lie of the land. Rivers, clay. A basin of eels and veins.

A short puff to the summit for a large reward; even eyes as blooded and tired as mine can be scraped and rinsed. *The mound is an eye*: jacketed in mud, turf, beer cans and a light dressing of slush. Industrial quantities of shaving foam. I thought of a Los Angeles crime scene, described in a film book: a manager (pimp) who had shot his unfaithful protégée, before putting the gun into his own mouth. Sucking fire. The New York journalist, cranking up the metaphors, explained how the intimate blast had taken out so much bone, armature, that the face had slipped into a single-eye mask: Cyclops. A blind, black hole at the centre of the forehead.

Beckton was Cyclops.

Beckton was the missing eye of Rooster Cogburn (in Henry Hathaway's sentimental western). John Wayne's capacious socket stuffed with true grit.

White eye speared by Dennis Hopper: in the form of a raven. Odin.

Or Kirk Douglas, Jewish-Russian-Californian, as Viking beserker, showboating his deformity. (The missing hand of Tony Curtis. The stump waved at stalled motorists under the unfinished A13 flyover.)

Panoptic eye at the roadside, albumen and blacktop. Surveillance systems operated by the monocular dead of the Estuary, bomber pilots, accidents of heavy plant, gas explosions.

Ascending, sightless, we would learn to see: Danny by touch, Track by good-humoured detachment, and myself – by fear. Of age, death, impotence. The spectacle of open land denied. The click of the ski-lift. The creaking of panels in the protective fence. Hot steam from the retail park.

I took Danny's dowsing rods; my breath was coming hard, the climb was longer and sharper than I remembered. It was disconcerting, not being able to locate the summit, not anticipating the next blind corner, feeling the rods dig into the palms of my hands.

At the penultimate turn, the rim of the western slope, above the Alamo of the retail park, its imported eclecticism, Woolworths and Matalan, World of Leather, light overwhelmed me. I staggered, fell. Reached out for support.

By and by the heart's action seemed to fail, and I suddenly collapsed, slipped off the saddle and lay down on my back, my mule gasping for breath beside me. When I gradually came to myself, I could see around me the bones of many a good mule and llama, cleanly picked, while high in the air floated the ever alert condor, said to be the largest and most powerful of all birds; but I was not just then in a mood to admire his proportions nor appreciate his attentions, and, gathering myself together again with the help of a more fortunate companion, I moved on, but only for fifty yards, when I again fainted. This was repeated at least fifty times till the crest was crossed and some progress was made down the western slopes.

Limp as laundry, I sat, head between knees. Danny, tactful or unobservant, lumbered about the tree line, noting buried electrical cables, the lively detritus of the old gasworks. Track kept going too: under the fence, onward and upward.

DANGER/BATTER/UNSTABLE.

The ski-slope had been dismantled, asset-stripped. Waffle-texture matting peeled away, to reveal spoilt ground: deadwhite. Skin under plaster. The slope was no longer a slope, but a series of steps, wet concrete platforms. The lift mechanism had been excavated. The Swiss Chalet that served abominable hot chocolate (dun-coloured Swarfega) had been detonated. The scam was discontinued. The alp would be absorbed, no doubt, into the London Industrial Park.

But I couldn't see it. Couldn't work my eyes. Arthur Norton's voice, his ride across the Peruvian mountain range, altitude sickness, falling from the mule, still echoed in my head.

The mercilessly cold wind blew right in my face; I shivered and covered my head with the blankets ... It soon passed over ... save for the groaning of the poor restless mules, seeking in vain for food or smarting from irritating sores. Poor, starved, over-burdened mules! I shall never

quite shake off the qualms of conscience I carry through life on account of
these too-hurried rides.

Norton's journal fitted this place.

The thing I'd seen in the mirror at the Travelodge, my double, swung from the resurrected ski-lift: a Goya caprice that I imposed on this all-too-material mound (anticipating the Chapman Brothers). Sound was enough, bringing back sight, bringing back the patterned quilting of the vanished ski-slope, bringing back the gasworks, the complex industrial landscape that existed as a prime target for Goering's bombers.

Thick tongue rolled around a Fisherman's Friend, holding heat, I took my time, breath in the lungs, staring – for as long as it required – in each of the cardinal directions. Danny recalled the raids, one of the gas holders blazing after a direct hit. Beckton had never recovered. They'd brought down a few Germans, you might find shattered fuselages, hanks of propeller, buried in the mound. Bones and boots. Identity bracelets on sheep-yellow wrist joints.

Once war is declared, it's an absolute. So Danny believed. There are no winners. Stanley Kubrick picked up the marshal's baton, carried on where Hitler left off. Call Beckton Vietnam if you want, but you can't summon a vanished culture with a truckload of palm trees, shipped in as root-balls from Spain, and a few thunderflashes. Palm trees die. They scream in the ground.

It wasn't enough to lose a war (that you weren't supposed to be fighting), you had to be seen to lose: madness, psychosis, after-images. The last great conflict for American journalism, Michael Herr, Norman Mailer and the rest, rucking over the skull-splinters of Ernest Hemingway.

Beckton was the killing ground.

Compare and contrast: Coppola's lush palm forests, lagoons, beaches (Conrad's East, the Philippines), with Kubrick's Beckton. Like a Margate Dreamland. A painted set for a seaside excursion. *Apocalypse Now*, redux or dead-ducks, is not *Heart of Darkness*, it's one of Conrad's Malaysian tales, an upcountry yarn spun by lawyers and accountants on a yawl in the Lower Hope, the Thames Estuary. A different kind of colonialism. Jukeboxes, hot tubs slippery with seasonal Playmates, fleets of helicopters. Coppola gives it the treatment, overkill, hallucinogenic popcorn opera. Kubrick swoops low over Norfolk wetlands.

English light.

Full Metal Jacket is about English light, a fine grading of absence: shades of grey, low cloud, melancholy, forgetfulness. A documentary, with a real drill sergeant, happening in limbo: the Battle of Beckton. Anton Furst, set dresser, perfectionist, rigs up the doomed gasworks with avenues of sad and solitary palms; he fires unpeopled generating houses. He fires memory: Blitz nights.

Full Metal Jacket.

The alp becomes the helmet logo of Kubrick's prophetic English travelogue, Thames Gateway as a future American fiefdom: Exxon refineries, Dagenham motorplant, multiplexes, retail parks. Ford's water tower. The alp is a grass-thatched steel helmet (borrowed from Sam Fuller, Robert Aldrich). Manichean tag: BORN TO KILL – with peace symbol. Love and war. Snipers waiting at every window.

The Thames is untouched: 'Charlie doesn't surf.' Charlie works the flyover with the Kosovans, showing his wounds. Kubrick's explosions have shaken something loose, something unfixed between sewage beds and river. Over-actors, reaching for Oscar-gilt dildos, make too much of the crack between worlds. A nude Michelin Brando lisping his Eliotic pieties and splashing himself with water. Orson Welles, photographed, mouth agape, horsehair beard, snuffling through a prosthetic conk, eyes too young: as Kurtz.

The horror.

For the film that never was. A few test shots in a tank. They don't understand, the impresarios, Kurtz is the thing that cannot be seen. Kurtz is posthumous. Kurtz is place. Kurtz is not Michael Curtiz, Hungarian showman, soap sculptor. (*Kurz*, adj. short; short and to the point.) They don't get it. The Hollywood genius thing is never short and to the point. It's inflated, loud, destroying whatever it sets out to celebrate. The smothering embrace of respect. Crocodile tears of child-molesting Louis B. Mayer.

'Who's the commanding officer here?'

'Ain't you?'

As soon as Hopper appears, on the steps, on the Beckton pyramid, cameras like shrunken skulls, cameras all over him, I know we're in big trouble. Coppola's in trouble. Madness takes discipline. Eliot put himself together on Margate Sands. The poem comes later. Coppola feeds Eliot's lines, like birdseed, to his costive genius actor: to pastiche madness.

Wired Dennis, chilled Dennis. Dwarf Dennis: cameras, grenades, sweat-soaked faux-guerrilla headband. Doesn't cut. We don't see the photographs he took, we can't afford them.

The nightmare of America is the hysterical belligerence of non-combatants: excused service Waynes, flatfoot Nixons and flatulent L.B. Johnsons, the Bush baby in Texan reserve uniform. Faking orgasms of righteous indignation. At the perfidy of others who lie more effectively than they do.

Beckton Alp, as Danny the Dowser discovers, is replete with lies, substantial debris. Memory deposits of actual raids and staged battles are indistinguishable. Generators of false history. A viewing platform on past and future.

'Pernicious dust.'

That's what Kubrick said. Beckton: Hué. Coal-black faces of actors and crew. He wanted dignity, pathos. Andrew Joseph Russell's photographs from the American Civil War. The dead of Gettysburg recorded by Timothy O'Sullivan. He wanted the destroyed buildings of the Paris Commune of 1871 in an anonymous stereoscopic view. He wanted Roger Fulton at Balaclava. Reality with its faint ghosts (where subjects moved). He wanted Julia Margaret Cameron (soft at the edges) for his own portrait: serious man with beard.

And he got Matthew Modine, an actor. A well-intentioned amateur with an expensive camera (it passes the time). He got coal-dust. The print of mortality.

★

Turning at last to the east, the zone into which we will soon walk, our destination of choice, I am stopped, heart-struck, by the futility of it: my journey, the book. London is leeched from the chart. It *is* white, hazy, phantom forests of pylons. Upcountry, Essex belongs to the warring tribes, guerrilla killers, driller killers, Ecstasy bandits. I've written pieces slighting the Sleeman brothers, taking the mickey out of O'Driscoll. I was safe in Hackney. But footloose in Basildon? Petrified in Purfleet? Describe them, use them for local colour, but keep clear. I wasn't stupid enough to arrange a meeting with Mr Big, Declan Mocatta. Mocatta was my Kurtz. Off-screen. And best left there.

But what if it's already too late? What if, like *Heart of Darkness*, this tale is being told backwards? What if someone else, out on the coast, is the true narrator? Then I am Kurtz, gone native, addicted to savagery. Listening to drums. Waiting for the bullet. 'Terminate with extreme prejudice.'

Danny, face to the west, rescued me. He had a text for every occasion. A book of local history cobbled together by one of those green walkers who dedicate their lives to revealing the location of London's few remaining secret spaces.

The dowser read badly, no rhythm, no emphasis, gaps in the wrong places. The drone was soothing. He taught me what to do: abort, abandon. Head for home along the sewage outfall. Take a train from Fenchurch Street. Go looking for Marina Fountain.

Danny held his book at arm's-length. And he growled.

Leaning on a creosoted railing, London makes sense. There is a pattern, a working design. And there's a word for it too: *Obscenery*. Stuttering movement on the road. Distant river. The temporal membrane dissolves, in such a way that the viewer becomes the thing he is looking at. Green rays of the setting sun strip flesh from the bone. He's done it, vanished into a Jimmy Seed apocalypse, an epic painting, an intensity that the writer knows he will never achieve. So he settles for quotation, echoes of other men. For photographs. Documentary retrievals. Memory prompts. Useless. We are still on the inside of the outside, searching for fissures.

Trapped in an envelope of diesel dust. From the summit of Beckton Alp, view is raw and absolute and unappeased.

'Is there an author?' I asked. 'For this flannel?'

'Yes,' Danny said. 'A Mr Norton. A.M. Norton. Dead, I believe. Car crash on the M25. He was trying to read and drive.'

The cold did things to Track's hair, despite the pins, combs, clips. The Polynesian rescue kit. She was obliged to notice it, deal with it; pat, pluck, wrestle (like ironing seaweed). Her hair helmet was crisped with frost, dead weight. She was fit, strong-necked, but the mass of curls and knots was a nuisance, a burden. And, when the day, the adventure, reached that stage – self-conscious hair – it was time to quit. Regroup. Return home.

She had had enough for now, more than enough (of Norton and Beckton); she wanted to be in the studio with the heaters that didn't work. Her table: yellow pencils in a blue jar, black notebooks, tray of reduced (stamp-sized) colour images. Green ink and pens with nibs. The fuss of the road ordered, laid out in columns, pictographs, glyphs. Her words.

Quit. Right now. Norton's narrative was unravelling in a potentially ugly way. Sticking with him would be a folie à deux, collusion in his madness. The Vietnam film stuff, the mutterings about his fictitious grandfather in the jungle: it clogged the frame. Norton had his uses – as an unreliable guide, dredger of oddball facts and fables – but, in his mulish way, he wanted to take over the lives of those who accompanied him, the road itself, the weather. This nose-pinching cold was his doing: that line about 'fake alp under real snow'.

Track was sick of his consciousness: of being involved with it, implicated in its traumas. Everything that had happened to them, since that first afternoon walking to Aldgate Pump, had been refracted through Norton's fiction, his voice. The unplaceable accent. The half-truths. The bending and warping of a simple event, a walk.

She was unprepared for echopraxis. The mindless repetition of another person's moves and gestures. His road, her road. Their road. It didn't work.

She wanted to consider other things. Would she, for example, go back to Seattle in the summer? Her mother? The drapes, the net. A mistake? She'd been thinking of that place by the sea in Bergman's film *Persona*. Another male fantasy. Barbecued monks. Dykes on heat. But a good clean house in which to work. Should she go with Ollie to Sweden? Was she more like Liv Ullmann (height, lips, weight of hair)? Or Bibi Andersson? Apparently practical, actually out of it, on the edge: a reader of other women's letters. She'd read Ollie's diaries. The boy, Reo Sleeman, didn't send letters. Sweden might be good, expensive. One of the islands. Ollie had stolen her mac. That's where it had gone. Like Bibi Andersson, much too big for her. Never using her specs, except in the studio. Ollie's little vanities. She was one of those people. It was easier to talk to her, properly, on the phone. If she couldn't get a show, sell a couple of things, they'd have to give up the lease. There might be a message, at home, from Ollie. There would be, for sure. Ollie at the seaside.

'I think I'll walk back, up the Green Way. You know? To Victoria Park?' Track said.

Norton would come with her. He'd run out of steam. He said something about following up on Marina Fountain's story, a train. Danny would try to find the Miller's Well in Central Park. They might meet, on the road, in a week or two. Nobody knew anything about what happened between Tilbury and Southend, a catalogue of oil smears and marshes (Fobbing, Bowers, Hadleigh). And, inland, out of the way, the National Motorboat Museum.

There was a light in the church. We went over the wall, Danny with some reluctance, Track leading the way. She rapped on the heavy door. And we were let in – by the older woman from the East Ham café. The other two, the Italian boy (now in white overalls) and the redhaired girl, were up some scaffolding, picking away at the plaster of the rood screen. To reveal, after hours of intensive labour, a few inches of medieval wall painting, a tracery of leaves and vines; a tempera Book of Hours.

'Hey, that's it. What I want,' Track said.

Floating, rough-edged fragments, paradise echoes of the wilderness that enveloped the church, the wild garden. Tiny squares of colour on the dim, whitewashed wall. A burning bush. A bunch of grapes. A starved saint peering, like a fox, through a thicket of bloody thorns. A sprung locust. The Norman church was an enlarged page from Track's blackbound album.

Danny, tests completed, told us about the narrow, red (east-flowing) ley line with its deep-green (north–south) cross-strut: marking the place of the original altar.

'Immortal, that line. Even if the church is demolished. Shadowing the road, church to church. Dagenham, Rainham, Aveley. The route we have to take.'

The church in which we found ourselves, so unexpectedly, intrigued Track – but she didn't know how to behave. Museum stroll with fixed grin? Or synagogue awkward – under parental gaze? The Jacobean monuments were a small theatre of mortality, pink cherubs, grave-digging spades; love, death and plenty of gilt.

POSTERITATI: 'To those who come after.'

DIIS OMNIBUS MANIBUS: 'To the Gods in all the Shades.'

Norton admired a black horse's head nailed to the wall, the negative of the A13 post-decorations from Newham Way.

'Which movie?' Track challenged, coming up beside him – as he watched the redhaired girl, goggled against the dust, scratch with tender persistence at the plaster.

'*Don't Look Now*. Not the restoration, collapsing cradle, the scaffolding: the photograph that bleeds. Sutherland's eye, magnifying glass, contact sheet. It's like Danny says: "the persistence of red". A mother with drowned child in a red coat.'

'And did they?'

'What?'

'Do it. The dressed/undressed, going-out-for-dinner scene? Did Sutherland and Julie Christie actually fuck?'

'Nobody *actually* does anything on film. That's the point. We re-edit, according to taste, leave out the bits that don't matter. Film is vulnerable. It rots, mush in the can. Words stick and burn.'

This dialogue between Norton and Track in the church of St Mary Magdalene at East Ham never happened. Not then. No humans talk like that.

Norton, silent, walking beside Track, in the twilight, temperature dropping, replayed his fictional day. He improvised. Track *had* touched his arm (she wanted to show him the monument to William Heigham and his wife Anne). True. They looked up at the scaffolding and thought: *Don't Look Now.*

Norton said (to himself): 'Nic Roeg.'

Track said (to nobody): 'Donald Sutherland. Would you fancy him if you had to go to his hotel room to show one of your paintings?'

Clean cut or lap dissolve?

They were passing the silted creek at Channelsea. Norton remembered one shot (static) in Patrick Keiller's *London*. Fade to darkness. Before we tune in to the deranged precision of Paul Scofield's voice-over. Fade to smell. Two figures, hands in pockets, on a long straight path.

Coast

At around 2.30 p.m., give or take, a woman with a child came through the door, to gossip with customers (maybe off-duty staff) at the back of the restaurant; coat on, holding firmly, right to the point of nuisance, to the tugging, excited kid – then passing her over to the manager (who had already put on his jacket). Tidied his hair in the mirror. They kissed – and the child, chattering now, securing a few fingers of her father's large hand, led him through the close-packed tables, never looking back until they were safely outside, on the parade, when she turned to give her mother a wave, through a window, which had to be wiped and polished, daily, to counter the abrasive quality of the salt air. All of them, man, woman, child, notably, commendably, neat. Clean. Wholesome.

Kaporal, undomestic, incomplete in his bachelor state, sentimental as Ford Madox Ford (banished from Kent), approved. He liked family restaurants, chrome and Formica, paper napkins and pale-blue plastic tablecloths. With, freshly rinsed, every morning, artificial daisies in narrow, green-glass holders. Or daisy-type flora (Kaporal didn't do flowers). White and yellow, anyway.

'Allo, mister. You want sal-mon and broccoli? Chef don't 'ave broccoli today, very nice spinach.'

The broccoli was always off and the spinach never really worked (too bitter), but Kaporal didn't care. Warm, soft food on a pasta base. The woman was charming, the mother.

'Maria,' he said. For the pleasure of it. Having her name in his mouth. She smiled, came back.

'Which pasta?'

'I think . . . spaghetti.'

He laughed.

'Always spaghetti.'

She touched his hand, lightly.

'Something to drink, mister?'

'Carafe. Red.'

'Another . . . *litre*?'

'Litre.'

No hint of disapproval in her voice. Admiration. If he didn't fool himself. Collusion in her voice, her smile. All things being equal, she'd sit down. Help him to dispose of the second carafe (bevelled glass, hospital retort, sample).

Light and fruity (pink mouthwash), blushful Hippocrene. Purple-stained lips. Maria's fingerprints on the curve of the dusty glass.

Trying not to burn, mopping his brow, being decent about the cigarettes (limiting himself, two to the hour), Kaporal gazed out of the window.

Should I sit at the big round table and catch the lowering sun in my eyes? Or shift further inside – and risk scalding my back on a radiator? These were decisions, strategies, to be deferred. Indefinitely.

Pasta joint, seafront. Out of season. Tony Hancock in *The Punch and Judy Man*? Certainly not. Hancock was hopelessly exposed on the big screen. Black-and-white face like a map of Australia, blank with wrinkles. A radio face. Better to imagine than to see. Kaporal was John le Mesurier, afternoon bars. Cuckolded. Kaporal was the afterlife of Oliver Reed (*The Damned*, Losey not Visconti, Weymouth). Ollie Reed in his pomp: *The System*. Michael Winner with Nic Roeg as DOP. A between-movies actor wintering in Guernsey, cheap booze, empty annex of money-launderers' hotel.

So Kaporal romanced. Playing with the masks, ransacking buried memory files. A life lived by proxy.

David Hemmings, he was in it, *The System*, 1964. Two years before *Blow-Up*. Mike Winner to Antonioni. Culture shifts: beach photographer, marine melancholy (*I Vitelloni* re-made by Ken Russell), to urban chancer with studio and agent and primitive car phone in open-top Roller. Lunch with bundles of prints, a book about to be published, in a fashionable trattoria. Tasting sauce in the kitchen. (Kaporal could do that. He was five years younger than Hemmings.)

It could still happen. With Maria. If not Antonioni.

He was pissed, rambling. Muttering to himself. He fitted the environment. Non-judgemental, easygoing (plastic tablecloth). Noisy kids tolerated, reps and scammers (jackets off). Women getting squiffy on a succession of single glasses.

Open all day. Always busy. Not now.

The guy from the Adelphi Hotel at the window table (seats six): alone. Single coffee. It's like a uniform for those guys, black leather blouson, dark trousers, *new* trainers. Six-o'clock shadow three hours early. Mobile phone and cigarette packet on display. They're not allowed to take paid employment for six months after coming ashore, checking in to the Warrior Square hostel (decorative wrought-iron balconies, permanent building work).

The economic migrant protected his coffee cup with an arm, whenever Maria approached – another table, the door. He wouldn't let her view the brown stain, all that was left of his refreshment. Edgy, bristling. Missing a newspaper.

It was the mildest of environments: cup of tea, chocolate and pineapple *bombe*, meatballs and tomato sauce, any combination you fancy, no hierarchy of values for Maria. Eat or sit. Chat or stay silent. Smoke or sniff the plastic flowers.

The pink ones on the migrant's table, the vase he moved disdainfully, making room for his phone and fags, were carnations. Kaporal sported those in his buttonhole at one of his weddings – Kentish Town? Carnations, pinks. A froth of candy petticoats. Stiff petticoats, layered. Broderie anglaise. Gingham. Ponytails. Bardot. Annette Vadim (née Stroyberg). Mylene Demongeot: in an over-coloured pin-up postcard. On a swing? Gillian Hills (a Brit) in *Beat Girl*.

How well this pizza place represented itself. The kitsch Aztec mirror with the angular panels. The golden sunburst clock. The purple/red/blue Mediterranean seascapes: tame Fauve, unwild Derain. Matisse, with an ulcer, painting in snow mittens while

chained to a chair in a Beirut cellar. A sense of non-specific celebration: light, gilt, summertime, well-meaning but hopelessly unsym-
pathetic bands of colour (sour yellow with loud pink, red trim like
an aspirational migraine). The music, borderline Muzak, was getting
at him now, film themes, tribute bands. Times when he'd nursed a
second drink in a Streatham wine bar, waiting for a woman to
text-message the fact that she wasn't coming: not today, not ever.

Football. Coming over, walking the promenade, Kaporal had
perched on the railings to watch a kickabout. Balkan boys. On the
lower promenade and then, when the tide retreated, on a scraped
section of beach, a few yards of only slightly tilted sand.

Achmed watched with him. Drin played, participated. Kaporal
never had much time for organised sport, team games, but even he
recognised that the Albanians didn't go at it like, say, the black or
Turkish or black Irish or doughwhite Scrubs locals. The inner-city
tarmac firms and fence casuals, the red dirt-and-weed oafs. Arsenal
and West Ham tops with baggy, many-pocketed bottoms. Or tight
jeans, name trainers, steelcaps, loafers. Only the young kids had the
full kit. All ages swore and shouted. From the off. Screamed.

The Albanians on the pebbled beach never made a sound. They
took their jackets off (some of them), but otherwise played as they
were. The pattern was neat, discernible (even by Kaporal). A few
paces, short steps, neutralise opponent, pass. Move. Receive, pass.
In silence. With terrifying intensity and concentration. Triangles.
Back to defender, foot on ball. Pass, pass, pass. No shots on goal.
No hoofing. Tripping, shirt-tugging. No action in the penalty box.
An unwritten rule. Advance until you achieve a position from
which a shot might, speculatively, be taken, then let the ball go to
the opposition – who will return the favour as soon as they see the
whites of your goalkeeper's eyes. Backwards and forwards, slowly,
then at pace. Up and down. Without a word being said. Without
appeals to an imaginary referee. Without elbows in the windpipe,
shirt tugs, spitting, shin rakes, instep stamps, theatrical collapses, or
any of the sophistications of the English game.

Like manic t'ai chi, Kaporal thought.

'Is time. The café. We find you one hour,' Achmed said.

Time for what? Had he signed up for some mad scheme? Drin and Achmed were good company. They didn't drink. They smoked their own cigarettes. And they had nothing to say. His local research, loosely commissioned by Norton, wasn't advancing. The asylum-seekers didn't really *do* anything. They hung about, on the porch of the Adelphi, taking photos of each other. They walked, in pairs, groups, or alone, through the gardens. They made calls on their mobiles. They looked at the sea. Achmed punted some mad kidnap plot, but that, Kaporal decided, was a misunderstanding. Achmed was giving his version of what he'd seen on TV the previous night, a video. *No Orchids for Miss Blandish*? *The Collector*? *The Black Windmill*?

Snatch a celebrity from the White Queen Theatre – then what? How to transport him? Where to hold him? Who would pay money to get Max Bygraves back? Who would even notice he'd gone awol? The tabs would think it was a stunt, Max Clifford. *News of the Screws* doing one of their agent provocateur numbers, bunging a tame crim. *The Grissom Gang*. *Touch of Evil*. It was always a woman, a woman misappropriated. Baroque, rotten fruit. Armpits. Frying fish. Motel laundry. *The King of Comedy*. Who would be crazy enough to kidnap Jerry Lewis (apart from the French)? Take that doomed Scorsese flick as a warning. We'll all finish up in a dumpbin on London Road. £3.99. No film in the case. No takers.

On London Road, Kaporal found two books. Bookends of a sort. A themed pairing: Paris, bohemia. Between wars. American writers with cheques from home. An English first edition of *A Moveable Feast*, lacking dust-wrapper. Now sitting, boldly, on the table, the blue plastic cloth, alongside the blind daisy.

Kaporal, two inches remaining in his carafe, caught Maria's eye. He hadn't really grasped the concept of the 'all-day breakfast'. He thought it meant that you breakfasted all day.

'Mademoiselle. A *fine à l'eau*. Big brandy, small water.'

She laughed, came over. '*What?*' Touched his arm. Nice quizzical gesture, hand on hip, waiting for the joke to be explained, tossing her hair, glancing over her shoulder to see if the chef, smirking at the kitchen door, was in on it.

'Just a brandy, Maria. Please. And coffee. Black.'

He flicked through the musty pages.

Hemingway on Ford Madox Ford (a neighbour, Winchelsea, Hythe): 'I always held my breath when I was near him in a closed room.'

The guy from the Adelphi smelt good, from three tables distance; Kaporal got the duty-free, the splash of intimate aroma. The clean zone. UnEnglish.

Outside the window, not reading the unchanged menu – pasta pasta pasta – were two men, Achmed and Drin (hair wet, swept back, tango dancer). The other asylum-seeker, when he saw them, jumped up, left a few coins on the table, walked out. Nodding to Achmed, shaking hands with Drin. Gone. As if he had been employed to keep the table, keep the seat warm.

Or maybe, Kaporal thought, the room sliding away, panels of the Aztec mirror offering alternate scenarios, the studious migrant was studying *him*. A watcher. A snoop. A reassigned secret police-man from Tirana. Working for Achmed. Making sure that Kaporal was in place, primed to take on the role offered to him in the coming melodrama, the illegal seizure and forcible sequestration of Max Bygraves. Money with menaces. Ten years minimum. Parkhurst, Durham. The perfect opportunity to get reacquainted with O'Driscoll or Alby Sleeman. A nice double, one up, one down, with the gay psycho (Phil Tock).

The glitzy mirrors, the underoccupied (mid afternoon) res-taurant, indulged Kaporal, let him think of Brassäi, of Robert Doisneau. It was worrying, this inability to take anything on its own terms, treating the south coast like a Monday morning conference at Radio 4, broadsheets on the table. Nothing was, everything was *like*. Referenced, analogous. Parodic. Two men from the Balkans (might be Algerian in the earlier Parisian model) standing in the doorway. One woman, back in the shadows, keeping her own company – *waiting?* – with a canvas bag, camera bag. A woman who came to the pasta place on two or three days a week, always with the bag, always tired – as if she'd been walking the streets all night.

Kaporal remembered the first time he saw her. It was late afternoon, he was a newcomer, a stranger to the restaurant. His arms were overloaded with books. He had received an unexpected royalty cheque from America, a film about plane crashes.

She was waiting. He was waiting. She looked around quietly, appraisingly, but without obvious effort to attract attention. She was discreet and dignified, thoroughly poised and self-contained. He was curious to see who she was waiting for. After a half-hour, during which period he caught her eye a number of times and held it, he made up his mind that she was waiting for anyone who would make the proper sign with the head or the hand and the girl would leave her table and join him.

Kaporal, feeling what he felt then, troubled, hot-necked, legs in (theoretical) plaster of Paris, was quoting piecemeal from the second book he'd picked up on London Road. As you will have recognised. The previous para. A straight steal, twitched from first to third person, Henry Miller's *Quiet Days in Clichy*. Nobody reads Miller. Kaporal could get away with transposing chunks of the old rascal into Bohemia, Hastings.

A good title.

(*Quiet Days in Clichy*. Not *Bohemia, Hastings*.)

There was another bit in the book (green covers, white starburst letters) on surveillance. Stalking. He'd done that too. Which was when he realised that the girl with the shoulder bag was exhausted, not from her night's exertions, but from the train journey, down from London – the standing, the unscheduled (but anticipated) halts. The fear, well-promoted, of terrorist attacks, bugs, gas, bombs.

Coffee, soup. They fixed her up, *before* the walk started. The walk was night. The walk was the mystery.

Once he followed her for a whole afternoon, just to see how she passed the time. It was like following a sleepwalker. All she did was to ramble from one street to another, aimlessly, listlessly, stopping to peer through shop windows, rest on a bench, feed the birds, buy herself a lollypop, stand for minutes on end as if in a trance, then striking out again in the same aimless, listless fashion.

A dark girl, petite. With a sort of Louise Brooks, even Djuna Barnes, hair helmet – Sapphic? Eyelashes. Bright lips, pouty as the mouth of a red balloon.

'You have licence?' Achmed said. As they sat down, Drin and Achmed, one on either side of him. Close.

'Not just now, actually.'

'You drive?'

'Oh sure. Of course. Always have.'

'Theatre show finish ten. You drive car. Drin bring car, big car, the St Margaret, her road. You wait car. Drin and Achmed carry man, singing man. You drive.'

There was no relevant book, no text for this, the absurdity. Achmed meant it. He had leaflets from the White Queen Theatre: Stephen Triffitt *Celebrates* Sinatra; Halfway to Paradise (The Billy Fury Story); Puppetry of the Penis ('Two well-hung Aussies have turned playing with themselves into a hit show . . . A video camera projects every intimate detail of these incredible phenomena onto a large screen, ensuring little can be missed'). And. Highlighted box. Bermondsey's own Superstar, direct from the London Palladium, MAX BYGRAVES. FAREWELL TOUR, FEATURING THE FABULOUS BEVERLEY SISTERS.

He's taken his time about it, Kaporal thought. Old Max must have booked on Connex. He won't show, not in Hastings. It's a wind-up. Like getting a knighthood, if your war record is a bit iffy: you have to be at death's door to be booked by the White Queen. And, anyway, the Albanians will never lift a motor. They stand out in the town. Move away from Warrior Square and the seafront and they'll be tapped, dispersed to Ashford, a plague hospital on Dartford Salt Marshes: shipped out.

Drin, who was staring out of the window, grabbed Achmed's arm. Reaching across Kaporal to do it.

'He come. Mocatta send him. Is good.'

Good move.

The guy with the wheels, going for inconspicuous, had parked halfway across the pavement, right on the double yellows. A fat gull settled on the black roof, challenging the driver to shift him. Nobody would give this vehicle a second glance: in downtown Havana. A 1956 Dodge Coronet, two-tone. (Kaporal had seen the photo in an art book.) A smoke bucket. Delicious with chrome. Hastings cars were notable for their modesty, pre-owned Nissan Primera, Peugeot 309 5DR Saloon (£600 o.n.o.), Ford Fiesta. This thing, in the Old Town, by the shop that did jukeboxes and Jack Lord *Hawaii Five-O* shirts, might get away with it. Exposed here, on the Grand Parade, it was like taking a scarlet bubble car to a gangland funeral in Chingford Mount.

The driver couldn't even lock the door. He dropped his keys and spent five minutes crawling after them. He was totalled. He saw Achmed, through the window, standing up, waving. He ducked back into the car for cigarettes and dark glasses. Then, sniffling perniciously, rolling his shoulders, he made his pizza joint entrance.

Reo Sleeman.

Alby's little brother. The crazy one. The wet dream his old mum scraped from the blanket. *Reo was the reason Kaporal was on the coast.* If he didn't look him in the eye, the Essex boy might not remember. A London face in this setting. Reo was incapable of holding two concepts in his head at the same time. But here he was, on his feet, swaggering. Mocatta's man. With instructions for the hired help, wops, redskins. The traditional wrappers of bodies in tarpaulin.

The seagull.

On the car roof.

A steady gaze. Out of the window. That's best.

Kaporal knew just whose face it had borrowed. Supercilious, sub-aristo. Arsenic pale, awkward. A tourist and a local. The gull was a fugitive soul, a suicide. It might blink at the lowlife – or take off on the wing, swoop over the waves, return to the rock where the gang congregated, melting post-Permian stone with their acrid crap. Beautiful in a way. But trapped in the wrong species, wrong body.

The gull had the face of Virginia Woolf.

Night

Night in the Old Town. Livia couldn't shake off the feeling that she was being followed. In London – not her place – *she* was the follower, in control of the drama. Of her fear. Good fear, edge. She welcomed it. The purlieus of railway stations, parks under tungsten light, tower blocks in dark wildernesses. Queer domestic rituals, human glimpses, against a backdrop of monolithic alienation.

For example: a man asleep, head sunk on chest, in an underground train. Windows like portholes in a submarine.

Dusty curtains, folds on a sepulchre, framing the aperture of another window, half submerged, swallowed by the pavement, in a back alley of the City.

An egg-shaped table-lamp (seen from inside the room). A high window. Diffused light, the nimbus: blue dawn breaking over a railed and frosty garden.

A girl walking through an underpass. Three categories of illumination: wall lights (pearly as crushed aspirin), traffic (red/gold), night at a distance, in the tunnel's mouth.

Trees. Livia loved her trees. City trees. The isolation. Sodium glare on crinkled leaves.

Livia was good, better than her mentor. Better than Jimmy Seed. The photograph, in this case, outperformed (in subtlety, in *heart*) the mechanical intelligence of the artist's hand. Jimmy calculated, measured up, delivered. Livia waited.

Olivia Fairlight-Jones. Aspirational Celtic hyphen. Known to her associates as 'Ollie'. Father dead? According to rumour. Mother wasn't talking. It took Ollie years to tease out the real story. The reason for reverting to (and revising) mother's maiden name. A stepfather with marine-factoring business in Brightlingsea, sold up at the right time. Retirement to Portugal. Ollie also had a husband (acquired and lost at the University of Essex). The photography came later. As did Jimmy. The work as an assistant. Nights clubbing in Dalston and Shoreditch. Information of no great consequence to Livia, she left it out of her gallery biogs: date of birth, list of shows.

But these are the facts that should, in a proper work of fiction, be scattered decorously through the text; revealed, oh so casually, in oblique conversation. By letter, phone call or fax. Engendering necessary suspense, admiration for the technical skill, the discretion, of the author. There should be an element of uncertainty, tease. Let's get it out of the way. Norton, in his narratives, was a premature ejaculator. By conviction.

Know it, tell it. Blabbermouth.

Livia rather fancied doing a Julia Margaret Cameron. In reverse. Giving up photography when she lost her spark, when she was old (around forty) – moving to Sri Lanka. To marry and settle down with a planter (if they still had them), or scholar (Sanskrit, Pali). Children. And trees. Plenty of trees.

Warm thoughts on a cold night. Her visibility, despite the dark, gender-unspecific clothes, heavy boots, coming away from the railway station, was alarming. London didn't care. It was busy, preoccupied, on the edge of breakdown. Once the beggars, and the smiling, excuse-me-do-you-have-a-minute clipboard tarts, the chuggers, had packed it in, bedded down in doorways, the city belonged to anyone who walked it. The coast was a very different proposition, a half-life of tranquillised opportunism, reflex crimes enacted for the benefit of (out-of-service) CCTV cameras.

Glue-sniffers without the energy to sniff.

Scrawny youths who headbutted their way into already vandal-ised cars.

Ram-raiders who hit depressed video outlets. Without the car. And made their getaway with an armful of empty cases.

Coastal lowlife were under no obligation to disguise their inter-est, their fingering of the imaginary weft, the smooth pelt of this fragrant newcomer.

Their prey.

A young woman from elsewhere with a large bag. A bag loaded with readily puntable kit.

Jackal signals. Red eyes in the shadows.

Hastings had a tradition to uphold. Photoshops. Cameras. Racks and racks and racks of rectangular views. Self-regarding images of picturesque beauty. Hastings was the operational base of postcard magnate Fred Judge. And the amateur lensman George Woods. Who, with his unwieldy plate camera and sturdy tripod, did some useful stalking of fisherfolk and excursionists.

Hastings, Ollie recognised, was seductive. Arriving by car or by train, the same sudden hit: light. Shore and sky. Cliffs and steep streets, unexpected angles. Reflections in windows.

With his liking for half-plate negatives, Mr Woods was never less than half conspicuous. He favoured (as a subject) working men, their portraits being taken by somebody else. A local hack. Artisan in a cricket cap. The camera seen by the camera. Dissociation of sensibility.

The prints, unrecognised in Woods's lifetime, established a marine franchise, 'The Cockney Day Out'. Traditions have to be invented. The scenes he captured are the ones that disappear first: a quality in the live/dead faces, nakedness, exposure to that cyclopean eye. *Vulnerability.* As they ignore the monster, unconvinced by its potency. The pathos of this respectable man of business, bearded photographer, Victorian, trousers rolled up, standing in the sea, on a rock – so that he can catch the promenade, the loungers on the beach, the cliffs. Girls who have lifted their skirts to reveal voluminous underpinnings.

Three young ones, wild-haired. You can hear what they're saying. One of them looks at the camera, at Woods. The oldest girl, spotty ribbon on straw boater, is issuing instructions: her tragic spectacles and serious knees. Senior sister or young mother? *Mind your manners. Don't stare.*

At the end of the nineteenth century, as Livia (diligent student) appreciated, it was a very different game. The camera was part of the spectacle: visible apparatus wedged on its prongs, hydrocephalic, fixing time. Fixing: the Occasion. As unique, once-and-forever. The camera artist arranging his actors in poignant tableaux – in which they are invited to impersonate themselves. With heroic awkwardness and dignity. Self-consciously natural, hardly daring to breathe.

In the twilight, Woods walked back home (incomer), wife dead (breast cancer), living with his daughter at Mount Pleasant Road, on the heights above the Old Town. Chapel-going family. No question of a night shoot. Episodes of the afternoon, sun-blessed mornings. Quietly epic representations of the actual (contrived, unforced). The photographer was still a cancelled presence, without irony, no epiphanies, yet, of the instant (lightweight camera attached to head, one-eyed blink).

George Woods, gentleman. Fixed lens. Gleaming brass instrument. Human mass. Crowds going about their business. Which, in Hastings, as he represented it, was pleasure: watching others as they watched hawkers, peddlers, fishwives, performing dogs. As they were helped on and off boats. The black jackets. The hats. The polished boots.

Livia's heel rubbed. Time to kill. She couldn't, far too late, emulate Woods. Her abstractions – nocturnal beach as thread of green running towards black horizon, in which (after minutes of concentrated staring) pinpricks of boats might appear – would have mystified him. She had to hang about, waiting till the drinking schools dispersed, the last bonfire was extinguished. Therefore: she was tracked by naughty boys, cusp hormonals offering to carry the camera satchel. To place their hot, fast twigs in her mouth. Bracken-smelling yobs.

Darkness, which she relished, was tardy; confused by lagoons of artifice, neon, blinking signs, green-and-red spill on wet pavements. Arcades. The yawning mouths of pubs. Tarot and tattoo displays. The pier. It took *hours* for the town to shut down, cool off, decant. And, in that interval, Livia stalled, fumed, wave-watched. Like the others. She was distinguished only by the ferocity of her attention. Eyes burning. An addict of otherness. Connoisseur of the unsayable.

Incident.

Up among the layers and levels – narrow steps, skewed chimney pots, secret gardens, bowed fronts, terraces – Livia saw a hunched figure, early hours of the morning, pushing a funereal contraption the size of Mother Courage's handcart. An ancient (non-antique) perambulator. A thing sitting in it, stiff but alert. A child. An infant. *A doll.*

Livia and the old woman pass. They meet again, in other parts of the town, at different watches of the night. *The doll grows.* The old woman must have a collection, rags for each of them. Routes to walk, never resting. C-shaped spine, warped like driftwood.

This narrative is too baroque. Livia photographs a single lightbulb, unshaded, visible through the thin curtains of a terraced house. Peach-coloured wardrobe. Candlewick bedspread.

Incident.

Drinkers (hypersensitive to the click of cameras) spot her. Invite her to join them, around the fire. They become aggressive, threatening, when she (waving) declines. One man follows her, shouting.

Photograph: blue searchlights casting a pyramid shape on the rounded stern of the Cunard Court flats.

Incident.

The dead hour, two or three in the morning, Livia needs to take a pee, positive discomfort. And, at the same time, feels pangs of hunger. Desire for coffee. Nowhere open. A gay club she doesn't risk. Lurkers around every possible bush or concealed alley. A burger joint in a bad street. Five men upstairs. The toilet, reluctantly ceded, in an unlit basement at the foot of some narrow, rickety stairs. Heart beating. Stairs creak as one – more? – follow her down. To offer a fresh bar of carbolic soap, a clean towel.

Photograph: sodium light reflected in fissure of black limestone rock, its crumbling tobacco-cake texture.

After two months of minor nocturnal excitements, recounted in letters to Track, Livia found the pasta place on the seafront. Made it her base, straight from the train; food when she was flush, coffee; leave some of her equipment with Maria. ''Allo, darlin'.' Avoid the baggy-featured man who stared at her with eyes like a sad walrus.

She didn't dislike him, or worry that he would do anything more than trail after her as she killed time in the late afternoons; she had to avoid dissipating her gaze, getting sidetracked into conversation. If he kept to his own territory, steady drinking, unsteady sexual fantasy, she could live with it. But she would not accept his seeing her seeing, the *sprung* paranoia she needed to achieve, before walking into the night.

Livia did not want, on any account, this arbitrary person with the books and the carafe, to register her with Marina Fountain. She hadn't told Track, she hadn't told anybody, about Marina. How they'd met. In the museum, the gallery. In front of the Keith Baynes seascape, in pastel, *Harbour Scene with Yachts*. Livia had an interest in Baynes. He'd lived in Hastings – St Leonards – in some sea-facing Thirties flats, and then in Warrior Square. Baynes delivered a Francophile panache that set him apart from the rest of the marine painters, the English topographers who liked nothing more, following Turner, than to gaze *inwards*, on shore, fishing boats, parade, cliffs.

Baynes hung out with the very louche Edward Burra, at Rye, picnics in the Rolls, sailor boys in striped vests. He was known to the Charleston mob, the Bloomsbury home-decorators and pond sculptors (prophetic of TV makeovers of the New Millennium, farmhouse furniture ruined with sticky things, stencils, daubs). Duncan Grant, Vanessa Bell. White-skinned naturists, readers in deckchairs. Bored literary celebrities between mistresses or boy-friends. Sneezing, under the South Downs, in dappled sunlight.

As life folded in on him, decrepitude, neglect, Baynes moved away from that vision of the sea, too much, too bright; he retreated to a cluttered room above the public gardens. No more of those heartbreaking recapitulations, *View from My Window*. Remedial. Convalescent. Gay. Forlorn. Signalling breakdown (like David Jones in Shoreham). Damaged Brits holed up at the seaside. Three panels of a window. A comfortable chair with three cushions. Yachts like clown caps. *No middle distance*. For Keith Baynes, there was never anything between here and there: a frieze, dance, a lively notation of the inessential, the debris of visual delight. He had money, private means, enough. A bottle under the bed. A window.

The charity shops of St Leonards had been good to Marina. The district specialised in them. Livia was dazzled, remarked on it, by how well the coast suited the older woman, bright eyes, clear skin, colour in the cheeks. Her outfit, blind-selected as ever, worked; pillbox hat (rudimentary veil), ice-cream-pink duffel coat, black boho turtleneck, very short blue-black suede skirt, green stockings, crumpled red boots. The wardrobe, listed, reads like a menu of alternatives for an Albanian sex slave in a Finsbury Park massage parlour. In the flesh, the woody quiet of the Hastings Museum, it played.

'Lovely rings,' Livia said.

On Marina's long thin fingers, her thumb. Scarabs and twisted silver bands. Native American blue (the eyes of Lee Marvin). Coral. But her hands betrayed her, freckles and small brown stains.

'Is that Estuary gangster still bothering you?'

'It's over,' Livia said. 'Haven't seen Reo in yonks. He doesn't know I'm down here. He's not looking.'

Her fingers, teasing the new fringe, gave it away.

'Get rid, Ollie. Don't fall for that sick-puppy routine. Reo's trouble.'

Livia rubbed her Adam's apple with a knuckled fist.

'It's finished, truly.'

She hadn't thought about Reo until Marina brought him back. He didn't matter. At a safe distance, he was a not-unpleasant memory: hurt boy, hard boy. Someone to rescue. Someone who said that he would die without her. Someone who lived through his indifference for the world: nothing touched him. Except Livia. His obsession. The way he saw her as a sister spirit. Incest and revenge. His dopey Egyptian mythology: reincarnation, animal familiars, terrible music. Love me or kill me. A double suicide, Mishima. Bent narcissism, bent history: straight to video.

'I see why. Why you tried him,' Marina said, 'but, now . . .'

'Well, what about *you*?' Livia came back. 'What about you

and Hastings? I can't get my head around it. Track doesn't . . . I
haven't . . .'

'I've found the room.'

Marina took Ollie's arm, guiding her.

'The room where Baynes painted his *View from My Window*. I
want you to make some tests, photographs. And one other thing, it's
important. Tell me honestly . . . did you get my manuscript to Norton?'

'Track. I'm sure. She *must* have. Track had it. She understood.
Track's good at those things.'

It was agreed. They met, early, for breakfast, long before Kaporal
surfaced, at the pasta place.

Marina had acquired – sublet, borrowed, bought – a flat in
Cunard Court, a Thirties (De La Warr Pavilion era) block that
looked like a beached ocean liner. At whatever time Livia pressed
the buzzer on the voicebox, struggled with the doors on the
old-fashioned lift, walked down that weirdly familiar carpet, the
block was deserted. A nautical remake of *The Shining*. Glimpses of
revenants, tourist class, on a ghost ship.

Marina, cigarette in hand, waited to greet her, to shepherd her
past the flat filled with pigeons, pigeon dirt, needles and spills of
tightly rolled newspaper.

They worked their way – borrowed pass key, charm applied to
the old folk – through layer after layer of this crumbling cake;
corridor by corridor, room by room. Seventy-six checked, 209 to
go. Very *close*, no goldfish. Nothing fitted – precisely – the Keith
Baynes transcription.

And what, Livia wondered, would happen when it did? What
then? Her print, whichever lens she opted for, however she messed
around in the darkroom, could never replicate Baynes's painting.
There was no way of gouging out the middle ground, the space
between camera and seascape. Vertigo and nausea always rushed
in to fill the gap. The flats with their geriatric accretions, family
snaps in silver frames, hothouse temperatures, phantom dogs (no
pets allowed), left her dizzy.

Marina was merciless. When photograph fitted over painting,

like a Venetian carnival mask, she would step through. Into that space-time anomaly. The bit Baynes was so careful to leave out, the foreshortened *something*, between observer and horizon. That mysterious lacuna (the pictorial equivalent of the John Major premiership).

She made it, ahead of her watcher, the man with the books, to her table near the bar (the kitchen, the coat-rack). Now she was comfortable, being here, being alone. She glanced sideways, profile in the mirror, good, lips glossed, hair holding, and surprised herself. She was *waiting* for the man in black, the one with too much skin; flesh folding like rubber – his reflex attempts, slapstick, to iron out the creases, erase experience, touch solidity beneath sag, a fading memory of cheekbones.

'Has he been in?' she asked Marina.

'Today, no. Maybe later.'

I am nothing like those women in Paris, she thought. Jean Rhys, was it? The drama of being misused, spurned (they solicited it), abandoned. In this place, at this time, Ollie was perfectly at ease. Ready, almost, for the flirtation with her lugubrious admirer. A reversal, as she saw it, of the Jean Rhys/Ford Madox Ford story: older man (shell-shocked), frayed beauty, an affair, abortion – a narrative told from both sides. A true fiction. Publish your revenge. The long, woozy aftermath of poverty excesses and provincial exile. *See what you've done to me.*

He was there. In his usual spot. Eating her in the mirror. Getting quietly sozzled. She touched the rough canvas of the camera bag, stroked it. The man would make a good portrait – if she did portraits. But her technique was based on self-denial. Immerse yourself in floating matter – drunk man reading book, melancholy asylum-seeker at round table, tired waitress, photographer on run from unsatisfactory lover – and take it somewhere else: night town. The steps. The pattern of the tiled roofs. The panoramic window of the fishermen's club as seen from the beach. Plastic swans, shrouded, on the paddling pool.

Drama: the unexpected entrance of two exotic aliens in leather jackets. Nice-looking boys, fit. *They know the bookman.* They sit with him. He's nervous. He won't be able to make his move, his unsubtle (gently spurned) advance on the girl photographer with the Louise Brooks fringe. They're behaving like pimps. They warn the older man off. They notice her, admire her. Who is this beauty?

A car pulls up. An American car. So this is just another of Livia's tales, her adventures at the seaside? She wished, so much, that she smoked, that she was wearing something more suitable. Collar turned up. Dark glasses: like the man. Very mean and hungry, slightly crazy. Coming straight at her. Brushing past the Adelphi Hotel boys, pushing one of them aside. Yelling, furious. A madman. Mad for her. One glimpse and he's done for. She has him skewered. He'll kill for a single glance. The woman of his dreams.

'Get in the fucking motor, babe,' Reo said. 'We're going home.'

Fenchurch Street

She was wrong, completely wrong – the Fountain woman – about Fenchurch Street Station. Clean. Spacious. Departure notices visible. Trains to the Estuary, Grays, Tilbury Town, Shoeburyness, every few minutes. Even the light (filtered through glass, bounced from white stone) was nicely managed, abundant. There was, this premature spring morning, no embargo on clarity: razor-cut shadows, splintered beams through mean windows.

A lull in our argument with the city. This, I thought, is how it should be. A fiver for a return to Rainham? They were giving it away. The track, like a ladder of ice, rushed towards Limehouse; churches, warehouses, pre-war office blocks with quirky detail, Art Deco fans, orchestrated symmetries.

I basked. I gorged on it, the suspension of hostilities. The non-arrival of my pal Joey. Joey Silverstein. Joey the Jumper. With his babble, his yap. Gnawed fingernails. Yellow fingers cupped, clawed, leaking smoke. Joey was my guide into Rainham, the Jewish Cemetery. He was taking me to the grave of a legendary urban character, David Litvinoff. Gambler, wit, 'lowlife conduit' to James Fox, Donald Cammell, Mick Jagger (and the rest of the *Performance* team), Litvinoff ghosted the transit between Whitechapel and Chelsea, appearance and disappearance, celebrity and crime. He left two things behind when he killed himself (across the river): a shoebox of reel-to-reel tapes (drunken improvisations, midnight rambles, quality jazz) and a memory stain. A diminishing band of friends and lovers, acquaintances and dupes, ageing relatives who couldn't forget him, met to talk through his mischief, his stunts. The hurt. Wilting snaphots slide sideways into the underbelly of the culture (Ian McShane in *Villain*); a man with his head shaved, throat slashed, suspended from a window in Kensington. Marchers on the street

(Vietnam, CND, legalise dope), banners and whistles, they don't look up. Nobody notices. It doesn't register. In the margin of every great public event, some poor sod is catching it, sight unseen, a bullet in the teeth.

I'd been tracking the Litvinoff story since 1975, the year that he died. Every lead a cul-de-sac. Every witness removed to Australia, South Africa, Golders Green Crematorium. The waters muddied by second-generation stalkers, media-studies victims with Sony MD Walkmans. They thought they could do it all on the phone, the net, in a couple of weeks: anti-scholars saturated in 'genre issues, core components and dialectic exchanges'. The height of their ambition, 500 words, in a slack month, in *Sight and Sound*.

The good thing about Joey, you could always rely on him: to be late. Time out, hard won, is golden. The worse the night, the better the morning's walk. Run it backwards. I touched the dog. I lumbered across the road – twitching from traffic that wasn't there – to press my hand between the sharp brass ears of the wolf at Aldgate Pump. Begin again, another excursion down the A13 – but, this time, by train; following the fictional paradigm – I can do media studies too – of Marina Fountain's Conradian vampire tale. Fountain had been snacking, it was evident, on her namesake, the other Marina, Warner: freelance scholar, novelist, collector of folk tales, Visiting Fellow Commoner at Trinity College, Cambridge. Warner mainlined lamias and succubi, Keatsian narcoleptics, sleepwalkers with inadequate nightwear:

> The Lamia, Emblem strong of Sin,
> Does all her Charms employ;
> To draw the unwary Trav'ller in,
> And then the Wretch destroy.

The Aldgate wolf was stressed today, by the absence of aggravation; it strained to break free from its stone trap. Some political chicanery with hyper-surveillance, invisible barriers, congestion charges, had emptied the streets, returned them to a period when it wasn't compulsory to run a car. My walk from Hackney was unnerving: sun disk pulsing behind cloud, a hoop of bright beams, cold squeezing the lung. A silver sun (over Haggerston Park) duplicated the aureole of the inoperative brass nipple that floated above and between the wolf's ears at Aldgate Pump: 'press here' for water that no longer gushes from the open mouth. The pattern of flaws in the stone, rust marks, removed iron, sets an agenda for the territory I want to explore. Maps made by accident are the only ones to trust: no agenda, no special pleading, no obligation to show anything that doesn't matter.

Morning shadows in Brick Lane shaped right-angled triangles: across Rodinsky's loft in Princelet Street, across the marbled slabs in the premises of A. Elfes, monumental mason. An alphabet of symbols that might be withdrawn in an instant. A confirmation that this was the right day to be on a train.

I went out into the garden, frosty, sharp underfoot. A full moon. I couldn't pretend to sleep. Even if you don't watch television, it leaks: it watches you. In pubs, minicab offices, Chinese takeaways. Through the windows of tower blocks. From the bedrooms and kitchens of railway cottages in West Ham, visible from the c2c train. This necklace of not-quite-simultaneous imagery: fear. Even if you avoid newsprint, its gets onto your skin. Pithy summaries on boards outside newsagents' shops: LONDON THREAT ON SCALE OF SEPT 11. BLAIR FURY AT PEACE MARCH.

Yellow tin and carpets of celluloid flowers.

MURDER. A MURDER OCCURRED AT THE FOOT-PATH BETWEEN THE FLOWER GARDEN AND THE CHILDREN'S PLAYGROUND. DID YOU SEE OR HEAR ANYTHING?

Helicopters. Sirens. Car doors. Arguments. Slaps. Screams in the night. It leaks leaks leaks.

I shut my eyes and see a river of cars, stalled. Tanks surrounding airports. Runways on marshland. Drills, earthmovers, pile-drivers under flyovers. Mountains of landfill. But that's not it. That's commonplace, nuisance. All sentient beings live with inconvenience, irritation, sudden death (for the few, the others). The nightfear I suffered was more personal (it carried on through the day): someone was stealing my material, ahead of me at every turn, subverting my wives. He impersonated me with a flair I couldn't hope to equal, this thief. Trickster. And he was bringing criticism down on my head – for being what I was. Played out, hackneyed (in every sense); editors couldn't stifle a yawn. Feisty young women peddled appalling rumours (no matter if they were true).

Then the phone rang. When my defences were down, blood sugar at its lowest level. Ruth? In trouble? Hannah wanting to clarify a year-old argument? Did I say what she thought I said she said and did I mean it – *still*?

'Hey, man. Listen, right. You stitched me up, man.'

Joey.

That was one of his standard 2 a.m. riffs (but not this time). Drug paranoia, the lack of it, kicking in. Joey Silverstein was one of the resources of London, omnipresent, ever-moving, edge of the frame, out of focus: longish hair (a year or two after it went out of fashion), good clothes, proper cut (borrowed, gifted by a friend). The story. The word. *Hot*. Gossip. He'd read everything, seen all the films. *Monster, monster*. He never bought a newspaper, but always knew what was in them. You couldn't slip a reference to Joey into a book of poems, vanity-published in an edition of three copies in Finland. He'd be straight onto it, onto you.

'Listen, man. I was *really* hurt . . .'

His eyes. They showed the hurt, his age, the years on the clock. Otherwise: he was twenty-two. For the duration. Along with his handsome partner, Patsy. Swooping on markets, working the margins, at the party. A chipped glamour. Collars up, lipstick tidemark on American cigarettes. Peake, Punk, Portillo: Joey was there. The new in *New Worlds*, the young in *The Young Ones*. And he'd been playing it for thirty years. Production offices, fashionable clinics, scandal for gift and never for sale: Joey the Jumper. Wired. The conduit to the conduit.

'Let's do a walk, man.'

That's how Joey signed off. It didn't mean a thing.

'Couple of weeks, right? I'll give you a call.'

Sometimes it happened. Once every six or seven years. Smithfield. Spitalfields. Fleet Street. Anywhere with coffee stops (regular hits of sugar). Bookshops, monuments. A story. London was a spoken autobiography, told in fragments. 'That guy in the café, my dad. You'll have to meet him next time.'

Next time was now. Joey didn't deal in anything further ahead than three days: which was when he wanted to meet me at Fenchurch Street. I was honoured. He knew somehow, before I'd worked out the details, that I was attempting a book on the A13. We'd discussed David Litvinoff for decades, the scams, the stunts with the tramp Pinter used as a model for *The Caretaker*, the trips to the country. Now, out of nowhere, Joey was offering to take me to the grave. In Rainham.

Rainham. The marshes. The definitive middle distance between human and non-human landfill. The better life promised for slum-dwelling East Enders. The industrial dereliction visited on ancient riverside villages. I knew the car park, behind the railway station, the villains who used it as a convenient meeting ground: fabulous sightlines, roads spilling off in every direction. I remembered the threats some of them made, if I ever went back.

There's no copyright on paranoia: where is Joey? Fenchurch Street Station was too good to be true, it was a set, an advertising shoot for Railtrack. Joey had been webbed up with music-business hustlers, pill-peddlers – wouldn't he have come across the Sleemans? Mocatta owned a recording studio in Harrow Road. Joey probably owed him, favours for favours. Why, suddenly, out of the blue, in the early hours of the morning, would he suggest a trip to Rainham? Mickey O'Driscoll's favoured disposal ground, black bags on the marshes, heads in ponds. It was on the news, it must be true, they'd just found a man without hands in a park in Dagenham.

Where was Joey? Had he bottled it?

The only other clients of c2c were French businessmen – trying to check out sites for a new Disneyland? They had complicated requests for the ticket-peddlers. Who ignored them. As improperly languaged and therefore invisible. There were no women of mystery on the concourse (Conradian commentaries in their hand luggage). No one-way vampires for Grays.

Up the long steps, head bobbing like a cork in a stream of piss, comes Joey. In a trilby, a belted tweed coat. Looking more mature, certainly, but frisky, alive; gesturing, spotting me, suppressed wave, other hand in pocket. That classic London noir swagger (a torpedo out of *The Lowlife*): old Whitechapel, Middlesex Street, fast talking, fast thinking, dancing feet. Impossible to buy a suit or coat (postmortem) from one of these boys: wrong size. Broad in shoulder, narrow hips, no legs. Generations of humping sacks, in warehouses and wharfs, do that. Try a jacket, nice cloth, nice cut, and your hands won't reach halfway down the sleeves. Short-armed, long-headed Scots, lousy teeth (poor diet), can't aspire to Cockney schmutter. Even if they can wriggle into it, wrap it around them, it looks like fancy dress.

Joey in a hat?

Maybe it was a religious thing, for the cemetery. I knew a bit about that, I had a tribute for Litvinoff in my pocket, a black, limestone pebble. I wouldn't embarrass myself like that television arts presenter who swept the debris from Chagall's grave, complaining about the scandalous state in which it was kept. Kicking small stones, the marks of respect. Astonishing behaviour from a man of culture, a Jew (by inheritance and blood).

'Sorry, son,' the latecomer said, 'Joey couldn't make it. Got the tickets? Liberty what they charge. Any chance of a cuppa. I'm done in.'

Snip Silverstein, the dad. They were like brothers, these two, father and son. There were moments when light drained from their eyes, then back, at a rush, to language. The sustaining force: memory.

'Joey's not well.'

Not well? Joey was never what you'd call 'well'. Sniffles, smoker's throat, lip sores, scars on the backs of his hands, it didn't stop him. He should have been dead years ago, the energy he expended, the company he kept: the man was a promo for staying outside the system, unregistered, ex-directory, no library cards. If you're wounded, walk. Joey, bunged to the eyeballs with viruses, public transport, crowds, kisses, needles, blood exchange, was immune to everything.

'Heart.'

Impossible. Joey's vessel was a leather pump. 'All heart,' the boys in the caff said. 'That Joey, all heart. A diamond. Give you the shirt off his back.' They meant: emotion. Rucks. Embraces. Tears at bedtime. Recollections, fondly delivered, of those known but currently inactive, out of circulation: Derek Raymond, Alexander Baron, Gerald Kersh – and, always, back to him, David Litvinoff (unpublished and therefore unfixed).

Joey had been sauntering down the Embankment, between bridges, this meet and that, so Snip reported, when he felt a bit dicky. Like his tongue, all of a sudden, was too big for his mouth. Jumped a bus. Some schwartzer kid was kicking off, screaming. Did his head in. High Street Ken, he got off, stumbled into a bank, Jock bank, Bank of Scotland. 'Sit down. Loosen your tie. Have a toffee.'

Joey wakes up in intensive care.

'Last time we was in 'orspital together, we was lifting a bottle to Joey's mate, David. The scars on him, my life. Remember that little coloured girl, the nurse? I said to Joey, "If she only knew, right son? What you're thinking." He blushed. First time I seen it, red as the flag. Showing 'im up in front of David.'

The best of London: running away from it. Comfortable seats and a woman's voice (recorded) to let us know the names of the halts, ahead of time. Snip dozed, hat over eyes. I spread Danny the Dowser's notes, his A13 retrievals, across the table. Before West Ham, it was like a drowning man's dream: my previous lives flicking past in a pale procession. The wilderness of Tower Hamlets Cemetery where I used to take my sandwiches when I worked for the Parks Department. There was a new (to me) chalk maze laid out on a grassy knoll. Then came the islet of poplar and willow in the muddy reaches of Channelsea Creek, near Three Mills, among the gas holders and sewage beds. The site was mythic, soliciting Tarkovsky (the Zone), or standing in for Bergman's Fårö. But getting instead the 'Big Brother' concentration camp with its perimeter fence and thicket of CCTV cameras.

Danny had nothing much to say about Plaistow and West Ham. Dagenham aroused him. Dagenham and Rainham were remote villages, fisherfolk and esturine pirates settling on a gravel shelf, above the mudline, the fluvial slop. Chalk behind them, into which they burrowed. Lime kilns on the shore. Twin creeks exploited: the Beam at Dagenham and the Ingrebourne at Rainham. Bucolic survivalism, pigs and fertility rituals, to pass the time before Henry Ford took over and colonised the entire land-scape. Detroit-on-Thames: rolling mills, dock, railway, major league pollution.

Dagenham: birthplace of Sir Alf Ramsey, Terry Venables, and the Dagenham Girl Pipers (Congregationalists, unsullied). See them march (courtesy of Danny's video grab) through the Becontree Housing Estate (*c.* 1932), in formation, cold knees lifted in perfect synchronicity on a damp Essex morning. Like a Highland regiment in drag – lipstick, aggressively bobbed and permed, stamping off to repel the invading Fascist hordes.

The parents of Byronic (club-footed) entertainer Dudley Moore were the very first tenants of 14 Monmouth Road, near Parsloes Park. They had been willingly exiled to England's fastest-growing estate (precursor of Thames Gateway). Diseased slum to pro-duction-line Arcadia. Your own garden, broad pavements, easy access to Hainault Forest. Downtown Dagenham: childhood refuge of barefoot chanteuse, Sandie Shaw. *There's always something there to remind me.* (Thanks, Danny.)

What is it with Dagenham and feet? Danny's file carried a

report from another Norton (A.M.), no relative, into a previously undocumented episode in the life of David Rodinsky (again again). This hack had got hold of Rodinsky's *London A–Z* and walked over the feebly marked path through Dagenham. According to Norton, the town was almost entirely populated by hobblers, persons in invalid carriages (silent, deadly). Maybe that was part of the employment package, smashed feet meant more cars.

Everybody in Dagenham seemed to be on sticks, in electrified carts, padding down broad avenues in carpet slippers. The whole district was a homage to the car. Not as a method of transport, but as museum-quality relics. They parked, like votive shrines, along the pavements. Even mangled wrecks were lovingly preserved.

But this, apparently, was young Rodinsky's Purgatory, his expulsion from Whitechapel. Sent into care, mother incapable, into old-village / new-estate limbo, he never forgot the childhood episode and traced his autobiographical routes onto a pulp-paper map. He made Dagenham a mystery. And Norton (the other one, the literary vampire) dogged his footsteps. Which led to a museum, Valence House, and a primitive artefact. (Photo enclosed.)

Here I discovered, among the portraits of the Fanshawes and the period rooms, a dark wooden figure, which I elected as my spiritual guide. It had been found in the marshes in 1922 and was known as 'The Dagenham Idol'. It looked African, armless, with asymmetrical peg legs and a large, paddle-shaped head with deeply indented eye-sockets. It was thought to date from somewhere between 2350 and 2140 BC. The thin, diseased legs, good for hopping or punting on a stout stick, proved the authenticity of this figure: the primal Dagenham limper, the ur-gimp.

The three A13 tower blocks with the pink stripes, previously logged from Beckton Alp, are now seen at speed from the train: across colour-coded warehouses, railway sidings, thorn bushes, yellow hoists. Focus softens. Reflections of Snip, head bowed, mouth agape, on the dirty glass (etched with spirals of obscenity, an aerial view of the Bishopsgate Ice Rink).

DAGENHAM STAMPING OPERATIONS. The visible stink of harsh dyes and chemicals, money in the vat. Dagenham: world capital of asthma. Rhone Poulenc Rorer: identified by a 1999 television report as the principal agent of air pollution in the Estuary. The price of prosperity. TIME ENGINEERS.

Snip snores gently, mutters in his sleep. 'It's what Joey wanted.'

Rodinsky's *A–Z* expedition circumnavigated the borough, a beating of the bounds. He took in a school, Valence Park, and a march right down the centre of the A13 (Barking By-Pass). He even looped south to pay his respects to the oval of the 'Greyhound Race Track' and 'Fords Motor Works'. The seven wonders. Sights seen and noted in red ink, Rodinsky never again travelled so far east (he didn't make it to Southend). He returned to Princelet Street and stayed put – until they removed him to the hospital in Epsom.

Snip was a very different case. More like the gangsters and knocker boys of the Sixties, taking advantage of cheap petrol and a developing motorway system, he travelled the country. A widow in Newcastle, a lady from Boots the Chemist in Morecambe. He worked as a stagehand in Liverpool, a tout in Brighton. And he played the horses, dogs, cards.

He deserved a day out. I'd stand him a proper breakfast when we got to Rainham.

The woman's reassuring voice announces it: next stop. I shake Snip, gently. 'Right then, son. Lovely.'

The train's gone. The cold grabs us. A landscape to die for: haze lifting to a high clear morning, pylons, distant road, an escarpment of multicoloured containers, a magical blend of nature and artifice, greed and altruism. Bugger Conrad, Rainham is one of the bright places of the earth. Comfortable beside the Thames, between river and forest. And soon to disappear for ever down the black hole of the Channel Tunnel Rail Link. Struck from the map.

Rainham

Provoking Snip's visible irritation – 'brass bleedin' monkeys' – I climb the railway bridge: marshland divided by the new A13 relief road (old road banished to Purfleet, oil tanks, travellers and their horses). Away to the south, winter sunlight bounces from a swift river. To the north, the remnant of a lost Essex village: Norman church, regularly proportioned Georgian hall, several pubs, Thames tributary (the downgraded Ingrebourne). Quite enough to get us moving.

Snip is already moving, leg to leg.

'I'm busting for a jimmy, son. Any facilities on this poxy platform?'

Enough, I'd say, to launch a raft of essays about . . . borders, the middle ground. I'm revived, revitalised. That's all it takes, a new spread. Virgin turf. The A13 book will write itself; start snapping, Norton, get your camera out. And don't forget the car park: no cars (no commuters), rattle of trains, heavy plant, quarrying, yarns about villains.

Rainham Station car park is much more threatening (less obvious), as a site for mayhem, drug deals, porn shoots, than the urban multistorey. (Acceptable in *Get Carter*, done to death by TV cop shows. By the time the multistorey reaches the Mitchell brothers and *EastEnders*, sack the location scouts.) There is an *implied* risk in wide skies, undefined criminous business occurring at the horizon, the flick of constant traffic: no vertical humans, no voices. It's like that moment in film noir when German Expressionist interiors, tilted sets, give way to apparently innocent Californian landscapes: *Out of the Past*. The filling station and the breakfast bar come into their own. If nothing else is happening, a man will drive slowly into town and hit you with a back story: fate. Malefic as the kiss of syphilis at a high-school hop.

Talk about location scouts. Danny's file has a beauty, a photograph of a resting motorist: Captain Amies, land agent. Rainham, back then (early Twenties), was like the Wild West, frontier country; unexploited, inhabited by inbreeds whose ambition, after uncounted millennia, had allowed them to bellycrawl twenty yards out of the river mud. Amies, who must have served in the First War and lived to bring his traumas home, had the perfect job: scouting the middle ground, the gap between what was known (London, dirt, people-stink) and hazy distance (Turner's atmospherics, his showy skies). The London County Council commissioned the captain to cruise the lanes and farm tracks and river roads of the back country: genial fellow, military title, in search of, so it appeared, the perfect pub.

I don't know anything about cars, but this one looks very much like a Model T Ford; spare tyre (necessary) clipped to driver's door, canvas roof, detachable headlamps and a very impressive horn (scare the cows).

Prairie, cropped grass, a fence. And, almost lost in the distance, the silhouette of – what? The Belvedere Generating Station across the river on Erith Marshes? The captain is *placed*. He has been given a specific brief: find the right location for the Becontree Housing Estate.

This gentlemanly occupation, from those post-war years, has now devolved to artists like Jimmy Seed. Get out there. Take your snaps and bring them back to town. Jimmy reworks, recreates (cleans up) Dagenham, West Thurrock, the QEII Bridge, hypermarkets, fast-food joints, cinemas. He puts down a marker. When they exist, to his satisfaction, in the studio, they're done with: sell the painting (to America, to be stored in a barn in the Midwest), knock down the redundant actuality.

On other occasions, Captain Amies (pipe and trilby) was accompanied by his young son – and a photographer. Don't, please, think *Paper Moon*: pastiche, sentiment, Ryan and Tatum. Amies had no truck with any of that; he was still in uniform, dark suit, high collar, shoes like a shaving mirror. He poses, as if under orders to reveal nothing beyond name and rank, in the doorway of a clapboard Dagenham farm, alongside his tiny other rank (school cap, bare knees, sandals). This lad, a future favourite of the royals, also picked up a title: Sir Hardy Amies, Novocaine-lipped couturier.

At the end of the platform was a long mirror, like Dr Jekyll's cheval glass. Disturbing: twin panels. Mirror offering the view back down the platform (no Snip, he doesn't register) and the diminishing perspective of the long straight railtracks. Backwards and forwards, past and future. Seamlessly joined in my snapshot (I hoped the flash wouldn't blow the effect).

Snip was no vampire. The reason he didn't show up on the screen soon became evident: he'd ducked into the Gents. A long-term victim of the eroded social amenities of London, I'd forgotten such things existed. I had to experience this, the cold-weather micturation, when you fear for that merciless final spurt, after the shaking, and the folding back, the fiddling with buttons.

'Will you fuck me in front of Her?'

Graffito. The final pronoun capitalised as in the Francophile novel by San Francisco poet and publisher, Lawrence Ferlinghetti. This tease was not a literary *hommage*, inscribed by some ageing downriver beatnik. It was a direct question, a philosophical challenge.

The conjured scenario pricked me: which *her*? Until, ticket barriers navigated, down the steps, stride for stride with Snip, the gender of the actors in this erotic dramaticule became clear. Penned in the Gents, the artist was advocating male-on-male action: as a provocation, a way of neutralising female potency. Enforced voyeurism was not the game: trashing mum. I would ring Hannah, or stop off at the Travelodge on my way back, talk it out. The statement. And my reaction to it. Her reaction to both the tale and my telling of it.

Now there was heat in our walk. Rainham was classically English: closed for the duration.

A church: THE CHURCH PATH IS NOT A PUBLIC RIGHT OF WAY.

A hall: NO WC. CURRENT TENANT HAS DOG.

Shops. COLD BLOODED: SPECIALISTS IN BREEDING REPTILES, AMPHIBIANS & INVERTEBRATES. A pointless franchise. Rainham was over-subscribed in invertebrates, swampcreeps, folk who delighted in telling you to leave town.

Always optimistic, I tried the library. The hall opens when it wants to, by appointment, for card-carrying members of the National Trust: a leaflet might be found. There is a mulberry tree. A Victorian dog kennel, bigger than a terraced cottage in Bethnal Green, for the Dalmatian pack. An upwardly mobile grifter called John Harle dredged the Ingrebourne, shipped coals from Newcastle, and founded 'Rayneham Wharfe'. Thereby importing the signature 'e' that would prove so useful in heritaging the precinct of future shoppes – and predicting the career curve of chemical entrepreneurs like Mickey O'Discroll and the Sleemans. Harle's barges were ballasted with marble, iron, clinker, Delft. He married a wealthy Stepney widow.

Nothing else happened, until Harle's second son was horsewhipped in the back parlour, by his father-in-law, for the crime of associating with 'newfangled Methodists'. The line, unsurprisingly, died out. Leaving the house as a fretful ghost, occupied by invisibles, unheard melodies.

'Church?'

An old biddy in a rubber bathing-cap butts in. 'Once a week – if you're lucky. They have to lock the door on the cleaners. Kids round here. Give 'em two minutes and they'll smash the place, altar cloth, Easter display, piss in the font.'

Snip's belly was grumbling, but he wouldn't stop until we'd left the village bit, the original settlement, behind. He hammered, at a pace I struggled to match, down Upminster Road. The mounds behind the kiddies' playpark were neolithic; the ribbon development was more recent, speculative Tudorbethan chalets (Epping Forest pargeting), black horses' heads on gateposts. This was a notable example of social polyfilling, Essex's own Bermuda Triangle (Ingrebourne, A13 and M25). More khaki belt than green. Teasing glimpses of marshland in gaps between customised housing units, parks and cemeteries. Fields, if you spot them, are horribly naked, ironically named: THAMES CHASE. Hedgerow Improvement by Tarmac Quarry Products. Dust in the air, your mouth, your clothes.

We need a rinse of tea, something to line the stomach, before we plod on to the enclosure (end of the end), where they stack the banished Jews: the voices of London.

Upminster Road, like *The Godfather*, comes in two parts: South and North. (*Godfather III*, the Vatican opera, Robert Duvall holding out for more money, doesn't count. It's the equivalent of Rainham's Warwick Lane, a pointless third act, a trek through a land without soul or spirit. *Mistah Kurtz – he dead*. We can't afford him. When a performer of Brando's bulk rolls out of a project, you lose a lot of bathwater. Drowned land. Rich black alluvium. Three men dicing for rags: Eliot quoting Conrad, Coppola quoting Eliot and stealing from Conrad. Conrad, at the road's edge, in Stanford-le-Hope, anticipating both of them. A wall of skulls.)

'See that. I knew we should wait.'

Irritated by my (silent) cultural ramblings, gurglings of colonialism and prejudice, religion and representation (every high street a thunder of dialectics), Snip spurted. On elfin feet. Pulled ahead, tried to find where he was, who he was, what he was doing: rested, panting. Hand on hip. I loped, slowly, steadily, at a slight tilt (right leg shorter than left), came alongside him, moved ahead. Until he scuttled, crabbed, shot forward like an invalid carriage with automatic gears.

'*There*. Large as life. I'm no mug.'

A dark-blue awning proving the theory that if you persist in your folly you will be rewarded: BAGELS. Fresh filled bagels, sandwiches, rolls. Try our delicious salt beef.

'We're on,' Snip shouted, 'your treat.'

*

At the point where Upminster Road gives up its ambition – it knows it's never going to make it to the end of the underground railway (end of civilisation) – the pale green of the District Line leaks into the landscape. Fields marked out for development. Lighting poles beyond the last hedge.

On the west side of London, film studios occupied the villages, woods; safe and convenient country, just beyond the orbital motorway. Thespians, economic immigrants, exiles from Hitler's empire: the charcoal-burners of old. Encampments of millionaire gypsies in autumnal Pinewood. Borrowed country houses in which they trained you for the drop into occupied France (codes invented by Leo Marks, writer of *Peeping Tom*).

The north: asylums, madhouses, Italianate water towers.

And, to the east, where we find ourselves, a loop from Rainham to Waltham Abbey: cemeteries. Christian (backed by florists and monumental masons, displays of statuary, garden centres). Muslim, under the pylons, screened by the reservoir. Then, alongside the gravel pits, the Jews. Grey, white. Like seagulls on landfill. Memorial stones.

'He was a character, your David. Good to Joey, fond of the boy. I never come to the funeral.'

SLOW.

Large white letters. Pink tarmac like a welcome mat. The road narrows. A grand arch. A sort of municipal, red-brick Temple Bar. As we walk in, Snip, stumbling, takes my arm.

'Did him a trim, just the once. Well-set-up man, David. Lovely shoes, handmade. Mouth on him. Soft but sarky. "Snip," he says, "if you could cut hair as well as you rabbit, I'd let you loose on my poodle." Schneide bastard, lippy. Like a father to Joey.'

Thousands of white graves in an Essex field. Rules laid out for prayers to be said if you haven't visited a cemetery in the last thirty days. Hebrew. A chapel with offices. One of the gardeners, local boy in baseball cap, very decent, goes through the ledgers, the deathlists.

'What year did he pass over?'

Snip can't remember. *Performance* was released in 1970, but they had it sitting in the cans, cutting and recutting, for a few years. Litvinoff was still on the scene at that time. He had a biography of Lenny Bruce 'in development', commissioned and paid for. Never delivered. Never begun. There are photographs of him, quite dapper, down in the country.

'Mid Seventies?'

The gardener is willing. The office is too hot: Snip mopping his brow. I'm not sure if I have to keep my cap on at all times. A scorched smell, burnt feathers. The hiss of calor gas.

I think of the posh kid – Harrow? – James Fox, getting his mouth round David Litvinoff's dialogue. Quite effectively, as it happens. When I tried to transcribe Snip's rapid-fire utterances, it always came out like Pinter with loose false teeth. Fox and the other toffs, Cammell and Roeg, years later, reminisced about Litvinoff, how he took them deep into the East End, villains' dens, the Becket in the Old Kent Road. Dives in the Elephant and Castle. Whitechapel, Bermondsey, Deptford, Dartford, Krays, Richardsons, north or south of the river: all one to them. Mouthy Cockneys, hardmen with square-shouldered suits, polished shoes and buckets of respect.

'How do you spell it again?'

'L-i-t-v-i-n-o-f-f.'

Nothing.

He tried the late Sixties and the early Eighties, no trace. Loose pages in folders and leather-bound folios. Pen-and-ink ledgers. Name after name. Nothing.

A priest (rabbi, official), a heavy man in a dark suit, is summoned. Hat off, the heat, the gas. Embroidered skullcap. He has a bad cold, allergic to dust; he sniffles, turns away, sneezes. Big handkerchief. Courteous. Won't give up. It's oppressive, column after column of names.

'Give Joey a bell,' Snip said. 'He was there, the service. Me, I can't stand phones.'

I'm waved towards a Battle of Britain instrument. The kind you have to crank. Joey knows. Voice weak, distant. He has the letter and the number, off by heart. I have to get out of that office. The year of death – 1975 – is missing from the file. The binding is loose, a few pages have vanished. The official is perplexed. I don't need directions. I know exactly where the grave will be. I've dreamt it, time and again. Joey standing beside me, smoking a cigarette.

Near the end of a row, grey – morning shadows from Brick Lane made solid – the same right-angled triangle. Headrest. Portland stone pillow.

IN EVERLASTING MEMORY OF DAVID LITVINOFF. SON OF THE LATE SOLOMON & ROSE LEVY. BORN 3rd FEBRUARY 1928. DIED 8th APRIL 1975. SADLY MISSED BY HIS FAMILY AND FRIENDS. SHALOM DAVE.

Shalom. I add my pebble to the pattern already on the grave. Six small stones, local, sandy, arranged at random; four in a group, centred, and two away at the edge.

A quiet and ordered place, unnoticed behind high walls, pad-locked gates. Uniform memorials, nothing excessive. A tractor preparing the ground, to the west, for future burials. A faint blue line of pylons revealing the position of the A13. Bare trees. High thin clouds in a bright sky. The temperature beginning to drop. Time to get Snip back to the train.

He's gone. Not there. Wandered off. He was standing alongside me when I took the camera out – perhaps that offended him? There might have been other relatives, friends, he wanted to visit; pay his respects.

Snip isn't a big man, not as tall as the gravestones. I walk up and down the central avenue, checking the aisles and tributaries: no Snip, no visitors, nobody. The sound of the tractor. I'll have to try the office.

The coincidence of a name catches my eye: Silverstein. IN LOVING MEMORY OF SAMUEL SILVERSTEIN. DIED 23rd DECEMBER 2002. MAY HIS DEAR SOUL REST IN PEACE.

The skullcapped official, overwhelmed by his allergy, racked with sneezes and splutters, is still brushing through the pages, running a thick finger up and down the columns. He won't give up.

'One day, God willing, all this will be in the computer.'

He waves me to the phone, holding up a hand to refuse my offer of payment.

'Joey,' I said, 'listen. I'm really sorry. I seem to have mislaid your father. He can't have gone far. I won't come back till I've found him.'

Joey's voice is very faint. He says something about how cold it is, he can't go out until the weather improves.

'My dad, man. He died just before Christmas. He came out of Rossi's, sat down on the pavement, died. Gone before they could call an ambulance. I still can't believe it.'

Gulls take flight, hundreds of them, from the field that's being improved by Tarmac Quarry Products, wheeling against the sinking sun. Long shadows on a narrow, mud-spattered lane. I have to go on. I made my promise to Joey. The perimeter road, between cemetery and gravel pits, loops back to the old A13, and then, by a complicated junction, to the new. I would walk, no choice, towards West Thurrock; maybe link up with Jimmy and Track at the ibis hotel.

If Snip was a fetch, a fictional device to get me moving, he had served his purpose. I'll risk the Sleeman brothers and their territory: Purfleet pubs showcasing darts, Lakeside retail park, new maisonettes in Chafford Hundred where they butcher unlucky associates with electric carving knives. After Basildon, the heat was off. I looked forward to a Canvey Island detour, a pedestrian circumnavigation of the flood defences and caravan parks. Then: Southend. The finish. Thorpe Bay, Shoeburyness. A heritaged nuclear power station.

Lurching lorries spill toxic waste in clouds of yellow-grey dust. Poisoned hedgerows. Bark peeled from trees. The only vegetation is the ubiquitous plastic sheet, stained viscera crucified on thorn bushes.

Think: *Hell Drivers*.

Stanley Baker, Patrick McGoohan, Herbert Lom, William Hartnell. Lumberjack-shirted realism (British homage to Warner Brothers B-features). Rattletraps jockeying on short-haul tours to quarries – much like these: Havering Aggregates. Didn't O'Driscoll (and Mocatta) own a fleet? They worked the golf-course scam. Planning permission for leisure developments leading to apocalyptic war zones of landfill holes and steaming bunkers. (Blacklisted American leftist Cy Endfield, the director of *Hell Drivers*, had to be credited as: C. Raker Endfield. 1957. Another era entirely. Available only to those prepared to risk Launders Lane.)

Reunited with the displaced A13, its verges, walking was once again a possibility: a glorious spread. Horses. Transport caff with net curtains.

Think: James Curtis and *They Drive by Night*.

READY FOR WORK. TAXED & TESTED. Resprayed Transits at £225. Tinkers' camp (on a traffic island). A roadhouse, supporting the firemen, and offering: LIVE GAELIC GAMES.

The new, improved, slipstreamed A13 is up on stilts, an elegant preamble to the M25 and the QEII Bridge. Traffic at a standstill. Nothing unusual in that. *Silence*. A few cars out of Rainham, burning rubber, not knowing what's ahead of them. Then . . . nothing. Ticking engines. I swear I can hear running water – a hose in the lorry park, the Ingrebourne?

An evening panorama. Frozen like a dream. Oneiric omnipotence: the stalled circuit of the M25, London's heartblood. Everything, it's clear, plays into the loop. That motorway circuit is the great contemporary narrative, track it if you can. All the tributaries, arterial roads, dual carriageways, links and runoffs, are supplementary chapters, additional files. Dreams born of dreams.

Then I hear, in the distance, in stereo, the sirens. Police cars coming from both sides of the river. Converging on some unknowable accident. The mess of blood and oil, shattered glass. Wind in the wires.

Coast

Ebiz. E-biz.

'I'm not going to talk about it,' Livia said. 'Don't ask me. I've nothing to say, nothing.'

Ebiz?

The asylum-seeker, the one with the moustache, followed them into the street. He was knuckling the nearside window. 'Ebiz?' He tapped his gold watch, held up five fingers.

Ebiz, Ebiz.

Reo Sleeman was a nodding dog, the spring gone in his neck. He beat his head against the wheel until there was a red groove in the skin, a sort of McEnroe headband.

For Livia, a decision taken. The last time, the very last time. She would take this ride, back to London, see Track.

'I am never ever getting in a car with you again.'

Seeing the Basildon boy on the coast, in daylight, was quite a shock. Livia twisted the driving mirror to check her hair. The moustache, the irate man from the pasta place, wouldn't disappear. He gestured with a bent arm, his watchface thrust at Reo. He shouted, with greater urgency. 'Ebiz.'

In the soft cell, the padding of the American car, Reo's body heat was oppressive, syrup. Like burnt hair in honey. Long hours on the road, held up by lights, diggers, accidents, weight of traffic, left a stringent sourness in his denim jacket. Stiff on him, freestanding, a skinny boy bulked by weights and steroids.

His face, there, in the mirror strip, staring at itself, through itself, eyes like pinholes. Cheekbones. Hatchet-shaped. Julia Margaret Cameron's *Iago*, Livia thought. The Italian model, Angelo Colarossi, used as the cover image for the catalogue, the recent Cameron show at the National Portrait Gallery.

Old brown leather, slightly tinted windows. Reo's car had a period varnish. The interior was beautiful, curvy, plush as a customised hearse. Reo was beautiful too. The mask of him, pale flesh stretched over a hot light bulb, stubbled. The effect Cameron achieved, inadequate lenses, sunbeams through shutters, of focus loss, slippage. A concentration so intense that it blurs and becomes painterly. The intimate portrait. Human face as landscape.

Male face, its inappropriate, undeserved beauty.

Reo's mouth. Sulking. Gondola lips. Jagger lips. Dry foam at cracked corners, pink-white, reflex sneer. Muttering to himself.

'Totally out of order.'

Last night, up in Cunard Court, she remembered Marina watching a film on television, in which a police car cruises deserted city streets – near the river? – chasing, following, a bandit, stick-up man, solitary walker. Three beautiful things. The engineering of the car. The images from the film: hunted man ducking behind pillars. The *silence* of the streets. Static and the moving camera. Livia went out on the balcony, sliding doors open, watched the sea, listened to the soundtrack. Deep American voices. Lurid orchestration.

And Reo. In profile. He was the third thing.

This drama was ridiculous. If she were not involved, it would be hysterical. Track would love it. She would absorb the whole story of Livia's 'capture'; Reo's spittle-flecked fugues, the romance of the road. It would make a great print: the sweep of the bonnet, reflection of setting sun, the red spill of traffic lights. Get Reo out of the car and everything would be perfect.

. . . not conned she's clever tricky her talk her books
      DRIVE . . .
            SPIN THE WHEELS . . .
               BURN RUBBER . . .
won't be taken for a cunt not this time not by her not again doesn't matter what she says I'm not listening . . .

Uphill. Let him. Let him shoot every light, straight over every pedestrian crossing. Squash cats, dent women, kill kids. *I won't speak.* They're waiting in little concerned groups outside the schools. Solitary men at the edge of it. Some of the mothers yawning. Tired. I wouldn't want kids – *would I?* Hadn't thought of it before. So much traffic. Won't say a word.

. . . car slides no problem I'm in control under the bridge road's ridiculous cunts don't know how to dip their headlights turn off get out of it narrow bridge not slowing slow down cunt back off back off arsehole cunt

   lights flashing . . .

    horns . . .

sun in my eyes trees arching overhead a tunnel that's better much better her legs she's got hands digging in her legs kick your shoes off you used to like being driven that's what I like best you said when you drive me somewhere the chance to talk have a proper conversation

   lovely clear road . . .

    Roman . . .

     would you . . .

fancy being a driver like Chas in the Jagger film Performance *not his motor not responsible out in the country at the beginning flash cunt beats a woman with a belt marks her I never shit on the sheets I never . . .*

Won't speak. He's been this way before. Don't know where we are. Slowing down. Might stop at a pub. The Curlew? Not sure. Could do with a drink. If I concentrate. If I *will* him to do it, he'll stop. Lights in the window. People. Get away. Ring Marina. Order a cab. Would they come this far out? Can I afford it? Money in my purse?

. . . never hit a woman before never have never will call it a Jagger film Alby does Kray bollocks Maidstone old days he's taking the piss it's Chas at the end when they put him in the motor they're going to do him out on the marshes last drive brings up the bile shit in your throat senses on alert synesthesia taste sound smell colour might have been Rainham I know

they're fucking upwest Notting Hill shithole studios upwest Johnny Shan-
non's from over the water Old Kent Road the one they say wrote it he's
Whitechapel Jewish feller I done paintings of Chas into Jagger like boxers
a fight poster yellow and red with lettering ultra bold mug to mug face-off
metamorphosis *too much charlie should have stuck with her best thing*
I ever done Jagger and Chas that terrible fucking syrup when Chas comes
down the steps at the finish they're putting him in the motor Mocatta's
boys he's dead meat he looks out and its Jagger fucking bollocks Jagger
down the pan finished from that moment innit smirking bastard wasted
had it coming she's got the look Livy of the French bird the tart the one
in the bath what was her name Lucy Livy Livy Lucy same hair no tits
mouthy full of it meat she's dead the French girl must be old now topped
herself Bindon he was tasty they say Alby knew Bindon the stories hung
like a donkey nutter dead now they're all dead Bindon stabbed some geezer
in a yacht club did a painting of Bindon too in a Jag from another film
fat dead hypergolic *rocket fuel ignites spontaneously on contact with a*
complementary substance how I feel how I am on fire open the window
wind down the window wind turns to fire oneiric *pertaining to dreams*
Dreamland Margate the beach the sea sand in your shoes makes skin burn
I can form a pool of saltwater in my cupped palm holy water my own
fucking bodily secretions cunt like a frill of different blue and pink rashers
the slippery sac of a squid inside out stinky fingers salt . . .

Solitary motor, American, in the parking space behind the roadhouse. Platform carved from the hillside, the escarpment. Overlooking the A21, not far from Riverhead, Sevenoaks. Woodland.
Lights of traffic, long beams, heading for the motorway, the M25.
A cold, clammy evening. Mist taking the lush from the landscape,
the Weald.

Reo slams the door and strides off towards the bright building.
She won't talk, move. He's mad.

The camera. She's wants her camera. In a bag. From the boot.
Panoramic window of the roadhouse, bluish striplighting, red sign,
in the twilight, across the damp car park: it might work. A quiet,
meditative print to offset Reo's *stupidity*.

His physical anguish is palpable. Lights on but the place is closed, closing up. A big man comes to the door. Reo backs off, swearing. Stands there, at a safe distance, doing silly karate kicks. Come on come on gestures. Bottles it.

Get out, run. Half-dark, trees the other side of the road. He'll never find you. Wave a car down, get away. Ring Track. Ring Marina. Ring the coast.

Or drive off. *Now.* Why not? Before he turns round. Leave him. Leave him to it.

Livia slides across the seat, feels for the keys. He's taken them, locked the door, locked her in. The padded rim of the window. She tries the handles. All of them.

The door opens.

He sees her. He's coming. She stands waiting. The smell of the fields, the woods, earthy, heavy. And the smell of the road. It's that blend, the tension she tries to impose on her prints. Unreal nature and natural artifice. He grabs her arms, hurting her. He slaps her, once, twice. Drags her around the car, pushes her in. He starts to cry.

. . . Racinage *the decorative treatment of leather a branchlike effect overhanging branches reflected in the windscreen like it's smashed with a hammer striking a woman a child's hand I can't forgive the feel of your jacket soft baby leather when I touched your shoulder you could have said something now it's too late I'm like he is* Performance *fucked flesh sick twins brothers artist and face villains all fucking villains family innit blood thicker Faversham was it definitely Faversham Bob Geldof and Paula Yates pills overdose sick games they brought it on theirselves totally out of order done it in another geezer's house across the Swale from Sheppey Swaleside the prison six months away I worked through the fucking dictionary big red book nothing to read better than weights the size* autodidact *lifted weights too wouldn't touch novels give up painting Jagger was done the minute he gets in that fucking motor Dartford the bridge coming up six miles crawling Bluewater wanted one of the nobs country place* fatal transit from document to allegory *white roller like*

*the old funeral trains like abos plastered in gypsum Harry Flowers good
name for a villain better than Alby Sleeman Mickey O'Driscoll Phil Tock
the train robber geezer Buster Edwards he had a flower stall Waterloo
hanged hisself in his lockup they're all dead Flowers in the Attic film
about car crash incest Alby's not so hard see him work on an engine
whistling purring along driving itself 'Allo Chas into the tunnel under the
river orange nicotine lights muddy on car windows slippery on polished
metal tiled bore drop a coin in the bucket and you can come back to Essex
until she speaks until she says it keep driving . . .*

'Stop the car,' Livia said. 'Now.'

She put her hand on Reo's bony shoulder, denim. The tunnel
had been superb, an experience. And now this: power station, tall
chimney, oil tanks, marshes, the elegant span of the bridge at night.
'I want my camera.'

Her voice brought him back, brought him out of it. They had
made it to the north shore, home turf, the A13. He was a free man.
He could swing into London, a club, or out to Southend, fish
supper. He could take her home to Mum and be out at the quarry
with his rods within an hour. He could stick with the M25, chase
Alby, Epping Country Club, the chaps. A reunion. Kiss and make
up. Kiss and tell.

How he'd blown it with the dagos, the snatch. The two Albanians
were down on the coast, potless, waiting for a motor. Max Bygraves
would be taking his curtain call, bringing the house down, right
about now. Stage buried in daffs and M&S knickers.

There's a spot, the filth love it, where you pull off the road, park
up at a vantage point, view of everything – Essex, Kent, bridge.
Space for two cars, nose to tail. Right by the section of motorway,
up on stilts, where pill-runners get a tug: nowhere to go, jump sixty
foot or hold your hands up. Smiley tabs down your Y-fronts, stuck
in the thatch. Pills in your pubics.

Reo and Livia sat, the lovers, side by side, taking in the flow, the
lit road, the mean windows of the hotel that looked straight out, a
few yards from the cabs of huge lorries. They smoked, they shared

a cigarette. Then Reo, reflex courtesy, opened the door for Livia, walked her to the back of the car. His hand on her elbow, the cool texture of her leather jacket. He fumbled with his keys. He reached into that big dark space for a torch.

Rubber matting, rope, spade. Spare trainers. Fishing box, rods, stool, maggots. Livia's yellow camera bag.

The beam of the torch flashes on metal, a blade. Reo's martial arts kit, Livia thinks. Samurai sword. He bends forward, gropes.

Ebiz.

Across six lanes of perpetual traffic, backdraughts that push them against the crash barrier, the hotel. Its name: *ibis*. Ebiz, ibis. So that's what the man in the pasta place was going on about. His hand, five-finger spread. Thick gold watch nestling in black hair. The ibis hotel. Thurrock, Lakeside. Ebiz.

White Queen Theatre

Kaporal sat in the car pretending to be Bob Mitchum, but it didn't take. 'Baby, I don't care.' His slack features had undergone the same substance-abuse landslide, everything flowing downhill, flycatcher's pursed mouth, autopsy eyes. Dimpled chin like builder's bum. But the *weight* wasn't there, the bulk. The psycho stare (unblinking) of a man who enjoys his work (getting drunk, causing trouble). The timing. Kaporal's yawn was a couple of beats too eager, a yawn of panic not boredom.

The hair.

The hair was the real story of Mitchum's heroic anti-career. It out-acted him. He could do absolutely *nothing*, sharkmeat on a slab, better than any other leading man (Dean Martin, William Holden). Wrecked or sober, Bob could do the voices, the yarns, play it forensically cool, cervical nerves twitching in a lordly corpse. Great gift, sleepwalking through our collective memory. But the hair gave the game away, contradicted the pose. The hair was hot (Elvis loved that pompadour). Sculpted. An art work. A national monument. Somebody was employed, paid cash, to work on the hair, plough and water it, arrange for a single greased strand to fall in a fuck-you droop. Wayne and Sinatra, with their dinky rugs, couldn't compete.

Kaporal patted his male-pattern (Prince Edward) bald patch. Forget Mitchum. This kidnap caper was crazier than any of those quickies shot in Durango for Howard Hughes: spook script-doctors rewriting on set, juvenile lead in hock to the Mafia, bagmen paying off local cops, whores, pinkos who named names, faggots, junkies, astrologers, blind cameramen, rodeo riders, grips who worked once with Bill Wellman – and all of them, night after night, expected to drink until dawn. Drink and bull. Tequila and horseshit. Unstructured monologues of global conspiracy, Illuminati, Jews, bankers, vampires, alien invasion of body parts.

Who snags the worm?

The Bygraves snatch should have been aborted as soon as Reo Sleeman lost it and took off for London. The girl was trouble. That was the thing that caught Kaporal's eye, her penchant for romance. The way she sat at the back of the café like Jane Greer in Mexico. Willing him to make his move. But Achmed wouldn't give up, he sent Drin to find a man with a lock-up, off the Bexhill Road. And now, in place of their lovely, roomy Detroit motor, the silent Albanian arrives with a two-door Verve (100,000 miles on the clock). He has to stick his head out of the window to drive. It's like trying to pack a slaughtered steer in a tumble-dryer.

Poor Kaporal was trapped in a Mike Leigh script – dysfunctional lowlife, bad food, wretched weather – directed by Michael Winner. The only part of it that played was the location. The theatre itself, Hollywood Chinese without Rin-Tin-Tin's paw prints, was a relic of the Thirties: freshly painted red lacquerware, wavy orange roof tiles and pointy bits (like German helmets).

The sea.

The cliff with the tropical gardens.

The hump of hill on which they were parked.

A long straight road with views right back to St Leonards and down to the theatre, fire exit and stage door.

Plenty of good directors had worked with less. If it was a question of waiting, watching – fine. Kaporal was up for that (if someone brought him coffee and burgers at regular intervals). But, sitting alongside Achmed, he couldn't breathe without synchronising his intake of air (window wide open) with the Albanian's openmouthed gasps.

'Ebiz otel. You drive. Meet mens. Count money.'

Simple. Kaporal stays in the car, alert, engine running. Achmed approaches Bygraves at the stage door, says he's the driver. And, meanwhile, the real driver, official driver, another economic migrant, has been paid off. Away.

'Where to? Who do we contact? Where's the drop?'

'Ebiz. I say you. Ebiz otel.'

Drin, from the backseat, passes over a leaflet. A promo for Dagenham Gateway, a new riverside city on the ruins of the Ford motorplant.

FUTURE PROSPERITY FROM PAST GLORIES

England soccer stars, including 1966 World Cup winner Martin Peters and legendary Chelsea star Jimmy Greaves, were born here. Punk band the Stranglers named one of their songs after a fan they called 'Dagenham Dave'. Dagenham was the birthplace of comedians Max Bygraves and Dudley Moore.

No photo of Max. They went with Sandie Shaw, long-legged, minimally skirted, on the bonnet of a production-line Ford with winking headlights.

'Dig-en-arm.'

Grab Bygraves – if anyone can recognise him – and on for a meet at the ibis hotel, West Thurrock, with Mocatta's men. Kaporal (English-speaker) will make the calls. Return Max, drugged, to his birthplace, Dagenham: an industrial unit. Hold him until cash is forthcoming, counted and bagged.

'You like?'

Pick up the dosh at the ibis and then to Mocatta's house, on the coast. Idiot proof.

And they were proven idiots, all of them.

Drin was nodding. Kaporal liked Drin. He never spoke. Achmed said something to him. Drin was nervous. He fiddled under his shirt, an amulet. Good-luck charm. Like a man unscrewing a prosthetic nipple.

'What's he got?' Kaporal asked.

'Air,' Achmed said. He gestured. Drin reluctantly fished out the private talisman: a circlet of golden *hair*.

His wife.

His luck on speedboats, trucks, trains, containers. His luck in England. His memory, stroked and savoured. Tasted.

Kaporal liked Drin. Loss, hurt, he knew about those things. Exile. The researcher had never lived in a place he owned for longer than six weeks. Wives were messy, they got involved with other men. They never learnt how to sit still, to wait. Drin knew. He twisted the hair ring around his little finger.

They were coming out onto the streets, dazed fans, with that shriven, after-church look: mute, slapping their hands against their sides to get the blood circulating, clouds of pink talcum and flea powder. There were a surprising number of kids, blank generation slackers, arms hooped for missing skateboards. Was Max suddenly hip on the coast? Had he done an album with the Manic Street Preachers? *I wanna tell you a story.* Jos hadn't kept up with the retro scene. He remembered Joan Collins in the early Fifties – *The Square Ring*, written by Robert Westerby – before she decided to stay there for the rest of her mortal span, fifty-three and holding.

This Bygraves thing needed somebody like Westerby (leftist, prole, strong on detail) to lick it into shape. Jack Warner, Robert Beatty, Maxwell Reed, Bill Owen, Sid James. Half of them economic migrants, colonials on the make. The other half music-hall turns. Men die, but Joan Collins is fifty-three for ever and doing Nöel Coward in the West End. A lamia in a black basque. With pink ribbons. Pinched flesh. Loose arms.

'Now, now you go. *Please.*'

Achmed, smoking hard, waved him on. But Kaporal couldn't move. A black road. Puddles of yellow light. Cypress trees on the cliff path. A sticky pine scent, after rain. Nasty looking razor-wire spinners. Meshed windows. A sudden block of light as the stage door opens.

'I'll be Maxwell Reed.'

Wasn't Reed married to somebody? To Collins? Probably, most of them were. Or Diana Dors? Cuckolded, of course. Irish. Appeared with Dors in *Good Time Girl*. 1948. From a novel by Arthur La Bern. *Night Darkens the Street*. They don't do poetry like that any more.

'Go go go! You go!'

Was it based on a real newspaper event, that film? Yank in Britain on crime spree? GI and an English girl who saw themselves as Bonnie and Clyde? La Bern had a background in journalism. Bad karma in that loop between reportage and fantasy, Odeon sweethearts on a killing spree. Flashbacks. Through those wobbly, nitrous oxide visuals, a dying man revises a wasted life. In pin-sharp focus. Involuntary flashbacks: the story of the Forties. Of Kaporal.

Drin is shaking him. Achmed's going mental. The streets are completely deserted and the celebrity, unaccompanied, is standing on the kerb, toking on a very fat cigarette. Kaporal remembers how to turn the key. Putting on the headlights is beyond him, Drin helps out. In the masterplan, Bygraves would be tucked away in the capacious boot of Reo Sleeman's Dodge. This motorised bucket has no boot; enough space, at a pinch, to stack just one of the seven dwarfs – if you folded him, carefully, like an army blanket.

Achmed made his oblique approach. Bygraves listened. He didn't seem fazed at finding his usual conveyance chopped in half. The man was tired, coming down from all that twinkling, storytelling, hoofing and crooning. A trouper. Old school. Singalonga Max: the prototype of mid-Atlantic man.

The Super Furry Animals T-shirt was unexpected – but, hey . . . Max was showbiz to the soles of his lifts. He had a reputation as a dresser, a pro who knew his value, brusque with underlings who couldn't match his own high standards. This must be the chill hour: baggy denim jacket lettered with: TERRE HAUTE PENITEN-TIARY. HARD TIME / HIGH TIME. The sneakers were unlaced and none too fresh.

Max looked ten – fifteen? – years younger than Kaporal expected: thick hair, nice smile, walnut tan. He looked familiar in the way stars do, faces from tele who infiltrate your consciousness like thieves in the night.

They had a bit of a problem, the Albanians, working Max into the car. He took the seat next to the driver, to Kaporal, leaving the ledge at the back to Achmed and Drin – who squashed together like a Siamese Twin novelty act. Two heads on a single contorted trunk.

'Nos da, Jos boy,' Max said, offering Kaporal a hit on his herbal cigarette. 'You still alive, bach? When was it, '73? Blake's Hotel? The interview for *Time Out*. So what happened, then, to the photos you promised to send?'

Max bilingual? Spanish picked up from his pool boy? Didn't sound like Spanish. Albanian? Was there a living Albanian language, Indo-European? *Nos da*. Nos da was the wrong Max, Max Boyce. The clowns had got the wrong comic. Most of the population, this side of the Severn, would pay good money to get rid of Boyce.

Even the Balkan bandits looked shocked when Max started to fiddle with a three-paper roll-up. Kaporal knew about Bob Mitchum's habits, brown bags of dope, intravenous tequila, tumblers of straight vodka, but that was Hollywood, *Confidential* magazine, a bad-boy franchise to maintain. One of the English elite, a diamond of family entertainment, practising the same self-destructive indulgences, was taking a mid-Atlantic stance too far.

'Albi. The name you had to use at Blake's. For the interview. Remember, Jos? Two rings, put the phone down. Ask for Albi. I loved all that.'

He cackled, coughed. Spat out of the window.

Albi.

The man with a dozen passports. Multiple-identity felon. Albigensian. Manichean: darkness and light. Anagram of alibi: *I, Albi*. The stupid fuckers. They'd misread the poster outside the White Queen, misunderstood the minicabber. Not Max but *Marks*. Achmed had grabbed Mr Geniality, the spliffhead businessman and all-round Celtic charmer, Howard Marks. The smoking man's Tom Jones. Mr Nice.

Marks was Kaporal's last gig for *Time Out*. The photos had been mislaid. Jos's stories were always photo-led (polyfilling gaps between snaps). And not just the photographs, the camera. They tried to charge him. He moved on. Creative differences. Filed a couple of pieces for *City Limits*, unpaid, then relocated to outer-rim TV (Highways Agency – involuntary retirement after drink-driving charge). Unfairly, he blamed Howard. And that long, long afternoon in Blake's Hotel.

The pitiless affability of a man who pleaded guilty to everything. With a twinkle in his eye.

There's a point, Kaporal decided, beyond which nice is too nice, arteries fur up, your mouth tastes like you've barbecued your own tongue.

'Kabul, boy,' Howard said, 'navel of the world. All my schemes start there. Lovely climate, lovely people. Statues of Buddha carved from the cliffs. Magic. A rocket-launcher under every market stall.'

The virus entered Kaporal's system. And he had never, subsequently, shaken it loose. Marks as a spook. He kept a place on the coast, Sussex.

'Know Nicky van Hoogstratten?' Howard asked. 'Everybody does. Nicky *is* Brighton.'

Kaporal, as soon as he got back to Streatham, checked the file: property man, sharp dresser. Old hippies, hanging around Bill Butler's Unicorn Bookshop, reckoned Nicky based himself on Mike Moorcock's Jerry Cornelius character (*The English Assassin*): a dangerous dandy. Or was it the other way round? Hoogstratten and the Weavers, they ran the town. James Weaver was old enough to have been sentenced to death: for kidnapping and murder.

'Hoogstratten's a thug, slum landlord. Stamp collector,' Kaporal said, on the phone, getting back to Marks. Answering the unspoken challenge.

'Oh aye, quite right. Keep clear.'

Hoogstratten was one of the reasons Kaporal settled further to the east, in Hastings, out of harm's way – with the geriatric farms, charity shops, de-energized bohemians.

Kabul, arms, drugs, oil, John Lennon, van Hoogstratten, rogue IRA, Mexicans, MI6, phony films that were never made: Marks's yarns (stand-up routines in rehearsal) were very like late-Mitchum, shrivelled-brain delirium, paranoid-visionary riffs, punctuated by inappropriate laughter. Reducing them both, interviewer and interviewee, to boneless husks.

The joke had soured. Kaporal went to work for Norton, a burnt-out ghost in a seaside flat. Who wanted him on the case, ear to ground. Hanging out in pubs. Gathering intelligence the hack could cobble together into a book that would sell enough copies to get him back to town. Instead of which, Kaporal found a sweating wheel in his hands. The car, heady with sweet smoke, was driving itself through the Dartford Tunnel.

Under the river. River of no return.

What did Mitchum say, the one time he refused a brawl? 'Never fight when you see death in the other man's eye.' Kaporal caught, and was transfixed by, a vision of Norton – an old man staring blankly out to sea, death lodged in the corner of his one good eye, waiting. Waiting for a call in a room with no phone.

Howard had nodded out, joint still fixed between smiling lips. Achmed told Kaporal where to come off the motorway, down the ramp, Junction 31, circle back under the road, and straight into the parking bays outside the ibis hotel. By the flagpoles, the spiky plants in woodchip beds.

Then they sat, nobody talking, timing the intervals between Marks's gentle snores. Achmed texted a message on his mobile. Drin played with his hair charm. Kaporal watched the windows of the roadside hotel. He saw them as a chessboard. He worked on his moves – as lights went on and off.

Checkmate. Endgame.

The windows were like hundreds of TV monitors, playing real-time films, synthesising boredom. Sensors hidden in tarmac firing small dramas, sexual fantasies of long-distance hauliers enacted in a dream hotel. Reveries inspired by topshelf service-station novels: underwear models, whips, boots, brass beds, designed after the style of the New Orleans brothel photographer, Bellocq. Without the pain. The scratches. The gold brown of alchemised river mud, tobacco. The blood of slaves.

A book by Michael Ondaatje.

Who is Bellocq.

He was a photographer. Pictures. They were like . . . windows.

Louis Malle made a Bellocq film: *Pretty Baby*. With Bergman's cameraman, Nykvist. Barbara Steele was in it. Kaporal met her once in Rome, nice girl. The profile was never written, he drifted on to a festival in Palermo. Then back with some German bums to Cologne. Malle wanted Mitchum for *Atlantic City*, but it was far too late. The point where elegy turns sour. Oxygen mask, emphysema, shrunken head.

We know too much – of trivia, gossip of our gods, the lazy Valhalla of private members' clubs, red plush, gold-plated spittoons. It would have been better, Kaporal thought, to have stuck with the image on the screen: young Mitchum in *Out of the Past*, old Mitchum in *Dead Man*, pained Mitchum in *The Friends of Eddie Coyle*, sleep-walking Mitchum in much of the rest. The architecture of the thing. What happens outside the limits of the screen is none of our business. Kaporal wanted his ignorance back. No knowledge, false knowledge, of the actor's life, the bile of racism, conspiracy theories. The day he first set foot in Bob Hope's mansion. Alcohol is a bad voice when it gets out, takes over. Jack Kerouac's wounded tenderness spilling acid, splashing solder in his own lap.

Mitchum's bulk turns to ash. They cook him. The family – plus Jane Russell (Howard Hughes's most monumental engineering project) – put out from Santa Barbara in a rented boat. Dust on the waves, in the air. Gritty grey powder on water. Dispersed, brought to shore. A small contribution to the landmass of California.

They were being watched, filmed. The conspirators. From behind muslin. From bushes. From that too-clean Transit van out in the road. Kaporal had an instinct for these things. Treachery, he majored in it.

A curtain, four floors up, twitched. A naked man – other figures, clothed, behind him – was staring down. *Norton*. Translated. In the wrong place. Staring at the motorway as if, somehow, without prior warning, his sea had frozen over.

Harsh blue light. Loudhailers. Hooded men with flak-jackets, hair-trigger paramilitaries, surround the car.

And limping into the frame, this brilliant pool of artificial day, is a man with a rucksack. Norton. *Another Norton*. Equally distressed. Ignored by the gun-toting heavies, men with cyclopean lamps fixed to their heads. Coalminers up from the underworld.

Norton plods on, and through, into the shadows. Towards the hotel. Which never sleeps. Another chapter. Fate revised.

ibis hotel

Through a nightland more object-led than expressionist, Norton dragged himself, his purple rucksack. Emotions, his emotions, were unreachable: replete hunger, sweating cold, aching knee, sore spine. Black charcoal outlines defined stalled cars and lorries. Framed travellers profiled in their pods. Snaking columns of dead smoke. A slick sky made from shoals of lurid fish (river of soles): their eyes set too closely together, glass beads anticipating pain.

Norton walked, walked.

Necessary heat was conjured by images of misplaced wives (the lovely Ruth, the lively Hannah); by pre-visions of the carnival family of Jimmy Seed, their black rubbish bags, plastic trumpets, tin drums, layers of summer and winter clothing: orange fur over polyester, plastic boots, purple stockings.

Norton walked towards the ibis, a roadside hotel. A museum of memory. A gallery where guilty artists were confronted by the evidence of their art.

A brothel of the senses.

Jimmy Seed: the tight skin of a former drinker, his trembling hand reaching out for an empty bottle. The artist, Track, a tall girl slumped in a hard chair, at the window table: nanny, pupil, surrogate mistress. Mistress of magic. Flaming hair. High, smooth forehead. Amused smile.

Track and Seed were waiting for guidance from a man who might never arrive. The ibis was a frontier post (like that town of prostitutes on the borders of the old Czechoslovakia).

Walking down what had once been the A13, and was now a detour, a wrong decision at a roundabout, a penitential drudge into Purfleet, Norton lost the arch of the QEII Bridge, the lights of the cars. Tonight's accident had brought the road to a standstill.

Nothing untoward in stasis. London's orbital motorway had absorbed the congestion-charge refuseniks of the city. A satellite band of black cabs making their circuit between Epping Forest and the great metropolitan railway termini. A necklace of hammered metal around the throat of London, its ugly sprawl.

For a short, good time, Norton enjoyed river breezes: rough grass, Armada fire beacon, cargo sheds. Gliding tankers, midstream, out in the darkness.

Then: helicopters, sirens. Something exciting in the way of meat and carnage, roadside mayhem, was being enacted, up there, on the concrete pier of the motorway.

Norton relished: the silence of the marshes.

Cross the tracks at Purfleet Station, enter the principality of Count Dracula (oil tanks, razorwire, pulp paper yards), and you are implicated. In on the crime, the highway accident. A photofit monster. A suspect in the event that brought the nexus of roads (M25, A13, West Thurrock Arterial, Purfleet By-Pass) to a troubled immobility.

Andy Norton, broken pedestrian, the only moving cog in the wheel of transcendence. Another return to nineteenth-century gothic, he thought, to scientific speculation: invisible men, post-apocalyptic survivors, mutants, suspect prophets condemned to live out their own fictions.

Horror on the motorway: an event horizon. The dimly lit block of the ibis, the port hotel, is an anchored space platform.

Walking, limping, out of the darkness that shielded and protected him, Norton blinked, closed his eyes against the shock of this overpowering ring of torches and tungsten. Paramilitaries. Rapid-response units had surrounded, with their usual excesses, one small, dirty, over-occupied car.

'I don't have any papers.'

He lied. To the officials. The half-hearted challenge. Preparing his response to a question that hadn't been asked. They weren't interested. They were acting for the cameras, tipped-off news crews. Something was being done about terror and Thames Gateway, about roads and men with moustaches who pitched up, uninvited, outside respectable Essex hotels.

Norton had nothing but papers. A rucksack ballasted with pulp. He had Danny the Dowser's copious files: Rodinsky and Dagenham, Captain Amies and Rainham, Sandie Shaw and Terry Venables. Ford's motorplant and Ford Madox Ford on *The Soul of London*.

Great fields are covered with scraps of rusty iron and heaps of fluttering rags; dismal pools of water reflect on black waste grounds the dim skies. That all these things, if one is in the mood, one may find stimulating, because they tell of human toil, of human endeavour towards some end with some ideal at that end. But the other thing is sinister, since the other influences are working invisible, like malign and conscious fates, below the horizon . . .

He will almost certainly not know that, in the marshes round Purfleet, he has factories larger, more modern, better capitalised, more solvent, and a landscape more blackened and more grim.

He was tired. A bed, any bed, would do. Better to dream this place, Purfleet, Thurrock, than experience it.

So much experience and so little of it experienced, lived through, understood. Nights, like this, when he couldn't sleep and came naked from bed, to pee or to drink, walking unsteadily to the window. Nose squashed against cold glass, former novelist, A.M. Norton, watched the bad cinema of the arrests in the car park.

He laid aside the book, his personal Gideon bible; he took it everywhere: Beckmann. *Heavy-paper catalogue edited by Sean Rainbird (good name), from an exhibition visited, for the duration, on a daily basis. Beckmann and the ibis hotel were made for each other.*

Norton sipped watered whiskey. There had been something of the sort, cars, guns, on television – news show, cop show. Time was running, counterclockwise, down the plughole, navel fluff, cigar butts, the oaty bits your digestion can't dissolve, washed from shitty fingers.

ASYLUM-SEEKER GANG SNATCH CELEB. The plot had been

sold out, obviously. A farce. Albanians under observation from the off. 'That's why I gave up fiction,' Norton thought. 'The banality. Everything's been done. Realism, such as it is, reprised as a game show. Big Brother at the Adelphi Hotel, Hastings. One lucky immigrant gets a passport, the rest go back to Sangatte.'

Tough to live, aged sixty, in a culture dedicated to trashing memory, elective amnesia – the back catalogue of Norton's Hollywood classics raided for remakes, ghost shows with grinning imbeciles, feelgood conclusions. You have to travel to somewhere as obscure and uncooked as the ibis hotel at West Thurrock to exist in real time: the right-hand panel of one of Max Beckmann's gloomier triptychs.

West Thurrock is where bad things happen, limbs hacked off, chained women, bondage corsets, stinking fish. Beckmann's myth stuff, kings and golden children, is out on the river. Past, present, future: three windows on the third floor of the ibis hotel. Revolve your head, slowly: river, motorway, chalk quarry. When society matrons came calling, wives of Party members, directors of I G Farben, Beckmann would only show them the river panel of his triptych, the one based on Shakespeare, The Tempest. *The side-panels, in their articulated cruelty, were left in the cupboard.*

Where was Hannah? Norton's conscience, his lover.

He'd come to the ibis for an assignation, a meet in the cafeteria, a bottle of chilled wine among the potted plants, a conversation. Hannah could, so she'd intimated that night at the Travelodge, help with his blockage, his inability to put pen to paper. A nice situation for a young photogenic millionaire novelist, moved sideways into three-page film outlines, no use to Norton. Silence, poverty. Too much world, not enough words. No time.

Hannah arrived late. Road at a standstill. Cab abandoned. Train from Rainham. Walk from West Thurrock. Hopelessly lost. Stockings torn, shoes ruined. Propositioned by unidents and glue-sniffers. No food left: lifeless sandwiches, lettuce like a bin of snotty tissues.

'Could we go to your room? You do have a room?'

She asked.

She couldn't get back to London. The gridlock scenario had finally happened. Norton gave her the number, went upstairs for a shower – to wait while she made a phone call. The cafeteria had been taken over by a family of transients, black bags, rattled husband, exhausted kids, two women. One of them with a camera.

Norton, abandoned by the muse, scoured his body, drank weak whisky, stroked the glossy cover of his Beckmann, fell asleep. No Hannah. Hours later, painfully tumescent, he waddled to the window.

A shock to himself – and probably to the cops, out there in the cold night, at the scene of the non-crime. The car. The spread-eagled miscreants. The pressmen.

He saw: that other Norton creature, the one with the purple rucksack. The pest from the Travelodge. His double, his doppelgänger. His uncommissioned portrait. The ugly walker who ram-raided Dorian Gray's attic. The fetch who sodomised his inspiration. Foreclosed his memory bank. Ripped off his research. Stole his women.

He'd warned the clown in Docklands, tried to shove his mendacious reflection back into the mirror. Thurrock was the end of it, the end of London. By the time he returned to the coast, the second Norton would be buried on the marshes. Death would have his eyes.

I saw the man with the cock standing at the third-floor window. But I didn't believe him. Do you know about tulpas, psychic offprints? My malignant duplicate was associated with cheap, off-highway hotels. He didn't walk, he didn't drive. He hung about, picking up women, eavesdropping on other people's conversations: flogging my stories before I could finish them. One question: was he the tulpa? Or was I?

Tired, hungry, confused, I found Jimmy at the bar, checking his wristwatch by pretending to fix loose cuffs, waiting, thick-tongued, for the first drink. His wife rounded up the kids. Track made annotations in her notebook.

'We're meeting Danny tomorrow. In the Plotlands. He's taking us to Canvey. You coming?'

I drank with them. I watched the screen, weather systems, blocked roads, terror rehearsals. Tibetans believe that it is the mind that creates the human body. We move among masses and shadowy shapes that are not mere hallucinations, they float, they subscribe to the theory of gravity. They obey natural laws. They are as real as the mind that forms them. The body we delineate does not vanish at the moment we recognise that it has been brought into being by an act of mind. *I am here.* I will hold this glass in my hand, even if the man upstairs refuses to allow me into his world.

When Jimmy returned to the bar with our written orders (that's how they worked it, knowing that the worst drunks would be incapable of scribbling legible instructions), I took Track's hand. Surprising her. Causing her to laugh and cover her mouth.

'Could we go upstairs? There's something I want to discuss – in private.'

She slipped me a swipe card. I pushed back my chair, picked up the heavy rucksack. Made for the back stairs.

The stairwell is cavernous, dark, unused. The steps are stone. Norton listens to out-of-synch sound, footfall, the feeling of touching the next step, quitting it, before sound reaches him. Vibration precedes confirmation. A fire door separates him from the corridor that contains Track's bedroom.

A sudden view of the road, up on stilts, heading for the river, tunnel space beneath it, the edge of the car park. Space sucked from the scene, a vacuum. Norton – gasping, toppling, hands on brass rail – is trapped in an air pump.

He misses his copy of the Beckmann catalogue, stolen by one of Hannah's more deranged clients. A multiple-personality journalist (who operated a bookstall).

He calls up: *Self-Portrait in Hotel* (1932). The artist weighed down by a lead hat. Strangled in a scarf like a rubber tyre. Hands in pockets of coat. Space cropped, titled. Stairs like sheep hurdles. The back way, rear entrance. Keep off the streets, ugly things are happening. There is a woman upstairs, waiting, her wrappered nakedness playing against the painter's hunched bulk.

In the 1941 *Double-Portrait, Max Beckmann and Quappi*, there is another hat. The word LONDON visible on the brim. A secret message, coded desire. Love for the city of Blake, seen in 1938, never forgotten. The eros of a sweaty hatband.

The view from the end of the ibis corridor is faithful to Beckmann's interpretation of space: absolute, terrifying – if it isn't blocked, doctored by verticals, dressed with telegraph wires, roads, railway lines, ladders. Space is the horror. No limits. Norton seeks relief in casual engineering projects, protective fences, thin trees, the tall chimney of the distant power station. Stalled traffic. Blue lights flashing. If the orbital motorway is fixed, then stars are fixed, gravity is suspended: *Norton floats.* The transients in the ibis hotel drift through the corridors like paper goldfish.

He makes it: Room 234. Swipe cards never work, not for Norton. He usually sleeps in laundry rooms. *He's in*: tight cabin, wall-to-wall bed, TV. Clean. Lovely view of the motorway. Save it. He unpacks his papers, Danny's files. He fishes out the whisky bottle. Takes a shower.

Under sharp needles of scalding water, Norton is descaled; blue flakes stick to plastic shower curtains. The fishiness of Rainham Marshes is boiled off, pores open, his scalp is massaged. The shower cabinet looks like something seen by a Beckmann fish-eye. Norton's features sprayed on an expanding beachball, flaws magnified: elongated skull with indentations of the tongs with which he was dragged into the world, unforgiving light. His frequently broken nose. In the cloudy mirror, among the pharmacopoeia of complimentary soaps and unguents, a softness of vision flatters incipient cataracts: he looks bad, but it's going to get worse.

Stretched on the hard bed, whisky by his side, TV (silent), Norton is about to read, work through Danny's files, preparing himself for the next stage of the walk. He knows Track isn't going to come. She'll bunk with Jimmy. He's better for her career. A family man. Man of property.

The film's *Macao.* A post-war industrial flick made with funds syphoned off from aircraft kickbacks, Commie witch-hunts. Conradian white-suit dreams of the South China Sea exposed to rabid American colonialism: Howard Hughes. Giganticism in place of human imagination, personal fetishes inflated to the size of monstrous hoardings: an adventurer, a torch singer, a boat . . .

And then they ran out of ideas.

One of those projects where the hook is an interesting past, soul damage (where no past exists): false memories, holes filled with booze, paranoia, cigarette smoke.

They sent for the wrong German (Vienna + Brooklyn): Joseph von Sternberg. Good old Joe. A ghost brought out of retirement. Replaced by Nicholas Ray (before the eye-patch). When all the time, it was obvious to Norton, they should have cabled Max Beckmann. Robert Mitchum, Jane Russell, William Bendix. An ocean liner. Think: Beckmann's *Departure* (1932). Three screens. Live action. Beckmann and/as Mitchum. The woman with the exposed breasts in the right-hand panel. Max and Howard Hughes, they were made for each other. Hughes was putting all the loose Germans on contract, rocket-propulsion scientists, torture mechanics, men with black books.

The ibis hotel: Room 234. Beckmann's address on East Nineteenth Street, Manhattan. His last exile.

Track isn't coming. Beckmann would enjoy Track, her intensity, the camera (carried around like a musical instrument). Her solidity. The red hair.

Norton drinks. He reads. *Basildon Plotlands*. Then a few pages from a novel by a woman called Barker. Then the next manuscript in the Marina Fountain bundle: incomprehensible verbiage. Vampires in Chafford Hundred, a cannibal stalker (female) loose in the Ikea warehouse at Lakeside.

And, finally, eyes drooping, photocopied sheets attributed to Michael Fordham, but of distinctly ambiguous provenance: reportage or fiction? *They called it 'the M25 Murder'*.

Norton flipped the page. A typo: dateline 'April 2003'. The murder hadn't happened yet. There was still a year to go.

A soft knock at the door. Norton's attention was engaged, he kept on reading. The story had the ring of truth.

The predatory tabloid's picture desk had rented a helicopter. They hovered so low over the scene that the tarpaulin which obscured the view had been blown away. The photographer must have used a polarised lens to capture the image through the windscreen of the large American car. It was big news that morning, because the police had shut down the entire north-east section of the motorway.

More knocking. The door – or something outside? From the window, Norton could see the helicopter, the vertical beam of the searchlight, the American car on the hard shoulder.

They had been going out for four years. Ever since they met at Epping Country Club one heady summer night in 1989. She'd seen this boy, absolutely caned, going for it on the dancefloor in his dungarees. He was lean, wiry – long dark hair in a ponytail. Kung fu kid, they used to call him.

The older brother, it appears, owned a martial arts club in Hackney Road and a pub in Woodford Green. The girl was an artist, an art student. A photographer.

Ecstasy was everywhere and it was mad. Twisted a lot of brains. Mates of theirs who had been strictly into lager and football, who had good jobs in the City, earning decent money, all of a sudden started wearing luminous long-sleeve T-shirts, tracksuit bottoms and beatific grins.

The boy, the kung fu kid, burnt his fuses, lost it. The lovers separated, tried again, before she got rid of him.

He helped his big brother put on parties. There had always been plenty of cash around. He'd do a few things at the boozer. Looked after the gym every now and then. Money was never a problem. He had never had anything of his own, except this beautiful young girl, the art student. He lived for training, the gear and the girl. In that order.

You can see it. You can hear the thump of the helicopter blades.

You can anticipate the conclusion of a story that is both banal and terrible. The physical excesses, steroids, cocaine. Brain shrinking like microwaved chicken.

A bloke from Walthamstow he knew started a kendo workshop. That was when he got into swords. He started spending serious cash on swords and other ninja paraphernalia. He gave up drinking, started reading books on the codes of Samurai honour.

The door, he had to answer it, bollock naked. Track. Agitated. With Jimmy.

'Switch channels, *now*. It's Ollie. Out there, in the car, with that madman. With Reo.'

You can't see much on the fuzzy porthole screen of the ibis TV set. They're stretching a tarpaulin over the Dodge, roping it. The helicopter is staying overhead. The motorway is at a standstill. TV is just a mirror of what's happening outside the window.

Norton remembered: the future tabloid story, how it turned out. Drug-crazed psycho, head filled with John Woo and Mishima, kidnaps former lover, an artist (journalists relish the implication). He drives out to the M25, parks up. Strips to the waist, produces a Samurai sword. Then blows it. Seppuku aborted: in favour of a merciless killing. Murder. The decapitation of the girl, the student.

His stained shirt was found in bushes by the side of the carriageway, as was a Japanese sword dating from the Meiji-restoration period. The sword was estimated later to be worth over eighteen thousand pounds. The police identified the antique as part of a collection stolen in a hold-up on a famous antique house delivery van earlier that year on the south coast. During the post mortem a number of incisions were found in the stomach area of the killer's body. His blood contained a massive amount of cocaine and amphetamine.

The killer, Reo Sleeman, hacked off the woman's head and ran into the road, brandishing it like a lantern.

He stepped in front of a Dutch HGV carrying 25 tonnes of plasterboard. The time was 4.15 AM.

4.12 on the bedside clock, red figures glowing.

'Do – *something*.'

Track shaking Norton. Jimmy flexing his cuffs.

Stars are our eyes: Beckmann.

'Take long walks,' the painter said, 'and take them often, and try your utmost to avoid the stultifying motor car which robs you of your vision, just as the movies do, or the numerous motley newspapers.'

Falling Man (1950).

Norton, naked, at the window. Two figures, clothed, behind him. The frame seen from the car park.

If you revolve Beckmann's painting, stand it on its head, it works. A swimmer plunging, arms outstretched, into a flower-strewn river. Feet like paddles. Out of the clouds: boats of angels, fires in windows. Down from heaven into the lifeless earth of a motorway hotel.

Beckmann understood, better than anyone, the mystery of the middle ground: *he abolished it*. The falling man, painted in New York, in the last year of his life, has no middle ground. The naked figure, close to the window, losing his green robe, bath towel, dominates the foreground. Black hair like the painter's favourite skullcap. The flying man – man who has forgotten how to fly, lost his wings – reaches out to touch, with thick, vegetal fingers, 'unknown space'. His soul transmigrates into the absence of middle ground (a collar like the orbital motorway).

4.13 a.m.: Track propelling Norton, wheeling him, stiff as a corpse, towards the liquefying barrier of the window.

'Time,' Beckmann wrote, 'is the invention of mankind; space or volume, the palace of the gods.'

Mitchum and Jane Russell: the posthumous embrace of mastodons. *Macao*. Lovers entombed in a block of Jell-O.

Wassily Kandinsky: 'Space is death.'

*

Cameras pick up a running figure, a naked man; out of the ibis car park, over the fence, across wasteground. Up the long ramp, sliproad – logged on surveillance monitors. Through six lines of stationary traffic.

The night of West Thurrock is not *The Night* (1918–19) of Max Beckmann; no bondage (except on digital channel, by supplementary payment); no Lenin, no pipe (smoking forbidden). No candles of lard in the electrified motel.

A.M. Norton has found his muse: murder. She is upside down on his bed, red slippers, scarf around neck, voluptuously nude. Her hand rests on her own gently heaving belly. Hannah listens to his story: seaside, failing eyes, failure of imagination. Standing member, huge, aubergine-purple.

Twin windows – sex rituals, falling man: side-panels of an unfinished triptych: *The M25 Slaughter*.

A naked runner, exploiting the corridor of the middle ground, between actuality and fiction, arrives unmolested at the American car. He opens the passenger door and taking the woman's hand leads her through the lines of stalled traffic to the ramp (an Expressionist motif).

To Track. Who has run down the back stairs, out of the hotel, across the waste ground. To embrace her lost friend.

So it is Norton that Reo Sleeman strikes (it always was). A clean cut. In the green glow of the dashboard. Norton: Green Knight. Spouting blood. Like a petrol pump gushing over the forecourt.

The radio in Room 234 acts as an alarm. A wake-up call for the walk to Canvey Island. Capital Radio's Flying Eye announces a twenty-eight-mile tailback, the worst in the history of London's orbital motorway.

Severed head in hand, grasped by a thin crop of neck hair, Reo Sleeman ran into the road. 4.14 a.m. *It hasn't happened yet*. Night traffic in spate. Clubbers from Basildon. Reps from Chafford Hundred. Lakeside deliveries. A Dutch HGV loaded with plasterboard, watching out for a difficult turn.

The impact barely felt. Driver in shock. Sweet tea. Sleeman tossed aside, crumpled. The head rolling, rolling, rolling. Eyes like fiery coals. Into scrubgrass. Down the embankment. Into the dark. The whole performance, captured on surveillance monitors, became a legend among snuff movies: the *Citizen Kane* of necrophilia, death of a nation.

Sleeman's funeral at Chingford Mount was well attended by men with shaven heads, sovereign rings, dark glasses and long black coats. Crocodile limos, nose to tail, stretched back as far as the North Circular. Florists were denuded. Notable among several highly inventive floral tributes were wreaths shaped like boxing rings, Mount Fuji, like jukeboxes. Respects were offered, upper-case carnations, by the serial mourners of gangland: Freddie Foreman, Tony Lambrianou, Dave Courtney (in charge of security), Kenny Noye, Bernard O'Mahoney (author of *Essex Boys*), Howard Marks and half the cast of *EastEnders*.

It was decided, after consultation with the family, a visit to Alby Sleeman in Maidstone (two counts of life imprisonment, armed robbery, assault on security guard), that the song for the crematorium, to play Reo out, would be *Wheels (Keep A-Rollin)* from the album *That Man Robert Mitchum . . . Sings* (Monument Records).

Forensic examination of Reo's Samurai sword led to the capture of the perpetrators of a south coast raid on a van of antiques, 'mainly from China and Japan', conservatively valued at half a million pounds. A subsequent search of Alby's London Fields lock-up recovered three kilos of cocaine, 7,000 ecstasy tablets and numerous bundles of very damp cannabis resin.

Of Norton, his head and his torso, there was no trace. The man had vanished. Some commentators doubted that he had ever existed. There was no entry in the register at the ibis. Katherine Cloud Riise (32) and Olivia Fairlight-Jones (30), despite substantial offers from the tabloids, were not giving interviews.

All too late. Norton was destined not to discover the thing that troubled him most – as he ran, naked, up the ramp: where Track got her name.

COAST

Allegories of Insomnia & Continuous Sky

A. M. NORTON

HAMISH HAMILTON
an imprint of
PENGUIN BOOKS

naked in the sea air and amongst the dead

– Catherine Millet

Cunard Court

So much experience, and so little of it experienced, lived through, exploited. So many broken phrases. *Failing windows, failing eyes. The moon is a suicide's eye. The missing eye of Rooster Cogburn.*

The way we repeat ourselves, dust down the same lifeless metaphors: discovering old notebooks with abandoned versions of new stories. Too late to be picky.

There is a certain pathos, a degree of comedy, to be wrung out of physical decay, stalled ambition, inappropriate lust: the skeleton propped on the balcony like a wind chime. Hollywood contrives an upbeat ending, dignity for the carcinogenic gunfighter who has to be winched onto his horse. The south coast is crueller, more practical. Home helps in the lift, the compost of memory packed away in hutches for the elderly, Edwardian and Victorian mansions on high ridges – the sound of the sea fading away by barely noticed increments.

The glass is smeared, clean it as often as you like. Something wrong with my eyes: no middle distance. Heavy clouds coming in on the curve. Toy boats, twelve miles out, on their superhighway voyages.

There were other rooms. From the kitchen I could gaze back on the Old Town, the cliffs, the pier; the sun, on good days, rose over that skeletal structure, polishing its black bones. Every new morning, light returned, a golden rule across the crests of wavelets. I stood at the sink for hours, at the day's end, when the fading sun had moved on towards Pevensey Bay and Beachy Head. I watched the lines of traffic, red lights and dirty gold. I noticed windows, shadows of people, blue television screens; the occasional solitary came out to test the evening air. There were always couples, all ages, moving along the seafront. Drinking schools kept their heads down, in caves and shelters beneath the promenade, unrowdy, working hard at the complex business of taking the edge off things.

You see? It's impossible. Flaccid prose dragging itself across the page. The Conradian era is over, leisurely paragraphs, tracking shots punctuated by elegantly positioned semi-colons. English as a third language, after Polish and French. Time to read Flaubert, Turgenev.

Conrad did. And Henry James. They lived around here, down the coast. I remember something Iris Murdoch wrote (in character) about liking women in novels by James and Conrad because they were 'flower-like'. And miles from reality, anyone met or known. 'Guileless, profound, confident and trustful,' say the writers. Deep as the sea. 'Inarticulate, credulous and simple,' replies Murdoch. 'Unbalanced by the part they have to act.'

I can't do local colour, topography, scene setting. I'm just not interested. A room is a room. The 'film essayist' Jamie Lalage, who tried his best to synthesise one of my baggier fictions into twenty-seven minutes of deathwatch television, limitation as the sincerest form of flattery, told me that he moved house, an arc around north London, on a regular basis. 'You can get one book out of anywhere. Even Willesden. Especially Willesden.'

He's right. Consider *London Bridge* (no UK edition) by L.-F. Céline. House of mad inventor in suburbs. Wild trajectory, through Soho, to the still-functioning chaos of the docks. Or, bypassing the drudgery of writing the thing yourself, you can always inspire books in others: Dennis Nilsen, Scottish conceptualist, body sculptor, mass murderer. Show-stopping footage, from the fat-clogged drain, by a miniaturised camera on wheels. Unedited, it would have walked away with the Turner Prize. That's more Willesden than any reasonable culture is ever going to absorb.

Who am I? What am I doing here? Where am I going? Read the press. 'Bohemian Atmosphere Attracts Literary Gent'. The *Observer*, 17 January 2003. *The Hastings and St Leonards Observer*, that is.

And that's where I'm going now. Down to the corner shop, the Purser's Cabin. To pick up a copy for the scrapbook.

Five rooms: kitchen (overlooking Old Town), sitting room (table, deckchair, combined TV / video – for video only), bedroom (mattress on floor), work room (table, antique word-processor, orange boxes filled with books), shower cupboard. The Cunard is a Thirties liner, part of the package that comes with the De La Warr Pavilion in Bexhill-on-Sea and much of Frinton: alien notions imported by exiled Germans and Russians, Mickey Mouse Bauhaus. Crumbling, expensive to maintain, destructive of the original fabric, rapidly adapted to proper Englishness: sticky brown paint in lifts, Ali-Baba-on-acid unmagic carpets, deck walk (around flat roof) given over to radio masts for minicabs and cellphone boosters.

Easy to negotiate. Easy to remember where you are (waking to traffic noise, sea on shingle, gull scream). Easier to leave behind.

By lift or on the stairs (seven flights), I never met another human. Cunard Court, as they always say, the visiting journalists, would give the off-season resort from *The Shining* a run for its money. Steadicam corridors through which the undead can't be bothered to promenade. Viewpoints, on each landing, looking straight into the rusty cliff face.

Hiding out in just such a place, mad Jack Nicholson got to spend quality time at the typewriter. Hammering out his Borgesian finger exercises, his concrete poetry repetitions. (In my opinion, nobody's asking, Cunard Court is more like *Rosemary's Baby*. Brownstone satanism gone white with shock, generations of seagull shit.)

My morning stroll, under the columns, was a delight. Sticky piss stains in doorways. Oddball commercial enterprises: furniture that looked as if it would eat you alive (Naugahyde recliners to be buried in), wedding dresses for American-size brides, leaky wet suits (reduced), fundamentalist electrical repairs, incense, bowel remedies, cheap booze and a boarded-up (rates refusenik) Dr Who ephemera franchise. An unfunded heritage operation that peddled the back story (mouse mats with maps of James Burton's St Leonards), lectures on local history (Monday mornings only, Easter to September) by a whistling lay preacher.

RESPECT OUR WRECKS.

BLOOD LUST – A NIGHT OF VAMPIRE GOTH. ADMIS-
SION FREE, EXIT OPTIONAL.

LIVE FOOD. REALLY CHEAP PRICES: CRICKETS,
LOCUSTS, MEALWORMS & WAX WORMS.

KEVIN CARLYON: WHITE WITCH, HEALER, TAROT
CONSULTANT, EXORCIST. FREE ADVICE.

The ads in the newsagent's window were an accurate reflection
of local culture: benevolent occultism, used white goods (wreckers'
plunder), New Age exercise bicycles.

I don't know what I've done to rate a mention in the fright sheet,
a slack week between machete raids on offies, pitched battles –
Russians and Afghans – down by the pier (homage to Mods and
Rockers, *Quadrophenia*), wrong-man-shot-in-drugs-raid and 'Tories
call for probe into property sales.' I hadn't enjoyed such a mix of
high-baroque actuality (rendered in two-finger prose) and shotgun
morality since the golden era of *The Hackney Gazette*. Pit bulls and
property supplements.

This is how it happened. Hastings is an elephants' graveyard for
science fiction and fantasy writers. I've heard the names of the
famous living ones (the published): Storm Constantine (a Moorcock
collaborator) and Christopher Priest (aka John Luther Novak, Colin
Wedgelock, etc.). A town of slippery identity, clearly. A place for
disinvention, winding down, cultivating writers' block as a definitive
condition. Earlier romancers included: Aleister Crowley (*Moon-
child*), Sir Henry Rider Haggard, George MacDonald and the aunt-
visiting Lewis Carroll. I discount the excursionist Charles Dickens.
He went everywhere.

A sharp-eyed journalist, contacts in outer limits websites and
subterranean genre magazines that specialised in not appearing,
caught on to the fact that I'd been forced to abandon London. He
was too young to remember anything I'd published, but the relevant
information could still be dredged up in a long morning on the
telephone.

We met in a pub in the district known as Mercatoria – pleasant, unthemed, big tables, all the real ales required and requested by the smocks and beards. This was a two-way thing, he might fill a corner of the page and I might acquire a useful contact, background information on some of the crimes, corruptions, local mysteries that I would attempt to shape into a saleable narrative. We came together, therefore, with no great expectations on either side. He was on time, nursing a pint of orange juice and lemonade, and I, panting, was ten minutes late, after a detour around a set of steps that were up for renovation.

A vicar strangled in the bath and then butchered (axe and saw) by his teenage lodger. The paedophile riviera: the *Observer*, London version, revealed that 'as many as 30 child sex offenders live in the Hastings area alone'.

'Nobody more alone,' muttered the fresh-faced journo. Who reported that rundown hotels and boarding houses were being exploited as holding pens for special-category prisoners released from Maidstone and Albany. The Wonderland child-porn ring, recently broken, had been traced back to emails sent out from a Hastings computer. Hastings, in receipt of various improvement grants and Euro funds, saw its future in terms of media enterprises attracted by the provision of broadband internet providers.

I fed him, in return, some tired stuff about drift bohemia, labyrinthine streets, cheap and none-too-cheerful bookshops, periphery as centre.

'Will Hastings become the new Brighton?' he asked.

'God forbid. With luck it might become old Hackney.'

Here was the article:

A once familiar name in the literary world is living in St Leonards after falling in love with the town.

A.M. Norton, 60, is making a new life on the coast after buying a flat in stylish Cunard Court.

Mr Norton is the author of several novels, hailed by the critics, and set in the smoky streets of London, where he uncovers layers of the capital's dark history.

Mr Norton first visited Hastings as a book dealer in the 1970s and has been attracted to the town since then.

He said: 'I need a new beginning, virgin territory. In London, I am written out. I'm sure that Hastings will provide an abundance of mysteries among its steep steps and narrow alleyways.'

Although Mr Norton is not entirely convinced by the town's ambitions to become a media centre, he does think the future for Hastings is bright.

He said: 'The potential for regeneration is massive.'

Mr Norton's current project, untitled, is partly set in Hastings and takes in everything from the history of Victorian photographers and painters to the killing of the Reverend Freestone, the friendly vicar who was dismembered in 2001.

A.M. Norton, 60. Sixty miles out. Leaning on the balcony at the stern of the white boat, Cunard Court, staring at the long, slightly bent road; at dog-walkers, cyclists, stern-featured joggers (yes, he has a pair of binoculars). It's good, he thought, to have someone to look down on: the television researcher Jacky Roos, his attic room in a hotel favoured by kitchen staff from other hotels (seasonal) and economic migrants freed from their six-month prohibitions. Roos, in his turn, could look down – in a physical sense – on the *Hastings Observer* journalist (escapee from Rainham), who lodged in a pretty, but overshadowed, undercliff terrace. The hierarchy was in place: blocked author, troubled researcher, perky legman (too young to know better).

They all needed one thing: a story.

When everything else fails, fall back on doctored autobiography: audition friends and acquaintances as fictional monsters, twist facts, push them as far as they'll go, distort evidence, leaven the mess with half-truths, public scandals, real landscapes. I'd tried that before and it hadn't played. Roos, a master at retrieving documents, a whiz at the keyboard, was my precise contrary: he never, if he could help it, left his room. He could find anything he wanted on his computer. He collected wives like air miles and then lost them. He loved art and respected artists. He had a tenderness for the world, moist eyes (sober). No memory, none at all: yesterday didn't exist unless he made a hard copy.

Facts sucked from the Mediadrome, the aether, excited and oppressed him: congenital paranoia. Conspiracies everywhere. Nobody who couldn't be reached in three phone calls. The web breeds its own cancers, cancers of the eye. A torched warehouse in Shoreditch. A man in a white suit pissing against a Californian redwood. A nervous Libyan buying six identical shirts in a tourist shop in Malta. An election address, by a Liberal politician in Taunton, ghosted by a bankrupt sword-&-sorcery author. A ringing phone. Roadside kiosk, no house within two miles. A golden torc, La Tène period, recovered from a peat bog in the Isle of Harris, during the search for a black box flight-recorder.

Roos made lists. He passed them on to his sponsors. Left alone, he would draw up charts and paste postcards, newspaper cuttings, around his walls: the past was optional, subject to revision. I exploited Roos, I admit it, putting him into a novel about the Jeremy Thorpe murder trial (in the character of 'Jos Kaporal'). It took Roos to run the barrister George Carman to ground, in a Dean Street drinking den, boozing on credit, shoulder to shoulder with petty villains, pimps, existential novelists. Roos unpicked the maze-like complexities of the financial scams set up by Thorpe's ill-chosen associates, Peter Bessell, David Holmes and their offshore bagmen. Without leaving Streatham, Jacky found me the address of Thorpe's Somerset hideaway.

I did the driving, the hard miles. The door-to-door stuff. To no purpose. Three years' graft and what are you left with, strip away the tricks of language, the narrative games? Jacky Roos's list. Thirty pages of unconnected facts. My novel was greeted, if at all, with well-deserved apathy (derision from old acquaintances who picked up the occasional nostalgic gig from the *Guardian*).

Three strikes and you're out, three duds and you're back to self-publishing, creative-writing classes in Southampton, book fairs in Bloomsbury hotels that look as if they're fronts for the Russian mafia. That's what it used to be like in the old days, lunches kept alive until it was time for a drink before dinner. Literary agents (male) of a certain age still make their phone calls between five and five-thirty (returned to the office for a jug of black coffee). They can barely remember who they're talking to. 'Waiting on . . . the cheque, the contract, the call from New York. They're all in Frankfurt this week. Spanish holiday. Divorce courts. Paris closed down. Strikes wars Easter Christmas.'

The Hastings book was my one and only. I refused to have any truck with novelists who lost their nerve and tiptoed into non-fiction, dinky little things about Regency snuff-dribblers, science as anecdote, First War diary, madhouse meditation, incest recovery affirmation, swimming to Scotland. Or, worse than those counter-grabbing booklets (which won't spoil the line of your suit), baggy horrors about stinky, seething, Elizabethan/Victorian London, poverty porn – illustrated from archive. Wormy history cooked up to make us feel good about the thin air of the present. Books about pain: crimes reinterpreted, battles refought. Books about roads (for those who will never have to use them).

Jacky Roos was part Belgian. A rim of brown froth around a fancy beer glass. I liked that about him, his strip of otherness; the time he spent, between projects, in melancholy resorts among the sand dunes (locations favoured by Essex smugglers with their high-powered dinghies). On unlucky weekends, the Belgian coast played like a rerun of Dunkirk, in reverse, an invasion of random craft, disqualified crews, amateurs with attitude. Wounded men. The casualties of misunderstandings with Euro-scum people-smugglers and drug barons.

Not Roos. He favoured the quiet life. Hastings suited him, greys and browns. Polyester and corduroy. (He should have been a literary agent.) His Belgium was like Max Beckmann's Holland, a tragic vacation, a sliced view through a convalescent window. Think Beckmann's *Scheveningen* (1928) and know Hastings (2003). Deserted promenade, pedestrian crossing, beach swept of pebbles by spring storms, merciless sea. Two panes of glass, soul-trapping, between painter and world. A high view into a dark bedroom (the absence of J.R.).

Even Jacky had to eat. Think: Beckmann's *The Artists with Vegetables* (1943). Grim concentration, contemplation of improbable foodstuff – which contemplates right back. Artists with trap mouths (gone in the teeth). More of a séance than a convivial interlude. Tense exiles, in an occupied country, waiting for the midnight tap on the door.

I met Jacky in the pasta place on the front. He was going hard at his second breakfast, a glazed pizza the size of a cardinal's hat. He was sweating and swilling from a carafe of iced water. He flinched, pushed back his chair, tried to get up, as I approached his table.

'No formality, Jacky. Long time.'

It didn't take much to get him on the payroll. We never socialised, or made phone calls. Once a week we ate in silence, watching the window, manoeuvring to avoid the mirror. Jacky drew up his list of local prospects: decapitated vicar (got that), Aleister Crowley's final boarding house (check), Brink's-Mat bullion buried in builder's yard (yawn), property scams and the BNP (dead TV), rumours about an Albanian plot to kidnap an unnamed celebrity at the White Queen Theatre (too preposterous for fiction), the woman at Pevensey Bay who had found the lost clerical head, while walking on the marshes. She might be prepared to talk.

That's more like it, I thought, a trip out, fresh location.

'Fix it for tomorrow. We'll walk over.'

'*Walk?*' Roos flinched. He'd given up planes (research on crashes, terrorism, corporate malpractice). He wouldn't go near a train (fifteen box files prophesying and confirming disaster, criminal incompetence). But he was wedded to his car, like a soft green snail to its shell. Antennae quivering in the breeze. Eyes shut.

'Nine-thirty. By the fountain in front of the Royal Victoria Hotel,' I said. 'Be there. I'll write it down for you. On the back of your hand.'

Sunlight in rough patches, like spilled solder. A grey sea. The curve of the bay, towards Bulverhythe and its wrecks, the small cliff at Bexhill. I sat drinking on my balcony. I had no idea how the disparate elements would fit together, but the heat was on me. Voices were beginning to whisper. Lies were warping towards their own fraudulent conviction.

I opened my great-grandfather's book (gone in the hinges) and began to read.

There was a legend in the family that Arthur Norton's portrait had been taken by Julia Margaret Cameron, in Ceylon, somewhere about 1877. Arthur, I knew, because I'd seen the letters they'd exchanged, was a friend and colleague of the botanical painter, Marianne North. Could he have met the Camerons through North? He had included Julia Margaret's husband, Charles Hay Cameron, in his list of 'Extraordinary and Eccentric Personalities Met During the Course of my Life as a Planter in Ceylon'. But although he took the story right back to the P&O liner and the voyage out – *'What do you think of Aden?' I said to a Yankee tourist whom I had observed stalking over the place for half a day without opening his mouth. 'What do I think of Aden? Why, I guess Satan must have somewhere to throw out his cinders!'* – his tendency to digress, chase any detour that might lead to a terrible joke, meant that Cameron's potted biography (after the style of John Aubrey's *Brief Lives*) never appeared. We have to make do with a procession of forgotten Scots, drunks, gamblers, rogues who went native or, worse, became Papists. The man had a fatal addiction to the picaresque.

I can't confirm it, but I'm sure there was at least one meeting with old Charles Hay Cameron, a man who spent years in Freshwater (on the Isle of Wight) without quitting his room. He lived in a quilted blue dressing gown, brooding on his abandoned Ceylon Estates; white-haired, affable, preoccupied, up for a cameo as King Lear. I believe that, like my great-grandfather, Cameron lost a fortune in the coffee blight of 1875. Certainly, Arthur Norton would never touch the brown stuff after that date. We thought once that it was South African gold that ruined him and sent him off on his fatal expedition to Peru. On consideration, I believe it was something much closer to home.

In his journals Norton compares the fever of speculation in coffee with the Californian gold rush. I think he is describing a meeting with the venerable husband of Julia Margaret Cameron, a dire weekend party at Little Holland House in Kensington.

Yes! I well remember meeting in London an old gentleman who had suffered much by this wild rush. His reminiscences of Ceylon were evidently anything but pleasant to himself, and certainly were not encouraging to those about to embark. To change the subject from coffee planting, a young friend, with antiquarian proclivities, enquired if there were any interesting relics there, such as tombs of the Kandian Kings. 'I don't know,' was the curt reply, 'but there are the graves of many a good English sovereign!'

A frayed postcard among the pages of Arthur Stanley Norton's travel journal, his portrait: author as bookmark. A reproduction from Mrs Cameron's albumen print? The slackness of focus, which we had taken for incompetence, might now be interpreted as the signature of the style, the intensity of gaze Julia Margaret inherited from her one lesson with David Wilkie Wynfield. Her cyclopean engine, the great camera box, driven close against the subject. Weak eyes, they reckon, a family trait among the Camerons. Damage inflicted on the print by the tropical climate.

Arthur's bright eyes. Out of the sepia fog, cold blue.

Laughter lines. Despite the effort of endurance in sitting motionless in that heat. (Marianne North moaned about the noonday sun, a faint breeze stirring the breadfruit leaves.) Norton retains his good humour, Aberdonian scepticism for highborn ladies and their art. (A thumbprint floats over his right shoulder like an ectoplasmic double.)

Arthur's beard, greying, was too well trimmed for Mrs Cameron's purposes. More Professor Challenger than Alfred Tennyson as 'dirty monk'. No cloak, a heavy jacket.

The trick she worked so often: mortality. A stare that empties the soul. Arthur's barely suppressed smile breaks the spell. A failure. On the artist's terms. *Portrait of an Unknown Man (Ceylon).* 1875–9.

My challenge was to integrate the private, family story – unattributed photographic portrait, collapsed investments, fatal expedition, lost camera (with Peruvian film still inside) – with the material

Jacky Roos was gathering for me in Hastings. And then to find a suitably Scottish form for this double tale. I rejected the alternate chapter technique, much abused by recent practitioners: historical pastiche interspersed with unconvinced passes at contemporary life. Those exhausted tropes: miraculously discovered journals, photos in shoebox, invented poems (in strict imitation of the period pieces they parody). Tick tock. Then now, now then. Until you end up with Nicole Kidman in a putty nose. The past as a website you can access for a small fee. Password: Metafiction.

And there was one other minor irritation: I was going mad. Nothing serious, a single, recurrent delusion. Another writer, with my name, my face, was trailing me; stealing my research and peddling it as documentary truth, a short film here, an essay there. That's why I left London. The creature had ruined my reputation, invading and capturing (so far as the critical consensus was concerned, Radio 4, Channel 4, the four broadsheets) my territory. He had forced me to flee to the coast, to begin again from scratch. At my age. Knowing nothing. No contacts. No money. And the fear that one morning he would be there, grinning, standing over my mattress, watching me as I slept.

Beach

Do I partake in the existence of gulls? High gloss, yellow beak, fishbreath? Timid dance at tideline, a sudden swoop, catching the wind, wings outspread, bones light as drinking straws? Up and away. Out over the Channel. Do I fuck.

The discomforts of childhood, itchy wool, sunburn, they never disappear. Half drowned by a hairy man teaching me to swim – by letting me sink. The sea was always cold, salty, opaque. You couldn't breathe and it hurt to try.

My first photographic portrait: perched on a stuffed lion on the promenade in Paignton. Brass rule between the animal's front paws. Disney cruelty, I thought. Hobbling the beast when it returns to life. Glass eye: the colour of vinegar. Mane that came away in your clammy grip.

I took Ruth to the seaside once, in the early days. Things weren't going well. You know women. I couldn't begin to figure out the source of her discontent. It was my fault, obviously: something done or undone, a grievance nurtured and unsmoothed. Actually, it occurs to me now, there was no single reason (unpaid bills, failure to alert her to a change of time for *Coronation Street*, bad sex), no unaired grudge: she didn't like me, simple as that. I was a mistake about to be rectified.

I asked her to drive (another black mark), so that I could film the full moon bouncing, a pingpong ball on a water jet, over the endless rooftops of the A12, the apotheosis of ribbon development (aspirational suburbia masking country parks and cabbage patches). We stayed at Orford, a gloomy choice in the circumstances. I wanted to check out the tower where Mike Reeves filmed the climax of *Witchfinder General*: Ian Ogilvy going nuts and butchering a faintly shocked Vincent Price – who realises, too late, he's in the wrong movie. The tower was shut, out of season. Autumn storms off the North Sea rained frogs and stones.

We drifted on to Southwold, where the white lighthouse, seen from an attic bedroom, over a Cubist scatter of red roof tiles, might have been an unfortunate symbol. We breakfasted, like all the other English couples, in a silence broken only by the chomping of dry toast and the ruffling of the *Telegraph*.

I still have the snaps. Ruth on the beach. Ruth among the stilt-shacks of Walberswick. Ruth in a pine forest. Such things, eventually, become a fetish. Long hair, long coat. Long legs. Why is this beautiful young woman *alone*? Who is stalking her? It hurts, seeing what she was, and what I was too stupid to notice at the time: resignation, distaste for the camera's obsessive attention. The tightness in her shoulders, how she draws herself into her coat. The futility of fixing the present moment, instead of experiencing it – experiencing it, always, with one eye closed.

I get the same feeling from Julia Margaret Cameron's portraits of housemaids and compliant relatives. Let them be. Leave them to their fate. A commentator, writing about a subsequent Southwold pedestrian, the late W.G. Sebald, said that photographs were a device 'whereby the dead scrutinise the living'.

Edouardo Cadava (in *Worlds of Light*): 'Photography is bereavement.'

Young Ruth lost to old Norton. It requires her physical death to bring my grey images back to life. Ruth, my one and only passion (unrequited), left early. And it still hurt. Not the fact that she'd gone (if I'm honest, I provoked it), but the manner of her exit. A trip to the magistrates' court, in support of a friend. And she never returned to the basement flat in Chepstow Road.

Coming from Wales (birthplace) and the West Country (education), I was lazy. I settled in West London; first Paddington, then South Ken (schoolfriends) and (mid Sixties) Notting Hill. It was the era, before the film, when it was just about possible to read Colin MacInnes, *Absolute Beginners*, without wrapping the book in brown paper. A teenage snapper and his verbals (penned by an old queen from Spitalfields). Street kids could be photographed without a visit from the sex police, a one-way ticket to Hastings.

Joey Silverstein, who was knocking about with Mervyn Peake's daughter, knew MacInnes (knew everybody). He was my first contact with London literature (humped in a Fortnum & Mason carrier bag): Gerald Kersh, Alexander Baron, Patrick Hamilton, Sarah Salt, Robin Cook, Robert Westerby and James Curtis. Joey wore a belted coat, summer and winter, he didn't sit down. As soon as he finished talking, he moved on. 'I'll call you next week, man. We'll do a walk.' I never saw him actually *read* a book, but he knew where to find them (Bethnal Green to Friern Barnet). He also knew, by touch, what was inside. And what it was worth.

It was years before I met a published author. The closest I came was watching Heathcote Williams spray Michael Moorcock graffiti around the borough, giving away the reclusive celebrity's current address. Bringing Hawkwind fans and geeks with typescripts to his door. Future wives. Dealers of every stamp. I was too proud to join them.

There was something about the concentration with which Ruth made up her face that morning, it troubled me. It was like watching Lucian Freud through a two-way mirror. One mask, attempted, revised, scratched off. Begun again. I should have guessed. (And now, years later, I can imagine where those little chats in the café with Freud led.)

Women, as well as men, were always congratulating Ruth on the smoothness of her skin – achieved without the use of powder or paint. If they'd known! The hours it takes to produce the natural look. You'd think they might have noticed eyelashes thick as flea combs, the black rings (Mandrake Club pallor on eight hours' dreamless kip). Her model: Anna Karina in *Vivre sa Vie*. Ruth took up smoking, French, unfiltered. She cultivated that slightly goofy, shortsighted stare that lends itself to misinterpretation: the spirituality of glycerine tears.

I met Karina once, with Godard at the Academy, Oxford Street. Permission to translate an interview. Quite a hefty lady, actually, in the flesh, nothing like Ruth. I thought: Sandie Shaw in Dagenham, much more like. Long legs, large feet. Slight stoop, curvature of the spine, from hunkering down to hear what short men with hairy backs and heavy gold identity bracelets were proposing. Secretary to a music publisher in Denmark Street – so she said. Could I believe her after what happened?

Ugly suspicions. I broke off my work, mid-morning, couldn't concentrate, a film treatment going nowhere; Cliff and the Shadows. They wanted a hip new image, Dick Lester jumpcuts, newsreel camerawork, South London one-liners – as a response (a rip-off) to *Hard Day's Night*. I slaved, uncredited and pretty much unpaid, for a composer of advertising jingles who wanted to go legit, screenplays, production. With one drawback: he was illiterate. Couldn't fill a speech bubble in a *Sergeant Rock* comic.

I started walking, jogging, around Paddington Station, up Praed Street, towards Marylebone Road. A group of them were coming down the steps, outside the court, laughing, heading off, so I imagine, to the pub for a celebration. One of the men, a longwristed *String Band*-type freak, was puffing away on a monster joint. Ruth, hanging back, not wanting to be associated, publicly, with such excesses, was being tracked by a very nasty piece of work. My mirror image. Same clothes, same Buddy Holly spectacles, same squint. It was the first time I encountered my double, the other Norton. The one who put the hack into Hackney.

You can imagine the rest. Ruth came back one Saturday afternoon, when she knew Chelsea were at home, and removed all her things. Two suitcases and the Dansette. I couldn't keep up the rent. I shunted, by way of Park Royal and Cricklewood, to West Hampstead – where I finally lost it, went into therapy. I was convinced that Harrow was the site of a holy mountain, a radiant city, the temple of the west: dappled light in a churchyard overlooking the valley through which the M25, London's orbital motorway, would one day pass. I suffered a pre-vision of this river of gold. I wandered the streets around the shopping centre, the wrong part of town, asking if anyone could direct me to the lodgings of the Cockney-Welsh mythographer and poet, David Jones.

They sectioned me to Shenley. Where I met several writers and a few psychotherapists. Cornflakes, funny-tasting tea, acid and vegetable gardening.

Laingian community life followed my first encounter with the East End. I met Hannah Wolf. We took a room together (very convenient for the North London line) in Compayne Gardens. As friends, colleagues. She wanted to monitor my voyage through insanity. I should have talked my trauma out, but Hannah was too busy, meetings every night, readings at the bookshop, running around doing bits and pieces for Doris Lessing. The writers in West Hampstead were serious. They meant it. They enjoyed company, feuds, affairs, meals eaten off your lap while you talked opera and Angola.

I started to embark on monumental walks; do it that way, I thought, work the gap between *personal* psychosis and psychosis of the city: the crisis of consciousness lives in faulty synchronisation. Sometimes the city was crazier, sometimes my fugues leapt ahead: fire visions, sunsets over King's Cross gas holders. We are part of the madness. Monitor *everything*: weeds, green paint on a wooden fence in Maryon Park, swans hooked by Kosovans on the River Lea, the way an Irish barman in Kentish Town stubs out his Sweet Afton and scratches a cut that never heals on his right wrist. When there is sickness, misalignment in the city, I sweat. I feel warts cropping on my tongue.

I had my first conversation with a living writer, the *Guardian* columnist Jack Trevor Story, a pub in Flask Walk. He was often there with a large dog and a small woman. He stood out from the usual Hampstead depressives and crossword-fillers. He had style. His mania, evident but lightly worn, convinced me. I decided to move to East London and take up fiction. Those twinned ambitions, symbiotically, brought the world together.

The day after I'd met him, Story rang me – offering, for a very reasonable price, the typescript of his first novel, *The Trouble with Harry*. The same one I'd seen him sell, twice over, to the bearded man who kept the bookshop on the corner.

Bo-Peep Inn

I began to wonder, witnessing the man gulp his pint of tomato juice, the blooded mouth, if Roos was not that terrible thing, a reformed drunk. The sweats, the trembles. The compulsive gorging, even in this smugglers' den, of microwaved bangers and soft white bread. Layers of grease combed into thinning hair. Fat fingers gripping the table's edge. A hard swallow, a dry heave disguised in a fit of coughing. The eyes had it, panic, frantic attempts to summon memory: *what am I doing here?*

We met on the Marina, by the pink granite fountain; Roos was almost on time. I hadn't wasted my thirty minutes watching the waves, the lateral drift, the heaping and scattering of small stones. Squadrons of gulls, legs retracted, rising and falling on a fierce tide.

I read: 'In Affectionate Memory of his Beloved Wife EDITH'. A sturdy pillar erected by James Castello, a Viagra afterthought. I'd known an Edith once, another graveyard, obliterated inscription, a lost woman reborn in one of my fictions. Title forgotten. Her name remains with me: Edith Cadiz. Is emotion for one who never lived, a spectre of the multiverse, legitimate? The fountain was unusual, by London standards, it worked, spurted to order, brass spigot: I cupped my hands and drank.

The marine parade, as Roos and I strolled west towards Bexhill, gushed with water, charitable taps, civic art (concrete disks), toilet facilities with operative basins and clean, flushed troughs. Hotels and tall houses were being restored, paint-licked, made ready for the season, the speculative developers. Old folk, weathered, hand in hand, kept each other upright. Young women, burdened with plastic bags, butting into the wind, left us limping in their wake. Roos, it has to be admitted, was not much of a pedestrian: he was affronted by this sudden loss of status, being naked (unmetalled) in a world of sunlight, sea breezes, dog accompanists, cycle lanes, salt-scorched palms and limp fronds. He wobbled, rolled his shoulders, hoping that the rest would follow. He worked his right foot, speculatively, as if reaching for the accelerator. He squeezed the knobs of the guard-rail like a gear lever. He stood, blinking furiously, waiting for the landscape to race past him.

History was lightly worn in St Leonards. James Burton, in his dotage, carved a town, a post-urban estate (with Classic pretensions), out of the hillside. His son, Decimus, on a commission in Tunbridge Wells, persuaded some free-floating royalty to winter on the coast: the Duchess of Kent and the young Princess Victoria. The usual riffraff – jaded aristos, Irish adventurers, gamblers, pimps, cooks, theatricals – followed. Crescent parks with Gothic follies. Masonic temples. An ugly church, designed by Burton himself, was replaced by an uglier one by Gilbert Scott (the power-station man). During the Second War, a V1 rocket, heading straight for Cunard Court, where a dance was being held in the Grand Ballroom, skidded down the promenade and blew up the elderly architect's turreted pastiche. Albert Speer in the wake of Sir Walter Scott.

St Leonards was protected from the Old Town (fishermen, street photographers, privateers) by an elaborate, Doric-columned arch that made Temple Bar (in Fleet Street) look like a frame for runner beans. The scale was such that a person called Ballard took space on the south side for the sale of 'Ladies & Gents Worked Slippers'. When the time came, there was no Temple Bar reprieve (removal to Theobald's Park, return in triumph to the piazza of St Paul's): the St Leonards arch was demolished, covertly, in a single night.

Much of the rest, pompous as it appeared, crumbled and cracked. Burton, pinched for funds and credit, dug out local stone (soft, red) for the construction work. He took his sand from the foreshore. Structural faults were soon apparent, blocks laid in the wrong grain. The charm of the natural landscape, woods, modest chasms, sylvan glades, the full Keatsian apparatus, was attacked, denuded, improved. To the point where, at the start of this new millennium, teams of police in masks, anti-bacteriological suits and white rubber boots, are picking through a monstrous landfill site for body parts, weapons used in the slaughter of a local businessman.

None of this mattered. My reflex scepticism was charmed by the seascape, views into tall-ceilinged houses, New Orleans balconies with ornamental ironwork, pink paint: the past as an asset, a free-and-easy marriage, give and take, not an accidental resource to be exploited. The grot and the gracious in perfect harmony: old motors decanting young hopefuls with black bags. Chipboard window panels being taken down. A long-serving Greek restaurant instantly reinvented as a Chinese takeaway. And one vast red box, windowless, like a giant container unit, to oversee the lot. The future in the shape of: CARPET RIGHT.

Jacky is lugging a camcorder but he doesn't use it. He can't talk when he's walking, can't think: nothing works. The in-flight computer is out of commission. I'm feeling generous, the mood of the morning, so I nudge him towards a pub I've spotted, early lunch at the Bo-Peep Inn.

But first: some necessary record of this evocative plaster statue (whitewash over grey conglomerate). The moss, the brown pox. A couple on a raft or bed, unemphatically pornographic in a Tennysonian sort of way: at it. Exposed. Drapes torn back. In the public gardens.

She is bent over his reclining (droopy, sapless) figure. His naked knee (above surgical support stockings, varicose veins) is crooked over hers. She kneels; her arms tight around his neck. His grip has not yet slackened on the long sceptre. A short skirt barely covers the darkness between spread thighs. Her nose has gone, tertiary syphilis. His eye socket: a lichen pad. King Harold and his mistress; another Edith, Edith Swan-Neck.

Very affecting. They say a Norton – Henry of St Clere – handed an archer the fatal arrow. Hastings, battle of: 1066. Up on Battle ridge, where the toffs now live. Normans and Saxons in combat. Henry was one of the uninvited tourists from across the Channel, eye (pale blue) to the main chance. There's always one of us about, a faceless Norton, putting a cynical spin on triumph or disaster. I inherited the temperament. The inability to take public art on its own terms. Nothing that a few drinks in the Bo-Peep couldn't cure. If you can't resolve an argument, photograph it: in the country of the blind, the one-eyed king is the proper symbol.

The lovely Edith: a white vampire ducking to get at that exposed neck. The fatal infection, love, that passes from generation to generation. Eros and Thanatos.

It didn't seem to matter where he was, if Jacky had a plate in front of him, he was happy: he gobbled and yapped. He knew about Bo-Peep, the facts. Smugglers, wreckers. The nursery rhyme decoded: Bo-Peep as excise man, sheep as criminals, contraband. When the phone shrills at the bar, a man with tattooed earlobes, neck like a capstan, has to answer, in an embarrassed growl: *'Allo. Bo-Peep.'*

Swallowed by Bexhill Road, umbilically attached to Hastings, Bo-Peep has ceded its outlaw status: rotting craft, decayed fore-shore, cheap brandy. Or has it? Checking the bar, I'm not so sure. Solitary session-drinkers marking out their territory with plastic lighters and fresh packs of cigarettes. The bar stools have backs to them, to stop the punters sliding, unexpectedly, to the stone floor.

Women. A couple of near misses. Masses of hair, industrially bleached, teased and tossed. Healthy skin and tidy features. Full slap: as for studio lighting. One of the pair had been mistaken, so I overheard, for the TV weather girl: a boast? But sweet-natured too, talking of their kids, putting it back, licentiously, forking down cod platters with peas and chips. Plum suede: boots and token skirts. Hoop earrings. Dressed for the occasion, this lunch, where their companions, the men, stayed with T-shirts (clean), low-slung jeans – and comfortable silence.

Sunlight filtered by dirty muslin projected the pattern of the arched windows across the table. Roos and Norton: part of the spectacle. The general amnesty. Laughter. Families. Coins rattling in machines. Dogs sleeping under tables. Ordinary, contented humans at their leisure.

And one face that didn't belong. A woman, by herself, writing at a round table. Postcards spread in a semi-circle. A large glass of yellow wine, untouched. Coup de foudre. Her full shape would all his seeing fill. John Keats, poet: *Isabella (Or, The Pot of Basil).*

Keats, knife. The words went together.

'*Knife?* You want a knife?' Roos offered. He hadn't used his own, the one wrappered in a paper napkin. He'd forked, split, speared – licked up the last crumbs. His oval plate was so clean it didn't need to be stacked in the dishwasher.

Lick. Stack. Dish. Split.

'Keats. Know the story? Keats in Hastings, the woman?'

(Roos again, picking his teeth.)

All I wanted was for Jacky to shift himself, his imposing bulk, so that I would have a clear view of the woman at the window table. These things don't happen every day. Ruth was the last time. I remember – *stop it, stop it* – having her pointed out to me at a poetry reading. (Robert Creeley, since you ask, an art school in Gloucester.) The poets I was with (self-published, private means) were obsessed (it had lasted three weeks now) with one of the students, a great beauty. They never exchanged a word with the woman, knew nothing about her, beyond her looks: her *look*, its potential. Mysterious – if you were hellbent on mystery. The youths, half crazy, hand-addicted, found her an irritation – of just the kind they thirsted for. Her inaccessibility (untried) was her charm. Dark, full-lipped. The sort of character they'd been told about in Wilkie Collins, *Woman in White*. Blonde = virtue, dusky = vice. A kind of masculine strength in female form. No form: they knew nothing about previous lovers, previous history. My take, I glanced away from the stage, was: analgesic, spiritual diamorphine, soul drip. Not even, not then, the beginning of something, a flicker in the heart's muscle. The end, I didn't know it, of one kind of selfishness, self-absorption.

I really was there for the poetry. Or the prose. The way Creeley, the Black Mountain man, paced his sentences. Husbanded tension. You could hear commas fall. He played the pauses with consummate technique.

And his eye. I was interested in that too, the missing one. Accident. Permanent wink. An asymmetrical Cyclops with a nicely considered beard. The Wyndham-Lewis-like Spanishness of Creeley's portrait in photographs. The 'wife' mystique: always a handsome woman in the frame, wide-eyed to emphasise his loss. A language dandy folded around ocular absence. *Le Fou. The Whip. For Love.* Close things touched and distance properly registered: an exemplary career.

'Another?'

It was the only way to see around Roos: by walking to the bar.

'I couldn't, not yet. Go another banger.'

'Drink?'

'Right.'

'What?'

'Tomato. Pint. Plenty of Worcester. Ice.'

While I waited (without annoyance), I turned towards the window, the source of light, the backlit woman who was scribbling in her notebook. Which was, of course, the biggest provocation of all. The amateur existentialists back at the Gloucester reading were driven to frenzy by their desire for women who wrote; they panted like Sicilians on heat, in the wake of a rich young widow in tight black.

Creeley, as he told us, had the thing all poets suffer in youth – and which I was enduring now. 'My dilemma, so to speak, as a younger man, was that I always came on too strong with people I casually met. I remember one time, well, several times, I tended to go for broke with particular people. As soon as I found access to someone I really was attracted by – not only sexually, but in the way they were – I just wanted to, literally, to be utterly with them.'

J.G. Ballard has a nice line about characters moving through a crowd on their 'private diagonals'. That's me. I passed the table close enough to sneak a look at the ring of postcards: London. At night?

Jacky's tomato juice is solid, pulped gruel, two blots of brown sauce floating on the surface like a bad conscience.

'Pud?'

'I think not. But thanks. I don't really do puddings. Not often, not every day.'

'Coffee then?'

'I *could* try the cod. If you're sure. It looks flaky and damp, the peas too. Proper wedge chips. OK, I'm on. And bring a couple of sachets of tartare. And maybe one of mayo.'

This time my diagonal sliced across hers, a run at the Ladies: our eyes (if mine hadn't been afflicted with strabismus) might have met. Recognition. Challenge. An indication that the leopard-print top (sleeveless, straight neck) was a genuine artefact, Fifties, not like the rubbish the other Bo-Peep women found on a rack in Matalan. Scarlet mouth. Expensive smell.

Jacky Roos, *his* mouth filled with cod (a nasty silver tone in the white), was at his most Belgian: belly satisfied, tomato juice swilled with chasers of black coffee, he wanted to talk. Loosen his belt, strain the bracers. John Keats at Bo-Peep.

Let me summarise. JK, Book II of *Endymion*: 1817. Poet aged . . . twenty-two? Delusions (founded and confounded) of eternal fame. Actuality: funds stretched, uncomfortable in his skin, flogging himself from place to place (each worse than the last).

His conviction (the Romantic franchise): 'I am certain of nothing but of the holiness of the Heart's affections and the truth of Imagination – What the imagination seizes as Beauty must be truth – whether it existed before or not.'

Big question: 'Have you never by being Surprised with an old Melody – in a delicious place – by a delicious voice, felt over again your very Speculations and Surmises at the time it first operated on your Soul – do you not remember forming to yourself the singer's face more beautiful than it was possible and yet with the elevation of the Moment you did not think so – even then you were mounted on the Wings of Imagination so high – that the Prototype (*sic*) must be here after – that delicious face you will see.'

Consequence? Hard travel, coach, foot, sea. The curious notion that a new location would provoke poetry, that's all it takes. Get out of town: Isle of Wight (agoraphobia), boat to Margate (claustrophobia), Canterbury (Chaucer lost). Hastings. Quitting London, always a mistake: especially for a man lucky enough to be born by one of the City's ancient gates (Moorgate, future tube disaster). A failed medic who couldn't cure himself (his poor brother): the lamia waiting, the blood kiss.

Endymion, that epic of ambition, white light, immature rhetoric, is also a map of Keats's travels. A road book.

> Swart planet in the universe of deeds!
> Wide sea, that one continuous murmur breeds
> Along the pebbled shore of memory!
> Many old rotten-timbered boats there be
> Upon thy vaporous bosom, magnified
> To goodly weapons . . .

That's Bo-Peep. That's Hastings. Wave-watching. Mooning about the cliffs. Until Keats sees the woman in the pub: Mrs Isabella Jones.

'Isabella *Jones*?'

'Right.' Roos said, wiping his nose. 'She was travelling with an Irishman, decrepit, uncertain temper, dubious connections. And –'

'My mother was a Jones.' Typical non sequitur. Deflecting attention from my interest in the Isabella aspect. The only line I could quote from my own work, the first in a rambling fiction about the Thames, time travel and secret railways: *'And what,' Sabella insisted, 'is the* opposite *of a dog?'* Dull question, but showy: I knew the answer now. The twin statues in Victoria Park, the Dogs of Alcibiades, with their snouts smashed. Letting in the wind. Overseeing future crimes.

Young Keats met this woman, his own age, was attracted. There may or may not have been a physical relationship (probably not), an exchange of 'heat'. A kiss. A single embrace. And then she, very obligingly, vanishes. With aspirations to muse status. Or: like the first manifestation of tuberculosis, the lacing of the lungs, the red cough on the sheet.

The dog riddle didn't matter to me. The pain came from the Sabella part. It's one of those names I can't shake off. Like Marina. And Edith. The daughters of Lear in Julia Margaret Cameron's carbon print (1872) are played by Marina, Edith and Alice Liddell: the Lewis Carroll gang, *Alice in Wonderland* jailbait. River sirens. Joseph Conrad's fatal (and invented) islands in *Nostromo* are called the Isabels.

The Bo-Peep episode settles into chalky whiteness. It's Whit-week, the poet is hungry for moon metaphors. The dark lady walks in his sleep like an audition for Vadim's *Blood and Roses*. The poem is completed. He returns to London.

But that's not the end of it, not quite; Keats chances on Isabella in a street 'which goes from Bedford Row to Lamb's Conduit'. She is still an 'enigma', but now she has been 'in a Room' with Keats's brother, George, with his publisher (Taylor), with Reynolds. She enjoys a close relationship with Taylor. Who writes terrible sonnets, infected by his passion for a woman who is suddenly everywhere.

Isabella allows the hot poet to accompany her on a walk to Islington, a social visit; she lets him in to her apartment: 'a very tasty sort of place with Books, Pictures a bronze statue of Buonaparte, Music, aeolian Harp; a Parrot, a Linnet – a Case of Choice Liquers'. Then, and this is the sinister part, she gives him a grouse, unplucked, to take home for his brother Tom – who is fading fast, consumption.

There is a night, just one, when they sleep together, before Keats goes off again, Chichester. Or do they?

> Hush, hush! tread softly! hush, hush, my dear!
>   All the house is asleep, but we know very well
> That the jealous, the jealous old bald-pate may hear,
>   Tho' you've padded his night-cap – O sweet Isabel!

Too close for comfort. The pneumatic thrusting of those hushes, the 'bald-pate' and his jealousy. I was fighting a long-dead poet – for possession of a ghost.

The woman at the window table had evaporated. Leaving behind her newspaper. I scooped it up, shoved it into my rucksack. Along with the postcard she had mislaid. Even Roos, by this time, wanting to reach Pevensey Bay in time for dinner, was glancing at his watch.

'A brandy for the road?'

My head hurt: voices, broken lines that might play some part in my projected fiction, but which I would never be able to write down or recall. Was this a meditation on time and memory? A guide book dressed with cheap quotations? An undercooked Mills & Boon romance (Hastings: home of Catherine Cookson)?

The mystery woman's postcard was London. Night and fog. 'Fred Judge': repro signature (1923). A murky print like early Gainsborough Hitchcock (the studio by the canal). But on location. *Sabotage* (1936): Hitch's version of Conrad's *The Secret Agent* (dark deeds, family quarrels, pornography and terrorism). Shot in the same year, confusingly, as *The Secret Agent*, Hitchcock's translation of Somerset Maugham's *Ashenden*.

Stop it. Stop right there.

Let the postcard sit on the bar. Alongside the brandy glass. Run your finger around the rim. Make that sound. Dip your finger. Taste it. She's gone. Leave it there.

Fred Judge, a Hastings man, was very active in the exploitation of memory: a prolific jobbing photographer. Rectangles of stiff card. Weather. *Having a lovely time. Feeling much better now.* Sales accelerated by war (Hitler rumoured to be major card collector). Great boost to correspondence. *Keep your pecker up.* Early cards – pre-cinema, pre-radio – as news. The fire. The burning boat. The freak storm. Forked lightning. Trams. Views. Fred's slogan: 'Over 100 Medals & Diplomas Awarded'. Cards pinned to weatherboard, a fisherman's shack on the beach. Like whitebait, flounders, plaice.

Millions of places: England. Judge or his representatives went everywhere. Even Whitby (rival turf). Ludgate Hill. What an archive!

Until Fred (moustache like the Kaiser, pinstripe suit of an acid-bath killer) decides he must *do* London. He changes his winning formula, and – influenced perhaps by Alvin Langdon Coburn, those long shadows – attempts the 'uncharacteristic' bromoil process.

Slipping away from the coast, on a late train, Judge made camera studies of London at night, blending Coburn's high style with the canny postcard promoter's staple of taxis, buses, policemen in uniform, equestrian statues.

Businessman first and artist as a consequence of that, Judge didn't waste time on such wonders as Coburn's cloud studies. He didn't have access to Henry James, Mark Twain and Ezra Pound. His runs on London were covert, fifth-columnist, Hitchcockian: men in coats and hats, sinister crowds. Hastings by day (picturesque, charming) – and London by night, West End, river (you can follow the route he took).

Camera Pictures of London by Night (1924). The book. A collector's piece. £350 or more for a fine copy.

November evenings. Stalking the action. Holborn Viaduct, Temple, the Embankment.

'Movement, life, and mystery,' Judge wrote. 'One can almost imagine one's self transported into another world, strange and alarming, alluring and sometimes fearsome.'

He wanted: an antidote for colour. A painterly funk of greys, crisscrossing vehicles, solitaries pursuing their 'private diagonals'. Drama exaggerated by low-angle POV. The more you hide, the softer the focus, the better it plays. Bromoil soup against the clarity of coastal light.

Stop it. Jacky is trying to haul himself out of his chair, wondering if he'd better sort out some crisps for the walk to Pevensey, a family-size pork pie.

The lacquered surface of the bar, its puddles of spill. Brandy glass with one last swallow. The leopard woman's postcard, her choice: 'A Night Arrival at the Grand Hotel'. Very *Thirty-Nine Steps*. Very

. . . *Grand Hotel*. Garbo, Joan Crawford and a squelch of Barrymores. I approve the setting – cab with open door, mysterious stranger (collar turned up, leather bag). Illuminated triangle above dim entrance. *Where is the photographer?* What did society make of this provincial lurker? Private detective? Government snoop? When it was all over, did he slip away to the station?

STOP.

It was the bromoils that slipped, leaked. Go to Judge's archive (Roos did) and they'll tell you that prints can no longer be taken from those glass negatives. London has reverted to its original fog, memory devoured by fungi. The night city is an involuntary collaboration between what Judge saw and shapes like fingerprints. A superimposition of gas clouds, smears, phantoms of future terror. Soon the glass will be clear as water.

So turn the bloody card over. Read what she says.

Something's dripping into my brandy. I could fill the glass in a minute. Vein pulsing like an over-generous optic. A new cocktail: 'Bram Stoker's Vortograph'. Mongrel blood, very fresh and red, with a shot of *fine* and a dash of Worcester sauce. The point of my chin, the old shaving wound, has spontaneously unzipped. I'm like a Romanov, a haemophiliac.

STOP IT.

'Stop that right now. You can't bleed here.' The barman rushes me with an ice bucket. 'Try this.'

Don't try it. Ice pinks as it melts, a fistful of cubes. Like a butcher's bin. Splashing over the bar, the carpet. My shirt, my jacket. The colour is extraordinary, too rich for an old man. I must be fresher than I thought. I'm emptying, fast, in a lunchtime pub on the hinge of a seaside town that has seen better days: the road to Bexhill retail park.

'You'll have to go, mate. You can't stand here bleeding. We don't have a licence.'

I snatch up the Judge postcard. Swab it with a dirty rag. The woman has stamped it, ready to go, addressed it and written a few words.

Now you're back – and when you're ready – come and see me in Cunard
Court. I've found out something very interesting about KB.
   Love, Marina.

We could deliver the card by hand. The name of the addressee
meant nothing – but she lived in Pevensey Bay.

Pevensey Bay

It was almost dark by the time we got there, twilight thickened around us like a comfortable wrap, muffling the shame of the territory we had to cross. I'd been prodding and poking Jacky since Bexhill: an endless marine strip. Caravan parks for the expelled of Lewisham and Eltham (community orders). Beach huts. Martello tower. Railway line. Low hills. Marsh. You might consider this a proper location in which to debrief a Soviet spy, a double agent, but *live* here? They hadn't heard, most of them, old ladies (fit as gibbons) peeping out from behind lace curtains and wooden shutters: the invasion was off. Hitler wasn't coming this year. And Napoleon was doing a time-share on Elba.

A high shingle ridge that would never be high enough, Roos reckoned, to keep out the sea: mortgages refused on asbestos properties, strictly cash. A constituency therefore of Londoners (barbecues, beer, boats) of a particular stamp, sturdy individualists with interests in the motor trade, plumbing, taxidermy and other outreaches of the free market. World-class wet suits: wind-surfing, sewage-dodging, messing about on boards, in dinghies, making plenty of noise. Melancholics too. Non-commissioned documentarists, painters without galleries, writers who didn't write. The holiday home of Peter Sellers (pre-Ekland and still the plump gadget freak with the 16mm camera): sober records of present malaise and future despair. A beach, a bungalow, a family. Spike Milligan hammered out a few episodes of *The Goons* between breakdowns.

It helped Roos to talk. If he couldn't rabbit, he had to confront the reality of where he was, this ribbon-development POW camp – tolerated (for now) because there wasn't quite enough land between sea and salt marshes on which to put a superstore. Pevensey lifers were the equivalent of the human shield in Baghdad.

Donkey sanctuarists: dressed down and prepared to castrate invaders on sight. Feisty old dames who looked as if they swam over to Dieppe every morning for a cup of coffee. If a life sentence means what it says, Pevensey Bay has cracked it: a leathery immortality (animals included), clumps of sea kale, uninterrupted contemplation of the great fact of the English Channel.

We started to worry about house numbers. I tried to remember the address on the fugitive Marina's postcard. Roos had *his* number, the home of the woman who found the clergyman's severed head, written on his palm – but it was too dark to read. Buzzed by speeding cars that either travelled full-beam or didn't bother with lights, we struggled to interpret the scrawl on the Belgian's yeasty paw.

Snap! You guessed. Our numbers were the same. But impossible to make out from the road. Bungalows (three-deckers stacked one on top of the other, Spanish arches, papal balconies) were set way back, up on the shingle ridge. We had no view of the sea, but took it on trust, that rumble; wind howling through the narrow gaps between properties. Down where we walked, there was nothing to help us: garage doors, painted dustbin lids and a commendable absence of novelty nameplates. Pevensey Bay was strictly word of mouth.

Which meant that, every fifty yards or so, one of us (me) would open a garden gate, negotiate a set of steps, feel for numbers – or peep through an uncurtained picture window. I saw things that should remain private, between consenting adults and pieces of electrical equipment (television sets). I found the magic number: 147. (Like the catalogue entry for Max Beckmann's *Young Woman with Glass*). I knocked.

Luckily, Roos was following close behind on the slithery wooden steps, a plump cushion. I might otherwise have tumbled right back into the prickly plants.

Blaze of light. Glimpse of nightkitchen. Laurel and Hardy in bowler hats. With none of their celebrated slowburn gravitas. Wrong shape, wrong size: Hardy was petite but padded, very pretty

– despite the grease moustache. While Laurel was tall and strong; anti-gravity hair, black bowler perched like rowing boat on sandbar. They did the walk quite well – for women. The tie-wiggling. With camply extruded digits. Voices too: like folk who had come late, and reluctantly, to sound.

Long jackets and smooth bare legs.

'Another fine mess,' Hardy, the little one, piped; after some fastidious pantomime, removing a speck of dirt from the corner of her eye. Geisha blink of a whiteface transvestite with padded belly. 'What took you so long?'

'Don't say a thing,' Roos whispered, 'about the head. Not yet.'

The odd couple – each to his own – bowed us in: through narrow kitchen to sitting-room (cushions, clothes, boots, sandals, scarfs, flatscreen TV, leather couch, pyramid of video cassettes).

'We're having a bit of a Bergman binge,' the redhead announced. 'Girls-together weekend, pigging out. Wine, chocky biscuits, black Pak. Find yourselves a glass.'

On the flatscreen, in morbid colour, someone had been killing sheep. A woman on crutches was having a bad time. And a cigar-smoker showed off an archive of gloomy photographs that he kept in a barn.

Jacky perked up at once. '*The Passion of Anna*. Great. Anything to eat in the fridge?'

'I think we've finished the last packet but you're welcome to look. And bring another bottle while you're out there.'

I followed the waddling culture freak into the kitchen, a glassed platform on unequal stilts over a rough garden. I wasn't in the mood for movies, Baltic angst (coals to Newcastle); mad women watching other women go mad. This pair looked just about capable of following the pictures in Rick Stein (pristine copy on shelf, along with the *River Café* thing). The only literature was a Zelda Fitzgerald biography and the grey Penguin of *Nostromo* – with nicotine-tanned pages. The girls were smoking their way through Conrad's mythical South American republic of Costaguana. I checked. They'd reached the bit with the eyed-patched general, Barrios. *Extraordinary night*

*rides, encounters with wild bulls, struggles with crocodiles, adventures in
the great forests, crossings of swollen rivers.*

'Shit.'

A dozen bottles of Pinot Grigio. A frond of black lettuce that was
starting to sweat. A tub of margarine. Two bullet-like olives in the
salad tray. Roos was furious. 'We'll have to use the phone. They
must have an Indian takeaway in the village.'

I could hear low, miserable voices in the next room. And women
laughing, gossiping, heart-to-heart: sisterly confession, moral support,
futures mapped out.

Jacky wrestled with the cork. 'We'll get them pissed, right, then
ask about the head. Who found it? Where? Human interest stuff.
You can change a few details and call it fiction.'

When I came back, with the new bottle, the little one was
shoving Marina's postcard (which I'd placed, without comment,
on the coffee table) under a cushion. She was wondering, quite
reasonably, how we fitted in. The tall girl kept up a kind of rapid-fire
commentary, the small one fell asleep.

'Livy's pregnant.'

'Livy?'

Names offered. Ages withheld.

I wrote them down to keep the record straight. The little one is
known, perversely, as Ollie. Livy, Livia. Olivia Fairlight-Jones.
Border Welsh? Same background, I guess, as Tiggy Legge(over)-
Whatever. The royal thingummy. Stan, the oversize Laurel, is
Katherine Cloud Riise – or, more familiarly, Track. Got that?
Friends, artists. The woman called Marina (who sent the card) is
older, a benefactor, former teacher, something of that sort. She
owns the Pevensey Bay bungalow – which she generously offers
out, sanctuary for associates, damaged urbanites in need of R & R
– while she rents a flat in Hastings, where she is supposed to be
writing a book, a novel. Her first.

I felt some sympathy for those French hacks, *nouveau roman*, who
didn't bother with names: single letters were usually enough. *R
watched at the window as the woman undressed . . .*

The Passion of Anna was winding down, the suspected sheepkiller had topped himself. The cameraman, so Roos informed us, was suffering from vertigo. Bergman was plagued with stomach ulcers. And Max von Sydow, commuting between the island location and Stockholm where he was doing theatre, was thinking wistfully of a Hollywood future and *The Exorcist*.

Anna wasn't one of my names. Thank god. They can't make a European art movie without her (character or star); it's the symmetry, the loving gasp in the sound of the thing. I had my hands full with recurring Marinas, Ediths, Isabels. Annas were altogether too much. From the woman who disappears in *L'Avventura* to Jean-Marie Straub's *Chronicle of Anna Magdalena Bach*. From Magnani to Karina: a terrifying absence of invention. Track had four or five names without resource to the Anna thing. I never met a bona fide Anna, which I'm sure you'll agree, given the weight of potential cross-cultural references, was just as well. One Anna and I'd be lost for life.

The Marina person who owned the bungalow had produced a very fine series of images, seascapes, views from a speeding car, retail parks: video-pulls (hence the expensive kit) reworked with paint. In the tradition, so I thought, of all those anonymous women who laboured, retouching Fred Judge's anaemic prints. Or the colourists of *Apocalypse* (1941–2) and *Day and Dream* (1946), portfolios for which Max Beckmann took all the credit.

The women made a pet of Roos, they had him smoking, doping. Instead of getting them drunk, he succumbed to herbal frivolity, descriptions of favourite meals. He was as high as a man of his bulk, stuck to quality leather, can go.

'You have such a lovely lovely little moustache, Ollie. Like a lobster. Let Jacky stroke. Talk to me – about that nasty old head on the marshes.'

'I'd rather talk about dreams.'

She cupped her belly, the hard round shape, no cushion, the restless foetus in its saline pouch.

Track, so Ollie whispered to her new best friend, was sticky with love, a man who taught her how to dowse, they slept together in the car park of a Travelodge. Now they were going off on a circumnavigation of Canvey Island, part of an art project, a walk down the A13.

Livia enjoyed the fruits.

It was illogical. Even in Jacky's current free-associating state. Track feverishly conjoined and Livia pregnant? Another Bergman on the screen, black and white. Track was opening the door, sliding it across, letting in night air, the roar of the sea. Its throat of stones. Roos snoring, heavily. And Livia breathing hard, resting her head, tenderly, on Jacky's soft, paternal shoulder.

I had a dream and this was it. Nothing made sense.

The new Bergman: a burning monk, a child caressing a projection of his mother, an actress struck dumb. Roos told us earlier that *The Passion of Anna*, conceived in a dream, was itself a dream: the only way of resolving the pain, by acting it out. 'A landscape,' the critic said, 'is a state of soul.'

I was with Track on the sofa, a little drunk, very confused, pressing my face into her hair – while she, watching the sleeping Roos, the REM-flicker of eyes behind heavy lids, reached beneath the leather cushion for Livia's postcard.

Pevensey is a hinge place. Future and past balanced on the head of a pin. On Track's decision: *will she remove my hand?* Which I have allowed, innocently, to rest on her thigh. Checking that Livia is still asleep, before bringing the postcard up close to her face, Track slides away – without discourtesy, otherwise occupied.

The blonde in the black mac gets out of the car. She's been trusted with a letter to post, her friend. She is going to break that trust and suffer the consequences. Swedish weather. Bad dreams. Sleepwalkers. A slap. Confessions of her own. Incidents on a quiet beach.

I kept an eye on the flatscreen, that magic window.

'Was it you?' I said. 'Who found the vicar's head?'

'It's still out there.' Track took a drag on her spliff. 'Or it might be under Ollie's dress. In her belly.'

She rolled from the sofa, crawled towards the open door, the night air, calling after her friend.

I stayed with the TV. Bergman's women, Bibi Andersson (talkative nurse) and Liv Ullmann (mute actress), were on the rocks: dappled sunlight, cold rain. The generally intense, static, interrogatory momentum of the piece was interrupted by a lateral tracking shot, the calling of a name. A Scandinavian scream moment.

'Don't hurt me!'

Track searching for tiny Ollie, her woozy and slightly pregnant chum. In the moonlight. Aware of the absurdity, the drama she should have left on the flatscreen, the false window.

'Ollie! Ollie! Forgive me.'

She means the confession about the head. It was never on the marshes, these marshes; it hadn't crossed the river, left Rainham. The head was lodged in Ollie's belly. A thing with gills. A ticking wonder.

I was half in love with Ullmann. I admired Andersson. Serially wonderful, both. But I was suspicious of this performance, the showy silence brought on by newsclips, burning Buddhists. The story Andersson has to tell, the episode with the boys on the beach, the small orgy, is a gift to an actress of her intelligence. Most of all, I doubted the great manipulator, Bergman himself (growling stomach): dark Prospero on his private island. Guilts and calibrated ecstasies. The celibacy of true authorship. Hunger for wives.

I was completely pissed, staggering. Had Ollie found the vicar's head, out there, across the busy road, in the darkness of the marshes? And, if so, how did that advance our case – if she wouldn't talk? If she wouldn't supply the details – fingerprint bruises, maggot patterns – that would allow me to shape a convincing fiction.

Ollie was sitting in a deckchair, nursing a bottle. The presence of the sea, as soon as you stepped out of the bungalow, was overwhelming: sound, weight, distance. Stones dragged, released, dragged again. Sorted and scoured. Beach defences bolstered by tons and tons of sand hosed from off-shore dredgers: the heroic attempt to retard the inward invasion, land piracy.

To be here, child in womb, was heroic too. Swift transitions between dream and place, mother's memories, the prompting of the curled unborn. All those ancient riddles that require no answers.

Track and Jacky Roos, sturdy silhouettes at the tideline, found something to say to each other. We could hear them, over the shingle, the slithering stones, as they went out of sight, down behind the protective bank, in hot debate. Before they returned, in silence, to the bungalow.

The women shared a bed. Roos helped himself to the sofa. I settled in the big chair, letting the film play itself out. Alma and Elizabeth, Bergman's fictions. Alma and Lizzie. Anna and Ollie. Anna is the palindrome. Pevensey Bay, it struck me, is the palindrome of my unwritten novel: confusion behind it and confusion ahead. I took another drink.

There was nothing, within reach, to read – except a battered Iris Murdoch. *Under the Net.* We were, all of us, hopelessly tangled: films with more substance than life. *It was not of course that I had the slightest intention of looking for Anna, but I wanted to be alone with the thought of her . . . I had found Anna deep. I cannot think what it is about her that would justify me in calling her mysterious, and yet she always seemed to me to be an unfathomable being . . . Few things disgust me more than these pretended profundities.*

I yawned, groaned. Threw the book aside. Failed to sleep.

The events I'd laid out with the help of Roos's file – unsolved murder (perpetrator in custody, motive obscure), gangsters and property rackets, botched kidnapping – would exist on either side of this lost night: untouched by me. Reality was unstringing like a necklace. I could run the Bergman video backwards and forwards at whim (I did, I do). Livy's pregnancy can't be undone. The Pevensey landscape is an absolute (changing before our eyes). The rest depends on my mood as I sit down at my word-processor, inspiration or otherwise. I must talk to Hannah Wolf. I must play that scene again, try and make sense of it, our night at the Travelodge.

*

Slatted light across the woodblock floor gave me fair warning: one of those days, so unexpected, so feared, so perfect. Impossible to live up to, impractical to celebrate. Gentle zephyr, kind haze. Soft air. Warm enough to take my coffee onto the stoop, doors wide. To read Track's letter, while Roos tosses and snorts, dreaming of American breakfasts, hogs and grits, sunnyside-up yellow eyes winking from a blue plate.

We decided your coming helped. We can't stay any longer in Marina's place. We're very grateful, please tell her, and send our love – but we feel, talking it over, that living in Marina's house is also living in her story, doing what she thinks we should be doing. So it's back to Essex, to our unfinished project, the road exhibition. Canvey Island (you should read Behindlings *by Nicola Barker) and Southend and Shoeburyness and wherever the A13 finishes.*

Please lock the door after you and leave the keys with Mrs Orwell in the papershop (Coast Road). Turn down the fridge (dial on right) to No. 2. Put the wine bottles in the green tray and carry that down to the gate.

Jacky, it wasn't your fault. Don't fret. Well, it was your fault, but it doesn't matter. It was my fault too. And not all bad. Yes, it was all bad. But no scars?

love, Track XXX

We returned, by the same route, to Hastings – and it was totally different, a different day. The road had shrunk, we marched, one behind the other, with our own thoughts.

'What were you talking about, last night, with the redhead – on the beach?'

'She claimed, she might have something, that we were married once,' Roos replied. 'Definitely familiar, that woman. I'm still paying the standing orders.'

'Worth it though, would you say?'

'No visible scars.'

'Fancy following them, the station – Essex?'

'Wouldn't go that far.'

'Right.'

I tried to limit the damage, Roos's cultural retrievals, but I had to let him function, to keep his mind off the hike. He said that J.G. Ballard called madness 'an undeclared war'.

Bexhill was sandbagged, pensioners and displaced persons worked on strategies for avoiding the sea. The De La Warr Pavilion, recalling happier times, other conflicts, featured grid paintings by a Norwegian – like pages of Track's notebook (shown to Jacky) blown up to fill a wall.

We sat on the balcony and imagined this place in more gracious days. Afternoon concerts, tea dances. From his satchel, Roos (recovering fast) dragged out a book: *The Liturgy of Funerary Offerings* by E.A. Wallis Budge. London, 1909. Light-brown cloth, minor foxing prelims, otherwise mint.

'Shall I recite the Forty-Third Ceremony, "The Cake Offering"? Or would you rather treat me to a Full English?'

The point of this reflex bibliophilia was the provenance. Book purchased Bexhill-on-Sea, April 1982: £6 (reduced, on demand, to £4.50). Bookplate of photographer Alvin Langdon Coburn. White circle with arrow, black gates.

Coburn retired to the seaside (Colwyn Bay) in 1918 and pursued other interests: Freemasonry and Buddhist meditation. Image-making, after the First War, was redundant. He was tracked down in September 1966 by poet Jonathan Williams. A stern old man in red-brown three-piece, watch-chain and insignia.

Among rhododendrons and azalea, Coburn twists, reluctantly, for the snapshot: creased brow. The photographer's shadow, afternoon sun, is a minor intrusion. Coburn knows all too well what the granting of this final portrait means.

The view from the rise, by the coastguards' house: Cunard Court and the double curve of the bay. Better than Naples.

Closer to home, we noted Judge's current premises, Italinate, an archive of postcards by the Bexhill Road. Then: ruins. Boats with burst ribs. Sewage outflow. A rough paddock where a lido had once been. A lockup, such as you might find under the railway arches in Hackney, stacked with canvases. Paintings of eyes. The solitary graffito on an abandoned concrete pavilion: I DONT BELONG HERE.

A small boy on a bicycle, blowing a policeman's whistle, calls after us: 'In twenty-four hours, you'll be dead.'

We parted, gratefully, at Entrance A of Cunard Court. I wanted a shower, something to eat. The last thing I needed was the heavy package left at my door. Unstamped, personally delivered. You weren't supposed to get in without permission. We paid a premium for security, service charges. Men in uniforms who smoked in a cubbyhole at night. I moved to St Leonards to escape unsolicited Jiffy bags.

No incendiary devices, no biological weapons. Worse: a novel or set of linked fictions, crudely typed on some charity-shop Remington. From that much-discussed person, Marina Fountain.

This is the book that the angel made John eat.

A hefty sandwich and a jug of coffee. I took them out to the balcony. My eyes hurt, the glare of the midday sun. The sea, with its reversed-loop sound, was all skin: wrinkled, feathery. Petroleum jelly on which gulls skidded.

I started to read. Words swam. Obstructions floated across my field of vision like ectoplasm in one of Fred Judge's nocturnal London prints. I fetched a magnifying glass – progressed, slowly, with agonising difficulty, a line at a time. Much harder this, interpreting alien fiction, than walking barefoot around the M25.

Marina Fountain

View from
My Window

Blind first. Then light, a quiet drizzle through dirty muslin. He sits, head throbbing, head in hands, back against wall. Trapped in the window frame, a fishing boat. Movement taken on trust, on previous experience ... before he risks it, draws back the sliding door. Experiences: a new day.

Who else, Stephen brooded, would appreciate this thing? Appreciate it enough to commit it to memory. Restless wavelets. A boat, riding the swell, circling back towards the red pier, the smudged sunrise.

A privileged viewpoint on the broad sweep of the bay, the English Channel. Keep it as a picture, in chalk and crayon. A composition in noisy segments. Colour independent of line.

That's all. Nothing else worth retaining. Last night's full moon displacing a thin coin's depth on his memory-screen. Satellite hung on wire over a lifeless sea. Two scenes, then, moon and morning. Equally painful, equally persistent.

The first thing that hits you, walking out of the station, is the light, the light of the

coast, the sea. Warrior Square, it says. But
there is no sign of a square. Or of a warrior,
an equestrian statue. A deserted piazza in
which you might expect to find taxis, touts,
runners sent out by hotels. Nothing of the
sort. Distant shufflers moving off, rapidly, to
avoid eye-contact with this alien life-form; a
person from elsewhere. A woman.

You don't need to be told where the sea is,
you start, without considering other possibilities, in that direction. The ground in front
of the station organises itself into a single
street, the usual hopeless non-enterprises.
Ghost architecture. Benevolent obituaries in
which the posthumous casualties of contemporary
life find shelter. And purpose. A daily round
for the desperate: the circuit of charity shops
and indulgent cafés.

Marine speculations, station to seafront,
have gone wrong, but they're not bitter.
There's nothing sour about this street. The
balcony of the station hotel, encrusted with
seagull shit, is crumbling. Hungry vines eat
into sick plaster. ALES & STOUTS: faded script
on washed-over brickwork. The town could go
either way, development (poop-scoops, heritage)
or entropy. She hasn't decided, this traveller,
how to cast her vote. The citizens - exiles,
inbreeds - don't recognise her. Don't understand that she holds their fate in her pocket.
That her slender, unostentatious elegance is
immortal.

The railway pub has beautiful, syrupy-brown
tiles, a foot-bath. She laughed aloud. SHOP-
LIFTERS BEWARE! CCTV INSTALLED. On premises

that stock nothing except dog baskets and rusty tins. She stopped, hand on hip, and cackled. Moorish arches, obliterated in generations of paint (canary yellow, burnt orange), jungled in greenery. Tobacconists coming to terms with dope culture. Graveyard of the antiques trade. Milk bars with subdued chrome and greasy Formica. Calendar views of Turkish beaches.

Huge gulls, incognito albatrosses, scream the news. They know she is in town. They shriek and warn, skid on roof slates, bombard bald skulls with white-green droppings.

One or two locals, clinking carriers keeping them in balance, assessed the incomer: smoke suckers. They swallowed blue-grey clouds: anachronistic residue of the age of steam, belching locomotives, care-in-the-community casuals encouraged to take up the weed. As a substitute for everything. They leered, politely. Without dissimulation.

She was something new, heat. A different smell. Beneath travel-dust, exotic combinations of body sweat and precious golden essences. The remote possibility of future sexual congress did not concern them – fantasies of the fed and fallible, the eros of employment. Congress. Fresh blood. Novelty. Repetitive playlets of seduction or seizure: not for the seasiders. Drinkmoney. No point, down here, in begging openly. Sitting pathetic on the curb, propped against a shopfront, the wall of a bank. Banks operated without cash-dispensing hatches. Marksmen on roofs waiting for the next raid; a shooting-gallery with live targets. Wall machines, if they had them, would choke on cancelled plastic, chewed-up fakes, revoked credit.

The woman was too tall for the watchers. Her eyes too sharp, all pupil, no cornea. Black. Then grey. Then blue as everything that's been forgotten. The vagrants withdrew their minimal interest. They knew when they were out of their league. They valued blood deposits they hadn't yet sold. They pinched pulses in their necks. Her long stride, childless, took her so rapidly along that straight street, down the retail canyon, towards the sudden slope that led to the sea. She was unimpressed, they understood, by charity bazaars, dealers who peddled versions of the same necrophile stock, price-ticketed refuse. Nothing of now, today, was on offer, everything had an erased history. Some of the shops were innocent of product, giveaway paperbacks in a plastic tray, empty video cocoons with misleading labels.

The town was its smell. Fried fish, dead clothes, seagull shit on windscreens. She didn't belong, among the professional scavengers, the bag carriers; too many fingers, feeling, stroking, pinching sour nylon, testing the stretch in wool, sniffing lycra.

'Cora' - she picked the name at random from a label - would do. For the moment. More than an alias, a fresh chapter. Anyone who steps from a train becomes, with that first breath, a character in a novel. Here was a good town and a good season in which to lose yourself; to stay lost, that was the pitch. Cora wasn't buying. Wherever she washed up, that was the story.

A location where her crimes were beyond the imaginative capabilities of the inhabitants – and the authorities.

Shoes were difficult. The skirt, the pale linen jacket. Easy, accommodating. Appropriate to the sticky, unsettled weather. She didn't need stockings or underclothes. A green canvas satchel with yellow leather straps. She changed, screwed up her old things and forced them into a plastic bag, which she left in a refuse bin. Where it attracted the immediate attention of a group of rag-pickers.

She was thirsty, suddenly, for milk. The idea of it. Creamy moustache, elbows on table. Milk and biscuits. Nursery food. Nursery food in an empty nursery.

She went into what might have appeared (to a writer of guide books) as a period piece, an old-time bakery with marble tabletops and wooden benches, frosted partitions; lovely galumphing girls, in white overalls, talking among themselves, ignoring the crusties, brandishers of single coins. You could conjure up, if you pushed it, a cow in the yard.

Pensioners, unculled, day-released from hostels, hanging on in dowdy seafront flats (owned and operated by teenage villains), hoped they were unnoticed. They mobbed and clustered, heads wobbling, knuckles swollen, joints creaking. The girls behind the counter couldn't hear what they said. Cuppa. Cuppa. No choice about it. Cuppa to grow cold on a ledge at the back, out of sight, away from the street. The tolerated at the limits of their liberties.

Cora, in her charity-shop outfit, shoes

pointy and pinching, linen impregnated, not
unpleasantly so, with another woman's cheap
scent, opened her satchel. Took something out
and laid it, between a mug of milky coffee and
a large, sugar-glued oat biscuit (dry as hemp
and half as appetising). She dipped and
nibbled, flakes lodged between sharp white
teeth.

She tapped the edge of the postcard against
the marble, tested it to see if anything would
fall from the picture. A seascape: yellow,
blue, green, orange-red on the sail. A signature in the bottom-left corner: <u>Keith Tollund</u>.
This was a Keith who painted like a Raoul,
breezy, confident. Beach boys stripped to the
waist, fishermen in brown trousers straining at
the rope. Wavelets jaunty as wind-in-corn.

Befriended by Dufy. Holidays in Dieppe, so
they said. Keith Tollund, dead and forgotten,
honoured in a municipal gallery (that nobody
visited). Keith was her project. Cora would
comb the junks pits of the Old Town, talk to
pickled men in blue jerseys, haunt dealers,
hoarders, guardians of backrooms: in search of
Tollund. Some word, whisper, of a man who had
lost his reputation. Another life to be rewritten, invented. Another skin to occupy. A room
to be found. Cora traded in discontinued biographies, a cultural bounty-hunter.

Barging in mobhanded. Trampling evidence into
the carpet. Setting up blue and white ribbons.
Noises in the press, Londoners. Cockneys on
expenses. Day at the seaside.

'Bloody mess, boy. Take my word.'

Stephen wasn't listening, he revolved the narrowed base of his thick white cup against the saucer. Spill of weak tea. Squeak of protest. The bent copper liked the place, his choice. Stephen was easy. Cups rather than mugs, fine with him. A touch of class, his informant, the shamed DS, reckoned.

'Old bugger was purely asking for it. Key in lock? Kids all knew, knew him. More cash than corduroy. Dressed like tramp. Bloody disgrace, man of the cloth.'

'Anything of value?'

'Druggies had him over. White goods, not worth fencing. Microwave his daughter gave him, never took it out of the box.'

A woman, walking past the window, the open door, took Stephen's eye: purpose in her stride. She stood out. She knew where she was going. The rest of them, street flotsam, were unanchored, they floated. Stephen watched and didn't listen, using the vision of this woman to detach himself from the copper's drone. He pressed a dirty tissue into his saucer, stared fascinated, as it changed colour, soaking up the tannin spill.

'Old sod like that, wants putting down. Asking for it, boy. Didn't know if he'd shaved that month, scraped one side left t'other. Parkinson's. Cornplaster dripping blood on dog collar. Odd socks. Piss-stained cricket flannels, pyjamas underneath. Give him his due, had some fair gear. Before the kids got in.'

'Do you have a list?'

Stephen waited until the ashtray was full. The detective was fat but he didn't eat. Or sweat. Cold grey skin under one of those calculated haircuts. Untrustworthy on TV: loud-stripe suit, Masonic ring, brutal slash of collar.

DS Krater, who kept cigarettes for professional purposes, non-smoker in his married days, was now addicted. He hated the taste, but liked the risk. Giving god the finger. His hairy digits were yellow as permanent bruises. The old tricks were second nature – shove the packet towards the child molester, then grab his wrist when he reaches out to take one.

The bent vicar, the one they'd chopped into segments and scattered over half of Sussex, knew Tollund. Both poofs, brown-hatters. Small town. Not enough talent to go around, shirtlifters relied on runaways, Balkan gippos. Stephen wasn't prejudiced, he didn't care what they got up to. There might be a story in Tollund. Krater's homophobic rants were reflex, they didn't mean much. By the standards of the force, down there, he was a liberal. He was talking to Stephen, wasn't he? His former colleagues wouldn't wipe their boots on him.

The others, the outpatients in the café, the freaks? Stephen couldn't avoid the long mirror. Prime examples of the tattooist's art, blue mermaids, dragons, barbed-wire hearts. Grafts and erasures. They held an absolute fascination for the displaced Londoner. Stephen saw these exhibitions as phantoms brought to life in the smoke of Krater's cigarettes. Women, more sensitive, went in for removal, discarded lovers, names sandpapered from a fleshy forearm.

Thin gold necklaces, rings, piercings. Orange

skin: part weather, part stain. An illusion of
well-being, health – as you see them walking
towards the marine parade. Dealers from the
hill carried a cellphone in one hand and a
packet of ciggies in the other. Dark glasses,
collar turned up. One of them, Stephen
believed, would have a cache of unrecorded
Tollunds.

Seasiders spat at cancer. Down here, in all
probability, they hadn't heard the rumours.
Cell damage. They smoked as they drank their
tea. Smoked as they tweezered ice buns from the
display case. Smoked as they passed water. They
woke in the night and lit a fag. They smoked
instead of breakfast. They smoked as they swam.
Or jogged. Or cycled. Or went to the surgery,
the school. They lit up every time they got
behind the wheel. They dragged deep when they
spoke on the phone. They didn't share. They
nursed a pack in the hand, spare in pocket.

But the thing that intrigued Stephen, on the
coast for six months now, was the oddity of the
couples. He couldn't imagine how they got
together. They didn't fit, any of them, men
with men, men with women, old with young.
Midwives and garage-mechanics in desultory conversation. Pill-peddlers and Joan Collins
matrons who flogged painted plates, sepia nudes
in pine frames. One very dapper gentleman, seventy-plus, carnation in buttonhole, was
escorting a black female body-builder in a leopard-print sheath, worn off-the-shoulder. Nothing made sense. Like Stephen and Krater.
Different cultures, different origins. Different exiles. They both, if it came to the pinch,

had East Sussex addresses. Neither of them belonged.

Krater shot a smalltime drug-dealer in his own bed. The wrong man. At the wrong time. When the council was going progressive, Euro-friendly: white paint and teams in orange jackets cleaning the beaches. Wrong house, wrong day. Head throbbing, breath like ullage. On early call after a weekend's boozing. The nationals picked up on it. One-day filler on the inside pages.

'Something and nothing, boy. Should have been sorted. Queer vicar, big house, takes in your average teenage psycho. Wants to teach him – about art. Gaff stuffed with portables. Strangled with the cord of an electric iron while he's lying in the bath. Butchered like the Sunday joint. Blood all over. Kid tries to flog the paintings in Bohemia. Vicar keeps boat, over in Eastbourne. That's where they find the torso. More prints than Fleet Street: oars, tarpaulin, arsehole. Hands and feet on Pevensey Levels, chewed up by sheep. Head still missing. Like the paintings. Nobody gives a flying fuck, tell the truth.'

'What did the boy say, when you got hold of him?'

'Sod all. Topped himself on remand. End of story.'

A hooded woman, old, twisted in the spine, dwarfish, stared in at the window. Hanging on the crossbar of a large, dirty perambulator. The infant, Stephen was horrified to notice, to notice himself noticing, was dead. Skull like a bunched fist. Close-swaddled in rags. Cholera case. The glass in the café window, the barrier between them, turned woman and child into an exhibit. The woman wasn't looking at him, but at Krater, her lips mimicking the movement of the disgraced copper's slack mouth, pursing to blow out spittle in place of cigarette smoke.

When Krater lifted his gaze, she turned away, moved off down the hill. Stephen, throwing a few coins on the table, got up to follow. When he came alongside, wondering if, despite himself, he would say something, he saw that the dead child was a doll. A doll that was propped up, staring at him, holes for eyes.

She progressed around the museum, among the seascapes. Provincial museums never fail to charm, bell jars of borrowed air: no expectations, no agenda, no obligation to inform. Time, in dusty columns, too lazy to advance.

Cora advanced, the sound of her heels (toes pinched and blistered) on the wooden floor, on soft linoleum, clicking against the metal trim of the rather pompous stairs. Culture for the edification of the unedified, the lost. The middle classes at a loose end, with children.

A woman, unevenly stained, hauled her partner in from the street. So that she could find a place in which to squat, pass water. And emerge, as Cora noticed, with talcum powder across her broad bottom, dark-blue denim – as if she'd been dusted for fingerprints.

'Come on. Come on then, come on.'

The man, drawn on the leash of domesticity, was slow to respond; he had actually become interested, pricked by, this display of ration

books, tickets, ribbons, tin badges. He tried
to justify his queer enthusiasm for the cases
of reserved, improved ephemera. But he knew
better than to speak. His partner, cuffing one
child, dragging another, was already returned
to the fresh air.

The hall of paintings, upstairs, was
deserted. The last visitors had tramped
through, without pausing, completed their circuit, earnt their pit stop. Seaside places are
big on memory, bits of wood dug from the sand,
spars, fragments of pots rescued from the deep.
Albums of dead sailors, faces peeled by experience, layers of wrinkles and ice-bleached whis-
kers. Piped and sweatered. Faces too strong for
the technology.

Seascapes. Arty visitors to town: as a fishing village, a resort. Essence lost or
absorbed. An accident of geology, a break in
the cliff, a harbour. The Cockney Turner takes
himself out to sea, looks back, across pitching
waves, green-and-black peaks. The yellow cliffs
are a barrier. Minor romancers and journeymen
set up their stools at prominent places and
limn the picturesque, an ordered landscape of
small craft, pulled up on the beach; two men at
the cliff's edge, sheep daring the drop.

Rossetti drew sickness. Lizzie Siddal twisting her pain against a hard chair. Lucien
Pissarro nibbling at particulars, a church,
found something worth retaining in the haze of
light; a premature pass at pointillism.

Then: Keith Tollund.

Gay in all seasons. Quarters of creamy
colour, honey you can lick. The man didn't

paint, he dabbed at the canvas, using face
powder and dry cosmetics. He waxed seascapes,
as he waxed his legs. He made them up, pretty
as a picture. He crayoned them with yellow lip
gloss. Combed waves to curve like eyelashes.
Cora loved what Tollund did. Chalk and green
crayon: sand, sea, air. Blues, yellows, chocky
browns, rouged keels. Self-portrait in seaside
boudoir, attended by sailors (pulling limply on
tarry ropes). Toy yachts sailing across a Thirties bathroom. Just enough puff to fill sails,
stiffen flags. The squadron flounces west like
a chorus line. A cargo boat, twelve miles out,
on the horizon, contradicts Tollund's speculative meteorology with the direction of its
black smoke.

A scene observed from his balcony. Soft
muscle under brown-and-green sweaters, the bare
backs of fishermen. Sand like brown sugar.

But the picture Cora wanted, the one that
would identify Tollund's room, the flat where
he lived before moving to Bath for the final
phase, was missing. Stolen. Mislaid. Loaned out
and never returned. The collection in the town
museum couldn't offer anything better than a
monochrome photograph in the catalogue: window
frame, armchair, yachts in a rectangle. Three
panels of salt-smeared glass: three seascapes.
A perspective she could judge, read back from,
an elevation. At least five floors up with
south-facing view.

This was the hint Cora had been looking for,
a coded inscription on which she could work.
She would check out the west end of town, along
the front, under the hill on which the vicar

lived – that friend of Tollund who had himself
been quartered and dispersed, decapitated. Murdered by a lad who might have reached out of
one of Keith's sketches.

A stiff climb, if you weren't used to hills, if
you lived in cities, riverside places. Cora
sweated lightly. It was not unpleasant, this
absence of underwear. She paused to admire the
eccentric detail of some ghostly Edwardian mansion. They didn't build on this hill, they
colonised it. Parks, crescents, balconies,
sloping lawns, azaleas. The favourite set-up
for future exploitation, quacks and charity
cowboys. Those who used seaside property portfolios to fund fantastic palaces in the neighbouring countryside.

The vicar's house had been Cora's first
choice for the room from which Tollund painted
his <u>View from My Window</u>. Tollund, in his cups,
<u>could</u> have been patronised, offered living
space, by the unworldly philanthropist. He was,
by that period, overplaying his acquaintance
with Eddie Burra, the runs out from Rye in the
Roller. 'The last time I saw him,' the barman
at the Royal said, 'he was dressed as a
Marseilles gangster with a burnt-cork hairline
moustache and toes painted on his shoes. He was
swigging vodka.'

The two dead men, vicar and painter, were
characters at a Chelsea Arts Club ball, entities brought together by their secret life: as
aesthetes. As extrovert inverts, lovers of boy
flesh. All the vicar wanted was to be allowed
to watch his guests bathe. Tollund had differ-

ent tastes, but he let himself be housed – for a time – by the wealthy clergyman. Of late, the retired C-of-E functionary, denied preferment (which, in truth, he had never solicited, too well-born for that), had lost his faith. In the town. In his ability to give shelter and support to the right sort. Boys, just now, didn't want to be taught how to sail, to handle ropes and rudders. They weren't interested in visiting galleries or looking through his albums of fine-art postcards.

He let the wrong sort in. The kind that didn't know how to use a bathroom.

Cora identified the house: a mausoleum, Bates Motel in Aberdeen granite. Stone like the absence of love, grey as unwitnessed ice. Colour hadn't been leeched by local conditions, it never had colour. There were livelier properties in Kensal Green Cemetery. Keith Tollund, sprawled in his armchair, chopping-board across knee, had stolen colour – by fixating on sealight, making regular trips to Dieppe. The vicar's mansion was god's obituary.

The view from the top-floor window, Cora recognised, turning before she reached the crest of the hill, was nothing more than a traffic island, fork in the road, telephone box. Terminal farms where melting flesh condensed on dirty glass. Memory hutches. Language schools. Suicide hotels.

Youths occupied this lozenge of grass, trees like mutated weeds. Broad avenues – of potential escape – radiated out from the scabby island, which became, by default, a place to chill. A suspended bus shelter. A vandalised

phone kiosk: every call an unpunctuated emergency, single parents with scabbed and weeping
arms trying to explain themselves before the
coïns ran out.

A bit of a ruck was occurring. With the kiosk
acting as bunker, into which the victim
retreated. Cora was close enough to be offended
by sound as well as sight of this ugly affray.
Stupidity annoyed her.

A tall thin lad, baseball cap, sporting goods
for non-sportsmen, was ranting, headbutting the
panel. Leaving gobs of yellow-white spittle,
which slithered thickly down. He turned away,
whipping himself up, before his next assault.

'Talk to me talk to me like that knock you
fucking out, spark out cunt. Truth. Cunt.'

He kicked, harder than his soft shoes
allowed, copycat karate. Pain devilled venom.
He stumbled into the road, as into a lava
stream. He hopped, blistered, onto grass.
Charged again, blaspheming, at the kiosk. The
shuddering victim.

What struck Cora, as she moved in on this
futile episode of urban theatre, was that the
gang with the loudmouth, the ones near him,
waiting for a phantom bus, weren't kids, but
an orthodox middle-aged couple, man and
woman, wearing the same shapeless, colour-
uncoordinated leisurewear.

'Kill you bitch you say you say you say that
again kick your head in.'

The experience of the world for this dislocated trio came down to a traffic island and
the capture of a phone kiosk, the only means of
communicating with the outside, with other

intelligences capable of giving judgement – or, at worst, listening to their complaints.

The object of the youth's demented monologue, Cora saw, was a child, a young girl. Partner, possession? Incestuous lover? He was out of control, backing into the road, ignoring awkwardly swerving local traffic, smokers, without cellphones; cars grinding uphill, leaking oil, trailing exhaust pipes. He had to watch his step, onto the high curb, the slippery grass. He screamed at the cowering girl. Who was chewing on a strand of loose hair.

The older couple, at the edge of the island, one foot on the grass, one on the curb, kept their backs to the action, shamed by it. They stared down at a massive, ugly, unused church.

Cora touched the mad boy's shoulder, and when he spun, disbelieving, mid-rant, she brushed the base of an outstretched hand against the ball of his throat. He jerked back, scalded, opened his mouth to scream and couldn't, something blocking the airways, a knot of pain around which breath failed to find passage. He dropped to his knees, red-faced, humiliated by dry tears. She kicked him and he slumped, slithered, spark out, against the kiosk. Now the girl, trapped inside, head barely reaching the panel from which the phone hung, took up her defeated lover's threnody, his screech.

'Bleedin' cunt. Mind your own bleedin' business.'

She hammered the snotty glass, ranting, gesturing. But, even when Cora walked away, she wouldn't step outside.

*

HEALTHY BOWELS? No problem in that department. Quite the reverse. Eyes: like looking out of week-old milk bottles. Ears clogged and sticky, nose broken. But bowels ticked like a German motor: Stephen X, age unknown: writer. Marine exile.

His walk, the colonnade. Wet suits for scuba divers. Yellowed wedding dresses. Black god franchises. Fast food. NO CASH KEPT ON PREMISES. The shops, beneath the hulk of the Ocean Queen flats, dealt in negatives, prohibitions – fear. They kept no stock beyond instantly forgotten memorabilia, concrete floors. Stephen releases a clutch of bad wind.

He had never, before this night, considered taking a drink at the Royal Hotel. Imposing facade, late breakfasters noticed when he crept out for his newspaper (London evening tabloid – of previous evening). More of a temple than a pub. Steps up from street, revolving door. Disconcerting reception area, woman behind desk, dim lights, panels of illusionist glass doubling the stairs, throwing back an atrium of wilted greenery.

Krater was nowhere to be seen. Nor was the bar. The street-level Palm Court, to which ordinary drinkers were admitted, was closed. The upstairs cocktail bar, fairy lights and heavy carpet, was defunct. Approximately-French chairs, Louis-something, faced the sea, occupied by couples who had slept together without being introduced. Stephen couldn't begin to read them. An ominously benign woman of the Rosemary West type, teacher in provincial comprehensive, who had run away with a pustular and hormonal fifth-former (incapable of sitting still): twenty years on. The mute afterlife of a misconceived romance. So Stephen, ex-author, improvised. Even the drinks were out of kilter, lager and pink gin, rum-and-pep against repeat orders of stout. Smokers, of course. All of them. Even the ones in uniform, veteran bell-boys, smoke leaking from cupped fists as they hung around the lift, hoping to pimp for the definitively de-energised.

Stephen hid, close to a pillar, and watched the window. This sea town, as he reported it to himself, fictional enactments of each lost day, was his cinema. A narrative of clouds and surfaces, uncalibrated evolution: he lived in what he saw. <u>As long as he himself was unobserved</u>. When his consciousness froze . . . that was the painting: window/frame. This was such a moment. A painting based on cinema, reflections, cigarette smoke, lights of passing traffic.

Two tendencies, Stephen noted, from his own flat, the high balcony where he flinched from the morning air. Fitness masochism and elective cancer. Obsessive hard-track joggers, hitting against the wind, tough women (weights attached to wrists) and old, weathered men (fit paunches, curved but unwobbly). Tanned, stained, toasted: by hazy sunshine and nicotine. Active early, die late: the concept.

'The motherfucker won't read it, fuck him. We don't need him, right? Script is king. He won't fly to Hong Kong, fuck him. We take it elsewhere.'

Stone-bald, ungay, an American Jew. In black T-shirt, white trainers. Talking to - what? - a

blond German accountant. Young, clean. Disturb-
ingly good-looking. With overdefined, spookily
well-distributed features. Actor turned to
script doctoring? Executive producer (without
product). A deal-maker in a third-class hotel
with an optional view of the sea.

A patrol boat, out of Dover, the kind Charles
Windsor once skippered, which had held its position, close in to shore, all day, was riding
at anchor. Lights on the bow. Rocking gently on
the evening tide.

'We're here, on the spot. We've wasted months
in this craphole reading transcripts, inter-
viewing witnesses, going through the goddamn
files. What we got? The fucking story, man. The
story. We got reality. This is a headline play.
It happened, right?'

'No, actually, I would not say so. I don't
for sure see that. He won't buy. It is still, I
think, too loose.'

'Loose? Fuck you loose.'

The bald man tried to push back the table,
spilling his untouched drink. He stood up, a
stain (the shape of Cuba) in the lap of his
sand-coloured shorts. He stormed the corner,
disappeared from Stephen's view. And was still
swearing when he returned with a fresh cocktail, which he put down beside the other. He
brought nothing for the German, who was scorn-
ing a cup of cold coffee. Pleased with his
reflection in the long window, comfortable with
his partner's discomfort, the accountant lit a
fresh cigarette. Long and very white. The
atmosphere of the upstairs lounge was freshened
by this novelty, American tobacco.

For the first time, Stephen couldn't take the sea. Even of favourite things, you can have too much. The sea was a cipher. It was implacable. He'd interviewed, out at Pevensey Bay, the woman (without a dog) who had found the butchered clergyman's arm. Stephen had been admitted to a beach hut on stilts that, miraculously, became part of the beach, the pepper-coloured shingle shelf.

An unbroken spider's-web protected wooden steps that led up from a bare garden. This woman, quite evidently, had not been out for days. One of those non-eaters, non-movers, who find their place. And abdicate. Turn away, reso- lutely, from other potentialities. Sniff creo- sote and ozone, sit by a half-open door, freshening a large blue mug of tea.

The kitchen door was wide to the road and the marshes, the Pevensey Levels – where the crude- ly amputated limb had been discovered, lying across the path, dragged from the undergrowth by some animal.

She saw what it was, but she didn't react. She listened to the noise the wind made in the reeds – and tried to think of a way to remember that sound. If she accepted the validity of the grand guignol token, she would have to <u>do</u> something. The blue arm was a barrier, that much was clear. But she was reluctant to abort her walk, the two hours in the weather that she allowed herself. On a weekly basis.

The view through that door, democratic shingle, curve of beach, would act as a prompt. For Stephen. Let her bring out the story in her own time. His book, his comeback, was already in ruins; a thing of fragments, false starts, muffled echoes. The Pevensey woman, in her unconvinced actuality, was a sidebar. And better for it.

She wasn't dressed, dressed to receive visitors, when Stephen knocked. She'd forgotten the appointment. Another woman, stepping out of the dim interior, took over. And Stephen played along. Shock, trauma, terrible thing to witness. He toyed with his striped mug (she'd omitted to add the tea bag which would flavour the hot water).

Stephen sipped and waited. Something was wrong. Nobody was smoking. The furniture was unsaturated, minimalist. Londoners in retreat.

After an hour or so it became obvious, even to Stephen, that the women were not in shock, or in any way distressed. They were drunk – just slightly, becomingly, a day or two into the session, pacing themselves. It was Stephen who was edgy, a non-smoker hurting for a passive blast of nicotine (plus woman-breath).

A heavy glass of cordial, Ribena, baby juice, turned out – as the woman confessed, giggling – to be kir. She dosed herself at regular intervals. They'd been indoors, so the friend said, for the entire weekend, snacking on junk TV, voting celebrities out of self-inflicted hellholes, reading extracts aloud, celeb-lit, Zelda, Jean Rhys, Djuna Barnes, all the wild women. Time out, away from the metropolis, relationships. In their own bodies. Relaxed to the point of becoming invertebrate.

What, the friend wanted to know, book in one hand, drink in the other, was Stephen doing

here? Who <u>was</u> he? The period of comfort and
sisterly support for the woman who had found
the distressed body part was coming to an end.
Outsiders were invading their sanctuary. The
friend pulled on a child's anorak when she
heard the knock at the door.

'When I was young, so high, and saw the sea
for the first time, so my mother said, I threw
open my arms and rushed at it. I wanted to
embrace the <u>whole</u> affair, take it home with
me.'

She laughed. And went outside to smoke, sitting uncomfortably on sharp stones.

Stephen, starting a head cold, remembered
this, the woman's words, that night in the
Royal Hotel. The way she clicked a loose sandal
against the sole of a bare brown foot. The sea
would outlive him. 'And ten,' he muttered. The
meter was ticking. But the game wasn't over
yet. Four score years.

'And ten. Ten for good behaviour.'

Returned from his mildly erotic reverie,
Stephen understood that the sea would never be
anything but itself. It resisted simile. The
lights of small boats, out there, winking. He
couldn't face that window a moment longer, the
cinema of ghosts. The unsynchronised conversations of lovers and film-termites, couples
who shared tables like prisoner and escort,
like day-release lunatics. They were, all of
them, unfit for society. They used the seaside
hotel as a decompression chamber.

The cocktail bar, hidden around an L-bend,
was the only viable solution. Almost empty
bottles hung like deserters, dirty glasses

caught by the heels. Varnished cherries left so
long in the pot that they congealed into a
tumour, knobbly cancerous balls. A plastic
pineapple, open, in which the ice had melted
into slush.

Stephen couldn't bring himself to register
any of it. Everything was looking, looking at
him. The bottles, the sticky-slick bar surface,
the mirror strip. How was it managed, this
exchange, seeing and being seen? Remembering?
Describing? Editing? Peripheral vision, field
of vision; looking and not looking. Looking
aslant, slices of the actual: bamboo-faced bar,
red leatherette stools (with chipped chrome),
the absence of the sea.

The painting. Stephen noticed the painting. A
way out of his dilemma, a false window. A view
of the sea. <u>View from My Window</u>. A Tollund.
Tollund's painting. He did not notice the tall
woman in the white linen jacket who had stepped
up behind him.

'So there it is,' she said. 'It had to be
somewhere. But somewhere is never where we
expect to find things.'

Stephen had lost interest in Tollund. He
despised the man – for trying to fix the future
by nailing the absolute to a significant
moment, a view. Tollund complemented the murder, a parallel narrative: that's what he was
trying for, just enough artifice to give spice
to a shilling-shocker.

The painting dressed an ugly set.

'Shall we go back,' she said, 'to your place?
And decide what we're going to do about it?'

*

On the balcony: Cora in a borrowed coat, lifted from a peg by the door, Stephen shivering. They face the sea, a narrow shelf over the coast road, ambulances and squad cars with sirens blaring. The building was floodlit from below, turning Cora, collar up, into a film-noir beauty, a figure of fate. Rain fell in discrete beads. Stephen reached out for them. Before they disappeared into a fuzz of white light. Heavier beads ran along the balcony rail. The sea was a separateness, in which they were joined. His eyes were scratched like old celluloid. Intimations of advancing cataracts.

It wasn't working. Stephen was aware, for the first time, of his own smell, that he inhabited it. It had never bothered him before; living alone by choice, it didn't register. His refusal to bathe, shower, began as distaste for squandering natural resources. The foible matured into habit, obsession; he arranged his life by such minor and unconsidered resolutions. If he looked at the sea, he should respect that substance, water, by leaving it alone. He shaved in whatever was left in the kettle when he'd brewed his morning tea.

Cora's essence, her 'principality' as some film buff used the term (in relation to the young Jane Fonda), extended a few inches from her skin. This was her place, moving as she moved: rain beads running down a slick collar. Inviolable.

The great landlocked mass of the flats, the Ocean Queen, was a speculation that had foundered, too tired, post-historic, botched and patched, even for south-coast property sharks.

The white-stone liner was loud with silenced
voices. Its client base: the Undead. Very old
people, worn to their last layer of skin,
keeping deathwatch on a fading sea. Veterans of
the Thirties, confined to their cabins, outlived by arthritic pets. Pigeon-squatted shoot-
ing-galleries with broken windows. Art Deco
cells for asylum-seekers and economic migrants.

Red sails too close to the glass. Tollund, by
that time, couldn't do middle distance. His
armchair floated out over the ocean. The busy
little yachts of the sailing club were gulls'
wings, blades on an oily sea.

'Deferred immortality,' Cora said. 'Empty
chair: death. Yachts: messenger birds, hope of
resurrection and eternal life.'

Back inside, they saw that Stephen's chair
was the right chair. Tollund's chair. The
inspiration for the painting that now hung
above the bar in the Royal Hotel. Their twin
quests - art and murder - fused and fizzled
into nothingness. The butchered priest, the boy
who hanged himself in his cell, the machinations of bent antique dealers, reduced to fiction. A life, Stephen improvised, to stand for
his own.

The woman, spectre or culture vamp, could
carry this no further. Two dimmed conscious-
nesses, in the shadows of an unlit room,
focusing on a bright morning scene that had
once been captured and was now forgotten,
irrelevant.

Tollund's seascape, Cora understood, had hung
in the study of the vicar (private income,
hilltop mansion). The painting concealed the

peephole through which the murdered man watched boys bathing in the great green enamel tub in which he himself would be strangled and drowned.

Out in the Channel, the boat with the lantern rocked backwards and forwards on the night tide. In a locker, wrapped in tarpaulin, was the head of the painting's last owner, the benevolent vicar. His eyes were open, clear, blue as a Mediterranean sky. The head faced the scene the painter had sketched for him, on commission, all those years ago. A chair with twin indentations, the wrinkled cheeks of the pillows.

'Endless,' he said. It said. 'I have had a good life.'

Cora sat down, back against the wall, wrapping Stephen's coat around herself, searching the pockets for a match with which to light a fresh cigarette.

Hackney

This was the place: Schizophrenia. A New Labour council window-dressing Old Tory corruption: holes in the road, burnt-out wrecks, hooded tollers on bikes, red cones for four-wheel drives. Mid-Victorian squares blithely ignoring bandit estates. Pubs demolished. Cop cars screeching. Old folk, unminded, trying to navigate a passage through boarded-up, council-funded enterprises – Kurdish wine bar, Nigerian financial services, nail-extension parlour – that disguised a Sixties piazza, one of those slabs of awkward geometry that operate as rat runs (war-zone rehearsals) for accidental criminals.

How to play inconspicuous among so many professional exhibitionists, the casualties of peace? Mid-road pedestrians. The voices-in-the-head brigade (who now have mobile phones to excuse them). Plotters. Twitchers. Watchers (sponsored and amateur). Skip-raiders. Natty tourists (the shoes give them away) with black cases and clipboards. Those who live far from the action but are paid to find a solution. Taggers who get CUNT back on walls before the whitewash masking their offensive slogan has dried.

Hackney, a Romance. A lifelong affair for the naturally monogamous Mr Norton.

This was the house Hannah Wolf occupied with her paramour, the journalist. The so-called 'London writer'. A front garden with burger cartons and holes from which bay trees had been lifted. She had left him and moved on, I knew that, further east – Poplar, Bow? I was meeting Hannah at the Docklands Travelodge. I needed to talk. Marina Fountain's *View from My Window* typescript was the last straw. It was obvious that the woman had somehow broken into my flat – key from porter? – and found the preliminary notes for my Hastings novel. Then typed them out, fast. The old Borges trick: reproduction as composition. My work became her work – if she was prepared to take that much trouble. She couldn't resist a few flourishes of her own (the hotel bar I'd never patronised), but what really bothered me was the account of the visit to the women in Pevensey. Fountain must have written it *before* it happened. Much of the rest felt uncomfortably like dictation, poorly transcribed, from a long-distance telephone call. The marine painter Keith Baynes was nakedly pantomimed as 'Keith Tollund'; the hints I intended concerning his sexual preferences (Jamesian and oblique) were exposed as *Carry On* crudity.

I was angry. The victim who had been watched, for so many months, would spy on the person responsible for this web of conspiracy: my namesake, Andy Norton. I had found his house. (Address in phone book. Can you believe it?) If I strolled up and down the road, day and night, mumbling to myself, nobody would notice. I'd fit right in.

No lights, no sign of occupation. Milk hasn't been delivered. Nor post. The only postman I spotted left his sack on the street, let the buggers sort it out for themselves.

I copied Norton. I tried the walk.

Within seconds, I was hit on for bus fares, taxis for partners who were seriously ill in Tottenham (cash returned within the hour). The time was demanded (no watch) by gum-chewing jailbait in vestigial skirts. Cigarettes were solicited by pre-school toddlers. Lights for beslippered outpatients. I understood all too well where Norton, lazy as most of his profession, found his material. He found it, but didn't know what to do with it: let it breathe, let germ cultures form their patterns, shape a coherent narrative.

Later that evening the man returned, limping. Rucksacked. With female company. Back from one of his walks. *I had him.* It was so simple. Try and remember the order of events plotted for my aborted A13 novel: a drift through Whitechapel, a secret stone, Sebald-influenced meditation on Conrad (*Heart of Darkness* and Hackney's German Hospital), with mini-climaxes (patterned after Basil Bunting's mountain range diagram, drawn for his long poem,

Briggflatts) at the Travelodge and Beckton Alp – before the big finish (comedy and tragedy, sex and surveillance) at the ibis hotel, West Thurrock.

I agree: predictable, linear, boring. That's why I abandoned the scheme and took off for the coast, new images. But knowing now that Norton – through some freakish space-time anomaly – was able to read my mind, anticipate my imaginings, steal my glory, I resolved to play him at his own game. I would use insights gained from the Pevensey women, the Bergman films, and rewind the tape: travel back down one of my spiked narrative's tributaries. Road as river. Walking as the only method of escaping from fate's gravity.

Through willed remembrance, I could anticipate (and prevent) Norton's crude plagiarism. What had happened once would happen again: but not necessarily in the same order. Different storyteller, different story. I should have attended more carefully to what Bunting said. He proposed a work in four sections (Spring, Summer, Autumn, Winter), but arranged for the symmetry to be dislocated by an ambiguous central passage, the equivalent of my Pevensey hinge.

'Take the middle out of it,' the moustached and bespectacled poet told me, eyes glinting, when I interviewed him for a radio programme (never broadcast). 'It's a different thing. The middle one is a nightmare or a dream or whatever you fancy. But once you've got that, of course, the chronological structure is obvious.'

I'd worked most of this out on the train from Warrior Square Station to London Bridge (not appreciating that this would involve a tour of Kent and the Isle of Thanet, a two-hour halt in Ashford, a section travelled by bus, change of engine and lengthy halt within sight of our destination). Time enough to think. With nothing to read but the newspaper left by the provocative Marina Fountain (avatar of John Keats's Isabella Jones) at the window table of the Bo-Peep Inn, Bulverhythe.

You'd forgotten? My obsessive-compulsive desire to hoard scraps of paper (for future interrogation)? The conviction that a coherent explanation of the contemporary world might be assembled from news-clippings, video-pulls, buried quotations. Marina Fountain's abandoned newspaper was a holy relic.

Bunting too was much on my mind. His lifelong allegiance to shape. Old rogue. He had to play at journalism (alongside the teenage prodigy, Barry MacSweeney): the *Newcastle Chronicle*. They watched shipping, boats coming up the Tyne. They filed tide times. Bunting was meticulous. MacSweeney learnt the value of getting the smallest details absolutely right. No compromise with reality.

Poets and war. Newspapers and their contraries. Deep truth, the only kind I cared about, belongs with the poets. Basil Bunting, prisoner of conscience in the First War; Quaker, skipper, spy. He worked for *The Times* in Persia. You want to know about Baghdad? Forget rolling TV reports, fixed documentaries. False authority. Read Bunting's translations from Firdosi, Rudaki, Hafez. Read *The Spoils*:

When Tigris floods snakes swarm in the city

Appreciate the vulgarity of the present conflict, study that ancient poem, *Gilgamesh*. The rivalry and love of Gilgamesh and Enkidu.

'Even if I write about brothels in Baghdad,' Bunting said, 'they are brothels I've been in.'

Beyond the train window, a field.

I could learn from the poets, rigour, discipline, attack. Secret structures of rhythm (my ear was tin). But most I could appreciate how, by intense concentration, seizure of the moment, they moved ahead of time: to tell it *as it should be*. Read the Denver man, Ed Dorn, on the Bush boys, the sleazy politics of compromise, perpetual Balkanisation (trashing of memory). Poems are memory-systems. Dorn, on the cone of time, sees what is coming:

. . . the curvature of the earth
from the obscure Islet of Diego Garcia East of
the Arabian Peninsula an experimental

missile vibrates and then launches
from the carrier, and Oh Good Lord, minutes later,
. . . American dumb missile arrives with punity
in the southern suburbs of Baghdad, ruined Cradle of Civilization,
just north of the Garden of Eden which looks, I must say,
rather abused and tacky now . . .

Dorn was locked into the chemistry of the thing, from a hospital bed, years before it happened – seeing through walls, reading the future on TV. Destroyed topographies. Futile sacrifices. Abused language.

I shouldn't read newspapers, it's not good for me (for you). Especially the concerned ones, the ones the hucksters and crooks are always suing for libel (career suicide). Newspapers don't know what to do about poetry, they ignore it – unless there's a prize attached, money, prestige, campus preferment. They might sponsor the other stuff, reflex verse, cheap war rhetoric: the easy way out. Anti-poetry. All too available. Nasty little satires and bleeding hearts. Language is a lump on the tongue. A tight throat. You can't spit it out, unless you rip flesh. Drip blood on paper.

I used to start with the back pages, in my sunny, geranium-on-sill, pigeon-watching, West London mornings: football, rugby, cricket scores. Then the art: book, film, theatre reviews. Junk the rest. One cup of coffee, finish. Get back to work. One chapter – off to the tube.

I dropped the *Guardian* (never a love affair) when they shafted Jack Trevor Story and started using Andy Norton (pit bulls, gangsters' suits, barbers, forgotten London literature). On the evidence of the copy picked up at the Bo-Peep Inn, Marina Fountain (leopardskin pillbox hat, French cigarettes) was a new *Guardian* reader. It didn't matter to her if the paper was out of date. This was an ironic gesture, a style statement. Life on the coast. Last-gasp Art Deco (1938) revamped for property supplements and second-home runaways: worst of both worlds. Marina had the look down pat, the apotheosis of transience. Blink and you miss her. Paint-blistering perfume in a seafront pasta joint.

If, these days, a newspaper left its grubby traces on my hands, it would be in an optician's waiting room, on a train. And I started with the obituaries. Moved on to New Age quackery: fruit for cancer, expensive trainers for ruined knees, torture chairs for wrecked backs.

A book review caught my eye, the title. *Madness: A Brief History.* Wonderful! Like: *Immortality: An Instant Sketch.* Or *Starvation: A Diet of Contemporary Views.* The author of *Madness* was the prolific and respected Dr Roy Porter. His 'eighty-somethingth' book. His last. 'The delusions of the insane can stretch our definitions of the word,' wrote the reviewer. Porter, London writer, broadcaster, raider of lost libraries, decamped to Hastings: a new life. He died, heart attack, cycling uphill to his allotment.

Porter's thesis, distillation of many years' profound study, was troubling: treatment is pointless, madness cannot be defined. 'Aetiology remains speculative, pathogenesis largely obscure, classifications predominantly symptomatic and hence arbitrary and possibly ephemeral and subject to fashion, and psychotherapies still only in their infancy and doctrinaire.'

What point then in my consulting Hannah Wolf? What useful account could I give of my condition? What diagnosis could she form from a single consultation at the Travelodge? The world was the problem and the world the cure. The long march of the A13. The remorselessness of the sea.

The big obit – poached face, candystripe jacket, badger beard, hair like Hokusai wave – was for an artist. A friend of poets. An 'American film-maker who brought a unique eye to his craft'. Another Cyclops, evidently. James Stanley Brakhage (1933–2003). Born in Kansas City: as 'Robert Sanders'. Adopted, two weeks later, by Ludwig and Clara Brakhage.

Stuck there, nowhere, in Kent on a stalled train, by that dull field, the news, not unexpected, was a blow. Stan Brakhage, author of the ultimate autopsy movie, *Act of Seeing with One's Own Eyes*, was himself dead: exposed to obituarists. Biography glossed. Achievements listed. Standing evaluated: 'a kind of poetry written with light'. Brakhage taught *seeing*, fault, flaw, scratch, mark of hand. Layers and shifts. The living/loving family, its ground, at the centre of everything: childbirth, friendship, death. 'An eye unprejudiced by compositional logic, an eye which does not respond to the name of everything but which must know each object encountered in life through an adventure of perception.'

Brakhage wrote so tellingly about the moment when film-pioneer George Méliès watched a static image of waves projected on a screen, and how they suddenly began to move. To *breathe*.

I was diminished by this loss. Marina Fountain, leaving her newspaper folded to the obituary page, had set me up. The catalogue of those who mattered in the world, by whose words and images I had navigated so long, was being rationalised, trimmed. A bad year for poets, now this. They put the bladder cancer down to the coal-tar dyes Brakhage used when he handpainted strips of film.

You can, if you're braver than I am, give your tumour a name – Rumsfeld, Cheyney, Perle – and live with it, reluctant companion in a white marriage, for the time that's left; live with the knowledge that the lump, the cell cluster, is going to die when you die.

Ed Dorn, visiting Rome, took an interest in 'Keats's struggle to die . . . almost visible through the window of his somber room'. The problem of separating ourself, in full consciousness, from the anchor of the body. Dorn's tumour was female: 'she detests who and what I detest'.

The lesser obits didn't hold me. I was running on empty, crocodile tears. The train seemed to have been chartered by Jehovah's Witnesses, the grateful dead on an awayday, crawling towards heaven. Ghost Dance Sioux of the 1870s (courtesy of Buffalo Bill's Wild West show, precursor to the tent show at Guantánamo Bay) saw the railroad as a ladder up which returning ancestors would climb. Justified corpses in the radiance of eternity.

In the bottom-right corner of the newspaper, somewhere between an obituary notice and a news filler, were a few lines penned by a person called Johnson.

ROAD WRITER DIES ON M25

A.M. (Andrew) Norton, 60, bookseller and occasional author, died last Friday in a freakish accident on the road which was the subject of his best-known book, *London Orbital: A Walk around the M25*. It is thought that he was intervening in a road rage incident when he was attacked with a machete. The site of the affray, the West Thurrock approach to the Queen Elizabeth II suspension bridge, had previously provided the climax to his pedestrian circuit – an over-complicated collision of antiquarian retrievals (Bram Stoker and *Dracula*) and hysterical satire (Purfleet oil storage facilities and Essex drug-dealers).

Norton, recently unpublished and retired to the south coast, was revisiting Essex with an eye on turning his earlier documentary research into a novel or film.

Born in Wales, educated in Gloucestershire, his work was largely set in East London. Standard figures from the Gothic catalogue – Jack the Ripper, Sherlock Holmes, Dr Jekyll – make frequent appearances. After some early success, as a latecomer to the school of Ackroyd and Moorcock, his adjective-heavy style with its verbless sentences passed into disfavour and critical neglect. He returned to his original occupation as a used bookdealer. Much of his material had the authentic musty tang of the book stacks and street markets. Norton, according to Calcutt and Shephard's guide to cult fiction, was 'an archivist of omens and the occult past'.

He was unmarried.

When Norton – the other, living one – came out, booted and rucksacked, low morning sun over Hackney horizon, I was ready for him. I knew just how it went. There was a woman. I expected that. Andy never walked without a companion: he needed a stooge, someone to bear the brunt of his 'humour'. She was strong-shouldered, tall as he was, long-striding. I pictured her, nude, in one of those photo-strip sequences by Eadweard Muybridge: *Woman Sprinkling Water from a Basin*. She had lovely thick red hair. She was, or rather she would be, the non-pregnant Pevensey woman, Track. The American. Jacky Roos's former wife.

They came down Queensbridge Road and into the Bethnal Green

labyrinth, Brick Lane. He was snapping away. She, a proper artist, waited. He missed the plaque for Bud Flanagan ('Leader of the Crazy Gang'), high on the wall, above Rosa's café in Hanbury Street. They took tea, chatted to a rather natty schnorrer. An old Jewish feller who fed them a succession of tall stories – which they lapped up.

I caught the name 'Litvinoff', the mention of Rainham. They were headed east. I anticipated every move, every move he made on her: an oblique advance on the golden wolf of Aldgate Pump. They were following, like sniffer dogs, a trail: pre-tarmac, post-development. The soul of the A13. And I was right with them, dictating the script. If I imagined a turn, a halt, a digression, they made it.

I don't think Norton spotted me. Maybe once. In Whitechapel, on Vallance Road. Or a reflection among nautical charts in a shop-window in the Minories. If he did, it was a bad dream, footsteps on his grave. He was dragged forward by the epic gravity of the fallen standing stone, on that bald patch of grass, behind Commercial Road. Who should I throw in to greet them, a dowser? A dowser who just happens to have worked for Ford's in Dagenham. Would *you* believe it?

Norton had no choice. I invented a bit of business to hold him back, while I scooted ahead to the Travelodge. My tryst with Hannah Wolf, lover and therapist. It was her story, really. The disentanglement of dream, reverie, landscape. Freud, Hannah said, was the first great novelist of the twentieth century.

Travelodge

It was in the car park of the Docklands Travelodge, as I paced, restlessly, waiting for Hannah, that I developed my notion of composite landscape (leading to composite time): skies from one exposure (Hastings) laid over another shore (Bow Creek). Characters from a deleted narrative could be given a second chance, revived in order to 'rescue' a dull passage of prose. The entropy of the road, the A13, invited this multilayered approach: documentation, in its absolute form, as pure fiction.

Give me a pen and a pad of paper and I would be totally incapable of sketching Hannah Wolf. My Identikit portrait was blank. She existed, if at all, in random memories: pouring water in a doll's cup for her sister, the way she clung, even now, to the rituals of childhood; her unlooked-for liveliness at the seaside, the rush, screaming, at the waves. And how she bristled, clicked her tongue, when she opened an official letter.

Hannah wasn't happy about this meeting. She had problems of her own. There was no question of letting me into the high tower, Goldfinger's flats with the view over the entrance to the Blackwall Tunnel. A quick drink at the Travelodge would have to suffice. We would meet, at twilight, in the car park (neither of us had cars). Hannah didn't want to listen to my dreary confessions. She wasn't a priest and she had no intention of dressing up, for my benefit, in a cassock. Or any other kind of frock. Of course she would recognise me: the one whose eyes shone in the dark like a photoflash vampire.

A procession of reps in grey suits (carrying other grey suits in protective wrappers), all going *out*, quitting the place, looking for action, gave way to nothing. Baffled road noise. Gritty breezes. A felt, but largely unheard, hum of bad electricity. Boredom would have to be redefined for the A13: it was no longer the precursor to retail terrorism, the void. Something worse. Shadows etched into tarmac. Hours and hours of CCTV footage rippling into orgasmic excitement: with the arrival of a crew of transients carrying black bags.

Like the Keystone Kops invading Tarkovsky's 'Zone'. The confirmation of my landscape thesis.

I ducked behind a car, a Nissan Primera. I had time to read, by braille, the letters in their circle, before this distracted man, his family, followers, children, hauled themselves into the lobby of the hotel.

He looked quite like the hyper-realist painter Jimmy Seed – about whose work I had once written a few thousand undistinguished words. We spent a long afternoon in his Hackney studio wrestling over a bottle. I wasn't much of a drinker, up until then. And he was trying to quit. Most of his recent work was predicated on the absence of booze.

When Jimmy went dry, so he told me, he started leaving people out of his paintings: neck-biters, slags, dog lovers, derelicts. Women with fat legs, visible pantylines and rucksacks. Men pissing on fires. He was right on the money. Out of Hackney and Limehouse and onwards to the A13. Cinemas, bingo halls, drinking clubs: waiting for demolition. His canvases were too big for the studio. They belonged on hoardings, advertising things that had already been sold.

Jimmy was the death of narrative. If you saw a photograph of the painter, hands in pockets of raincoat, up against the wall, towpath of canal, white shirt buttoned to the collar, he resembled a political prisoner. A man in the wrong place, Belfast. Waiting for a bullet. Friendly fire.

So here they all are, the unpainted of lost London. I watch them stagger across the car park, my cancelled fictions: the American woman, Track, kid in one hand, black bags in the other – and sullen Andy Norton (fink, liar, thief). He fancies his chances. A new location, a road for the morning. Troop of bohemian vagrants (artfully introduced). A strong woman to temper his culpable misogyny. He can't believe his luck. It's almost as if somebody is pulling the strings. He talks about 'tapping territory', mediumship, ley lines, possession. He's even come up with a tame dowser.

Hannah caught me by surprise. I think she'd been spying on me for some time. She kissed me full on the mouth. I tasted her. Then she broke away, skittering off towards the picture window, the bar.

It went well, the evening. I thought so. A place nobody would ever find us, dark alcoves, soft Muzak. We drank steadily. I learnt, with gritted teeth, how to listen. Hannah had access to material I knew nothing about: communal life, post-Laingian politics, Poland. Poplar.

The more she talked, the happier she was. Between fugues, we necked. I let her run. I was beginning to enjoy it, being an audience. Freud, she announced, was an artist, a myth-maker, a proto-novelist fixated on sexual drama (place him alongside Ibsen, Strindberg, Bergman). Jung was a premature Californian. She had a postcard of a rather wonderful painting, *Freud and Jung Leaving New York*, by one of her clients (don't call them patients, nutters). A beard called Rhab Adnam. Wild seas, off Manhattan, the great psychologists hand in hand on a slippery deck: tall towers trembling. Impossible not to read this naïf apocalypse, painted thirty years ago, as prophetic (all good art *begins* there).

'Either you make reality an object of pleasure, if you are powerful enough already.' She quoted Jung. 'Or you make it an object of your desire to grab or to possess.'

There was no difficulty in avoiding Jimmy Seed's gang (it *was* him), they were getting loud and plastered. Jimmy was back on the booze, stress had driven him to it; taste and warmth on tongue and throat, glow in belly, welcomed him like an old friend.

I liked Hannah's voice, disparate elements of race and place had come together to form her disguise: Whitechapel, Hackney, Bow and the real east, Kraków, Kishinev, Kurdistan. Her eyes shone and her hands moved. Enthusiasm (too light a word): possession. The yielding up of self. Touch. Her hand alighting on my thigh. My arm closing, quite accidentally, around her shoulder.

In the long mirror above the bar I caught the other Norton's eye: mean-spirited, voyeuristic. *You looking at me?* Another round: Kummel, lemonade and ice for Hannah, while I stayed with the whiskey. Norton pretended to be absorbed in the TV film – *The American Friend*? Betrayal. Double-dealing, trains, sickness, borders. Fellow director Nicholas Ray guesting in an eye-patch. Avatars of death everywhere.

I asked the barman, a man who looked like an air steward who'd been found out, if I could get a room for the night. It was going to work with Hannah. She couldn't, at this hour, walk back, alone, across the A13 into that estate. Talking made her affectionate. It might have happened too – but for Norton, the smirk with which he watched Dennis Hopper's exploitation of Bruno Ganz. America and Europe. Revenge, I suppose, for the adaptation of an American original by a German: the disapproval of Patricia Highsmith. Her crooked mouth.

Wait for him in the Gents, then finish it, stuff his fat head down the bowl. Repossess my own story, clear the road. A night of love with Hannah – then, unbathed, a walk to the limits of the A13, Southend, the sea. Beautiful shifts of energy: fresh images, fresh prose.

Meanwhile, to pass the time, I told Hannah one of my dreams. Do you ever read the same book twice? And wonder at the changes? Hannah was always asking, if a film came on, late in the evening: 'Have I seen this before?' The answer is always 'no'. You redirect, respond to trigger images, throwaway gestures, the clothes they wear. Dreams should never be recounted – because you shape them, smooth out glitches, apply logic, search for the kindest camera angles.

Hannah broke away, detached my arm. Took fierce spectacles out of her bag. She swept the room, as if seeing it for the first time. She noticed other drinkers, pulled down her skirt.

'I dreamt that I cut off the little finger of my left hand.'

'Please,' Hannah said.

It did sound gross, banal. The first fascination of dream-revelation, like seeing yourself on television, soon fades.

'And next morning, cutting bread, I really did slice the thing, to the bone. Here, look.'

'Don't. One more word and –'

'A woman I met on the south coast recommended a novel set on Canvey Island, which involved a guilty walker – responsible for his brother's death – feeding his fingers to an owl. I think it was an owl. I can't imagine how he trained it to stop there.'

'This is perfectly disgusting and quite pointless. I'm not and I never was your therapist.'

I stopped, of course. Stopped speaking. The trance of tender forgetfulness, between Hannah and myself, was shattered. But the finger theme wouldn't go away. Gestures. First finger and little finger, outstretched, warding off the evil eye. Eye in the palm of the hand. Eye of Horus. Eye in a triangle: Aleister Crowley. Tattoo parlours of the Old Town. A barber on Cambridge Heath Road putting a new blade into his razor, missing digit, tight-skinned, raw.

My great-uncle (on my mother's side), I'd forgotten him, a ghost in the attic, simple-minded but without harm. My grand-father shaving the old man, towel around neck, on a stool, outside in the sunshine. Soft bristles. Toothless, grinning, he shows me his stump.

And *Struwwelpeter* by Dr Heinrich Hoffmann. Those German doctors! Another nightmare. The smocked boy on the cover with his blond Roger Daltrey afro and fingers like branches. Brightly coloured woodcuts: masturbatory warnings.

> The door flew open, in he ran,
> The great, long, red-legg'd scissor-man.
> Oh! children, see! the tailor's come
> And caught out little Suck-a-Thumb.
> Snip! Snap! Snip! the scissors go:
> And Conrad cries out – Oh! Oh! Oh!
> Snip! Snap! Snip! They go so fast.
> That both his thumbs are off at last.

Robert Mitchum in *The Yakuza* (1975). He hacks off his pinky, a point of honour, gangster-Samurai thing. I thought about continuity problems: how they'd keep the hand out of shot for the rest of the film. Somnolence and celibacy, Mitchum's schtick. Japanese buddy (Ken Takakura). The symbolic castration helped.

The images kept coming. Hannah moved right away.

William Burroughs.

Bill took off the top section of his finger with poultry shears. ('Stainless steel, sir. Never rusts or tarnishes.') He set the saw-tooth lower blade against his little left finger and squeezed. Blood squirted. He wrapped the joint (no longer part of the story) in Kleenex and went out to a bar for brandy. He brought the severed fingertip to his analyst, Dr Wiggers. Who was sure that Burroughs was undergoing a psychotic episode (as I was, now, by proxy).

The Beat Generation finishing school: Bellevue Hospital. His shrink, a 'lady', taps a yellow pencil on her teeth.

'Do you hear voices?'

'When people talk to me, I can hear them talking, yes.'

'No, I mean, do your hear voices talking inside your head?'

'I suppose you could say I have a vivid imagination.'

'Now, what about this self-mutilation?'

'Oh that. Well, that's part of an initiation ceremony into the Crow Indian tribe.'

People like to be photographed with Burroughs: celebrities, movie stars, aspirant writers, painters. Mick Jagger, David Cronenberg, Francis Bacon. It's a genre: skull and flesh. Burroughs: memento mori to twentieth-century culture. I'd been snapped with him myself, beside the goldfish pond, a couple of weeks before he died. By one of the young men, the carers. You could hold that photograph in your hand and watch the lineaments of the face disappear (mine before his).

Hannah yawned, cumin and caraway seed. I could see the capillaries on her tongue, tiny hairs: rough pink fur. I wanted her to be my owl, claws and feather cloak. I wanted to feed my fingers into her mouth. But she was tired, preoccupied. It wouldn't play, the scene I was scrambling to write.

Poor Conrad. How would he open his sauce bottle without thumbs?

Norton lurched after Jimmy Seed, out of the bar. I followed. Anger boiled in me: off-road rage, Travelodge temper tantrum. Smash his skull. Splinter his face. Stop the story right here. Cancel the stupid drama that is still to come at the ibis hotel; complex diagonals of action I'd never be capable of articulating – killer in car, watchers at window, Albanian kidnappers. (Are you sure they weren't from Romania, Moldova? Mountain men. Catholics not Muslims? Economic migrants sending money home.)

'What's your game? Staring at a strange woman in a hotel bar?'

We wrestled. I drove his face against the mirror. I wanted to print the slogan – *Pastis* – backwards on his forehead. Absinthe. Absence. I wanted to push him through – into hyperspace. Let him splinter and fragment.

He vanished, I bled.

I filled a basin with cold water, splashed my face. Norton wasn't a cancer that would perish alongside me in the crematorium. Nor a double, Xerox, trial run. He hadn't filched DNA, grease from my poultry shears. Andy was certainly no parallel universe alter ego, fetch or substitute. Tanist. A simple grammatical error, shift of pronoun: he for I. Exit and out. Reality requires an even tone of voice. Fiction demands the courage to walk in other people's dreams: regime change. Know how to steal and when to keep it buttoned.

Hotels are always aphrodisiac: the barely felt vibrations of constant traffic. Barefoot in carpeted corridors. Lifts like safes: the two of you, close, sharing air, not touching, not yet. I was aroused, in the old days, by the corruption of the city, wealth, power, institutionalised mendacity: so fuck it away.

Ruth Alsop. The original. My one and only.

Ruth liked hotels: the anonymity. The simple fact of not being in a place of laundry baskets, ironing boards and shopping lists. A house where she was responsible for sheets, bills, toilet rolls. She loved, and kept, those little complimentary wrappers of soap. But, most of all, she loved the view from the hotel window; being able to sit and watch the town square, the river, somewhere she would never again visit.

Hannah was very different. Her home was the heart of things: the setting of the table, the polishing of furniture, the arrangement of books. In theory. In practice, domestic space was cramped and chaotic, tumbles of papers, clothes, meals begun, abandoned, preserved, forgotten. When the cleaning had been done and the room was tidy, cut flowers, music, she relaxed, relented, became affectionate. I was rewarded, confirmed in my human mess, surprised by the hunger she unfailingly located somewhere within me.

The Docklands Travelodge was never going to be right. It reminded Hannah of her internship, a hospital in West Texas. Troubled strangers, about to go through some bad experience, wondering if they could meet the bill. Would it be easier to die under the knife? Leave their hated relatives digging up the garden to find the cash.

I didn't know what to do, what to say, how to move. Hannah was brisk. She ripped off her skirt, strode into the bathroom (a cupboard), pissed loudly with the door open, ran the tap for a moment, came to bed.

I took a shower, but it didn't help. She was sleeping in white T-shirt and black bra (she never bothered with colour coordination). I wanted to talk, nibble, come at the business obliquely, as if by accident – but that was impractical. She was comatose, snuffling, and I was painfully priapic. Her bare legs and great thick bush excited me. I stroked, I nuzzled.

'In the morning,' she mumbled. Without turning to face me. 'Much better then.'

I loved the way her lips thickened, muscle, rind; thickened and became moist. As I was. In a state to crack windows, stop the traffic.

'Too tired.'

She rolled away, curled up. And there was absolutely nothing, I knew from long experience, to do about it. The road was out there, a few yards from our bed, I concentrated on that: remembering, step by step, every yard I had walked from Aldgate Pump. I anticipated the next day's march, Beckton, Rainham, Thurrock. I called up markings on oil tanks, graffiti on the river wall. Somewhere between Chadwell St Mary and Mucking Marshes, I fell into a shallow and troubled sleep. I floated out on a slack tide, pressed against Hannah, dreaming of Ruth.

Barking

Begin with a hollow laugh. I am walking in a south-easterly direction, at pace. Tin noticeboard on sewage outfall path. The oxymoron: 'Recent History'. Taggers, spray-can bandits, and their idiot revisions. How far back do we travel before 'history' kicks in? Allen Ginsberg, I remember, was very excited when the huge poet Charles Olson announced, on the crest of one of his more messianic episodes, that history was over. A summerhouse near Regent's Park. A middle-aged Jewish man with a beard. Being interviewed by a nervous youth, his first paid assignment. Ginsberg scratches, grooms, worried about his lover's breakdown, back in New York, smashed windows, incarceration in madhouse. A dark-green T-shirt rides over gently protuberant belly. Buddhist breathing, English cigarettes.

'Olson says that now everyone can select their own images, everyone is on to the fact that language is controlling them on a massive electronic scale. Olson is saying that history is ended in the sense that not only the old means of manufacturing history are called into question, but also the population explosion, the electronics information network, the fact of our leaving the planet, the atom bomb, the shortage of food, the ecological disturbance caused by heavy metal industries, have all changed the environment so much that the old conditions of history are changed. They are no longer like they were during what we know of as history, a place where the skies are open, where the sky is the limit.'

Wide skies over Newham, the valley of the Roding: wild skies. London shit running in torrents under my feet. I didn't expect, with my present duties (narrative and ethical), to be thinking of Ginsberg, 1967. Career journalist reporting on the underground scene, his own impotence. Poets sitting around: electing themselves as unacknowledged legislators, listening to scientists and street politicians, conmen, visionaries, state spooks in disguise. Drug-brokers, hustlers, innocents. Language still a weapon. The phrases of that time, after weeks of editing, looping, replaying, stayed with me.

History has ended. It was (and remains) a TV channel: shuddering videophone image from the war zone, desert or mountain cave. Ginsberg in heaven, yakking, scraping hair from his mouth, trying to make sense of it. But, if there is any history left, it is on a noticeboard, alongside the Northern Sewage Outfall. On the road to Beckton (aka Basra). Roads have to go somewhere (apart from the orbital M25, which carries you outside time, back to H.G. Wells and Bram Stoker). History, by definition, is 'a continuous, systematic narrative of past events'. Events that remain, are *allowed* to remain, in the thin air of our present.

Ginsberg's clear skies. Early mist. Cocktail of pollution. A man walking, creaking, stiff back, loose grip, wobbly knee – but lustful, hungry as an adolescent: hungry, in the absence of the desired object, the dark woman, for place.

'A giant public tolerance of all forms of madness and perversion,' screamed Ginsberg. I transcribed the tape, fingers blistered: stop, play. It was the beginning of the word thing, before documentation gave way to the easier path, fiction. On that long thin page (my first self-published prose work), I can see the text now: *a photograph of Ruth Alsop*. She'd come up from Soho, Frith Street (where she was typing out translations, Godard scripts), to join us, the TV crew, on Primrose Hill; carrying bananas, milk, bread, cheese.

'Who's *that*?' Ginsberg asked.

'A friend,' I said. 'A good friend of mine. She's brought some lunch.'

And there she is, the pain fresh after thirty-five years: that history doesn't behave as it should. You can't re-enter the frame, repair old mistakes. Ruth Alsop aged twenty-two, short blue-and-white spotted dress, straight-cut, bought in a Paris flea market. Long smooth brown legs. Long hair. And the look she gave: which I hadn't, back then, the wit to interpret. The look of Isabella Jones in Hastings. The woman writing in the Bo-Peep Inn. A face divided: easy smile, a gaze that goes on for ever without coming into focus.

The private woman and the public man, Ginsberg, united for one instant – when Ruth hands the compulsive journal-keeper a banana freshly bought, that morning, in Berwick Street Market, in Soho.

Primrose Hill lost. Beckton Alp achieved. Engorged, I walked with difficulty. I came alongside two razorheads, amateur Futurists spray-painting a stretch of brick wall.

'More purple – in the eye sockets?'

'Maybe. A squeeze.'

'More scarlet on the muff?'

Carrier bags clank with cans, paint not lager. Two artists, loaded down, on the road to Beckton Alp. Two aesthetes: tame, savage. The liminal places, across the Lea, beyond Abbey Creek, were loud with them; characters determined to revamp the landscape. That's why I kept off the A13. I could shadow Norton, Seed and the others from the high ground, from a distance. I knew exactly where they were going. No avoiding the golgotha of Rainham. The TV dramas of the ibis hotel. But the road itself, since my first pass, the fictional version in which the pilgrims ascended the alp and detoured to witness the wall-paintings of St Mary Magdalene at East Ham, had changed. For the worse. (As we, recent historians, always assert.) Respect for the three Es: Ecstasy, Entropy, Essex.

Some clown, or cabal of clowns, had decided that the way to soften up the punters for the exploitation of Dagenham, Barking and the brownfield acres was to treat the dirt highway, the A13, as an art work. Grunge giving way to glamour: 'Young Architect of the Year', Tom de Paor, has been invited to reconceptualise the hard miles.

'This is really charming,' he said – of the views around the Ford factory – to the man from the *Standard*. 'All roads lead to Barking. It's the belly button of England.'

He's done his research, this thirty-something Irishman. 'The place is full of gangsters. The Gunpowder Plot was hatched here.

Dudley Moore limped to this school.' The project, de Paor's make-over, will be called: *Arterial*. Drivers, drifting through the doctored ecosystem of recent history, alternating bands of colour-coordinated crash barriers, paths in green, white and gold, steel posts with blue landing lights on top (road as runway), will experience 'a perpetual rhythmic form whose movements are all of a piece'.

I'm still mired in the recent future. The 'shifting moiré pattern' of the road is at a standstill, while preliminary civil engineering work is completed. The award handed to the young architect (angular specs and reddish Stephen Dedalus beard) was co-sponsored by steel company Corus, who are currently downsizing unsightly and unprofitable rolling mills in South Wales. We're all advancing, like it or not, into projective time, visions that should never be realised. But this tops Gateshead, Glasgow, Liverpool, any of those cities of culture. No other spread of defunct industry and conceptual art, I must acknowledge, could offer a spectacle to compare with 'the oldest metal flyover in Britain' – alongside New Age geographer Chris Street's sacred triangulation (East Ham Church, holy well in Central Park, Barking Abbey).

I sat on an excavated tump of earth (still slightly hot), on the north side of the A13, opposite Beckton Alp. I wished that I still smoked cigars, Burma cheroots. Why not? What is there to lose? The device that Conrad exploits in *Nostromo* – call it breathing space – a group of men, Anglos, high Latins in dark coats on the harbour wall lighting up. Good punctuation. Suspension of narrative bluster. Sunlight dancing on wave crests. Silver ingots in a lighter – riding low in the water. Gentlemen who know how to smoke.

I watched Norton's troop, defeated cavalry, the mules shot out from under them, zigzagging (Herzog style) up the Alp; scrambling for footfalls, dowsing for heat. *Was I responsible?* Did I really write such nonsense? Norton, sweating, gasping for breath, trying to hold it together, this three-in-one narrative (great-grandfather, Joseph Conrad at Stanford-le-Hope, Stanley Kubrick), consoled himself with a single thought: *it's not true*. This never happened. I'm not here.

But it is. True as Herzog's films, as *Fitzcarraldo* or *Aguirre, Wrath of God*: recent history, recorded history, researched, re-enacted. They will build a boat and drag it through the jungle, over that slope. They will descend the precipitous path to the final river. Monkeys and arrows.

Wednesday, 26 March 2003: breaking off from writing, imagining this journey, a lovely warm, false spring afternoon, in a fug of rubber fires and yellow dust, I walk to Beckton Alp and on to Barking. It *did* happen, it is still happening – until I sit down at my desk to mar the purity of that day by straining after documentary truth. The unreasonable desire to convince strangers, editors, publicists, critics, readers.

I could do nothing about Track and Danny, a conversation I didn't hear. I couldn't help Norton. Or save Ollie from her fate at the ibis hotel. My only option was to swing away, let them complete their preordained trajectories, while I shadowed them, off-highway, through Central Park in East Ham and down Barking Road to the Abbey.

Central Park, unexpectedly, lives up to the brochure: out of the traffic, the nuisance, into urban tranquillity. A little Eden. Open railings, by some acoustic freak, muffle street noise. A limited green space expands as you walk into it. Elements, such as the standard war memorial obelisk, acquire an affecting gravity. Chris Street, promoting this obscure patch as a gateway to the stars, might be on to something. A celestial rival for the mundane visions of the politicians and city planners.

As promised, in the north-west corner of the park, I found a granite fountain that stood in for the lost 'Miller's well'. The fountain belonged in Hastings (it should have been filled with water). My twin tales were coming together: the fallen menhir of Amazon Street with the memorial slab outside the Royal Victoria Hotel in St Leonards, the Central Park fountain with the Castello fountain on the marine parade. Road and coast. Thames corridor and seaside: linked narratives. Maps of separate countries with the same symbols, the same plan.

If Hannah had been with me . . .

Young couples, Asians mainly, were canoodling, courting on benches. The park was shaded, discreet. Zones kept to themselves. Frutescent alcoves for lovers. If Hannah was with me . . . She'd snort – plupfff – at my notions of Jungian synchronicity. The psychologist's famous dream in which Liverpool is also Basel. 'The various quarters of the city were arranged radially around the square. In the centre was a round pool.'

Otherwise known as: the East Ham mandala. Absence of water. The perfectly round granite cup is a memorial to a buried well. *A fountain filled with bread*. The raised octagonal island at the centre of the bowl: an aperture blocked by a stale loaf. The outer rim of the dish is packed with brown and white slices, mouldy wads, pitta bread, liver-spotted nan, chapati, waffles, pancakes. This dry fountain swam with dough, untouched pigeon offerings.

And Barking Road, as I walked east in the soft twilight, shadowing Norton's fictional pilgrims on the A13, confirmed Chris Street's speculation: a busy pub, hanging baskets, gold lettering on deep blue. *The Miller's Well*, Free House. Make the journey and the tracings will always be there, not as history, but as parallel motif, random survival: a boozer, a drinking fountain, a dowser with kit improvised from industrial debris.

Barking Abbey, where teenage dealers make their moves among preserved ruins, offers spiritual benediction to a major retail park, a shopping city on the banks of the River Roding. The dead lie quiet. Gravestone craft, in relief, under full sail, make for the Thames. The Abbey was founded in AD 666 by St Ekenwald. A date whose ominous significance was justified by the pagan Danes: fire and sword. All the history that is worth retaining is etched into a tablet on an architectural fragment, a gateway known as the Curlew Tower.

A fat sun dropped behind bare churchyard trees, behind the MFI block, Paul Simon's Curtain Superstore, Powerhouse. 50 p.c. off everything. At the golden hour, I could follow Chris Street's theoretical alignment: through St Margaret's Church to Tower Hill, on to Southwark Cathedral. Nothing is lost, nothing is obliterated. No interlude in park or abbey could ameliorate the coming horror of West Thurrock. The nightmare at the ibis. Journalists and psycho-geographers, urban planners and venture capitalists: what difference? Spin as many versions as you like, the road will have the final word: Barking. The umbilicus. One stop beyond terror, two stops beyond boredom.

ibis hotel

The ibis hotel, West Thurrock, was corrupted with watching. Journalists were embedded in the ground-floor bar, admiring themselves on television, stuffing their pockets with vouchers. When something bad happens, they are there to confirm it: places, previously innocent of news, are granted a heritage identity (black plaque). Houses are demolished: in the city of Gloucester, on the West Bank of the Jordan, Afghanistan. Concerned men in open-necked shirts, women in combat gear (with optional pashmina), they articulate the horror: Willesden, Hungerford, bleak moorland outside Manchester. Now, for one night only, Essex. The approach to the QEII Bridge: a double-header. Celebrity kidnap (botched, sold-out) + girl trapped in car with drug-crazed, sword-wielding psycho.

Jos Kaporal, in his ambiguous identity as researcher/self-impersonator, had spent weeks in hotel bars, where the price of drinks leapt by regular increments as the journos poured in. He was usually there before the bad thing occurred (DV camera, Polaroids, tension-relieving duty-free cigarettes). A Belfast planner on an awayday to Birmingham. Being a figment of a desperate novelist's imagination, he was comfortable in his discomfort. The noise. The heavy drinking. Multiple screens. The twitter of mobile phones. Dry fucks of the Mediadrome. Bursts of brilliant white light around a roped-off section of generic car park. Loudmouths fighting for rooms that look down on the action (double-glazed windows that won't open).

As a long-term sleeper, an agent manipulated by a remote and disinterested controller, Kaporal was in his element. Jacky Roos, his alter ego, the demi-Belgian, was less happy. He was the model, it's true, for our binge-eating undercover man – but his cover was blown by this confrontation with the fictional double. If they find themselves in the same room at the same time, the world tilts on its axis. Rivers run backwards. And books are composed by clicking typewriters in empty rooms.

I didn't know where to begin. My instinct was to run upstairs, call room service; keep my door locked until it was all over. Roos was in custody (my fault). The Albanians were being helped with exaggerated courtesy into a police van. Drug-smuggling comedian Howard Marks was holding court like a rock star on sabbatical from the Priory: voice of Neil Kinnock, face of Bill Wyman.

The kidnap subplot collapsed because there was nowhere for it to go, the author lost his bottle. It was never much of a story in the first place and he was no Elmore Leonard. You pick up a paragraph, overhear something on TV, when you're shifting your weight, easing your back, at a crowded bar. Like now. One thing journalists are good at is catching a barman's eye. Waving a banknote and talking to the office at the same time. A gang of no-hope Albanians plan to kidnap Posh Spice. Stunt or scam? It ends, as these things inevitably do, in the parking lot of an ibis hotel (convenient for everywhere, a hundred yards from the orbital motorway).

A TV crew has been tipped off. The Beckhams, Essex to the core, up their security: CIA-approved bomb shields, blast-deflectors, for the limo. Higher-definition CCTV. A revised profile: more virtual, less actual. Body doubles (like Saddam). A shopping trip to Milan. MTV awards in Hollywood. Promo in Japan. Reassignment to Madrid. Economic migrants travelling club class with large men in suits and mirror glasses.

I logged the newspaper item, then, months later, in a weak moment, thought it might play with the Hastings novel (the gaudy necrophilia of the White Queen's coming attractions). I didn't have a clue how Albanians talked (even bandits, gangster associates), so I tried to keep them dumb: go with voiceover, the detached authorial overview. Manuel-speak (Jew playing Catalan): 'I lov-a you, Meestah Fawlty.'

No real harm done, not yet. Andy Norton goes upstairs, knowing that Track will not join him, *not* knowing of her liaison with Danny the Dowser (a future in the Basildon Plotlands). A.M. Norton, whiskey and water, is waiting for Hannah Wolf (the promise that she would try and make it, make up for the previous night's fiasco at the Travelodge).

Lights are coming on in the ibis. There is a car out on the road. A young man with a Japanese sword. A girl who wants to break with him. He drove her to the M25, near Thurrock, in 1989. It was on television. Breakfast radio explained the jams, miles of stalled traffic. Newspapers exposed links to Essex crime: drugs, protection, bent gyms, people-smuggling, record labels used for money-laundering, thefts of antiquities on the south coast, bullion robbery, timeshare in Spain, child pornography, massage parlours stocked from the Balkans, boarding houses given over to the involuntary exile of convicted paedophiles. The girl, decent, ordinary, bright, was granted an aura of sanctity. Her talent was talked up: hairier than Tracey Emin, more Mexican than Frida Kahlo. Beautiful of course. Radiant with future glory. And dead. Very dead.

The disturbed youth (steroid and ketamine habit) was, to the same degree, demonised: dole-bandit, psycho, expired road fund tax. He cut her throat, before running in front of a Dutch HGV which was 'carrying 25 tonnes of plasterboard'. Trauma of driver, 42, family man (two families). Foreigner.

Hacks like nothing better than life snuffed out, blink-of-the-eye tragedy; characters straight from stock. Further revelations promised. More arrests. Pages and pages of photos: weeping mum at funeral, white T-shirts with tattoos and blankets over their heads, youths in dark glasses holding up newspapers to mask mean faces, baying mobs of the righteous (gobbing, hammering on the van). Cellophane floral tributes scattered over an elevated section of the M25.

This was a true event, embedded in recent history (forgotten by tabloid grazers): girl murdered, suicide of killer, horror of truck driver, valuable Japanese sword recovered. I couldn't affect the outcome. It was a journalist who gave me the details, another Hackney narrative: he turned it into fiction, published the pain. The girl was his sister. So he was, at least by association, involved. He knew the participants. He understood the mechanics of the fateful night. It was his story to tell.

I had no such legitimate claim. But he inflicted it on me, lodging the details in my imagination, soliciting a new and revised version. 'Save her, honour the memory.' The unspoken agenda. As it appeared in my egotistical version of the world. A site to be written, blood and scorched rubber, rescued by language.

I failed. Two Nortons were never going to be enough. Andy in Room 234 with his files, his nostalgia. And his sterner, fiction-composing doppelgänger, A.M., sipping whiskey – and wanting, despite the unfolding horror, to make love again: with Hannah, the only woman to whom he had confessed his dreams. Severed fingers. Fantasies dressed as fact.

He didn't tell about Ruth, those dreams. Memories that wouldn't go away: a walk by watercress beds, clear pools from deep springs, May flowers on a Mediterranean island. A bed with rose-printed sheets, the bumps of her spine. His tongue tasting the skin. The crease of her bottom. Not a flaw. As she pretends to sleep, first light at the open window.

Now Norton's third mind had broken cover, the writer, the watcher. The other two could never be reconciled. No treaty between marine light and the A13 corridor (the realpolitik of a manipulated future). No tricks or shifts can slow the passage of the American car, killer and victim.

When a natural climax arrives, a crisis in the narrative, subvert it: pick up a book. Go with the old modernist strategy, quotation. Eliot, Pound. Yeatsian dictation. I didn't have a lot of choice, one paperback in each sidepocket of my poacher's waistcoat. I had selected, to help make sense of the recent history business unfolding in Babylonia, Andrew George's translation of *The Epic of Gilgamesh*. The map of the Ancient Near East worked better than the fancy graphics put out by TV networks.

'Let us wage war!' A martial illustration, Republican Guards advancing in formation, shields and spears.

> when he arrives why be afraid?
> That army is small and a rabble at the rear,
> its men will not withstand us!

Judicious misinformation, chest-beating: patriotism. Better to hate well than to die carelessly. Make the people more afraid of the monster they know than the dust armies who will burst through their cinema screens.

> 'Now make ready the equipment and arms of battle,
> let weapons of war return to your grasp!
> Let them create terror and a dread aura,
> so when he arrives fear of me overwhelms him,
> so his good sense is confounded and his judgement undone!'

The ibis wasn't suited to poetry. It prized its anonymity too much, company credit cards, the cleanliness of a Belgian service station – Roos was quite at home. Menu from Poland.

In *Gilgamesh* the dead return. But they are too discreet to gossip about their experience of the afterworld. Ollie, throat slashed, windpipe severed, can't speak. There is an eloquence in the position of her body, the way it has fallen and stopped falling. Eyes shut. Head turned from the road, back towards Rainham.

> 'I cannot tell you, my friend, I cannot tell you!
> If I tell you what I saw of the ways of the Netherworld,
> O sit you down and weep!'

You have a place, off-highway, on the borders of everything. You have the Thames. The road east, the A13. And the orbital motorway. At the ibis decisions have to be taken, difficult choices: meat or fish, red or white? *Express* or *Mail*? Lies have to be shaped. Time must be hobbled. It's a holding zone, a customs post with no customs, no form.

'If your eyes are of no more use to you than this, I shall have them put out.'

My second book, the spare: *Nostromo*. You recognise it? The copy liberated from Pevensey Bay? Where Ollie was slightly pregnant and drinking white wine. Now she isn't. That would be too much. I can't inflict further distress on the unborn. I stole the Penguin Conrad from the kitchen of the beach chalet. A weekend visitor had left it behind. The two women were never going to read it, were they? Small print, brown pages, thickets of lush South American prose (penned on the south coast). Verbiage. Józef Teodor Konrad Nalecz Korzeniowksi (naturalised Englishman): godfather of magic realism, cousin to Dostoevsky and Flaubert.

Appalling arrogance, I admit. Horrible attitude. The American girl (Track) might, for all I know, have a doctorate in post-colonial studies: 'The reassembly of chaotic events into a causal sequence exposes an author swimming against the tide, caught between a *Western* view of a non-Western world and a desire to reconstruct, as a mirror image, the Polish conflicts of his childhood.'

In *Nostromo*, that masterpiece of movement, shifting perspectives, romance, rebellion (intelligent, frustrated women and good black cigars), nothing affects me so much as the agony of its composition. The research, the libraries devoured. Maps, charts, engravings. Financial pressure. Small farm near Hythe (rented from colleague). Author (creased brow) knowing he has a vast undertaking on his hands, long, complex, laboured: it must seem easy, free-flowing as a swift stream in chalk country. It must divert a dull-witted readership. The pain of those paragraphs! Sentences. Syllables. Mots justes. Money money money. To entertain. Ford at Winchelsea. Henry James at Rye. Wells at Sandgate. Stephen and Cora Crane at Brede Place. Food on the table. Wine. The creaking study door. Forbidden entry. Family excluded. Nightwork.

A short story that got its claws into him, cells breeding like a cancer. It swells, unnoticed, into a novella: 60,000 or 70,000 words. Three months at the outside. Telegraph Pinker.

Six months in: '*Nostromo* grows; grows against the grain by dint of distasteful toil . . . but the story has not yet even begun.'

Black and bitter depression, fevers, troubled stomach. A condemned man writing against the clock to save his head from the executioner's axe. Hand trembling, palsied. Focus lost: that terrible image of the eyes being put out. Eyes on hooks. Eyes of the dead.

Two years from the start, the breezy, optimistic beginning, Conrad cracks: mounting debts, serialisation, finish the thing or starve. This obscure life, three miles from the sea, thirty miles from France. He scribbles by day and dictates by night: to Ford Madox Ford (his wife can't stand the fellow, perpetual guest and benefactor). Gout and the other attendant demons conspire to unman him: Ford has to doctor one of the chapters. Dual authorship, they'd done it before. Half delirious, like a skeleton on a raft, tongue swollen till it fills his mouth, Joseph Conrad completes the draft by working through the heat of August for eighteen hours a day.

Then what? Revisions, proofs, corrections. Editorial adjustments. Critical disapproval. Indifferent sales. Academic scavenging. Posthumous acclaim. Posthumous revisionism. The minutiae of books and life picked over by impertinent hacks. An overblown and wholly misguided television translation. A film that is never made, the obsession of David Lean in his Limehouse palazzo, brown Thames glittering outside the window. A man who does not know how to answer the phone. Scriptwriter Christopher Hampton banged up for weeks, months, years. A reprise of the original torment of composition. Finish it and die, Lean knows the story. And he strings it out: 'a book largely constructed out of other books'. Hampton's sequestration repeated by Norton – which Norton? – in the cabin-sized bedroom at the ibis hotel.

Language voodoo, a book opened at hazard. Room 234, p. 234: 'I spoke to you openly as to a man as desperate as myself.'

Nostromo, the Capataz de Cargadores, a self-regarding adventurer, is also known to the females of the harbourside inn at which he lodges as Gian' Battista. John the Baptist. Could I have been thinking of that? Prophet and road. The dark painting in some Maltese church, the execution in all its erotic theatre: man of the desert, half naked, glistening with sweat, decapitated for the delight of a courtesan.

A.M. Norton, the fabulist, had collapsed into a boneless heap, so much dirty laundry. News happened, it was nothing to do with him. Wait and see. Like T.S. Eliot, as it was rumoured, he sought sexual congress, with all its implied difficulties, as prick to his muse. Margate convalescence and *The Waste Land*. Neurasthenia, incense and a decent suit.

Andy Norton, urban topographer, blistered like one of those downland hikers of the Thirties, was more reckless: take the story as it comes. He sprung from the window, charged through the traffic, rescued the damsel. Who required nothing of the sort. It was her choice to be in the car, letting the high romance, of love and loss, play itself out. To be, once and for ever, rid of men and their fuss.

I ran down the stairs. Jacky was drinking again. Essex had that effect on him. The book he'd published on the Basildon Ecstasy bandits: the possible consequences. He had to get back across the river, fast. To Hastings. He was prepared to validate my reconfiguring of history, cobbled together from a couple of chapters of *Nostromo* and a quick glance at the crib he downloaded from one of the hotel's laptops.

Gian' Battista steals the silver. He pays court to the younger daughter of the lighthouse-keeper (the grand old Garibaldino), while he is betrothed to the elder. He is shot, killed. The critics call this 'Conradian transference'. You get what's coming to you, but you don't know when.

Hannah was still slogging from Thurrock Station, muddy, exhausted, when they brought Ollie in. Quite safe. Not yet pregnant. Rescued from her mad drive north: Reo Sleeman splattered across the tarmac with the stranger who stormed to her rescue – like Gilgamesh – and vanished into the night.

Fiction conquers all: the Bush/Rumsfeld doctrine. Keep saying it. A new world order. A road map for peace. Reality is infinitely malleable (given the budget and sufficient force of arms). As the tanks rolled across the desert (same shots repeated, flexible commentary, on different nights), as Howard Marks yarned and laughed (receiving a commission to visit Panama on behalf of the *Observer*), I took Ollie upstairs. To rest and recover. I gave her my bed. I had learnt to listen to women and not to watch. My dreams were unashamedly Freudian (forgive me, Hannah). My mouth tasted of Ruth: blood and sugar. The evidence of Pevensey Bay, which lay both before and beyond me, confirmed the fantasy: I made love to the young woman who was like a daughter, but who shared my mother's name. And through this intoxicating and stomach-tightening folly, I became my own father.

NETHERWORLD

THE
MIDDLE
GROUND

ANDREW NORTON

ALBION VILLAGE PRESS

Mr Norton knew that he must talk, and he and I spoke laboriously. It was a difficult duet . . .

– Virginia Woolf

Mr Mocatta

I came down to breakfast with real hunger. The journalists had gone, Thurrock was returned to its customised obscurity: a pot of steaming coffee, full English – high sheen on the elevated motorway. It is always better, when lodging in such places, to eat out. A log-cabin transport café, a mile down the road, near the river. My favourite section: soap factory, pilgrim church, recovered wilderness. Grays, Tilbury, Canvey Island, Southend. The resolution to the outstanding question left to my novel: *where does the A13 end?*

The Old Invincibles, my Aldgate Pump casuals, reconvened after many dramas and diversions, recent history suspended, were eager to finish the job: walk the road until it disappeared under the North Sea. The painter Jimmy Seed, Track and Ollie, Norton, Danny the Dowser: the Famous Five (with their imaginary dog, Borges). One step to the east, one step beyond the bridge, and it was over: my connection with the south coast, that mistake, the flight to Hastings. Beyond Thurrock, the broad Thames spreads its legs, divisions between Essex and Kent are absolute: sandbanks, oil tankers, unpredictable currents. No way (if you discount the eccentric Gravesend ferry) of getting over, interrupting a linear flow of narrative. A travel journal with a beginning, middle and end (in the right order).

Jos Kaporal, somewhat white around the gills after his outing as 'Jacky Roos', put away a preliminary breakfast while filleting the broadsheets and scanning the vine-wrapped TV monitors (winter sports, traffic, shopping).

'Jos.'

He flinched.

'Norton?'

I confirmed it.

'Any chance of a ride to – Hastings?' he asked.

'Sorry.'

'I've got the dosh.'

He patted his chest; searched, with trembling fingers, for that one forgotten cigarette. The reward for good behaviour.

'I'm never going back,' I said. 'The whole thing was a mistake, fiction. I'm ready to accept the consensus: I can't hack it. No talent for putting myself in other people's shoes, ventriloquising the voices. Strictly realism from now on: roads, retail parks, bunkers. Books that can be summed up in a sentence. If critics have to wade through four hundred pages to tease out a storyline, they'll kill you. And, oh yes, I'm thinking of getting married.'

Ollie, coming up quietly to our table, laughed.

'Anyone I know?'

I blushed. The blood was still there when required, the heat. Her kindness, last night in the small bed, brought me back to myself. To my proper business, the recording and interrogating of unloved territory. The anticipation of coming horrors alongside the exposure and ridicule of those that were already apparent. It was celibate work, I admit. But that could change. Ollie was fit, young, a walker. She could provide the illustrations. There was something different about her this morning; in another woman you might call it gloating. Four hours after the event, she knew she was pregnant. I'd seen the phenomenon before: seven minutes post-coitus, a woman smoothing out a map of Scotland.

'Shit.'

Refried beans, mushrooms, blood sausage. Kaporal let one rip: he browned it. 'Shit! Shit! Shit!'

Two men, busy eyes, were carving their way towards our table. Bouncer types in an excess of smart casuals: like ramraiders on the run from Matalan, Beckton Alp. New white trainers – on which the lightest spot of blood would register – replaced on a daily basis. Ikea wardrobes of cast-offs. Combat slacks with elasticated waists, too many pockets and no flies. T-shirts that strained around powerlift musculature.

'Jos, my son, thought it was you.'

Mock punch, genuine gasp.

'Mick-eeey.'

'On the tele. Shocking. Poor young gel.'

'Nothing to do with me, Mick. I live on the coast now.'

'Big Alby, Jos. He's in pieces. His little brother.'

'Absolutely certainly, yes. I was ringing for flowers.'

'Keep your hand in your pocket, Alby understands. We're the transport. Introduce me to your mates.'

Time for a change of trousers? Kaporal was ankle-deep in it, his worst nightmare, schlock fiction.

'Mickey O'Driscoll,' he said. 'The writer. *Rettendon Roadkill*. I helped with the editing. They made a film of that one. Mickey was played by Sean Bean. And Phil Tock. He's –'

'Doing a favour for an old pal. He wants a meet, Jos. Mr Mocatta. Bring the company. Make a day of it. Know what I mean? Nice run to the coast. Won't cost you a penny. Right?'

The vehicle was one of those blunt-nosed space-cruiser taxis, silver, the kind that shuttle between Gatwick Airport and the satellite hotels. O'Driscoll, the haulier, former HGV man, drove, watching a satellite screen, maps of virtual traffic. His minder, Tock, gawped out of the window: the cinema of the clouds. A special morning, perhaps unique, no early accidents, suicides, bridge jumpers; no problems at Junction 29 (the A127 inflow), no traffic stacked up all the way round to Junction 27 and the M11. No panic-buying war-fever convoys heading for Bluewater, no water-hoarders draining the plastic-bottle lake at Thurrock. A lull in the natural order of things, remission for bad behaviour. Sunbeams dancing on khaki Thames. Glinting on metal drums, the bald domes of the Exxon storage tanks. Casting long shadows (soap-factory chimney) on the striped wall of a huge block building.

Tock babbled. 'What's he like then, your gaffer?'

'Good as gold,' O'Driscoll said.

With false authority: his style. He had met a man who might

have been Mocatta – once: as an associate of an associate, making up the numbers. A pub near the Swanley interchange, not far from the racetrack: inscribed black-and-white photos of Mike Hawthorn, Jim Clark, Graham Hill, Peter Collins (dead heroes). Tasteful under-wear spreads in the Gents, no beavers. Pink soap and a working blower. One of those country places improved by the fortuitous proximity of the motorway.

The club-owner from Basildon accepted Mocatta's investment, his sponsorship of the coming motorway culture: noise like ampli-fied heartbeats, mood-enhancers, lots of driving with no fixed destination. Rucks, at odd times of day, in fast-food facilities. Aggra-vation at coffee stalls. Butchery among pristine estates where sound carries through six identical houses. Double-glazing for amateur torture buffs.

'True to form,' O'Driscoll laughed, 'Pat never paid him.' He twisted his head to see if the passengers in the back seat were listening. Eyes (on the glass of the driving mirror): black sea slugs.

'Pat Lyle? Haven't seen Pat since . . . Hollesley Bay. Keeping well, is he? The old ticker. How is Fat Pat?'

'Not too clever. Fell off a tower block in Dagenham. All the way.'

'Big send-off?'

'Ten cars, wreaths. The faces. Never got home for three days, did I? Filth waiting in the kitchen. Done for possession of a poxy firearm. I'm supposed to live in Laindon without a bit of insur-ance?

We had room to stretch out: Ollie was quiet but happy to be on the road again, heading south, to that promised weekend with Track in Pevensey Bay. Marina Fountain's bungalow. The point of bad behaviour, a one-night stand with a manic depressive in an ibis hotel, is to have something decent to chew over with your mates (much the same mix as a Henry James novel). Pregnancy, if it takes, is a bonus. Life, for these bachelor girls, was an interval to be endured between emotional binges, tears, giggles, videos, wine, chocolate biscuits. Deckchairs on shingle. Warm breeze from the Channel. Lovers traduced, put to rights, before the Monday-morning return to London, their inadequate embraces.

Kaporal, also delighted to be getting out of Essex, crossing water, was in a more troubled state of mind: escaping the poisoned territory of his past, but returning to marine exile in company with the very elements he had moved south to escape, Mocatta's goons. His belly rumbled, loudly.

O'Driscoll smoked, prison-style, but he wasn't offering. Jos licked nicotine stains, snacked on fragments of fingernail.

I asked him about Mocatta, what he had in the files, anything to keep him occupied.

'The astonishing performances,' he said, perking up, 'were in those early, black-and-white interviews. *World in Action*. Never shown. The height of his infamy – when the underground press were demonising him as a teenage Rachman and *Private Eye* kept banging on about his links with the National Front, connections with African despots. He was like an air-guitar, street-hustling imitator of Tiny Rowland. Carnaby Street not Savile Row.'

'Premature New Labour, then,' I responded. 'Tony Blair, thirty years ahead of his time. The nerd who blows up the world because he fails his Brian-Jones-replacement audition.'

'Vanity as style,' Kaporal reckoned. 'Hard-lacquer narcissism. Religion. The chosen one: untouchable, inviolate. Flicking invisible particles of dust from his lapels. Buttoned to the neck with high collars, stiff white, slashed wide. Thick silk tie. Waistcoat like Flashman. The dandy, the sadist.'

'What were the interviews like?'

'Amazing, electroplated ego. Mocatta boasts of anything they want to throw at him: Nietzsche, Colin Wilson. Beethoven on record sleeve, Hawkwind LP inside. He gets a real kick from saying the unsayable: "I am a superior being. Those who stand in my way will be destroyed." He relishes the tremors of shock that run through the liberal/left, dope-smoking camera crew. He admits, with a flick of his cuffs, to despising inferior races, using his heavies to shake out unwelcome tenants, killing and torturing associates who let him down.'

'So why isn't he in prison?'

'As soon as the editing is done (three days of wild excitement), advance teasers being prepared, his lawyers turn up with an injunction. No release forms have been signed. The interview was a wind-up, a piss-take. "Mr Mocatta is a respectable businessman with a substantial property portfolio and sensitive (government-approved) interests abroad." Forget it. Dead in the water.'

'Never shown? Even after the recent trial?'

'No chance. The last time I worked for Channel 4 they wouldn't let me say that the Bush family saw the Gulf War as a rerun of the cattle-versus-sheep business. Cowboy fantasies enacted on a global scale. Old George, the CIA man, in construction with the bin Ladens? Sorry, lads. Mocatta has lawyers like the rest of us have fleas. If he's gone down for arranging the death of a Hindu shopkeeper (fifty-four shops), so what? He'll be out on a technicality before Archer. That interview is buried, probably destroyed. I tracked down a pirate tape, warehouse in Archway. One viewing in the middle of the night, no copies, no transcripts. The owner hasn't worked since, can't get arrested. He's down on the coast, writing thrillers under a pseudonym.'

Movement, at this pitch of comfort, even allowing for O'Driscoll's choice of music (Irish showband and late Sinatra), is time travel – the warp; bright air parting in waves on our sleek prow. I could have crossed the Dartford Bridge for ever. My problems lay on the far shore. *So junk them*. Shift modes. Channel hop. Try documentation, a walk.

I was never going to reach the promised land: Canvey Island. Oil and caravans.

I could see the A13 pilgrims, Jimmy, Track and Danny, down there, far below, tiny figures on the river path, heading east, to answer my riddle: what happens after you take that last step?

They slept, our hikers, in Danny's Plotlands chalet. Most of the original structures, built by naturists and fresh-air buffs, had disappeared under tarmac, new estates. A breath of the countryside in the Langdon Hills for those decanted from East London by war or ambition: put up whatever you fancy, a small patch of ground. Walks, grass-cutting, singsongs. By motorcycle and sidecar, or train (with a hike at the end), they came in their hundreds. Woods and secret hills with a view of the coming A13 and the distant Thames. Paraffin lamps, chemical toilets, board games and burnt sausages.

Track, up early, photographed the survivors. She dowsed living traces. As Danny dowsed fossils, minerals, electricity and crime. They filled their plastic bottles at a tap, placed (in the Twenties) at the top of the lane, the unmade road. And they came over the hill and through the country park to join the A13 at Stanford-le-Hope.

Clouds of hawthorn blossom. Skylarks twittering. Heavy-bellied sheep. Then the diesel zephyrs, hammering traffic. And the decision (by Track) to detour to Canvey Island by way of homage to Nicola Barker's novel, *Behindlings* – which she was reading for the second time. She had the sense, again, of walking in a stranger's sleep, enjoying no free will, being fated to follow a path trampled flat by earlier, better-informed artists.

'The walks book,' Doc announced, sounding justly proud of his coup, 'the section on Canvey. All that crazy stuff about boundaries. I never understood a word of it . . .'

Barker, Hackney-based, wrote about islands (Hackney being the first). She had a thing for English eccentrics, decent but damaged, behaving oddly in small communities, navigating a slant through a warped topography. Canvey was the paradigm.

'On foot? Are you crazy?' she scowled over at him. Smoke in her eye again. 'It's a piss-ugly walk. Nothing to see.'
'I like to walk,' he said, 'I like the *fact* of walking.'

Nicola was right, Canvey was piss ugly and also beautiful. The beauty of accident. Isolated chalets organised into rows and ranks, a timid colony waiting for the return of the tide: the famous 1953 flood that did its best to scour the riverbank of unsightly human mess.

Jimmy Seed, excited by pristine bungalows named after shopping centres, started to sketch. Only in Canvey would you find a citizen prepared to boast of living in a dwelling called 'Lakeside'. Little lawns. Low walls. Tall aerials.

The island divides into two zones parasitical upon an imported high street (imported from the Fifties, Leytonstone). Charity caves, nail extensions, quick food. The Thames-facing section is oil tanks, a disused gas works, sewage and caravans. The strip that backs onto Benfleet Creek is recreational, golf and yachts. With the golf course doubling as a walk-through cemetery, bunkers with headstones, sand traps with memorial plaques to permanent 19th-holers: festooned in floral tributes.

Our trio of A13 walkers sat on a bench to look at maps (no help). Banks of buttery daffodils waved. The tide had retreated, beached wrecks faced a horizon on which flames from the Shell Haven and Coryton oil refineries never went out.

Danny dowsed and voted for immediate evacuation, Benfleet: a steady ascent, the high ridge, Southend and the finish. Jimmy, weary, agreed. Track, in a minority of one (but red-haired), triumphed. 'An hour,' she said, 'tops.'

A promotional poster for a film called *A Man Apart*, pasted to the side of the bus stop, featured a shaven-headed mercenary (scowling like Argentinian midfielder Veron on his way to an early bath). Smoking ordnance in one hand, badge in the other. Trucks on fire. Another burning city. Regimes laundered. Long march to the minarets and towers of Coryton. The above-title name: 'Vin Diesel' – dyslexic notice at service station? Mr Diesel wasn't happy. This shoreline – inlets, refineries, clusters of religious fanatics (Jehovah's Witnesses, Primitive Methodists, Latter-Rain Outpouring Revivalists) – was where invasion would come. *Had* come. Romans,

Dutchmen. King Alfred's tussle with the Danes at Beam Fleote, the 'tree-lined creek'.

In my extended reverie on the Queen Elizabeth II Bridge, my disinclination for a meeting with Mocatta, I tried to invade the consciousness of the most susceptible of the walkers, Katherine Cloud Riise (known as Track). I wanted to force them across *their* bridge, into Canvey. Please allow me to bask – while O'Driscoll searches his pocket for a pound coin, the bridge toll – in the exhaustion and triumphs of your epic march.

Without blisters. (Where *did* she get that name?)

WELCOME TO CANVEY, TWINNED WITH COLOGNE (DIST 3), ROMAINVILLE, ROSCOMMON.

That sounded about right: a traffic island. A raised strip of grass that summarised all any traveller would want to know about the estuarine settlement. Shark fin embedded in thin soil (silver bright): metaphor for lost fleet. Armada beacon. Loose rocks representing prehistory, Mudhenge. A beach of bird seed and broken shells. Drive around it in twenty seconds, appreciating the distant refineries, the big skies. A red rectangle planted by the sponsors: McDONALD'S EXIT.

Trapped in O'Driscoll's silver space-cruiser, my eyes bled with envy for that Canvey traffic island, the quiet climb through the village of Benfleet with its church (St Mary's), its graveyard and 'licensed' Dickens restaurant. Broad verges, bare trees coming into flower. The long curve to the red tower with its booster mast, the glimpse of the river and the sudden remembrance of the A13: back on the road.

The pilgrims – Jimmy, Danny, Track – ploughed on in grim silence. The job had to be completed, miles of suburban sprawl, half-towns, broken country. Shops and cafés they won't have time to enter. A day's walk. Shoulders chafing under the straps. Heads clear, eyes bright . . .

My own are failing. I blink hard against the repetitive bridge supports, the hawsers. Too much floating matter, too many scratches. Like film-stock from the year of my birth: 1943. Robert

Mitchum and William Boyd (Hopalong Cassidy) in *Riders of the Deadline*. There are gaps in the fog, clear pools of vision (the illusion that I can still make out the Southend walking party). The rest is completely lost.

Tock is staring at me, mouth open. They say he can catch bullets in his teeth (which might explain the state of them). A wad of gum like a cancerous growth on the pad of his tongue. 'Arright, son?'

Track's walk is right. But I'm not on it. Not with her. I can't hold O'Driscoll's cab much longer. In the clouds. Above water. Between Essex and Kent. The one section of London's orbital motorway that is not acknowledged as the M25, different rules, different space-time continuum.

Cruelty: they call the A13, at the point where it insinuates itself into the Southend diaspora, 'London Road'. Because, it is obvious now, the bias is *out* – west. Aspirational. Hadleigh is Mill Hill translated: Jewish colonial mansions, fancy ironwork, security cameras, multiple garages, gardeners. Pillars. Porticoes. Steps. Houses for retired dictators: Saddam Hussein, 'Baby' Doc, Idi Amin. (No, that's too fanciful. I'm imposing my riffs on the perceptions of the walkers. They see *new* things – absence of people, of noise, litter. They notice Shipwrights Drive, a striking Thirties modernist house. The quality of light and air owing something to river and hill and the long road that has snaked all these miles from the grime of Aldgate.)

Track's notebook is almost full. Her miniaturist grid: windows of colour. Half a page, she reckons, for Southend. With one left over for the sea. Tiny photographs smudged with blues and yellows. Words. And parts of words. A union flag at a leaded window: THE CON. (SERVATIVE CLUB deleted.) A mobile phone mast rearing above an A13 sex shop (with awning): INTIM (Eurostyle). FOR ADULT SINGLES & COUPLES.

Monumental sky with lowering cloud base, over the Estuary, the power station on the Isle of Grain.

Jimmy is still looking for prospects, cold irony, something to replace the warmth of booze, the missing madness. He spurns this entire run, the hobble from Leigh-on-Sea to Chalkwell: dull street patterns, too many garages, not enough dereliction. He lines up the Southend sign, deep blue on a bed of daffodils – then let's it go, too soft. WELCOME-TO-SOUTHEND, TWINNED WITH THE POLISH RESORT OF SOPOT. Too many words. Too many letters to paint. Too much hassle.

Two hours in, London Road endless, small shifts between swallowed villages, ill-founded optimism, they rely on Danny, his black bag, his brass instruments. *Is this still the A13?* Can Danny confirm the vein of heat running back to Aldgate Pump? This walk, with its false starts, detours, interruptions, dramas and fictions, does it play? And where is the wolf?

Humans were back: twitching junkies, pavement smokers, ponytails who walked very fast, with black bags, bumping into lost old folk on sticks. SEAFRONT RAPE TRIAL COLLAPSES. Frying fish, petrol, hyacinths, sea breezes.

Suburb to pre-urb to urb (sizzling like spit on a hot plate). Then suburb again, broad avenues, fields for sale (development plots), first rumours of the military (MOD).

Track spotted it and Jimmy took the photograph. He had been preoccupied, mid-afternoon, by jailbait, scarlet-mouthed on mobiles, mobbing bus stops, waiting for pick-ups, the family car. Blackcurrant outfits, loose ties and short skirts – like one of the pubs he used to patronise on the edge of the City. Swish, swish. The cars were good too. Large, shiny. German, Japanese, American. A few vintage pieces. All his fantasies congealing in this unlikely nowhere, Thorpe Bay to Shoeburyness. End of the line.

A pale-blue people-carrier parked in the driveway of a crumbling Art Deco house – the twin of the vehicle O'Driscoll was piloting into Kent – offered for sale. And on its side, Track registered the significance, calling Danny, was a hand-painted art work: the wolf pack. These were louche beasts, yawning seasiders, paying homage to their pack leader: the brass wolf of Aldgate Pump. (Jack London meets London Road, Southend.)

Message received, chase over.

It only needed Danny to confirm, after they crossed the railway, drifted into Shoeburyness, that the A13 had finally given up the ghost. Nothing dramatic. A zebra crossing, a bend, a turn-off down Campfield Road – vanished. Rebranded as the B1016. Who has heard of that? Who cares?

They kissed. Danny's beard. Track's scratchy red hair. Jimmy combing his bald spot. Shoeburyness Outdoor Leisure, Camping Showroom: they flopped into picnic chairs. They examined fire-sale flying jackets (£9.99) and laughed over Diesel boots at £39.99. This was MOD territory. A pub named after a character in *Dad's Army*. A railway station. Barracks. A bleak shore. Oil tankers blocking the horizon. Track searched for an unbroken shell, to be inked for the last slot on her grid, but she didn't find one.

They didn't know it, but they were out of the story: liberated. Danny and Track, no marriage, stayed together, private vows in St Mary's Church, East Ham. One on either side of the scarlet ley line. Under the restored wall painting.

Jimmy made his vows too, a betrothal to fame and property. (He got one of them.) The walkers, from this point, were on their own.

As the loving couple wandered up the hill towards Danny's Plot-lands chalet, in gentle twilight, rooks, midges, Track told him how she got her name. Katherine/Cat. A favourite film, favourite movie star: Bob Mitchum. *Track of the Cat*. Family drama with highly symbolic panther (like the wolf of the A13). Danny was happy to be entrusted with this secret, Track's heart. The lie meant nothing to him. And Track was glad, after all this time, to be rid of it.

As O'Driscoll's motor came off the bridge, my eye went out. The stronger one: capped, lens-hooded. The familiar pattern of encroaching motorways, low hills, chalk quarries, was soft, grainy, Impressionist. The abdication of the middle ground finally achieved: 'I can't see.' The windows failed. Bluewater became its celestial double, it shimmered. The salt mound at Swanley interchange was one of Monet's haystacks. The fuzz of movement uncorrected. North Kent: a film by Stan Brakhage.

'Could be worse,' Jos said. 'Welcome to the company of one-eyed jacks. Movie directors have always understood the glamour of the piratical patch. It keeps them in work.'

'Fuck you. The one-eyed jack, split Cyclops, is the penis. Brando chucking Kubrick off-set, out of America. On towards the black dust of Beckton, his Vietnam. *One-Eyed Jacks* is a gay western, written by Calder Willingham. Whipping, posing and moodying about with smashed fingers. A Hollywood Freud*fest*. Pat Garrett and Billy the kid in drag.'

Take his mind off the eye thing, psychosomatic, thought kindly Kaporal. Compile a list: one-eyed directors.

'I'll start,' he volunteered. 'Raoul Walsh. A bird, wasn't it? Smashed through the windscreen when he was driving to some desert location? Eye-patch adds character. The story Mitchum always told about Walsh spilling tobacco from his roll-ups. You can't judge distance, sorry.'

'André de Toth,' I came back. '*House of Wax*. A 3-D horror flick made by a one-eyed director.'

'Skiing accident. André started out covering the Nazi invasion of Poland, then married Veronica Lake. Can you tell, do you think, the before and after films? Binocular and monocular vision?'

'Fritz Lang,' I said. 'He gives great eye-patch in *Le Mépris*. That might be cosmetic. Fancied himself in a monocle. His Westerns are good and camp, but they don't do landscape.'

'Wayne as Rooster Cogburn,' Kaporal mused. 'Think Hathaway was taking the piss out of Walsh? The Duke as a fat parody of an eye-patched rival director? Or was it the great Ford? Old John in his later years?'

'Nicholas Ray. Guesting in *The American Friend*, he patched up.'

'And Jarman,' Kaporal trumped me. As we drove towards the coast, the fabled beach chalet in Dungeness, the rock garden. 'He went blind. *Blue*. The screen itself as subject. Voice. Light of projector beam. Blue on blue. Transcendence.'

We skirted Hastings on the high road, the Ridge, took to lanes and tracks between hedges. Ollie perked up at the reflected brightness of the sea. Kaporal's lists didn't help, the imminence of that mythical personality, Mr Mocatta, was overwhelming. I had nothing left to say. I experimented with partial and total blindness – without Jarman's puckish spirit, his poetry.

Fairlight. Good name. A Lookout Station. Military detritus. Country park. Olivia Fairlight-Jones. This was a sort of homecoming for Ollie, hyphen like an umbilical cord between present self and memories of childhood. Cliff walks and private beaches. Ships that had gone aground.

Phil Tock rubbed his hand, nervously, in circles on his bald skull, warming the ridges. O'Driscoll whistled. The gates were opened by remote control, an unseen electrical eye. The drive descended, by steep and slithery curves, through woodland. It seemed as though nobody had come this way in years.

'You sure this is right?' said Tock. 'Ask a local.'

'Oh yeah – and where you gonna find one?' O'Driscoll sneered. 'This *has* to be it. Rest of the village gone off of the cliff years ago.'

Mocatta's house was Manderley (Hitchcock's version). Or Welles's Xanadu. A fake. A fraud. A broken set (on which some schlock merchant would shoot a quickie over the weekend). A gothic monster still in development – with classical and Egyptian revisions. The only comparison, as an achieved structure, would be the front elevation of Nicholas Hawksmoor's Christ Church, Spitalfields: that is, three churches or temples, different eras, piled one on top of the other (but staying, miraculously, vertiginously, in balance). Mocatta, as his own architect, was car-boot Hawksmoor. Doric columns from a demolished Midland bank. Granite steps from a Gents' toilet in Bexhill. Landseer lions (repro). War memorial obelisks: erased names. A Mississippi mansion that was sliding, verandah first, into the English Channel.

Mocatta had builders instead of friends. They decamped, unpaid, when he went inside (eighteen months on remand). Much of the roof was missing, tiles stripped. Rain left puddles in the hall.

Tock stayed by the car, O'Driscoll lit a cigarette. Kaporal worked on his list. While Ollie, taking my hand, led me down an epic corridor; oil paintings in ornate frames turned to face the wall. She looked into many empty rooms, shrouded furniture, undraped windows. Expensive carpets into which sheep pellets had been trodden. Brisk bushes growing through the boards, strangling white statues of naked gods.

Deep in what might have been, in one of the establishments on which this folly was loosely based, the servants' quarters, Ollie located an occupied space, a kitchen: an old biddy, fag in mouth, gin bottle within reach, stirring a reeking pot. Carpet slippers, wrinkled stockings. Winter coat (coney collar) over flowered pinafore. A pale-green Aga, the only warmth in the place. And standing stiffly, well within thermal range, was a man playing cards. Playing with himself, Patience. Double pack spread across a marble counter: click click click. He didn't take his eyes from his apparently endless game.

'Hello, Nan,' Ollie said. 'Lunch ready?'

'Chicken soup,' the cook replied. 'Made with rabbit. Fowls sick, lost their feathers. Fox got most of them.'

The cardplayer, moving painfully (to studied effect), advanced on the stove, turning his head to evaluate, in turn, the intruders, half-blind old man and bright young girl.

'Daddy!' Ollie rushed at him. 'I'd like you to meet my fiancé.' There was a long, tense silence. And then, right on the beat, they both laughed. And went on laughing as my legs gave way.

Fairlight

'Over my dead body,' Mocatta said, tenderly massaging the small of his back. 'Or his.'

Brown suits, in the country, if inherited, are acceptable – but the Fairlight magnate had miscalculated both the cut (near Vorticist) and the *depth* of brown (Nuremberg, 1934). The effect, coupled with elastic-sided Chelsea boots, was contradictory and sick-making: Fascist mufti with Tin Pan Alley tailoring, Aldgate sweatshop ripping off a P.G. Wodehouse dustwrapper.

'Don't tease,' said Ollie, slipping her arm through her father's and leading him to the table, where he refused to sit.

He winced. 'This idiotic court case. Do I look stupid enough to hire a hitman aged seventy-five who lives above a launderette in St Leonards? A pensioner who sees a vision of Our Lady in a damp patch on the ceiling and walks straight round to the cop shop. Confesses, implicates me, and asks for seven other stiffs to be disinterred, Hastings to Horsham. I've been on my bloody feet since they let me out last Friday. Playing Polish Patience. You need two packs. Take my mind off the sheer fucking agony.'

'Poor Daddy.'

'So which of these cunts got you up the duff? Porker or egghead? Fetch O'Driscoll and sort the dirty little sod out, then we'll have some of Nan's soup. God help us.'

Kaporal's clenched buttocks were squeaking in the style approved by Sir Alex Ferguson: unlubricated penetration of a rubber woman. He couldn't eat a thing, even if Granny Mocatta fed him with a silver spoon.

And it was worse for me, the guilty man. I was quite prepared for a shotgun wedding: so long as they didn't pull the trigger. I find a third wife, new home, ready-made family, and it ends in farce:

clownish dialogue, tumbledown set, pantomime villains. And just when I'm kidding myself, a totally novel experience, that my Shakespearean symmetries are working out. Established world collapses into chaos (blood, madness, storm), before order is restored: winter into spring. Lovers pared off by hierarchy: king with queen, duke with duchess, peasant with peasant (comedy turns).

Mocatta fouled it up.

I tensed for Ollie's kiss of betrayal, my last. Under her father's stern gaze, she hugged the shocked Kaporal. Pecked his cheek. Winked.

'You know Jos Kapôral, the film-maker? You *must*. We're very much in love. And hope you'll help us buy a flat in Brighton. Eastbourne, if you're a meanie. Deal at a pinch. They're all gay there and Jos is trying to reform, stay off the booze.'

'Oh yes, I *know* Kaporal,' Mocatta sneered. 'I pay good money to have that fat whale write a book, he thinks it gives him carte blanche to speak the truth. Facts mean nothing, I told the cunt, what I want is style. Front, swagger. Not fucking statistics downloaded from the internet, gossip from disgruntled geriatrics in the Conquest Hospital.'

O'Driscoll, with Tock behind him, was at the door. Not sure if they were invited to break bread or heads.

'Chuck this rubbish in the boot, the pig. Bite his balls off first, for assaulting my little girl. Release the handbrake, run the fucker over the cliff. Then piss off. You can walk to town. Take the bus if you're feeling flush.'

Nobody moved.

'Which?' Tock whispered.

'Which *what*, maggot?'

'Which town?'

'Be my guest. Basra, Buenos Aires. Don't hurry back.'

That tone, Norbury Wildean, hernia-in-the-throat: Kaporal placed it straight off. Camp aggression, passive sadism. Tortoiseshell cigarette holder and haemorrhoids. It wasn't Nöel Coward in *The*

Italian Job: John Osborne as unlikely Geordie gang boss in *Get Carter*. Plenty of scope for drawling menace. Cards in the kitchen. Fancy house. Kaporal, yet again, was in the wrong movie. An oversize Cockney git who has run out of sarky comebacks. A landscape he can't read and raw nature hammering on the window.

O'Driscoll touched his shoulder. Sinews stiffened, he walked away down the long corridor (with the shadows of security bars). Jimmy Cagney in *Each Dawn I Die*. *Kiss Tomorrow Goodbye*. Christopher Walken in *King of New York*.

Mocatta's library: open to the weather.

The gentlemen had withdrawn and gran was catching up on the gossip, killing the gin. No cigars were on offer. But the bent plutocrat, understanding that Norton was a literary man, was keen to show off his trophies – packed shelves of pristine first editions, gleaming Edwardian bindings, good cloth. All of them feeling the effect of the rain, prevailing wind, the absence of a protective wall. That part of the house had collapsed, slithered into the sea. The books, acting as a final buffer, would go next.

'I collect local topography, Romney Marsh, Cinque Ports. The miraculous cluster of talents that found refuge here, between the turn of the century and the First War. I was lucky enough to acquire – from a one-legged man in New York (he had the full complement when I met him) – the cream of David Garnett's library. Henry James (you'll notice the presentation inscriptions to Edward Garnett), H.G. Wells, yards of Ford and, of course, my great weakness – Conrad. Recognise the suit?'

'Suit?'

He opened his jacket like a set of wings.

'The ultimate fetish. I'm *wearing* a sentence from *Nostromo*. I had it made up by a little man in Aldgate, Manny Silverstein. You might have come across his brother Snip, fund of information. Mostly libellous, all invented.'

'No, never.'

'Remember the quote? *The vigour and symmetry of his powerful limbs lost in the vulgarity of a brown tweed suit, made by Jews in the slums of London.* The chosen people are best incinerated, of course, but while a few of them hang on, rats in a drainpipe, civilised men should exploit the skills they possess: vents, cuff-buttons, linings and so on. I've stopped in Brick Lane for a bagel, I'm not ashamed to acknowledge, after a night on the town.'

Playing for time, I started to examine the shelves – with the reflexes of an old-time runner, rapidly scanning, left to right, high-lights identified (with a faint clearing of the throat): the first English (1896 Heinemann) edition of Stephen Crane's *The Red Badge of Courage* and Ford's first book, *The Brown Owl*, along with a lovely copy of *The Shifting of the Fire*. The better Conrads had been dispersed before Garnett's library was catalogued by Michael Hosking of Deal. The copy of *Nostromo*, which Mocatta had rebound in rather showy full-Morocco, was undistinguished: ex-lib with a label from *The Tabard Inn Library* on front paste-down. Many annotations (not thought to be in author's hand).

Morocco. Mocatta. Moorcock.

The letters of those words formed and reformed. Owlish ooos. My head swam. I couldn't decide if my host, the preposterous figure in the brown suit, who clearly modelled himself on the fictional Jerry Cornelius, had been invented by Michael Moorcock in his pomp. Or if the exiled editor of *New Worlds* had based his gender-jumping, time-shifting star on someone he'd met while visiting his mother on the coast in . . . Worthing?

Moorcock's Notting Hill, through the intervention of Mocatta and others, had migrated to the south coast: Brighton. Old hippies in the Lanes. Coke-snorting journalists wallowing in chichi flats. Resting actors. Peddlers of stolen property. Expensive restaurants with lousy food. Sad poets with leaking memories. Property sharks who learnt their lessons from Rachman: don't sleep with upwardly mobile tarts and never mix with writers. (Tender-hearted Moorcock was more forgiving of Rachman than any of his former collaborators.)

'I have . . . a thing . . . I want you to do,' Mocatta rattled: as his back went into spasm.

'I'm awfully busy just now,' I said. 'Fat novel months overdue. Publishers making unpleasant noises. You can't rack up advances these days and forget about them. I used to make a tidy living inventing titles over lunch in Charlotte Street. Now they send in the heavies or take you to court.'

Mocatta cracked his knuckles: a Moorcock villain from a shilling-shocker. He was much more like Jerry's evil brother, Frank. The wheel of fate had completed its spin: where Jerry Cornelius fought the Vietnam War in London (from the roof of Derry and Toms), Mocatta (arms dealer, land shark) brought Mesopotamia to Fair-light. Along with his flying boat.

Driving out of town, scarf blowing in the wind, Cornelius tuned in to Radio Potemkin, The Moquettes. See: *A Cure for Cancer*, first edition, p. 191. Moquette, Mocatta. Mock Hatter. The city was on fire.

Identity drifted. Titles were optional. Place was absolute. Mocatta saw himself as the direct inheritor of Ford and Conrad. A gentleman farmer who didn't farm. A writer who didn't write – but was the cause of writing in others (future memoirs). Mocatta, as a name, belonged in Conrad's fictional country, Sulaco. The Occidental Province where Hamburg Jews, Italian freedom-fighters, Masons, mad priests and men in love with silver were welcomed and absorbed.

'One question,' Mocatta persisted, 'before I make my modest proposal. Can two men write one book? I'm thinking of Ford and Conrad. The total collapse Conrad underwent with the completion of *Nostromo* – and how Ford stepped in, took dictation, even composing that pivotal section, the conversation between Martin Decoud and Antonia Avellanos, the dark spirit of place. Oh, the sub-tlety, the spaces around the couple, the shadows. The stage business with the lost fan. Ford's technique, barely perceptible, injects one drop of blood into the ice. The pure adventure story, *Treasure Island* revised by Dostoevsky, is lifted to another dimension. And I want you to play the Ford role for me. Write my story. I have the words, obviously, but not the time. My daughter can help.'

I thought: fantastic. This situation. A library of sodden books stuck board to board. The missing wall. Brilliant light from the sea. Two characters, on the verge of hysteria, testing each other out, arguing over authorship – when they are both ghosts, deletions, figments of nobler writers' fading imaginations. Skull talking to skull.

Mocatta was Moorcock's Jerry Cornelius (a character leased to many hacks and visionaries). I came to him late in the day, when Jerry was pretty much played out, cycle completed. (And not yet bought by Hollywood.) Moorcock, prolific composer of sword-and-sorcery epics, labyrinthine London tales, had retired to Lost Pines, Texas: cleaner air (so he thought), different prejudices, a gracious property (very much like this one). In his exile (compulsive consumer of British newsprint, addict of Radio 3), the great mythographer must have been amused by some piece I'd written. He made 'Taffy' Norton the bonehead sidekick of his 'metatemporal detective', Sir Seaton Begg. A muscular Christian pathologist in the tradition of Dr Watson. Norton puts dumb questions quite effectively and consumes hearty breakfasts.

'Who does the graft and who gets the credit?' said Mocatta. 'Orson Welles and Graham Greene arguing over the provenance of a wisecrack about cuckoo clocks. Pathetic!'

He pulled a slim black volume from the shelf: Nicholas Delbanco, *Group Portrait (Joseph Conrad, Stephen Crane, Ford Madox Ford, Henry James and H.G. Wells).*

A conscious and conscientious effort to subordinate his sense of self, the idiosyncratic diction that asserts identity. Or the opposed identities may have, momentarily, merged. It shows the degree to which collaboration can forge prose parts into a seamless whole. As Conrad was fond of saying, and Ford proud to report, 'By Jove . . . it's a third person who is writing.'

'That's what I require from you: the Harry Lime factor, the Third Mind. Keep me back in the shadows as long as you can, a cocktail of criminality and poetry. But stress my ability to notice the tonality of a marine sunset as I strangle a tart in an Eastbourne hotel.'

'Is there a fee?'

'Six months' rent on Cunard Court, I control the property. No junkies on your floor, I guarantee. And I switch the drum and bass operation – persuading wrinklies to move on – over to D block. Reasonable? You give Hastings a bit of literary varnish and Hastings gives you a living – fair?'

'Food, books, council tax, electricity?'

'You'll have to graft, bar work, minicabbing. The world doesn't owe you a living, you ponce, just because you've knocked out four novels in thirty years scrounging off the generosity of publishers.'

I walked away from him: the edge of the room, the edge of the world. With one soft eye, I was no judge of distance. This was my moment of choice, keep walking or sign another, probably terminal, Faustian contract. Unable to appreciate the detail in the cloud, pinky-mauve behind grey, breaks in the flocculent membrane, I went with fine gradations of sound: unfathomable depths grumbling and shifting, small waves breaking and dragging on shingle, gulls, rustling leaves, footfall on gravel, distant shouts, children's voices in the country park.

'Let's keep it simple,' Mocatta said. 'I see my story as a blend of documentary and *hommage* – what might vulgarly be called fiction. The model will be Conrad, *Nostromo*. Just call the book: *Mocatta*. Very much the Conrad feel. I'm the title part but I'm not always on stage, do the Harry Lime thing again – build me up through contradictory accounts, shreds of gossip, newspaper cuttings.'

'Is there a plot, a structure?'

Mocatta laughed. 'Brink's-Mat,' he said, 'the Heathrow bullion blag. Gold for silver – geddit? How the robbery connects with the construction of the M25, Falklands War, ecstasy trafficking, asylum-seekers. The large picture – politics, media, business – I'll fill you in. You can pick most of it up in one afternoon in the clubhouse of the London Golf Club in Swanley. They all belong:

Denis Thatcher, Sean Connery, Kenny Noye, Kelvin McKenzie, Kerry Packer (overseas member, obviously).'

'I don't play, never have.'

'Neither do they. Swanley's much too civilised. Think of it as an eighteenth-century coffee house. Investments and sex.'

'So gold is the motif. What about the characters?'

'You can do the lowlife, villains, chancers, artists. I'll point you in the direction of the serious players. And I'll be there in the wings, glamorous, well dressed – but obscurely troubled. The secret wound.'

'Which is?'

'Your business to find out. Succeed and I'll kill you.'

'Location?'

'South coast. The coastal province, the new republic: Pevensey Bay to Folkestone. Old freedom-fighters from the Balkans, bent doctors, retired mercenaries drinking away their guilt: it's on a plate. My life, I don't know what I'm paying you for. The *Nostromo* parallels write themselves. The search for the treasure? Coppers digging up builders' yards in Hastings. You can plant the gold bars in . . . Canvey? Isle of Grain? By the Dungeness Lighthouse? No, I've got it, one of those off-shore forts, Thames Estuary. Perfect. You'll sell hundreds of thousands, film's in the bag. Give it plenty of that magic realism, coke-skewed actuality, fast-breeding metaphors, and I may chuck in another six months in Cunard Court, gratis. A year if you're short-listed for the Booker.'

'Where *is* the bullion? It might help if I knew which areas to avoid. You don't want metal-detector freaks blundering over your property.'

Mocatta was gripping one of the shelves, his back again, spur of bone pressing on lumbar nerves. Interview concluded, time to be moving on. Why do we have to talk in the shorthand of comic-strip bubbles? Why can't we be granted the dignity of Jamesian paragraphs, the unspoken, flicks of hair, turns around the garden, silent contemplation of art works?

'You stupid, or what? There never was any bullion, cunt. Urban myth. Insurance scam from the off. Bit of business that grew out of the landscape of perimeter fences, bonded sheds, proximity to motorway. A fucking fiction. And we all did very nicely on it. Cops, customs, legit and semi-legit Kent and Essex entrepreneurs. Half the faces from the Elephant have brought property in Biggin Hill on the back of the Brink's-Mat scam. The rest are in Cyprus.'

I was too dim, too slow to pick up the connections: a fossil from the age of paper. Paper was truth. Touch it, smell it, always faithful. I knew how to navigate those tides, that sea: novels, essays, travel journals, poetry. Everything said that needed to be said. The clues all in place. Names named. Hastings had played its part in the invention of television, the whoredom of electricity. Now they were up for broadband internet connections, the world in your lap. I was finished, doomed like those decent, backstreet bookshops. Corrupted by a sentimental attachment to a past that never happened.

'I'll do it,' I lied.

He stared at my outstretched hand, a turd on a silver plate. He was a man of extreme, probably clinical, fastidiousness – camping in a ruin, a bombed-out palace: Blenheim as Butlin's, Camber Sands.

The genre he proposed was provocative: South American multi-layered fiction as practised by an alien (a thief). Revolution, colonialism, a fabulous harbour. Joseph Conrad's *Nostromo* (published in 1904) was not only the summation and synthesis of a number of white-world tendencies, but also a template for Marquez, Fuentes (pinch of Stephen Crane) and Jorge Luis Borges. (I remember the great Argentinian myth-maker being asked about his favourite films. 'Westerns,' he replied. Imagine that: a blind man in a half-deserted, afternoon cinema, confronted by widescreen prairies, mesas, buttes, rock chimneys. Films composed by directors with eye-patches, bandits. A theatre of sound, full orchestra and spare dialogue. *West of the Pecos*. Mitchum growling his way through Raoul Walsh's *Pursued*.)

Lists again (the defining contemporary vice). Compose a new list, best of, just like television, to stop my knees giving away. Before I run to the kitchen, make my escape. Let's see. What can you offer on 'South American' or 'Central American' novels (or films) by European writers and artists? They have to be authentic: texture and soul. Snake inside sugar egg.

I nominate: Malcolm Lowry for *Under the Volcano* (novel, not film). B. Traven for everything from *The Treasure of the Sierra Madre* to *The White Rose*. Werner Herzog, Luis Buñuel. R.B. Cunninghame Graham (mate of Conrad). W.H. Hudson. Daniel Defoe (*Robinson Crusoe* filmed by Buñuel). Georges Arnaud for *The Wages of Fear* (film and book: oil, nitroglycerine, sweat). William Burroughs for *The Yage Letters*. (I wouldn't, as a general rule, include Americans, but Bill's a dark twin of T.S. Eliot, same birthplace, so I'll make an exception. Apologies to John Huston, Sam Peckinpah and Budd Boetticher.)

Burroughs also qualifies as a Conrad obsessive.

'One of my favourites is Joseph Conrad. My story, "They Just Fade Away", is a fold-in from *Lord Jim*. In fact, it's almost a retelling of the *Lord Jim* story. My Stein is the same Stein as in *Lord Jim*.'

That's Burroughs in a *Paris Review* interview. A yarn he repeated when I met him in Lawrence, Kansas, second drink in hand, sun dropping, cat on lap. Minder moving in to whisper something in his ear.

My wild card is the little-known novel *More Things in Heaven* by Walter Owen. Owen, an initiate, lived for a time in Buenos Aires. He produced a sequence, linked narratives involving spontaneous combustion and a cursed manuscript, that seems in some ways to prefigure Borges (with a dash of M.R. James). Owen's book, difficult to find, has itself become a talisman, possession (unless it can be passed on to an unsuspecting recipient) conferring malfate, paranoid delusions, death. I rid myself of my original copy, but still have the second – which arrived, anonymously, as barter against a bad debt.

Mr Letherbotham, a middle-aged bachelor who for some years had earned a somewhat precarious livelihood as free-lance journalist and reporter attached to one of the local English newspapers, was found dead in his apartment on the fourth floor . . . The body of Mr Letherbotham was seated at a small writing-table. It was evident that he had been in the act of writing when death overtook him . . .

I was fascinated and appalled as I read and re-read the thirty or forty scribbled pages which had littered the floor of the room in which in the silence of the night death had come to their writer in a mysterious and dreadful form. And gradually I found the conviction forming in my mind that the story they unfolded was not fiction but a narrative of factual events, and that from them an astonishing inference might be drawn regarding the manner in which the tragedy had been brought about . . .

Mr Letherbotham's first name, I remember, was: *Cornelius*. Accident or warning? 'I was struck by the coincidence,' stated Owen, 'if indeed it was a coincidence and not a clue to some hidden connection.'

Back in the Seventies, when I had a cash-in-hand job, tracking down living associates of John Cowper Powys on behalf of a rag-trade millionaire, I got to know another member of the Kings Road retinue, the poet Hugo Manning. Manning, working as a correspondent in Buenos Aires, came across Owen. They shared an interest in the occult. In verse. Hugo showed me, with pride, the inscribed copies of Owen's translations of *The Gaucho Martin Fierro* and *Don Juan Tenorio*, which he later sold to the West Hampstead dealer, Eric Stevens.

Was Hugo, in fact, the model for Mr Letherbotham?

It didn't take much prompting to tease out the story. Hugo never came to terms with English weather; mopping his brow, he sweltered (visible vest, thick woollen shirt, tweed jacket, duffel coat), battling primitive central-heating systems. He was a man confused, as lost as Conrad's Captain Mitchell, returned, after years in Sulaco, to England. Hugo puffed away at his pipe, doodled with coloured pens in the ever-present ledger: portraits of hangers-on in his patron's office. He had the nautical beard, the garrulousness traditional in Ancient Mariners. There was always a yarn to be spun – in words whose order never changed.

Hugo was the conduit between Walter Owen and Borges

(although the two writers never exchanged a word). Memories of Owen, the mystical journalist – and even, perhaps, his cursed book – were passed on when Manning formed his rather one-sided acquaintance with the blind librarian. Living in Swiss Cottage, years later, as a humble member of Canetti's circle, Hugo published a private press booklet on Borges.

Yes, he told me, the Argentinian never tired of expressing his enthusiasm for De Quincey, Stevenson, Chesterton and the *Beowulf* epic, but his great love was . . . Conrad. Borges, according to Hugo, insisted upon the intimate relationship of document and fiction. He quoted Bioy Casares: 'I think Conrad is right. Really, nobody knows whether the world is realistic or fantastic, that is to say, whether the world is a natural process or whether it is a kind of dream, a dream we may or may not share with others.'

Borges and Manning. The blind man and the old sailor with the clear blue eyes. Long afternoons at café tables – neither man was a serious drinker – discussing the Kabbalah and Jewish mysticism. Hugo was a Jew and a scholar. They were, if you like, study partners. It was Borges's fancy to claim some Jewish blood, on the side of his Portuguese mother. I understood very well, from the things that Hugo did *not* say, that he believed his life's work, the writing, was pointless. In a world of correspondences and balances, demons and angels, everything worth saying had been said. His laboured verses were tributes to a music his ears were too thick to catch. Borges, on the other hand, fan of cowboys and knifemen, high romance and hermetic pulp, recognised the world as a labyrinth of texts and echoes, a forest where the blind were the surest guides.

The women were head to head over a plate of Marmite sandwiches (I could smell them); Marmite and anchovy soldiers – to provoke the necessary thirst, the pints of warm sweet tea. They were also, it was quite obvious, immodestly drunk: as the proper response to Mocatta's anachronistic withdrawal.

'Nice little chat, boys?' cackled the crone. 'I'd fetch your tea from the oven if my pins was still working.'

Ollie pushed herself up and came over to her father, hugging him, as he flinched. Crackled.

'Shall I call a cab for Mr Norton?'

'Let the slag walk. It's what he's known for.'

A walk was fine. Mocatta led me back through corridors that had warped and crumbled, slithered seaward, during the time I'd spent in the library.

'I don't go out of doors. Agoraphobia – brought on in Belmarsh. I'm like an albino in sunshine.'

The evening light, dappled leaf patterns, low gold, was inviting. I knew better than to attempt a handshake. Five or six miles back to St Leonards would give me an appetite. I might risk the Balti house with the photo of that satisfied diner, Lord Longford, in the window. The encomium from Cunard Court resident Leslie Ash: 'Unique!'

'Don't go tearing off. I've got something. Before you start on our book, a little bit of inspiration. You might find we've more in common than you imagined. I've always had a fancy for genealogy. What's your middle name?'

'MacGregor. Father's mother. Or was it grandfather's second wife? A proscribed name for centuries. Highland banditry, then strategic Jacobitism. Savage blood. We're proud of it.'

'We could be cousins then.'

'Cousins?'

'Name banned: MacGregor, Mocatta. All the proper Scots dispersed to the colonies,' he said. 'Ceylon, Canada, Panama. Why not? Haven't you come across coal-black Nortons, Nortons in skullcaps? I've heard rumours, put about by envious scum, that Mocatta might have a drop or two of the Semite, generations back. We're both Hebrews in denial, who knows?'

I was away, breathing rich moist earth, when he called out. The curse of having been a bookdealer left me with perfect recall of the shelves of his library. (The way we can walk into a shop, after three years, and know just where to put a hand on that second edition of Paul Bowles's *The Sheltering Sky* with the perfect dustwrapper.)

There was a gap in the M section: one volume missing between Carson McCullers, *The Heart is a Lonely Hunter*, first English in scuffed d/w, and Julian Maclaren-Ross, *The Weeping and the Laughter (A Chapter of Autobiography)*, first edition, nice copy, slightly faded on spine. Lavish presentation inscription to David Garnett. (I checked.)

'Norton. Wait!'

He was shouting, but I was around the first bend, out of sight, house gone for ever. I felt the hard shape of the brown parcel he'd given me: a book. A curse. I didn't want it but I couldn't throw it away. The provenance was too rich.

Cunard Court

Sleep knuckled from eyes. Doors thrown wide. And still the town wouldn't come into focus: so it wasn't all bad. Women lost. Threats from psychopaths. Bills, bailiffs. A tray of begging letters from maniacs who want a free ride into the writing game. Life as I knew it. Naked feet on rail, coffee cup in hand.

The sun rises quietly over the pier, a golden triangle dissolving across sleepless waters: the stern-wake of a white stone liner that only travels backwards. Paul McCartney (on Concorde) boasted of witnessing two sunsets in one day; at the rail of Cunard Court (last of the Atlantic queens), the sun *never* goes down, it solicits admiration – fetch that camera. One more panoramic view of the bay and Beachy Head.

If another person has been in the flat while I've been away, so what? They're not here now and they left no mess.

What seas what shores what grey rocks. What is this face, less clear and clearer?

Not Ollie, surely, not here? The day's first promenader: scuttling, slowing, breaking into a jog. The mysterious woman from the Bo-Peep Inn? A hot flush, memory spasm: stuck like a wet leaf to the window of a train. Except that trains, as we saw on our walk to Pevensey Bay, don't move; parked in sheds, in sidings, ancient, dirt-encrusted, with bright new logos.

Mistah Kaporal – he dead.

Unsecured tartan dressing gown, flipflops. Grumbling belly, manky hair: Norton aged sixty dripping from the shower. If he doesn't sit at his desk, six hours straight, what purpose to the man?

Coffee with just enough Colombian in the blend to make me long for a last cigar. Can I contemplate this temperate seascape ¬th equanimity – and, at the same time, pay my dues to the horrible murder (car over cliff) of an associate I've exploited for so many years? Poor Jos. Poor Kaporal. Poor Jacky. Adiós, Ollie (you're not responsible for your father). Another unfinished book. Draconian penalty clauses for non-delivery. Involuntary amputation, eyes on a skewer.

I'll slip out for a croissant, a newspaper. I'll open Mocatta's package before I drop it in the bin. I'm too superstitious to dump a book while it is still safe and snug, embryonic in its protective sac. A scarce Ford? An inscribed Conrad? Mocatta is sure to tell me later, when he knows the Jiffy bag has been discarded: he'll savour my anguish.

Kaporal's attic. A blue light. There is always a light – like a TV set that can't be shut off. Preserve it as Mr K's memorial. I'd be happy to pay his rent, lock the door, leave the room untouched for years. His legend.

The book's a dog. A demonstration of Mocatta's weakness for genealogical research (last refuge of the snob, the social climber). David Sinclair: *Sir Gregor MacGregor and the Land that Never Was (The Extraordinary Story of the Most Audacious Fraud in History)*.

Why not? I've nothing else to do, I've run out of characters (dispersed into more promising narratives). A morning on the balcony, feet up, picking at a book, watching a line of yellow plastic birds, strapped to the rail, spinning for their lives – and, away, away, in the gauzy distance, tiny white yachts. The reassuring hum of traffic, sirens. It takes me a few minutes to realise what's missing. Mocatta has been as good as his word: the rhythm of drum and bass, two floors down, has stopped. The bleepy silence of intensive care.

The point my Fairlight patron was trying to make, it soon became clear, was this: Conrad's Sulaco, a fictional republic based on substantial research, was anticipated in this person MacGregor's topographic scam. The Scottish adventurer (my relative) invented a real country. He commissioned a guide book and shipped boatloads of the gullible (who paid for the privilege) out of Edinburgh to the swampy and largely uninhabited shores of Poyais on the Mosquito Coast. Like Conrad, he drew from his imagination a coastal province with harbour, public buildings, churches, libraries, grand squares, distant hills.

Sir Gregor appointed himself General and Cazique, military and political ruler, a combination of the functions of three or four Conrad characters. City bankers backed him, South America in the period after the Napoleonic Wars was fashionable: the Imperium, glutted on military success, was greedy for profit. Sir Gregor Mac-Gregor was the author the times demanded, a literate Archer with a fragrant wife and a fluid sense of actuality.

I ripped through Sinclair's book: this was *personal*. Should I look on myself as a Norton (old Arthur lost in Peru)? Or a MacGregor (sitting comfortably in London conjuring up a fabulous Central American colony and persuading others to invest in it)? Amateur travel writer or professional fraud? In the fevers of these contradictory Highland bloodstreams lay the genesis of my delirium, my schizophrenia.

As I studied *Sketch of the Mosquito Shore*, the book MacGregor commissioned (with its engravings of the port of Black River), the final barrier between truth and fiction dissolved. MacGregor (coward and hero) fought in the South American wars of Liberation. He knew Bolívar and enjoyed the privilege of friendship with the legendary General Francisco de Miranda. He betrayed them both. MacGregor was no Garibaldino in honest retirement. And he was certainly not the model for Conrad's Giorgio Viola. The man who kills Nostromo.

MacGregor devised a form of fiction that paid, a premature assignation between Bruce Chatwin and get-rich-quick TV. The man was a genius. Poor Arthur Norton, botanist, gold-hunter, vanished into the jungle. His justification, if it lay anywhere, was hidden inside that early Kodak camera: the undeveloped film. Kaporal (on my behalf) had been chasing old ladies, second wives of third cousins, through the net: nothing. The trail was cold. No more Nortons. No relics dreaming away their twilight years in coastal retirement homes, villas and follies left by Scottish colo-
'ists returned from Ceylon and South Africa.

I put Mocatta's book aside: a Japanese flatpack table that threatened to buckle under the weight of a single volume. Nothing to be done. Close my eyes, feel warm breezes from the south-west. Brood on: James Burton (inventor of St Leonards), his pyramid tomb, white hotels, Masonic lodges, parks and crescents. He was as crazy as MacGregor (or so his family thought). Carving a town, a resort patronised by royalty, out of the cliffs: a vision (of fame, loot, immortality).

Sinclair, digging deep, discovers (to his own satisfaction) the source of MacGregor's 'undoubted attachment to South America'. One of his ancestors, implicated in the disastrous attempt to colonise Darien in the late seventeenth century, 'formed a marriage with a native Princess of the country, from which sprung our hero'. The conman's unusually dark complexion was therefore explained: his taste for the primitive, the baroque, his inability to discriminate between truth and fiction.

I leant on the rail, breathing deeply. Hastings shimmered. The height – seven floors up – offered an illusion of omniscience (toy houses in blues, pinks, yellows): more distant than the stars and nearer than the eye. Why not attempt a Philip K. Dick? What was that video? *Minority Report*. Eyeball recognition. So change your eyes. Pluck them out, score replacements on the black market. Replenish sight.

Lines from Eliot drumming in my head all morning, occupying the gap left by the spiking of Mocatta's amplifiers (thumpthumpthump). In Margate, as voyeur, the poet made his existential cri de coeur (or boast): 'I can connect/Nothing with nothing.' A bank clerk, under the paving stones of King William Street, looking up through green glass: the legs, the silk-sheathed legs, the clicking heels of typists. Tom Eliot the Nightstalker, his agonised peregrinations: doorways he can't enter. Libido and lethargy: the hair-shirt, pornographic imaginings in the Cannon Street Hotel. Eliot's breakdown and seaside convalescence were resolved: the publication of a masterwork. I couldn't help myself, everything connected with everything. And Eliot was the messenger: *Death by Water*, *The Hollow Men*, *Marina*.

The conspiracy: to write and rewrite Joseph Conrad, *Heart of Darkness*, *Nostromo*. A voyage, backwards up the birth canal, tagged with epigraphs from the master. *I will show you fear in a handful of dust.*

One of the letters on my tray was from a woman who had laboured 'for more than seven years' making an artist's book out of *Nostromo*. Squeezing ghosts of words, with infinite pain and care, until they become abstractions, wave patterns printed on tissue. 'I am badly distressed,' she wrote, 'by my failure to get the work out to even the modest public.'

But the public is never modest. Nor the writers, the initiates: the possessed. Why should they be?

Burroughs cuts up Conrad. Graham Greene follows his lawless roads, his journeys without maps (Burroughs cuts him up too). Conradians all: Nostromoners. The name of the society, the brotherhood, it came to me as I stood on the balcony, watching Kaporal's window, waiting to see what Ollie would do next, clutching my binoculars. (A telescope would be more use now.)

Nostromoner (*Nost-rom-on-er*), *n.*: physicist of language, anonymous disciple of the writer Joseph Conrad (especially *Nostromo*). One who is dedicated to reworking the major texts and adapting the masks of Conrad's characters, spurning novelty. Nothing to be written that is not written.

Grand Master: J.L. Borges.

The society never meets. No member must acknowledge another. Special interests: the alchemy of false memory, residues floating in the universal mindstream.

J.G. Ballard, who became a Nostromoner the moment he left Cambridge, was later expelled for announcing himself, to a well-connected television director (son of the Archbishop of Canterbury), on his arrival at Shanghai International Airport, with the words: 'Hello, James. Mr Kurtz returns to the Heart of Darkness.'

The expulsion was meaningless (like the mad pronouncements of André Breton and Guy Debord). You can't belong to a society that doesn't exist. This is a covert (and imaginary) association ⸱e membership is posthumous, invented by scholars hungry for tenure: forged documents, doctored photographs. Several of the more significant and prolific Nostromoners (Poe, Stevenson, De Quincey) *preceded* Conrad, contriving their imitations before the original was written or remembered. (All composition is memory.)

Forge/forget: the cannibalistic closeness of those words. If I lay the book, Mocatta's gift, *The Land That Never Was*, across my knees (bony, Quixotic), and remove the pretty dustwrapper (eye-gum) . . . well then, by weight and shape, you have a laptop. Lift the front board, the lid. Words fall in vertical lines, bar-code rain. Patterns not symbols. Visible echoes. Pattern recognition: the art of the bibliophile, the Nostromoner. It costs nothing to join. Pick up a paperback in any flea market, a cheap Penguin from a Hastings charity shop. Start there. Work up to the hardback (with its megabyte).

Ballard, serene in Shepperton, started to give away secrets. Book as computer. His story. Title ('re-memorised' from Borges): 'The Index'.

From abundant internal evidence it seems clear that the text printed below is the index to the unpublished and perhaps suppressed autobiography of a man who may well have been one of the most remarkable figures of the 20th century . . .

Who and what does he list? 'Eliot, T.S., suppresses dedication of *Four Quartets* . . . collegium of Perfect Light Movement . . . Limited Editions Club . . . Oswald, Lee Harvey . . . Sex-change, rumoured operation . . . Telepathy, conducts experiments . . . Zanuck, Darryl F . . .'

Private libraries, arcane societies, Eliot. Ballard might as well have published an article in the *Sunday Telegraph* (he tried that but nobody noticed). You have to chase remaindered editions to bring the story to closure: a copy of *A User's Guide to the Millennium* picked up in Greenwich, after a walk to the site of New Labour's Dome (closed while uninterested parties argue over the small print of the asset-stripping contracts). Greenwich is a place of pilgrimage for Nostromoners: an anarchist's bomb, lifted from newsprint, destroying the interpersonal dynamics of a fictional family: *The Secret Agent*.

Before you flip Ballard's millennial computer, examine the photo-collage dustwrapper (icons and influences). Check out the suspects: Graham Greene (top right, very shifty) and (top left) Robert Duvall in *Apocalypse Now* (Coppola's folly).

Conrad resists cinema: Orson Welles's aborted trial run (pre-*Kane*) at *Heart of Darkness*, the career suicide of Nicolas Roeg's straight-to-oblivion version. Welles was a lifelong Nostromoner (three Conrad scripts, all unmade). 'I don't suppose there's any novelist except Conrad who can be put directly on the screen,' he told Peter Bogdanovich. He smuggled *Heart of Darkness* onto radio (nobody listened), then conceded: 'There's never been a Conrad movie, for the simple reason that nobody's done it as written.'

Conrad, on a healthy retainer from the Lasky company, wrote a silent-screen adaptation of 'Gaspar Ruiz' (*Gaspar the Strong*). Lasky rejected the script, it was shelved. In company with his literary agent, J.B. Pinker, Conrad travelled to Canterbury to view Maurice Tourneur's film of *Victory*. *The Silver Treasure*, a film based on *Nostromo*, was made in 1926, and is now lost. There are no known prints in any of the great collections. Orson Welles's footage for *Heart of Darkness* can be found in the Lilly Library, Indiana University.

Affiliated Nostromoners who smuggled Conradian material into the cinema include: Alfred Hitchcock (*Sabotage*), William Wellman (*Dangerous Paradise*), Carol Reed (*Outcast of the Islands*), Andrzej Wajda (*The Shadow-Line*). Richard Brooks, Terence Young and David Lean are not Nostromoners. A fact confirmed by Lean, who died in his riverside conversion at Limehouse while labouring over his long-term obsession, a script based on *Nostromo*.

I didn't dispose of the *User's Guide* dustwrapper without scanning it for additional information. There wasn't any, a random (post-*Pepper*) iconographic sweep: Aldous Huxley, two (dead) Beatles, Presley, Warhol, Humphrey Bogart, Ronnie Reagan. Generic nec-
lia. Freud, Dalí, Marilyn Monroe: faces looking for T-shirts.

Torn newspapers. Motorways. A poster for Don Siegel's *Invasion of the Body Snatchers*.

Graphic scrim. Lose the wrapper. Flip the lid.

A real index to go with its fictional predecessor.

And, yes, you'll also namecheck: Eliot, Greene (and *Green Berets*), Hitchcock, Dennis Hopper, Howard Hughes, inner space, insanity, R.D. Laing, Fritz Lang, Chris Marker, Henry Miller, Michael Moorcock (p. 190), physics, Poe, Roy Porter, *Rear Window*, Carol Reed, relativity, Nicolas Roeg, Jack Ruby, Jimmy Savile, R.L. Stevenson, *Sunset Boulevard*, television (5, 11, 24, 73, 82, 89, 167–8, 173, 174, 225–7, 232, 236, 243), *The Tempest*, Vietnam War. And Darryl Zanuck.

Zanuck: Nostromoner? Old movies, run to the point of invisibility on the Irish provincial circuit, act like pre-electronic computers. Tap in wherever you like, surf the reference books, download the connections.

Zanuck in exile, Paris. Affair with Juliet Greco (model for Marina Fountain?). Zanuck as writer, his stories published by a hair-oil company. Talent recognised: scripts for Rin-Tin-Tin. 1924: *The Lighthouse by the Sea*. There it was, the *Nostromo* connection, bold as brass. The best place to keep a secret: in lights, the brightest bulbs you can find, above the marquee. Remember *Nostromo*'s last reel, the Isabels? The Capataz de Cargadores has arranged for the old Italian freedom-fighter to be appointed as lighthouse-keeper. He rows across the bay, courts the younger daughter, goes back for the buried silver. Is shot. Killed.

Zanuck works with Bill Wellman (*Maybe It's Love*, 1930). Wellman is a Nostromoner. Wellman directs Robert Mitchum.

WELLMAN: I make pictures. What do you do for a living?
MITCHUM: That, Dad, is a matter of opinion.

Mitchum, Wellman, Zanuck. They invade Europe. They smoke cigars. They talk Conrad. Zanuck cultivates the eye-patch directors – Raoul Walsh (*The Bowery*, 1933) – *before* they lose their orbs. John Ford, he was another pirate. Another eye-patch (painted by Kitaj). Fritz Lang (*The Return of Frank James*, 1940).

In Hastings, everything connects to everything. The British love their secret societies, confederacies of outcasts: Aleister Crowley expelled from most of them. The Hermetic Order of the Golden Dawn, O.T.O., Ma Ion, Kos: they make it their business to confirm writers in rituals of impotence, elective invisibility. Machen, Blackwood, A.E. Waite, Austin Spare, Walter Owen. The Redonda mob. Remember them? M.P. Shiel as 'King' of Redonda – an uninhabited islet near Antigua (map like *Treasure Island*, displacement like Conrad's Isabels). John Gawsworth, Lawrence Durrell, Dylan ͡s: all members of the cult. Poetry has to go somewhere.

W.B. Yeats, George Russell, Crowley: verse in freefall, from vision to bathos. Limping towards Hastings to die.

Ford Madox Ford: *The Shifting of the Fire* (1892)
M.P. Shiel: *Shapes in the Fire* (1896)
Walter Owen: *The Mantra of the Fire* (1947)
Jim Morrison (The Doors): *Come on Baby, Light My Fire* (as featured in *Apocalypse Now*, 1979)
Alan Moore: *Voice of the Fire* (1996)

Fire on water. Cults of the coast. Explain this: I was walking up the long slope of London Road, in the direction of Silverhill (and, ultimately, the Ridge), an early expedition to locate the house where Crowley gave up the ghost. Two men, with their partners, in a Thai restaurant. They know each other but they aren't sitting together. Nobody else in the place. One couple (J.G. Ballard and friend) in the window. With the other pair in the furthest dimmest recess: Nicolas Roeg (and protégée). Nostromoners in psychic communication? Regrets for Roeg's film of *Crash*: never made? A proposed Ballard script for *Nostromo*? As space opera.

I don't believe in originality, just product. The book I was about to abandon – stones in the throat – all my useless research, confirmed one fact: my failure to rewrite *Nostromo*. Yes, you could construct a graph of rough equivalents, but there was no elegance in the match. Something missing: life. Forward momentum, a reason to turn the page. An absence at the centre: the human heart (as factored by Ford Madox Ford). I needed a collaborator, badly. I needed Jos Kaporal. Reborn. Brought home. On the case.

This is what I scribbled in my notebook:

```
Hastings = Sulaco
    Brink's-Mat Gold = Silver Ingots
Mickey O'Driscoll = The bandit Hernandez
    Mocatta = Charles Gould
Norton = Nostromo
```

```
   Hugo Manning = Captain Mitchell
Jos Kaporal (journalist, exile) = Martin
Decoud
   Olivia Fairlight-Jones = Antonia
   Avellanos
Arthur Norton (great-grandfather) = Dr
Monygham
```

I'm not happy, for one very good reason, with this mirror-world: *I* should be Decoud – the cynicism, the fatal passion for Antonia (the dark lady). Antonia must be Ruth. Ruth Alsop. A splash of duty-free perfume (Calvin Kline One) on the inside of her left wrist. That man Decoud should never have left Paris. He should have retained Antonia: as a memory, a perfume to chase (through piano bars and bordellos).

His suicide, returned to Sulaco, is inevitable. The 'triple death' of Welsh mythology: gunshot while sitting on edge of boat (+ drowning) while dying of thirst. Decoud couldn't hack loneliness, the bitter Crusoe existence of the sunbaked islet: 'The solitude appeared like a great void, and the silence of the gulf like a tense, thin cord to which he hung suspended by both hands.'

I took a turn of the deck (the narrow balcony that ran from sea-facing view to town view). A photographer could do something with this, curves, sharp angles, balconies, railings. Whiteness. Light. Can't you imagine those haughty nudes – in heels and sailors' caps? Hastings was moving, walkers, cyclists, drinking schools. Kaporal's attic was still blue: an ultraviolet tanning cubicle.

And somebody – I fetched the binoculars . . . *Ollie!* – was in there, in the room. With a man. They were embracing. A large man in a black shirt: allowing himself to be hugged by a small, neat, agitated woman. A swimmer, who has been too far out, grabbing for a rock. If I didn't know better – and my ability to connect names with faces was famously awful – I'd say: 'Kaporal'. Another revenant. Another example of narrative punctuation refusing to stay punctuated.

Kaporal with Mocatta's daughter, my fiancée? Ludicrous. The mother of my first child? My daughter. Under sleep, where all waters meet. I hope they call the babe Marina.

Conflicting emotions somersault, shirts in a washing-machine, as I run down the stairs. Jealousy, anger, relief: that Kaporal should return from the dead to rescue the stalled novel, that he should take Ollie off my hands – leaving the way clear for my pursuit of Marina Fountain.

But why, I wanted to know, was Kaporal waving? Looking up at my balcony, waving his arms as extravagantly as the propellers of the yellow plastic bird.

The Ridge

The house had changed. It wasn't the house to which the journalist had brought me. This section of outer-rim Hastings, the Ridge, was dedicated to obscurity, anchored in failure: empty hospitals, retirement homes that had themselves retired. Laurel and bay. Ivy creepers. Planting strategies that screened detached properties, sparing them spectacular views of a glassy sea; saving them from the curiosity of the vulgar.

'Are you sure it's this one?' I asked.

Kaporal's black T-shirt was several shades blacker around the armpits, an inverse pyramid of bodydamp on his broad back: sticky and steaming. We were so close, I didn't want there to be any mistake. Close to resolution: a set of photographs to spread on the table. Those are the finishes to which I aspire – pictures, not words. Pictures taken by another hand. Found footage. The shock of recognition. Broken sentences knitting together like a stop-motion Polish cartoon.

'That's what the woman said. Stonestile Lane.'

Expectation, the rush, carried us to the top of the hill, more than an hour's hard walk – but Kaporal's interpretation of his phone conversation made me feel that there was no time to spare. This was a very old lady. The trawlings on the net, adverts placed in local papers along the south coast, the printed leaflets he had distributed in retirement homes and dying farms, had paid off. A relative of Arthur Norton, in possession of an early Kodak camera, had made contact. She refused the reward. She wanted to meet – in person – the last male Norton, to take tea with him. She lived in Hastings.

That's why Kaporal waved at me with atypical vigour when I stood on the balcony. Not, as I thought, because he was still alive. Nor because Ollie had chosen *him*. (He couldn't be sure they hadn't been married before, mislaid each other. Somewhere between the language student and the lost weekend in Las Vegas.) The researcher was ecstatic, he had found the final piece of the jigsaw, Arthur Norton's Kodak. He was off the case. He could return to London.

O'Driscoll wouldn't bother him now. Alby Sleeman was banged up. Phil Tock had decided on a sex-change operation, relocation to Thailand. They weren't killers. Like everybody else in Essex, they had ambitions to make it in the media (red letters on black gloss, hardmen doing the Look). When you've been banned for life from the Basildon Festival Park there's nowhere to go, not really, it's all downhill.

Mickey kept Mocatta's motor. He was intended to use it running passengers between the City Airport (Silvertown) and the ibis hotel (Thurrock). A circuit of Travelodges. Mocatta had lost the plot. The guy who wrote his scripts, back in the Sixties, had skipped the country, opened a breakfast bar in Corpus Christi, Texas – where he growled his way through sentimental border ballads and recited cowboy poetry. Without the paperback mythology, the romance of his career as hired assassin, rock star, property developer and cross-dresser, Mocatta was just another anal retentive who lived in retirement with his old mum.

Jos and Mickey parted on the best of terms. Kaporal promised to deliver the numbers of a documentary director, a production company, a literary agent. There might be a part, funeral scene, in a two-hour thing they were doing on the Swanley road-rage killing. A definite maybe, as talking head, in the reconstruction of the Rettendon Range Rover slaughter.

This climb was different. Kaporal, if he could help it, never walked; he waddled to the pasta place, sat on a bench and stared at the sea. With Ollie beside him, the man bustled like Werner Herzog on the snowy road between Munich and Paris. Up from the park through suburbs of quirky, non-regulation housing stock: villas, bungalows, castles, haciendas. Towers, conservatories. A restaurant that converted a Tudorbethan pub into the set for *55 Days at Peking*.

There were allotments (memories of Roy Porter), football grounds carved out of the high ground (Machu Picchu). A long leafy lane that weaved alongside properties customised by a benign plutocracy: the secret serenity of swimming pools, decks, pension funds paying off, golden handshakes for shamed quango vermin.

I couldn't help myself, I yapped about the Nostromoners: my theories. The former Kaporal had a taste for conspiracy. Now he frowned, let Ollie take his arm – as if she needed his strength to get her over the rough stones.

'So they're all male, your Nostromoners?' she said.

I was still a little raw, after our broken engagement, but I did my best to disguise it.

'Females and gay men use Virginia Woolf in the same way – as a portal. Headaches, seasonal tensions and so on. Hypersensitivity to loud-print dresses, vulgarity, the lower orders. Fondness for untipped cigarettes, hats, cottage gardens, painted furniture. They call them, Virginia's camp followers, the Wolverines.'

A silly revenge for my lover's desertion. Ollie was unimpressed. She had as much trouble as I did in sitting through stream-of-consciousness, multiple-narrative, death-by-drowning, putty nose Bloomsbury necrophilia.

'Was Kurtz a Jew?' Kaporal asked. The politics of colonialism, race and gender had, of late, called Conrad's status into question.

A good question. Conrad's Marlow, we know, was an Englishman. He was drawn from the novelist's sailing partner and fellow cigar smoker, George Fountaine Weare Hope.

'All Europe,' Marlow said, 'contributed to the making of Kurtz.' The anti-Semites of High Modernism ran with Kurtz, the upriver trader, as man of straw, stuffed guy, symbol of defeated capitalism and its blood-drenched voodoo. Was Kurtz based on Klein, the chief of the 'Inner Station', met by Conrad at Stanley Falls, on his own Congo expedition? Or on a fellow lodger in Stoke Newington? One of the Undead taking possession, slipping through at a time of weakness and malarial fever. Dark stains in the glass of the German Hospital. Stains shaped like a river.

I had a passion for maps. I would look for hours at South America, or Africa, or Australia, and lose myself in all the glories of exploration . . . The glamour's off.

Kurtz with his mongrel blood, his terrible end, troubled me. What images were waiting in Arthur Norton's camera – if that film had not already turned to mush, ink, mud? Kurtz was too close to the lovingly described horrors of the death of poor Hirsch ('a little hook-nosed man') in *Nostromo*. Hirsch is white-world Jewish, irritating, a leather peddler scorned by the silver mine magnate. A coward, a blabbermouth. A victim. The shadow of his broken body, swinging in the torture chamber, strung from a beam, beaten, brutalised, shot.

'The strange, anxious whine' of Hirsch (the third man in the lighter) wouldn't leave me alone. Arthur Norton met many such tradesmen and percentage-cutters on his travels, along with Jesuit missionaries and debauched Franciscans; his humour in these circumstances made me uneasy. It was too close to my travesty of Hastings.

The house was like Balmoral, but bigger and in worse taste: turrets, heraldic shields, French hipped roofs with conical spires and a flurry of exposed black beams. We stood at the top of the drive, looking for an excuse to give it up, turn tail.

'What did the old bird say?'

'Come to tea. Bring your young lady,' Kaporal replied.

They couldn't find stone as grim as this outside a Glasgow necropolis. The lawns, light stolen by dense hedges, were some consolation. A gardener was resting on his rake, staring at us in a manner that verged on autism.

We crunched gravel. The man, rake gripped like a Morris dancer, moved diagonally across his patch – to protect it and cut us off.

'My friend!'

His moustache, the absence of it, had me fooled. But Kaporal was better with Identikit portraits.

'Drin?'

The quiet man, it appeared, spoke fluent – if formal – English: after the fashion of Joseph Conrad. Another caricature I'd miscalculated.

'Jos-eph. And you also, Mr Norton. Mademoiselle, I am charmed.'

Drin, after the ibis fiasco, had returned to the coast. His six months' quarantine was over. He was legit: a gardener and handyman taking night classes to reacquire his medical qualifications. Drin was an anaesthetist.

'Achmed?'

Achmed, it seems, in partnership with some Russians, was managing a video shop in Southend. And telling his story to a scriptwriter who wanted to recreate the adventurous journey to Sangatte as a dramatised documentary.

We shook hands with the Albanian. He embraced Kaporal, kissed him on both cheeks. They exchanged mobile-phone numbers. And promises neither man would keep.

Lifting the weight of the brass knocker – a wolf's head – I had one of those moments: après vu. The conviction that I would be repeating this action for ever. It was so familiar, the way the knocker adhered to the paint. The absence of an electric bell. The longshot from the road: ash, ivy, laurel. That afternoon with the journalist, last year, searching for the boarding house in which Aleister Crowley died. We were, back then, on the wrong side of the Ridge – taking in the seaview, the spread of the town. The kind of houses that become prep schools, retirement homes, sets for *Fawlty Towers*. The hubris of Edwardian social mobility (cash from the colonies) brought down by a primitive ring road, the continuity of broken traffic.

Do you find, when you know an author, that you can see precisely how his fictions draw upon experience? The flat in Camden Town that he loans out to his female lead, after a thorough cleaning, belongs to an sf encyclopaedist. The lecture at the ICA – 'smelling of wet wool' – is one that he himself delivered, a year earlier. Life is an inadequate rehearsal for text. The unsuspecting reader decides to follow, one bright afternoon, a fictional trail along the canal bank.

A photographer, on a whim, after discovering that Compendium Bookshop is now defunct, walks back to Hackney. And notices, months later, toying with a box of prints, the way a woman with a rucksack, eyes on the ground, misses the sinister transaction whereby two men in hooded sweatshirts wrestle a typewriter from the grasp of a fat boy.

'Yes?'

A woman in black bombazine. Backlit in doorway. Waiting. Door open a slit. Fern in blue pot. Brown envelopes on small table.

An act of will, a nudge from Ollie: the gears click.

'Mrs Norton. We've arranged to see her.'

The length of the windows, tall and narrow – are they expecting an imminent attack by archers? The old folk, the few who are inside, are very dapper. The click of croquet balls on the lawn at the back. And the click of false teeth anticipating crumpets.

Mrs Norton promises a tour of the garden after tea. She's tanned, check shirt and jeans, and looks much fitter and brighter-eyed than anything I've seen recently in my shaving mirror.

'Sit down, dear.'

'What's that very pleasant smell?' I said. 'Leafy, woody. Bit like cinnamon. Wrong season for bonfires, surely?'

'Oh, that'll be the crematorium. Wind's from the east today.' She hoots at my discomfort.

Our precise relationship takes a while to establish, a question of memory: mine. Her husband is my father's first cousin. Old Arthur, who had six children (three of each, between voyages), was grandfather to both men. Mrs Norton, Winnie, was young Arthur's second wife. He'd been gone now twelve years. Tea-blender (family tradition) in the City. Winnie worked in the office. They lived in Wimbledon. For the tennis. Competed twice in the mixed doubles. Won a cup in a tournament sponsored by the *Standard*. She'll find the photo later. They retired to a house in Silverhill, near the park, the courts. It got too much when Arthur passed on.

'This is such a lovely place. I have my own bed, flower bed. And

I walk to town every Saturday for shopping and a drink. There's still a few of us left, the tennis crowd. It feels right to live in a house with a family connection. Even if it's not my family. I'm a Londoner, through and through, Sydenham to Norbiton. End of the line.'

'Family – in Hastings?'

'Oh yes, dear. Old Arthur built this pile when he left Ceylon. Before he went off on his travels. A Mr Stevenson, who was with him in Peru, bought it from the widow. He made the conversion. Apartments. Commercial hotel. Hospital in the Second War. Boarding house. And now apartments again. Some of the girls have been here through all the changes.'

One of these girls, seventy-plus and rattling the cups on an ebony tray, brought us our tea.

'Thanks, Naomi. Lovely, dear.'

Winnie Norton took over.

'She struggles backwards and forwards to Ore, poor old thing, every day. Won't retire.'

The cake was high-density fruit, black as anthracite. The tea, which Winnie took without milk or sugar, was excellent. It tasted of something strange, the leaf; it cleared the head, unblocked nasal passages, and was both flowery and bitter.

'So this is your young lady?'

Winnie smiled at Ollie. A conspiracy of diminutives.

'No, actually –'

'I thought not. She's got a lovely complexion.'

Winnie asked me to stay where I was, enjoying a second cup, while she took Ollie to her room to fetch Arthur's Kodak and the photo albums. It wouldn't be right for a gentleman, even a relative, to visit her bedroom in broad daylight.

When they'd gone, I walked to the window: a view over sloping lawns to woods and a shady valley.

'Shall I clear now, sir?'

Naomi appeared at my shoulder.

'Thanks, yes. I think they've finished.'

Naomi didn't move. The furniture in this room, older than the waitress, displaced its own weight in memory; indentations of those who had sat, dreamt, succumbed. I thought of movie stars in old age, letting the booze get its revenge. Mitchum. Sinatra with his rug and belly, broken voice. James Stewart and Richard Widmark on the riverbank in *Two Rode Together*: silly in hairpieces, unable to hear blind John Ford's instructions. What does it take to survive the death thing, the human contract? Courage. Forgetfulness. And an open-ended ticket to Switzerland, one of those lakeside clinics.

'He's there now, the old devil. By the ilex, sir. Staring in,' Naomi whispered. 'Eyes like a fox.'

I couldn't see anyone in the garden, resident or intruder.

'Where?' I said. 'Who are we talking about?'

But I knew very well who she meant, the Great Beast. Aleister Crowley. Only the dead see the dead. They don't go away, the more persistent of them, they hang about like old actors who can no longer find the route to the Green Room. Some moan and rattle, most are sad, waiting on the platform of a station where trains don't stop. Crowley with his glistening bald skull, his shrunken bulk, was trapped in the boredom of endlessness, in the shrubbery. The immortality he always solicited: suburban Hastings.

Visible to a crone in black. Who, as a young girl, had carried up his breakfast tray when the shakes were on and he couldn't find the strength to come downstairs. To make the performance, magus of the cold meats. Servant of Satan.

Even for those who love photographs, there comes a point of album fatigue. Too many beards, too many brides. Too many beaches. The faces of the dead, curated by the dying, solicit one last hurrah: *remember me*.

Arthur Norton with his laughter lines, hair, watchchain: I couldn't find anything to connect us. Paterfamilias. Property owner. Wife, children, servants. Arranged, time and again, for local photographers: E. Geering and Alexander Wilkie (615 Gt Northern Road, Aberdeen). Slender daughters, sons in kilts (the future Nostromoner has a fat book in his lap).

But one card, tissue wrapped, was of a different order: a portrait taken by a photographer who actually *looked* at Arthur, wondered what he was about and how to present him.

'San Francisco, we think,' Winnie said. 'It's inscribed but I can't make out the signature. Before the earthquake.'

'I didn't know Arthur was in San Francisco?'

'On his way, my husband decided, to Central America. Before Peru. I want you to have it. And the camera. You still do the writing?'

'I'd like to give it another shot, yes. Sometime.'

'Come back, please,' Winnie said. To Ollie. 'I like you very much. Bring your young chap. Or we could meet in town. Don't ring, I'm a little bit deaf. Just come when you fancy it, a lovely walk. *Do* come, dear. Goodbye, Andrew.'

I gave Ollie my keys. She was prepared (and qualified) to develop the film that had been lodged in the black box of that camera for over a hundred years. The instrument was the twin of the Kodak used by Bram Stoker's Jonathan Harker when he was prospecting for property investments in Thames Gateway on behalf of an overseas client, Count Dracula. Harker got there more than a hundred years ahead of Jimmy Seed.

'I have taken with my kodak views of it,' he wrote in his journal. Carfax Abbey, Purfleet. 'There are but few houses close at hand, one being a very large house only recently added to and formed into a private lunatic asylum.'

Arthur Norton's Peruvian film was the escape clause for my disintegrating fiction. Leave it with Ollie. She was right, I didn't deserve her. Give her to Kaporal, the better man. He would walk alongside this young woman to Cunard Court, take her to my flat. Then cook a meal, spaghetti with all the trimmings, while she converted my shower-cupboard into a darkroom.

What was the final entry in Arthur's journal? A ravine: *precipitous cliffs above, perpendicular rocks below, a roaring torrent at the bottom of the gorge, on the margin of which we could see gold-seekers washing out the mud.*

Arthur's party, diminished, exhausted, make camp. The gold-seekers offer no hospitality. The Indians vanish in the night. There is a cave in which Arthur finds shelter against a tropical downpour. The smell forbids sleep. *A poisonous gas that no bird or beast can live near. Rats running across the puddled floor drop down dead; the snake that pursues them shares the same fate; while birds flying above drop down and fly no more. The place is fatal to birds, vermin, and all creeping creatures who come across it.*

Now we were so close to a solution, I had to distance myself from the action. Give Ollie time to do her work. I was like an expectant father. I needed somewhere to pace, a bench on which to enjoy a cigar. This wouldn't be easy. I had a superstition about sitting on anything with a memorial plate: no names, dates, no more views (favourite or otherwise). The Hastings Museum then. Let Ollie take the direct route, the steep descent; I'll sidle, meander over nursery slopes, to the gallery in the park. Another encounter with my old friend, *Harbour Scene with Yachts* by Keith Baynes.

Because, very soon, one bright day, without warning, the painting won't be there: not for me. My good eye had closed and the weak one was murky. I couldn't face the operations, forms, bills, writing time lost. Baynes made colour you could taste, he was the Marine Ices of seascapes: buttery chalk, chocolate chip, melon green. He taught your eyes to salivate.

His story, like the myths of the chopped-up parson, the Brink's-Mat gold, would never be resolved. There were no hard facts, no secrets in museum files. But the gallery in which his painting hung was a fine place to visit, romancers and their circumscribed visions: the same shore with different characters. The same characters in different hats.

There was never anybody in the gallery. Before today.

'Have you noticed,' the woman said, 'those pencil marks? Go on, get in close. *There*. And again there. Top right, vertical. Bottom left, horizontal. Framing marks – which the framer ignored? A hint of the missing window?'

She was tall. I liked the scent of her.

The Baynes painting was swimming. I was losing it, colour without form.

Hat and decorative veil. Was this vision a wedding guest? Plum suede skirt with slash to show off the legs. Ankle-boots. Complicated scarves, rings, bangles. She was in good nick, but older than I had imagined – about my own age. The woman from the Bo-Peep Inn. The one who left typewritten stories at my door.

'Marina,' she said. 'Marina Fountain.'

And she shook my hand.

Royal Victoria Hotel

Walking down through the gardens with Marina Fountain, skate-board ramps, White Queen Theatre and on to the Grand Parade, felt right. The fret was stopped in me, the constant self-interrogation: a break in consciousness whereby old arguments faded into the tidal drag (motorway sound slowed to the point where it soothes). A skinned and glittering sea. The tottering hulk of Cunard Court as a reassuring ghost: deserted ballroom, cracked swimming pool (filled with bags of cement, mounds of sand), rusty balconies. One light on the seventh floor.

'Let Ollie finish the developing. We'll have a drink.'

I didn't say it. She knew what I was thinking. She knew the men from the Adelphi Hotel, pacing, agitated on cell phones. Drinkers, dispersed from their favoured sites on the lower walk, opposite the theatre, had atomised into smaller groups; ciderheads, dark-blue lager tins, silver tins. One school hung around the Gents, shirts out, ruddy, swaying and singing, a piss party. A family group with dogs and babies staked out the bus shelter. Trios, couples and solitaries balkanised alcoves, tactfully organised along the shingle's edge, carpets of pale-orange butts, punctured cans. 'Marina Marina Marina.'

They clinked in her honour. One of them tried to stand up, to kiss her hand. 'Have a wet, Marina. See yus Marina. Right, Marina, right?'

I assumed, with no good reason, that she lived in Cunard Court. Where else? That retro look. Those legs.

'I know where Baynes painted that view,' she said. We paused alongside the weather station: a decision about that drink would have to be made, the venue. Marina made it.

'Which floor?' I asked.

It didn't matter. My book was never going to work. I couldn't pull it together; as usual I'd gathered far too much material – incontinent research, undisciplined, reckless, a pyramid made from worms.

'Tell you on one condition.'

'What?'

'You take me dancing.'

My knees were gone. My legs belonged on an Edwardian billiard table. It had been years. I came from the wrong era. Proper dancing vanished with National Service.

The Royal Victoria Hotel, that iced cake with the tattered Union Flag, had a piano and a cocktail pianist with Jerry Lee Lewis hair and a greasy tux, the shakes under control, a limited repertoire: each golden oldie more depressing than the last. Unlikely couples with bottled tans, leftover from the days when TV announcers wore dinner jackets, went through the moves with robotic precision, before subsiding into their gilded coffins.

'I love to dance. Remember?'

Almost.

A warped Polaroid. A small fantasy: she touched my arm, coming through the streets of Notting Hill, late, after a boozy meal, in a cocoon of unconcern; knowing ourselves, one through the other, not knowing how it would go, what form our lovemaking would take.

Were we old enough – to dance? Old in habits, certainly. I scanned the ads in the newsagent's window, before he could pull down the shutters. *Historic steel boat once owned by Edith Piaf. Diesel Engine. 3 berths.* A photograph. Like a Dunkirk survivor. Seen some parties, that one, dancing to a portable radio on French rivers. We should learn how to leave the past alone, let light decay at its own volition. Maybe those New Puritans were right: no back story, no complexity, no adjectives. 'A man walks up to the bar and orders . . .'

Leave Ollie and Kaporal alone. Take them out of the story. Junk the A13 material. Grant Arthur Norton's Peruvian journey its intrinsic mystery. He was there, he vanished. So what? Nothing to do with me. I don't want the prints from the Kodak. I'll dance. We'll have a few drinks, walk across the road to the sea. You can still hear the piano from the hotel. Full moon. Crane up. Audience restless, glutted with references. Overload. Make it simple. Man, woman, bench. Finish.

I searched for the bar, someone had moved it (from its position in Marina's typescript). As in a temperance hotel, it had been hidden: alcohol available – if strictly necessary – on prescription. The barman was a person of restricted growth who had left a travelling circus and found steady employment staying out of sight. His eyes glared at you between the olives and the dead peanuts.

'Two gin and tonics. Please.'

'Ice and lemon?'

He made it sound like a perversion.

'No,' I said. I didn't have time to watch him mount his block, juggle with cubes, claw a sacrificial citrus fruit and massacre it with nail scissors.

Before I could sneak a look inside her bulging leather satchel, Marina returned from her face-repair operation. I wouldn't have done it anyway. I didn't want to know. For the first time, in months, I was perfectly content to be where I was: soft chair, attractive woman, warm gin.

'Keith Baynes worked from Cunard Court, it's true. You must have seen *View from My Window, St Leonards* (*c.* 1965) in the Hastings Museum catalogue. No middle distance: sofa, yachts. But that other, madder sequence, with the agitated cushions, choppy sea . . .'

It wasn't just her face, the whole look had received a major rethink. I thought I was safe with the ankle-boots, she couldn't dance in those. Marina had executed a complete costume change, Cyd Charisse heels, gardenia in hair, a spangly black number that flashed like a case of eels.

'It's our song.'

I held her, I knew that much. The white piano sounded like ice cubes dropping into a tin bath. Marina was enjoying herself. We performed – without flourishes, twirls, the moves you used to see illustrated in the picture strips, footprints only, with little arrows: one-two-three, one-two-three, one-two-three, one. She tucked her head on my shoulder: smoke and soap, nothing that helped me fix my memories of a past that hadn't yet happened.

'Baynes kept a room in this hotel. He entertained. So the skewed perspective makes sense: it never was Cunard Court. And there's something else. He fell out of a tree as a kid, haemorrhaged, lost the sight of one eye.'

I shouldn't squeeze so hard. I knew how easily Marina bruised. Knew? I met the woman for the first time today. Orange-brown marks slowly darkening, as fingerprints faded in the flesh of her arms, the remembered intensity of an afternoon encounter.

'A career of inaction,' Marina said. 'The doctors advised him to live quietly in the country, on the coast. Close enough to imagine France, but not close enough to experience it: drains, garlic, muscular sailors in striped vests.'

'Blind in one eye?'

'Nice man, by all accounts. Slightly bewildered, they say, by what was happening around him. Never quite sure if the yachts had sailed into his room, or if he had drifted out to join them.'

His friend Othon Friesz reported: 'Light is sometimes arbitrary and shadows omitted.'

One-eyed visions from an English hotel. Displacement strategies made possible by a private income too modest to draw attention to itself.

We returned to our table. I collected another round. Marina was smoking. She didn't share my inhibitions; she'd taken the portrait of Arthur Norton, the one from San Francisco, out of my bag, and she was twisting it around in her hands (purple-black nails), holding it close, holding it away. Everything short of licking it for flavour.

'Of interest?' I asked. I too had my secrets.

'Another dance. I'm enjoying myself. You think that's supposed to be Latin-American?'

She could carry it off, with her look, Mediterranean, sallow on the fresh side of jaundice, but it was too much for me. Marina didn't have natural rhythm, she had style: she shimmered. Men watched her. Women watched her. It never fades. I kept out of the way, making random gestures with my arms, listening to my joints creak.

'My great-grandfather,' I said. When we collapsed at the table. 'Arthur Norton. In San Francisco? I have no idea what he was doing there.'

'I know,' Marina replied. 'Read this while I freshen our drinks.'

She made it easy. Passages marked with coloured stickers. Yet another book. *Motion Studies: Time, Space and Eadweard Muybridge* by Rebecca Solnit. Muybridge, the stop-motion man, inspiration for Duchamp and Francis Bacon, didn't do portraits. What possible connection could there be with Arthur, the card that Marina was busily interrogating?

I ignored her markers and flicked idly through reproductions of naked women with basins of water, an old man (Muybridge himself) marching with formidable length of stride (fit but mad), a group of Shoshone Indians squatting alongside the Central Pacific Railroad. Great images. But no trace, thank god, of the Norton portrait. Muybridge kept the world at a distance, clouds, athletes, urban panoramas. Solnit had picked a good subject.

'Rebecca's a chum.'

Marina, saving time, brought the bottle.

'I stayed with her in San Francisco. She took me on the Muybridge trail. Read page forty-two. Then go back to thirty-five.'

'Later, perhaps.'

'Now, read it. Then we'll go up to my room. The one in which Baynes used to stay.'

He documented several groups of Native Americans, a few Chinese miners and city dwellers but made no known portraits. His photograph of Emperor Norton on a bicycle is as close as he got – literally as close, for though Muybridge photographed individuals a few more times and made hundreds of motion studies of men and women, he never photographed anyone as close-up as portraiture requires, never depicted them as expressive faces rather than representative bodies. It says much about him that he always kept his distance.

'Norton? "Emperor" Norton? Who is *that*?'
I had to know, the irrational impulse that keeps you going, to the very last page, when you understand, deep down, there is nothing ahead: banal twist, tawdry revelation, fraudulent closure.
'Norton is as close as Muybridge ever came to taking a portrait.'
The absurdity of this man's imperial title made me think of Conrad's silver-financed Central American republic (ingots shipped directly to San Francisco). It brought back my conman ancestor, Sir Gregor MacGregor, 'Cazique' of the Mosquito Coast. I fell for it, I reached for Marina's slender pink marker.

Norton, an English Jew who came to California via South Africa, initially made a fortune speculating in foodstuffs. In 1853, he tried to corner the rice market at twelve cents a pound, only to be ruined when Peruvian ships sailed in full of rice at three cents a pound. He apparently cracked under the strain of the crisis, then re-emerged in 1859 with a proclamation he gave to the *San Francisco Daily Evening Bulletin* to publish, announcing he was emperor of the United States. Later he added 'and Protector of Mexico' to his title . . . He wandered the city, graciously receiving homage, chastising the disrespectful, and taking tribute in the form of free meals, free clothes, and small sums of money given for his irredeemable bonds, printed free by local shops. His career as emperor was made by the collusion of the citizens of San Francisco and the newspapers that published his edicts,

the accounts of his fantastic and entirely fictitious travels to Ceylon, Australia, Tasmania and Peru. In the photograph Muybridge made of Norton sitting on a bicycle in the late 1860s, he is a solid middle-aged man looking down at his handle-bars with a frown of concentration, more serious than his gaudy uniform with its tarnished epaulets.

I undressed quickly and waited, trying not to yawn, while Marina went through the familiar rituals of preparation: knickers chucked away, the struggle to unfasten the dress (that might require my help), the sitting on the edge of the bed to unroll her stockings, shoes back on, selects a fresh pair of knickers (drawer left open), walks to window, no urgency, curtains open, full moon over the sea, the same expectations, her feet so cold when she does climb into bed, under the sheets.

It would sort itself out, eventually. The Norton story. The film Ollie was processing didn't matter. Emperor Norton never made it to Peru. The family fortune wasn't lost to the sharks of the financial markets: *he* was the crook, the spinner of fictions. A ganef, a schnorrer. A tolerated joke. Walking to hide his shame in pretended madness – until that became the only real thing about him. Ruritanian uniform and antique bicycle. A near portrait by Eadweard Muybridge: a man who, like William Burroughs, kills his wife and gets away with it. Who changes his name more often than his socks

(Muggeridge, Muygridge, Helios, Eduardo Santiago Muybridge). Who changes his personality, a double life brought on by a stagecoach crash.

I found a scar on my head. I had a double vision – saw two objects at once; had no sense of smell or taste; also had confused ideas . . . Then I went to London and consulted a physician named Gull.

Gull? Sir William. Royal physician and Ripper suspect. Gull specialises in injuries to the brain (Stephen Knight, who wrote a book denouncing the Masonic conspiracy, died of a tumour). Gull advises healthy outdoor activity, Muybridge begins to photograph landscape, cumbersome equipment dragged over the west, Yosemite. *(Yo! Semite. Yo! Norton.)*

Stereoscopic views that insist upon two good eyes. Middle ground vanquished. Panoramas that don't quite fit.

No portraits. Portraits give access to the disappeared. Subject infiltrates consciousness of observer. A conspiracy of soul-theft: like psychoanalysis. Freud never made love after the age of forty.

Two pan-scrubber beards: Emperor Norton and Eadweard Muybridge. Naked men walking. A flick book. Frozen frames, stapled together, create the illusion of movement. But Muybridge wasn't reliable, even with his motion-study sequences; he wasn't above slipping in the occasional duplicate, a retake from another run.

I was Jewish not Scottish. My Highland blood, if any, came through that fraud, MacGregor. My expulsion and homelessness predated the Clearances. Emperor Norton's San Francisco years, prophet without doctrine, living on his lack of wits, embroidering compensatory fictions, made more sense than the business with Peruvian jungles and undeveloped films. Muybridge's cruel portrait told the true story: a broken man staring at the ground. Two broken men: one with a bicycle, one with a camera.

After lovemaking: language. I'd forgotten how it used to work, the poetry thing. The gift of words, whether you like it or not. Marina, camel hair coat around shoulders, long legs crossed, sat smoking at the window. She had Ruth Alsop's habits, her gestures, perfectly imitated: thirty-five years lost. I struggled to invent our first meeting, the natural history of my destruction, the hole in my life. Those decisions are lightly taken, stupid argument, heat of the moment: one of you walks out. Thirty-five years before our narratives converge. If that's what is happening. If that's who she is. Who I am. Now.

The great stone liner, Cunard Court, was floodlit. My flat: the eye in a pyramid of yellow illumination. Marina pointed, thin wrist emerging from sleeve of charity-shop camel hair, to where the St Leonards pier once stood. So I had misidentified Hastings pier, visible in so many of Fred Judge's postcards. And from this error many incorrect readings accumulated. Moon shadows on ruffled water brought the pier back as a ladder of light.

I put my arm around Marina's waist.

'Ruth?' I said.

'Touch it.'

The metal plaque with its braille lettering. I ran my fingers over proud script: useful practice for what was to come. Cunard Court: refuge of the one-eyed artist. A tribute to the demolished pier. How the English love things when they are no longer there. A nation of restorers: bodgers, destroyers, resurrectionists. Skeletal platform on rotten piles: memories of the good times nobody had (Graham Greene, Patrick Hamilton).

The plaque commemorated the location 'where the first moving picture was shown 7th November 1896'. Precursor of what-the-butler-saw flickers. Rows of devices, like those X-ray machines in shoe shops, capping the eyes. Moon path as projector beam: true cinema.

'When did you realise?' Marina asked, as we walked slowly, arm in arm, towards Cunard Court.

'What?'

'That I was Ruth Alsop. And I left you, after Southwold, because I was pregnant.'

Her moods. Those photographs on the beach. The conversation, I hadn't taken it seriously, hadn't responded, when she talked about wanting a child. The smell of the pine woods, resin and soft paths after rain. I was too busy with my camera.

'And I was the one – dumping Jiffy bags on your doorstep.'

'Why?'

'They were your scripts. I was returning them, one by one. Hoping . . .'

'*Mine?*'

Coincidence, accident. The kind that happens a million times a day, people who once knew each other take flats in the same building. But nobody met in Cunard Court. Old ones who no longer went out, weekend sailors, speculators who passed on without making wills. Talking to a stranger in the lift was like holding a séance. What if they replied?

'Did you marry? What happened to the child?'

'Sort of. For a time. It didn't work out. She's fine.'

Marina noticed me in town, followed on a whim; remembered me. So she said. It had been easy, cultivation of Cunard Court handyman, to borrow a key: surprise for old friend, lover. She read my notes, the pages and pages of names, facts, prompts, false starts.

She was writing a book of her own.

'It was obvious you were blocked. I borrowed a couple of red notebooks and copied the stories out, your drafts. A provocation, really. A tease.'

'Why?'

'My own book wasn't coming. I couldn't find a form until you provided me with a title: *The Middle Ground*. It wrote itself – in weeks.'

She kissed me.

'I owe you,' she said. 'More than you know.'

The smell was heady: dying hyacinths in a bed around a table of black rock. Bang in front of the Royal Victoria Hotel.

**TRADITION SAYS THAT
WILLIAM THE CONQUEROR
LANDED AT
BULVERHYTHE
AND DINED ON THIS
STONE**

'You were never doing a novel. Barefaced topography. The names of your characters – Danny *Folgate*? Wink wink. Dowser as spirit of A13? Check out the City/Shoreditch boundary: Norton Folgate, E1. Drin? A river in Albania. And Mocatta, the W.R. Hearst of Fairlight? His drinking fountain must be all of sixty yards from Aldgate Pump: "In honoured memory of FREDERICK DAVID MOCATTA. In recognition of a benevolent life." People as spirit of place, Andy. The same old tricks.'

Not true. I had no idea. About Mocatta. The man's in the newspapers, on TV. He owns this building. He has a mother, a daughter. A library.

'And Marina,' I said. 'Marina Fountain. What about her?'

'The last pub before you get to Bo-Peep, as you very well know. The one under the cliff workings, near the statue of King Harold and Edith Swan-Neck. Marina Fountain is a splash of cheap gold paint on a black background. A boozer with a narrow garden, a pit stop on the road to Bexhill.'

Ollie and Kaporal, saucepan smouldering with the remains of burnt spaghetti sauce, had gone for a curry, leaving Arthur Norton's prints pegged out to dry in the shower room. A brief note gave nothing else away. We moved, down the corridor, to Marina's flat.

My head was aching, my mouth an asbestos sandwich. Marina had a bottle of Calvados. She kissed me again. Said that she'd slip downstairs to join the others, a coffee, so that I could decide, in private, what do about the Peruvian photographs. Give them, unseen, to Ollie: a future conceptual project? Or exploit them? If not as a conclusion to my abandoned novel, then as the start of something fresh. Like the Conradian postcards I found in Brick Lane Market and printed (as endpapers) for my novel, *Downriver*. The moment those negatives were transformed, they abdicated their power. Their hold over me.

The Calvados, with its lovely afterburn, did the trick. I mellowed. Marina had a studio flat, smaller than mine, but better organised. Her neat typescript had been left on the Ikea desk. Nothing to consider: *read it*. 214 pp., the length I'd aimed for, back at the start. Three sections (bright-yellow interleaves). Everything my chaotic novel failed to achieve: discipline, reason – inevitability. Themes stated, interrogated, resolved. She had a nifty title (like a white paper from the LibDems): *The Middle Ground*.

Hastings as Hastings. Her argument was shaped through unforced biographies of three men: John Logie Baird (first television signal), Fred Judge (photography and its limitations), Keith Baynes (view from a single eye). There were no awkward authorial intrusions, Marina was seductively present in every line. Her tone, her sureness of touch. The anecdotes. She left space around her characters that allowed readers to fill in details according to taste. Playful severity. Scholarly rigour without a blitz of footnotes. It was a fine thing, this book. I pictured the finished object with a dust-wrapper based on one of Fred Judge's fading bromoil nocturnes. Text double-spaced. Generous margins. Good cream paper. Dark-blue cloth. Stitched, not glued. Minimal cover copy (gloriously vague). Justified hyperbole from Susan Sontag, Anita Brookner and Simon Schama: in boxed quotes.

Recommended summer reading, pick of the year. Fame, prizes, respect. And more: a job well done.

John Logie Baird (born in the year of the Ripper murders, down from Helensburgh on the Clyde, unwell) scarcely registers *where* he is. An orthodox Scottish CV: poverty + the go-getting push of the permanently disappointed man. He's touchy, upset when journalists talk of 'seeing by wireless'. He picks this sleepy town with its crumbling sandstone cliffs (and, in future time, famously bad TV reception) as the place to attempt the first transmission.

Who will help him? Who is President of the Hastings Radio Society in 1924? William Le Quex: author, Ripperologist, spy, faker. (Marina doesn't tell you much about Le Quex, but I can't help myself. He's the kind of forgotten man who would, if the fellow hadn't turned up with a bulging suitcase, have invented Baird and his 'Shadowgraph' disc: primitive science fiction in a striking pictorial wrapper. Sold on railway stations in time of war.)

The threat to England and the British Empire from alien invasion (yellow faces, Mongol hordes) was a festering obsession: 200 books credited to this Londoner who died in Belgium. According to his faithful admirer, N. St Barbe Sladen, Le Quex never grasped the nice distinction, if any, between fact and fiction.

His publications include: *Beryl of the Biplane*, *The Bomb-Makers*, *The Bond of Black*, *The Broadcast Mystery*, *The Chameleon*, *The Closed Book*, *The Death-Doctor*, *The Double Shadow*, *An Eye for an Eye*, *The Spider's Eye*, *Three Glass Eyes*, *The Voice from the Void*.

Future war, radio waves, Whitechapel Murders and the green rays of marine sunsets: *Le Quex was a card-carrying Nostromoner*. He had himself appointed to the honorary consulship of the Republic of San Marino. If anyone had the time to wade through the morass of his paranoid fictions, the secret history of the period would reveal itself. He stood at Baird's shoulder when that first transmission was made.

Sound becomes picture: 'A curious high-pitched whistle, with a hint of regular and very rapid interruptions.' A large veined disc that looked like god's eye, spinning spinning, above a base made from coffin wood.

Marina was smart enough to spurn the Le Quex digression, but she rescues Baird and the era of backroom experimentation, driven amateurs. Rescues the man. And she is just as sympathetic to Fred Judge with his hunger for 'views'.

Her essay, measuring Fred's nightstalking of London against a project undertaken in Hastings by the Hackney-based photographer, Effie Paleologou, did justice to two very different sensibilities.

Judge, inspired by Alvin Langdon Coburn, wanted something more than commercial success, a definitive catalogue of the picturesque. He wanted: art. Loss of control, breakdown – the unexpected. Paleologou read Hastings as a theatre set: threads of rope, cobbled streets illuminated with puddles of artificial light.

'All eyeballs and head,' wrote Liz Kent in her introduction to the Paleologou exhibition at Hastings Museum and Art Gallery. 'The light is mute, the reddish cast of the colour so peculiar that we are left wandering through the image, asking ourselves: what exactly is going on?'

The Keith Baynes meditation, which concludes *The Middle Ground*, carries the three movements back to their starting point, the view from Cunard Court. Marina is working from the room that once belonged to a gentleman artist. She discusses Max Beckmann and his Italian marine paintings (coded biography, Kabbalah, premonitions of war); and argues that this lesser thing, Baynes's Francophile relish for sunlight on water, yachts, fishermen, is not to be spurned. There is a passage to be navigated into the 'middle ground', a corridor he neither delineates, nor understands. A space where lives can be lost. After improvisation and analogy, Marina comes to Baynes's last years, more or less forgotten, removed to Warrior Square: the man with one eye.

I had emptied most of the bottle. This book would make her name: *Ruth Alsop*. There it was in red letters on the half-title of her script. I was already mapping out an essay in her support. Would that be too intrusive? Drooling hack jumping on the bandwagon of a livelier intelligence. You had to be very careful, these days, who you puffed, or who you chose to libel. My fiercest critics were my oldest friends.

Postpone the decision, my trip downstairs. Handle the objects on Ruth's desk. Postcards: Baynes, Judge, Beckmann (*The Bark*, 1926). The invitation to the Paleologou show. The Remington on which she had, so laboriously, copied out my aborted tales. Maps. Books. Stones from the beach.

A tin with a paper label, yellow and blue, picture of the sphinx.

Finest Handmade AMBAR CIGARETTES. Philip E. Mitry. At the Anglo-American Bookshop Opposite Shepheard's Hotel. Cairo, Egypt. I had to sniff the interior. Photographs. Preserved. The lion shot, myself as a child, in Paignton. A photo-booth strip, Ruth mugging as I frown. A semi-tropical garden carved from the cliff: Fairlight! Ruth with a child, a girl. Mocatta's daughter. Ollie.

The story made too much sense, it hurt. A stone in the heart. Ruth with Mocatta. The flat in Cunard Court as pay-off, benevolent banishment. Child lost. Twice. My daughter and the other, the one Ollie was carrying. Fathered, head in the ditch at Thurrock, by Reo Sleeman. Resolution as pain postponed.

I couldn't go back to my flat, the darkroom, the drying prints. That was over, a discontinued and discredited narrative. I couldn't join the characters in the curry house. Relationships were too complex now – with Kaporal as a kind of son-in-law and Ollie a daughter, lost, carrying a child that wasn't mine.

I picked up a book from the top of the pile and brought it close to my face. Deep-blue cloth with five wavelines, top and bottom, on spine. Caress it, feel the heat, then flip the lid.

Afterwards his story was not so clear. It lost itself amongst the innumerable tales of conspiracies and plots against the tyrant as a stream lost in an arid belt of sandy country before it emerges, diminished and troubled, perhaps, on the other side. The doctor made no secret of it that he had lived for years in the wildest parts of the Republic, wandering with almost unknown Indian tribes in the great forests of the far interior where the great rivers have their sources. But it was mere aimless wandering; he had written nothing, collected nothing, brought nothing for science out of the twilight of the forests, which seemed to cling to his battered personality limping about Sulaco, where it drifted in casually, only to get stranded on the shores of the sea.

Acknowledgements

Marina Fountain's 'Grays' was originally published in 2002, in a slightly different version, by Goldmark (Uppingham), as part of a selection called *White Goods*. My thanks to Mike Goldmark.

Marina Fountain's 'View from My Window' was published by the Worple Press, 2003, as part of a limited edition of *The Verbals*. My thanks to Peter and Amanda Carpenter. And to Kevin Jackson.

The Publisher is grateful for permission to reproduce from the following: *Under the Net* by Iris Murdoch, published by Chatto & Windus. Reprinted by permission of the Random House Group Ltd; *The Epic of Gilgamesh* translated by Andrew George (Penguin Books, 1999), translation copyright © Andrew George, 1999; *Behindlings* by Nicola Barker, published by HarperCollins Publishers Ltd, copyright © Nicola Barker, 2002; *Motion Studies* by Rebecca Solnit, published by Bloomsbury Publishing, copyright © Rebecca Solnit, 2003.

Thanks to J.G. Ballard for permission to quote from his works, to Jennifer Dorn for permission to quote from Ed Dorn's poetry, to Lee Harwood for permission to quote from his letters, and to Andrew Dakers Ltd for the extract from *More Things in Heaven* by Walter Owen.